BY LAURIE R. KING

MARY RUSSELL

The Beekeeper's Apprentice

A Monstrous Regiment of Women

A Letter of Mary

The Moor

O Jerusalem

Justice Hall

The Game

Locked Rooms

The Language of Bees

The God of the Hive

Beekeeping for Beginners
(A Novella)

Pirate King

Garment of Shadows

Dreaming Spies

The Marriage of Mary Russell
(A Novella)

The Murder of Mary Russell

*Mary Russell's War and other
stories of suspense*

Island of the Mad

Riviera Gold

Castle Shade

STUYVESANT & GREY

Touchstone

The Bones of Paris

KATE MARTINELLI

A Grave Talent

To Play the Fool

With Child

Night Work

The Art of Detection

Beginnings (A Novella)

AND

A Darker Place

Folly

Keeping Watch

Califia's Daughters (as
Leigh Richards)

Lockdown

Back to the Garden

Back to the Garden

BACK TO THE GARDEN

A Novel

Laurie R. King

BANTAM BOOKS
NEW YORK

Published in the United States by Bantam Books, an imprint of Random House, a division of Penguin Random House LLC, New York.

BANTAM BOOKS is a registered trademark and the B colophon is a trademark of Penguin Random House LLC.

LIBRARY OF CONGRESS CATALOGING-IN-PUBLICATION DATA
Names: King, Laurie R., author.
Title: Back to the garden: a novel / Laurie R. King.
Description: First Edition. | New York: Bantam Books, [2022]
Identifiers: LCCN 2022010985 (print) | LCCN 2022010986 (ebook) |
ISBN 9780593496565 (hardcover) | ISBN 9780593496572 (ebook)
Subjects: LCGFT: Novels.
Classification: LCC PS3561.I4813 B33 2022 (print) | LCC PS3561.I4813 (ebook) |
DDC 813/.54—dc23
LC record available at https://lccn.loc.gov/2022010985
LC ebook record available at https://lccn.loc.gov/2022010986

Printed in the United States of America

randomhousebooks.com

3rd Printing

Book design by Caroline Cunningham

To the Independents: booksellers, thinkers, and spirits.

You inspire me.

So the Lord God cast Adam out from the garden of Eden, to cultivate the land he came from.

Why are you so angry? Why is your face resentful? If you do well, will you not be accepted? And if you do not, won't sin crouch outside your door, filling you with longing?

—Genesis

BACK TO THE GARDEN

PROLOGUE

Then

The man in the dripping Army poncho paused to shove back his hood and stand, head cocked, trying to make out the half-heard sound. A minute later, a car came into view, half a mile or so down the hill—a big white Pontiac, struggling to keep on the road. The man leaned on his shovel, judging the contest between the treacherous surface—the way up to the commune was unpaved, rutted, steep, and slick with the endless rain—and the determined car, which obviously had good tires.

The car slithered and flirted with disaster, but managed to avoid going off the edge or getting bogged down in the section where the culvert had washed out last month. When it came to the end of the clear section and vanished behind the trees, the man bent over to shake the rain from his long hair and beard, like a dog coming out of a river, then slopped the last shovelfuls of mud from the blocked ditch before walking down to see what the invader wanted.

The mud-spattered Pontiac eased into the farmyard, hesitating over the choice of targets: ancient woodshed or shiny new greenhouse? Psychedelic school bus up on blocks or geodesic dome layered in tarpaulins? In the end, the driver chose the aging farmhouse in the middle, pulling up close to the steps. The engine shut off, the music died—had to be a tape player, a radio would get nothing but static this far out. The person inside leaned over to roll up the passenger-side window, then sat, staring through the smeared windshield at the house as if expecting someone to come out.

The man in the poncho stayed where he was.

Eventually, the car door cracked open, emitting a figure who might have beamed in from another planet: a man in his early thirties with a carefully styled mop of red-blond hair, his mustache and sideburns trimmed just the safe side of emphatic. A large black umbrella poked into the air and opened, shelter for the wide lapels of his suit and the bright silk of his tie. The whole picture suggested a salesman who'd become disastrously lost—but when the salesman's other hand came into view, holding a sleek attaché case, the bearded man recognized what this man had to be: a lawyer.

Junior partner, early thirties, who hadn't really thought out the whole hippie-commune-in-Oregon thing. He made a noise of disgust as he noticed the muck swallowing the inch-high heels of his gleaming shoes. One foot came up, driving the other farther down, but as he looked desperately toward the farmhouse steps, his glance caught on the figure in the poncho.

"Afternoon," he shouted, his good cheer sounding a bit forced. "I'm looking for Rob Gardener? Robert John Gardener?"

For long seconds, the only sounds in all the world were the hiss of rain and the tick of an overworked engine. Junior partner on one side of the lonely farmyard, large bearded man with a heavy implement on the other. Representative of The Establishment, the law, the benefits of right behavior on one side, and across from him . . .

The newcomer cleared his throat. "Your cousin David—David Kirkup? Gave me this address, and—"

The voice that interrupted was gravelly, deep, and so rough it might not have spoken in days. "So," Rob said. "Has the Old Bastard finally died?"

1

Now

The day had been going so well, until the bones turned up.

It was a Monday, for one thing. Jen liked Mondays. The Gardener Estate was closed to the public, which always made it feel more like a family home than a place of work. The staff could park where they wanted, dress for comfort, and dive into their tasks without having to dodge the cameras and the clueless. Some of them even came in early, to work up an appetite for the morning break, and at noon they sat down together for an only slightly ironic communal lunch.

This Monday was also a perfect April morning on California's Central Coast: warm sun, blue sky, the formal gardens a mosaic of glorious color, the Great Field a sweep of brilliant seasonal green, thanks to the series of winter storms. The kind of day that tempted Jen to spurn office work and spend the morning in old jeans, allowing the real gardeners to order her around.

Except that those winter storms had created a problem.

Yes, it was great not to worry about drought for a change, to see the trees leaf out so generously and the nearby reservoir fill. Not so great was how the long months of sodden ground had toppled over three of the Estate's oldest trees, collapsed a stretch of century-old stone retaining wall, and—this being the matter that was keeping Jen from a day of nice, mindless weeding—lent a Pisa-like tilt to the biggest and most idiosyncratic of the Estate's outdoor statues.

Rafi, the head groundsman, had noticed the tilt back in February. It wasn't an immediate hazard, since the statue was outside the formal gardens and easy enough to fence off, but with good weather coming on, picnickers would soon arrive, and small children whose parents ignored the NO CLIMBING signs. Normally, a repair order would have gone through, a simple matter of choosing a contractor and having the Estate's art conservator there to supervise. But for this statue?

Manager, groundsman, and conservator, along with the hard-hatted driver of the big crane idling behind them, stood to survey the job.

"I could just finish tipping it over, so it's not a hazard," the driver suggested.

"Let the blackberries grow over it," Rafi agreed. "Call it environmental art or something."

"It is the weirdest thing on the place," Jen admitted. Jen Bachus had been the Estate's manager since the Trust took over, and before that, a neighbor and regular trespasser. Jen had definite opinions on the weirdnesses of the Gardener Estate—and a sixteen-foot-high, tile-covered figure with long skirts, an odd torso, and a trio of conjoined heads was a thing most visitors found unforgettable. And that was before they got to the expression on its face.

But the conservator was shaking her head. "You can't do that. It's a Gaddo." Although even her voice suggested a tiny bit of agreement: *Midsummer Eves* was kind of creepy.

Mrs. Dalhousie, the Estate's archivist and conservator, was only here because of the Estate's Gaddoes. She'd retired from New York's MOMA, moved west, and come with a ladies' group to visit the gardens—where she was astonished to find three (possibly four) sculptures by the artist known as Gaddo, a woman famous in the seventies, notorious in the eighties, and out of fashion by the end of the nineties, when her feminist outrage was superseded by Damian Hirst's masculine irony of rotting cows and formaldehyde sharks. There were signs that she was now, twelve years after her death, about to be rediscovered as the gynocentric precursor of bad-boy shock art.

Mrs. Dalhousie had instantly volunteered—rather, she walked in and took over. And once she'd sorted out the Gaddoes (which *might* include the Minoan snake-goddess figure they'd found gathering dust in the attic), she moved on to transforming the archives from a room full of memorabilia into a properly cataloged, scanned, and referenced archive of the Gardener Estate's century-long history. Mrs. Dalhousie approached every project, be it sculpture restoration or newspaper storage, with a computer's tireless energy, a monk's passionate dedication, and precisely nil sense of humor.

But not even Mrs. Dalhousie could claim that *Midsummer Eves* was the ideal ornament for a part of the Estate given over to picnicking families and long views over rolling hills. The *Eves* might have two other faces, but the massive laurel hedge made it impossible to tell. For decades, this face had loomed at the top of the Great Field like an avenging goddess, baring her sharpened teeth at passersby and frightening the more sensitive children.

Were it not for the inescapable fact that its creator later became famous enough to be known by a single name, the *Eves* might already have been allowed to quietly deteriorate, just one more piece of pretentious hippie junk from the Estate's commune era.

"At least it's an early Gaddo," Jen commented. "From her 'Menacing Feminist' phase rather than full-on gross-out. Unless you think the grout contains pureed placentas or ground-up human bones."

The two men looked alarmed. Mrs. Dalhousie looked thoughtful, but only corrected Jen's terminology. "It's known as her 'Sisterhood' phase, and the dates for this would place it early on, which makes it all the more important. As for the bones in that piece you're referring to, they were from a monkey, not a human child. At any rate, I shall be quite interested to see the other faces. Gaddo's sketches for the piece are surprisingly fragmentary."

"Whatever we find, this thing's costing us a fortune, even before we look at the renovation costs and security measures. Do you think . . ." Jen fixed her eyes on the statue and tried to sound as if this was something that was just occurring to her. "I don't suppose we'd be allowed to sell it? Like, to a museum? I suppose a private collector would pay more, but I'd rather see it in public hands. And if a museum—like MOMA—oversaw the renovations, they'd be done right. Do you think the Trust might consider letting it go?"

She could feel Mrs. Dalhousie's gaze, drilling into the side of her face.

Mrs. D claimed that the Gaddo would generate income from art historians and selfie-seekers—eventually. Jen wasn't sure the Estate's bank balance would hold out long enough to see a return on expenditures. However, if they could sell the *Eves,* there were any number of projects that had been pending for some time . . .

But in fact, the ultimate fate of *Midsummer Eves* was not up to Jen, or even Mrs. Dalhousie.

"According to the Trust agreement," Mrs. Dalhousie pointed out, "anything beyond maintenance and repairs requires Mr. Gardener's approval."

That reminder took some of the shine out of the morning.

Jen's gaze slid over to Rafi, who had worked for the Estate longer than she had. "Do you know when anyone last saw Rob?"

"Hmm. November?"

"Oh, right—when he took a shot at those hikers."

Mrs. Dalhousie blinked, the crane driver looked uneasy, and Jen gave them both an apologetic smile. "Mr. Gardener's private corner of the Estate is clearly posted against trespassing. Though it was only bird shot, and he wasn't actually aiming at them."

Still, the thought of setting off on a death-defying drive to speak with a famously irascible Gardener put a different shade across the job at hand.

"What about his cousin?" Mrs. Dalhousie suggested.

"David is still in Germany."

An odd silence fell.

The crane driver waited. When no explanation came, he took off his hard hat to scratch his balding head. "Well, anyway. Your problem's with the base. The thing is held together like crazy—forty years and not so much as a crack—but it doesn't look like they stabilized the ground underneath it at all, just wove up a bunch of rebar, slapped some forms around it, and poured directly on the dirt. And that's your problem. It's so close to that hedge, nobody spotted the stream under-mining the whole thing. Look, I'm going to have to pick it up base and all, anyway. If you like, I could just take it a little farther, to that flat place. It could sit there for months. You can even put up a scaffolding and do your repairs there."

Jen nodded. "That's probably for the best. In the meantime, Mrs. D, I'll pencil in a discussion on selling it on next week's Board agenda. Maybe when David gets back, he can go up and talk to Rob, see if he's fond of the thing. We might even be able to fit in a preliminary vote on Tuesday, if Rob doesn't mind . . . retiring it."

She could no longer avoid Mrs. Dalhousie's eyes.

The older woman's expression was clear. *I am the veteran of a thousand art-world negotiations. I am not deceived by your act of innocence.* At the same time, she was experienced enough to choose private conversation over public argument, so she added her permission for the crane driver to get on with the task of shifting the sculpture, base and all.

But as he began pulling out a series of straps and hooks, she spoke, for Jen's ears alone. "You've been thinking about this for a while, haven't you?"

"What, selling it? Not very long."

"Ms. Bachus, behind that wide-eyed manner of yours lies one of the most relentless forces I've ever worked with. Why are you so determined to be rid of the *Eves*?"

"I don't *want* to get rid of her. Honestly, I'd be happy to have her stand here and glare at the picnickers forever. But I looked up what a Gaddo is worth. And I have a dim idea of what restoring her is going to cost. If selling this statue means we don't have to sell off some of the Estate itself, that's a decision I could live with."

"Selling some land? Has it reached that point?"

"Our operating costs don't change much, whether we're open or not. After the past couple years, our cushion is nearly into the red. Something has to give. Unless you like the proposal David's bringing back from Germany."

The archivist winced. "That's going to be discussed Tuesday?"

"First thing on the agenda."

"Well," the older woman said.

"You think MOMA might be interested?"

"Let me know if there's any way I can help."

They watched the driver attach his cables and braces to the statue, wrapping it with the care of a Renaissance bronze, testing each strap before he climbed up into his cab. The great engine gave out a roar, preparing to rip the *Eves* from the earth. Lesser gardeners popped out to watch.

The driver was good, lifting slowly to let the weight settle into the cables, making his adjustments before they were needed, even giving the load a sharp little drop to shake off some of the heavily packed dirt—and, to Mrs. Dalhousie's distress, some tiles from the figure's skirts. The massive weight swung ponderously over the slope toward the chosen spot. There the three-faced *Eves* descended, touching gently down (dropping more tiles) to settle into its temporary home.

The younger audience members cheered, the engine coughed and died away. The driver let the cables go slack, then climbed down to begin freeing the *Eves* from their sling.

Mrs. Dalhousie set off briskly, stooping to retrieve bits of shed decoration, eager to assess the state of the sculpture's long-hidden side. Jen, Rafi, and the lesser gardeners followed behind.

The conservator had eyes only for her *Eves*, but Jen glanced accusingly at the square of raw soil that had last seen open air half a century before—then cried out and staggered backward. Rafi grabbed her arm, the others gathered round. Even Mrs. Dalhousie turned.

In the center of the dirt square lay a clot of hair and what could only be a human jawbone.

2

In a hospital bed some twenty miles south of the Gardener Estate, an old man made of bones and skin and angry eyes drifted slowly toward his death.

He was having what the nurses would call a good day. Oxygen hissed faintly through the nasal cannula rather than using the full-on mask. He'd eaten his breakfast, complaining all the while. Afterward, his vitals were steady enough for a sponge bath—by a male nurse, not one of the young women, and one who knew to keep his earbuds in and music playing so he didn't have to hear the old man's words.

When he was finished, the uniformed guard shackled the old man back to the bed and resumed his chair in the hall, closing the door in case the patient felt like calling insults at passersby. He was always worked up on the days the cops were coming. Especially the woman.

A *good day*, in the hospital, had a narrow and technically precise meaning based on oxygen, appetite, and wakefulness. *Good* had nothing to do with the man in the bed, or the staff's relationship with their patient, or their feelings about caring for him.

Frankly, most of them would not have minded if Michael Johnston's slow drift toward death speeded up, just a bit.

In a small windowless room some thirty miles north of the Gardener Estate, a woman walked an old quarter back and forth across her fingers as she studied the four photographs on her wall. Back and forth, went the coin. Back and forth.

Each photograph was 8½x11 inches. Under each was another sheet of paper that protruded exactly one inch. On each protrusion was a neatly printed name: Polly Lacewood. Sandra Wilson. Demi Scott. Windy Jackson.

The woman's eyes, a light amber color, seemed to be reading the photographs, shifting between one and another as if comparing a note on Polly Lacewood to something written on Demi Scott, then back.

It was the hidden lower sheets that had the writing on them: dates from the 1970s, place names from across the San Francisco Bay Area, enigmatic objects, personal names, arrows, question marks.

Back and forth, round and round.

When the cellphone on the desk in front of her flipped to 11:00, she set down the coin and opened the phone's text function:

Good time to talk?

A few minutes later, the cell rang.

"Hi, Al. Finished yet?" She listened for a time. "Okay, so maybe I should go down and see Johnston on my own? Why not? Al, we can't wait around for them to make up their minds. I'll just say I assumed I was cleared to work it on my own whenever you weren't available. And maybe not having a man in the room will tempt him into letting something slip. Yes, I know, but what can he do, anyway? He's a hundred years old and chained to a bed."

She listened, silent, for a time, her eyes fixed on the photographs. The one on the left had been there long enough that the tape was starting to peel.

"Al," she said finally, "you told me not to hand in my badge, and I said I wouldn't, but if my presence is getting in the way of—"

Again, she went silent, but for the occasional monosyllable. At the end, she nodded. "Okay, I'll wait till one of you is free. Just so they understand that we're running out of time."

She ended the call and stood, dropping her phone into her pocket. She retrieved a handgun from the locked safe in the corner, clipped it onto her belt, and picked up the cane propped against the side of the desk. She then looked down at the occupant of the room's other chair. "I'm not leaving you in here to mess up my notes."

The cat yawned, stretched, and paced in all innocence out into the hall.

The woman paused before she followed, to consider the four photographs on the wall. Polly Lacewood, Sandra Wilson, Demi Scott, and Windy Jackson. Smiling, blond, unsolved.

She turned off the light and shut the office door.

3

———

Jen Bachus would have expected that uncovering human remains—even old ones—might feel a little more . . . urgent. Yes, she understood that last week's triple homicide took precedence over some half-century-old bones, and she appreciated that the coroner's people were still here, but considering how chaotic her own last forty-eight hours had been—chaotic and apprehensive and filled with jolts of memory (*Are those* human *teeth?*) that stopped her in her tracks—she had not expected her initial skin-crawling shock to give way to something shamefully close to exasperation.

I should just accept defeat and close the Estate for a few days, she thought for the fiftieth time. Monday's police responders followed by Tuesday's reporters had brought today's unticketed thrill seekers and distraught loved ones (most of whom came looking for someone who had disappeared in the past five years, not five decades ago).

At least the gates would shut at 1:00 today. Wednesday afternoons were reserved for private tours—although Jen had canceled both of today's, then felt guilty at having hesitated over the loss of income. She also tried not to think of the cost of the extra guards, needed to keep the gawkers at bay, or of the psychologist they'd brought in both to dispense comfort and advice to the grief-stricken, and to counsel any Estate workers disturbed by Monday's events.

She'd discussed matters with her staff: should they close the Estate until it blew over, or simply deal with matters here and now? (She did not bring up any financial consideration: that was her problem, and she didn't want to appear ghoulish.) In the end, they all decided to hold out. The weekend would be nuts, but hopefully after that, interest would die down.

Jen tried not to wish for some other spectacular disaster to titillate the masses away from her door.

However, the day's endless stream of phone calls, text messages, and staff dropping by to consult did explain why, when the knock came at the half-open door of her office, the manager didn't bother glancing up from the printout she'd just dug out of the desk drawer, and her response was a touch impatient.

"Yes?"

"I'm looking for the manager, Jen Bachus."

"I'm Jen, but I really can't give you any information at this time, the Estate is closing for the afternoon. If you have questions, I'd suggest you talk to the police."

"I am the police."

Jen's head came around, her attention shifting from the list of backup guides to the woman standing in her doorway. Small, tough-looking, but with the most extraordinary eyes, a sort of translucent amber color. Tinted contacts? Unlikely—the rest of her was the very opposite of showy: cropped hair, no makeup, a teal shirt with rolled-up sleeves, khaki pants, sturdy walking shoes . . . and a cane.

The woman didn't look like a cop. Well, she did—of the granite wall school of cops rather than the swagger-and-brag school. And the cane wasn't necessarily permanent.

Jen realized that she was staring. She straightened, pushing back her hair and trying not to be drawn in by those eyes. "Sorry, we've had an endless stream of people looking for—sorry," she said again. "Yes, I'm Jen Bachus. How can I help you?" (The woman would have been striking even without the compelling eyes. Not beautiful, but vivid, with a sense of focus that would've been memorable. Come to that, she did look vaguely familiar, though not someone Jen had ever spoken to. Perhaps a visitor, glimpsed across the gardens?)

The policewoman took the question as a welcome and stepped inside.

"Raquel Laing, SFPD." She made no move to shake hands—but then, these days few people did.

"Oh, sorry, I figured you were here about the bones." *Stop apologizing,* Jen ordered herself.

"I am."

"Really? From San Francisco? Everyone else has been from San Mateo County."

"I'm with the Cold Case Unit. Consulting for San Mateo. More or less."

"Do you know who it is? The last I heard, nobody was even sure if it's a man or a woman."

"There's no ID yet, no."

"Okay, but I'm a little confused. I thought the police had to have a, well, a case before they could have a cold case?"

"It's complicated. Is this—"

"And aren't they usually murders? Have they decided that's what it is?"

This, at last, managed to sidetrack the cop. "It is difficult to envision it as a suicide or accident."

Jen gave her a crooked smile. "Yeah, but back in the seventies? The kind of people who lived here could have decided that this was the more ecological choice."

"The family was big on environmental responsibility?"

Jen blinked. "You don't know much about the Gardener Estate, do you, Ms. Laing?"

"It's Inspector Laing, and no, that's why I'm here. Is this a good time to talk?"

"Good? Well, I guess—oh Lord, is that the time? Look, there's two things I have to do first, and I can feel my blood sugar going nuts. I'll grab us some lunch and meet you in the garden. Go out the back of the house and make for the wisteria gazebo, I'll be there in ten minutes. Um, unless . . ." She looked at the cane. "Perhaps you'd rather do it here?"

"I'm fine, just not fast. What's a wisteria?"

Jen felt her jaw drop. "You don't know what— Sorry. It's that purple flower at the high end of the formal gardens. Oh, and here, you'll need a VIP pass so nobody tries to toss you out. Just clip it on your lapel."

Pass clipped, the policewoman stood back from the desk. "I'll meet you at the . . . wisteria gazebo."

She pronounced the phrase as if it were an unfamiliar taste in her mouth. Jen hesitated, then shook her head and trotted away with the list of possible on-call guides to use for the weekend.

Eleven minutes later, list delivered, Jen walked up the central path of the formal gardens. It felt like weeks since she'd taken a breath—two days in a maelstrom would do that to you—and in that time, spring had arrived. The earth smelled delicious, the greens sparkled. And the tulips were beginning to open, she saw—apricot parrots, new this year after much debate and looking very hopeful. Between them and the wisteria, weekend visitors would find plenty to post on social media that had nothing to do with bones, she thought with satisfaction.

The small woman in the gazebo turned at Jen's approach, to make her way down the steps and away from the heady scent. Jen wondered again if the cane was a permanent fixture. The deliberation in how she negotiated the steps suggested injury, not disability.

She caught herself before the woman could notice the direction of her gaze, and lifted her attention to the frothy sea of lavender blossoms. "Spectacular, isn't it?"

"Very pretty," the detective said.

Pretty? The Gardener wisteria was a showstopper! This time of year, it brought in half their paying visitors. It had appeared in every important gardening journal in America and half the bridal magazines. Printed on postcards, shopping totes, notebooks, mugs, and full-sized posters, it was one of the biggest earners in the Estate gift shop, second only to the image of Dylan driving the Revue bus.

"These vines are over a century old," Jen said tartly, "planted when the garden was first laid out in 1915. Half the wisteria in California comes from it." She heard the indignation in her voice, but was not about to apologize yet again. Instead, she held up the two picnic lunches. "There's a good table up at the top of what we call the Great Field—this way."

From a distance, the eighteen-foot-high laurel hedge around the formal garden looked impenetrable. A path through the structured beds led straight up to a wall of shiny green laurel, then at the last moment jogged left, and the woven bronze gate came into view—like one of those concealed doors in a library, Jen always thought. A magical place where shelves that looked fixed suddenly gave way—or here, a landscape that seemed formal and structured opened into sweeping near-wilderness.

The Gardener Estate was set in 3,500 acres of rolling Central Coast hills—low grassland dotted with live oaks near the house, higher coastal range covered with firs and redwoods beyond. Paths meandered over the slopes. Picnic benches invited visitors to appreciate the great central meadow. Discreet informational signs described the wildlife, geology, historical importance, and environmental projects of the Estate.

The gate was one of Jen's personal Gardener Estate treasures. With a creak of metal hinges, the visitor stepped from eighteenth-century England into the open expanse of California hills—the New World's reply to Capability Brown.

As usual, she turned to watch her guest's reaction—but Inspector Raquel Laing seemed as unmoved by the dramatic parting of the greenery to grassland and hills as she had been by the wisteria-draped structure.

The manager sighed, letting the gate swing shut as she carried their lunches to a nearby table. One of today's canceled groups had been a lunch tour, leaving the kitchen with the makings of thirty award-winning picnic lunches. Though the inspector probably wasn't going to be any more impressed by the meal than she had been by the view.

"Cheese or ham?" Jen offered.

"Either is fine."

So Jen set down the bag labeled HAM and carried CHEESE to the other end of the table.

Inspector Laing made no move to sit. She studied the colorful *Midsummer Eves* on its plinth of rebar-filled concrete, resting where the crane had deposited it on Monday. Its new position put it at eye level with the table—not that one could see the *Eves'* eyes at the moment. Instead, the long skirts and oddly-shaped torso ended in a lump of black plastic held together with duct tape.

Jen looked up to explain the trash bags, but saw that the inspector's gaze was now on the large canvas tent pressed up against the laurel hedge.

"The crime-scene people put that up," Jen told her. "Though I think they left for the day. Even with it, there's been a constant stream of people taking selfies where they found 'the girl in the statue,' as the papers insist on calling it. The sheriff had to leave one of his men here to chase people away. People are so macabre."

"I understand the remains were under the statue's concrete base."

"That's right. Turns out they poured it directly onto the soil—the reinforcing bars kept everything together, but there wasn't any base rock or anchor. This winter's rains were the final blow. We were lucky—the thing could have toppled over onto some family."

"Was the installation done without a permit?"

"A permit? Here, in the seventies?" Jen laughed. "We don't need no stinking permits."

"Still, I'd have thought basic engineering would be a requirement for monumental artists."

"The residents were probably too busy researching strains of cannabis to bother with how to keep a couple tons of art from falling over on their grandchildren."

The amber eyes darted over to Jen with something close to a smile, then took note of the waiting lunch. The small woman leaned her cane over the end of the table—something in the motion again brushed Jen with a sense of familiarity—and sat, methodically unfurling the lunch bag and laying out its component parts in a precise line. At the reminder, Jen did the same, with less precision.

"What is under the black plastic?"

"Three conjoined heads. Apparently based on the Hindu idea of a three-faced god, or in this case, goddess. A creator, a preserver, and a destroyer."

"Why are they covered?"

"Self-defense." Jen smiled at the cop's raised eyebrow. "Ours, not hers. Which is directly related to my short temper this morning. Are you familiar with the artist Gaddo?"

The inspector raised those remarkable eyes—golden now, in the full sun—toward the distant hills, as if retrieving facts from some inner storage facility. "Feminist collective and gender politics. Art depicting and occasionally incorporating women's organs and dead creatures. Worked with Judy Chicago. Arrested in France after throwing what was purported to be menstrual blood at . . . Dick Cheney, was it?"

"That's her. And that"—Jen nodded at the colorful figure—"is an early Gaddo. You probably saw our two other ones, up at the front door—*Adam* and *Eve*. They're so beautiful. All three were done in the seventies, before Gaddo went too bizarre. And although she's nowhere near as popular as she once was, thank God, our conservator is absolutely certain that once we show the art world what we have here, this week's madness is going to feel like a gentle drift downstream. We covered the heads before we opened Tuesday, so we could control when and how to make the announcement. We also put up some boring signs saying the plastic is protecting the heads from further deterioration."

"Did no one know you had a Gaddo?"

"Oh, they knew it was here—hard to miss. And you could sort of tell it had three heads, but it's been there for so long, and the hedge is so high, no one's seen the back for years. As soon as she saw them, Mrs. Dalhousie—our conservator—sent our gardening crew for a ladder and some trash bags.

"I thought she was nuts, because the hidden faces are amazing. But then Mrs. D pointed out that piling the artistic revelation on top of the news about the body would make everyone's life even more impossible—including that of the police. Some plastic trash bags would let us separate the two . . . upheavals. The sheriff agreed. Especially when we explained that, considering Gaddo's later reputation, someone is sure to suggest that she put the body there herself."

The eyebrow went up again. "Are you suggesting some kind of human sacrifice?"

"*I'm* not—this was a commune of organic farmers and their kids, not some weird Manson cult. But you know the internet, no rumor too wild. And Gaddo's fans are a little out there to begin with. However, no matter what happened, there's some family who lost a loved one and never knew where they were. So we decided that when that news is no longer quite so fresh, we can shape a separate announcement about *Midsummer Eves* itself. Because it really is an extraordinary piece, both as a piece of art and as a step in the artist's development."

The two women gazed down at the ugly black-and-silver lump atop the sweep of bright tile.

"Mrs. Dalhousie will have her work cut out for her. She's come across photos in the Archives that show the sculpture standing the other way around, just before it was installed, though it's half-hidden behind scaffolding and she can't think why they'd have turned it 180 degrees. Anyway, if the thing makes as big a splash in the art world as she anticipates, we are not ready for that now. So: trash bags. And later today, a nice tidy piece of cloth."

Jen sighed. "I hate having to be concerned about the Estate's reputation and convenience. It feels petty and inconsequential, compared to having some loved family member disappear. And if there is anything any of us can actually do to help, please let us know. In the meantime . . ." She shrugged. "I have a job to do."

"I understand. I would like to see those photos."

"Mrs. Dalhousie should be in the Archives until five o'clock—that's in the house, one of the upstairs bedrooms."

"Good." At last, the inspector turned to the containers arranged on the table before her. She picked up the menu card, which explained that the containers were compostable, the ham was organic and locally sourced, the herbs, vegetables, and olives in the pasta salad were from the Gardener Estate itself, and the dairy products in the sandwich and individual cheesecake came from a nearby, award-winning dairy. She laid the card aside and peeled the potato-based film from her recyclable bamboo fork. "Ms. Bachus, when did you first come to the Gardener Estate?"

Jen, surveying the elements of her own lunch, wished she felt some appetite. Maybe if she and this woman could talk about anything else . . .

She heard the silence and looked up, and gave a quick shake of her head. "Sorry—I was just thinking how difficult a cop's social life must be, when a simple question comes out like an interrogation."

"I suppose so."

"Well, I don't know when I *first* came to the Estate grounds, because we lived five miles away and my parents used to hike all over. I didn't know the commune itself—I was teeny when it disbanded—but even if it had been here, I'm not sure Mom would have brought me. She knew some kids who lived at Olompali, back in the Grateful Dead days, and she'd seen what could happen when things got chaotic. My dad died when I was nine, and she and my brother were both working, so I'd wander all over. Trespassing, of course. It was a different time then, you know?"

While Jen talked, she'd been rearranging the contents of her sandwich, but again, silence attracted her attention. The cop wore a look of polite incomprehension.

"'Olompali'?"

"You seriously *don't* know anything about the Gardener Estate, do you?"

"Well, you said it was a commune."

"I thought—you know. False modesty, police investigative techniques. So you don't . . . And you . . . Oh God. I've been going on about cannabis and cults and the Grateful Dead, and you have absolutely no idea what I'm talking about."

"I was only told about the bones here a few hours ago. Not much time for background research."

The cop's expression of polite bewilderment suggested that Jen had been speaking Turkish. Suddenly, she became aware of a bubble of emotion trying to push its way to the surface. Two battering days on top of several weeks of difficult conversations and year after year of having this place and its history the center of her every waking hour . . .

And the way the inspector had pronounced *Olompali*. With the same precise emphasis she'd used earlier on the words *wisteria gazebo* . . .

The bubble burst, coming out not as wild sobs but as a snort of laughter. Jen couldn't help it, couldn't help how the other woman's blink of consternation only made matters funnier. The most interest-ing person Jen had met in a long time, who cared nothing at all for the endless minutiae of an estate manager's life. Which might have been depressing, even insulting, but somehow hit her as absolutely invigo-rating. Like a jerk on the leash to her long years of self-absorption.

Jen threw back her head and laughed.

The outburst didn't last long, but as it trailed away, it left her feeling more herself than she had since the crane's engine roared to life Mon-day morning. She even felt the first vague stir of appetite.

"Sorry," she said, for what felt like the twentieth time since she'd met Inspector Raquel Laing. "I'm not laughing at you. It's just that, it's been a while since I met a person who not only knows nothing about the Gardener Estate, but who isn't even very interested in it. You, In-spector Laing, are a welcome and refreshing addition to what's been an extremely trying week."

4

Raquel Laing was not often surprised by people. Puzzled, certainly—she often had no clue why people did things, but as far as she was concerned, understanding the *why* didn't matter, so long as she could read the signs and anticipate behavior.

Jen Bachus had surprised her.

The moment she arrived at the door of the manager's office, Raquel had seen the stress: tight shoulders, wary eyes, an exaggerated twist of the lips for every minor challenge—looking for a paper, pushing back a fall of unruly hair, turning away yet another intrusive outsider. It didn't require her compulsive fiddling with her many rings or the flicker of disgust at the sight of lunch to know that the woman was near the breaking point.

Deliberately, Raquel had moved to counteract that tension, with a calm voice and the stance of authority. She'd managed to divert Ms. Bachus from the question of why a San Francisco cop was working a San Mateo case, and other than one minor glitch—something to do with the wisteria—the interview continued, despite the woman's distraction.

But then, when the next glitch rose up—Raquel's glaring failure to understand—instead of storming off and telling Raquel to go do her homework, Jen Bachus had laughed.

And continued to chuckle as she saw Raquel work to reassess the situation.

The relief of laughter had restored her appetite, as she picked up her sandwich with no sign of disgust. Her shoulders were relaxed, the muscles soft around her jaw and eyes. It made her look younger, more approachable, more appealing. *Dee would like her,* Raquel thought, then wondered where the idea had come from.

"I'm glad you find my ignorance amusing," she said. "Although I am actually interested in the Estate." *And I have been for nearly four hours now,* she did not add.

"It's okay. Most locals only show up here when they have some out-of-town visitor to entertain." Jen took a bite of her sandwich, chewing with a degree of relish.

Pushing brings antagonism; informality disarms. Raquel put on her most affable face. "Unlike you, who's been trespassing here since you were a kid. The roads would have been quiet enough that you could go all over on a bike, right? Let me guess: a red one."

Jen uncapped her bottle of sparkling water. "Blue. A hand-me-down from my brother. But yes, by the time I started sneaking in on my own, the Estate was more or less deserted. There were all kinds of falling-down huts and abandoned cars and school buses, places where they'd planted vegetables and pot, but The Commons itself was long gone. Putting the *Eves* up seems to have been one of the last things they did."

"Is there anyone around who would remember those years? Not necessarily who lived here, but nearby?"

But that was too direct. Jen's shoulders drew up and she concentrated on her sandwich, taking a deliberate mouthful too large to talk around. She chewed slowly, watching a hawk hovering high above the field. Eventually, she swallowed. "There's sure to be."

And sometimes you push. "Perhaps some of them still work here?"

"Could be."

"Ms. Bachus, do you have a reason not to tell me?"

Jen's face twitched rapidly through surprise to dismay, settled into an almost adolescent sullenness—then changed again as her eyes came to rest upon the handle of Raquel's cane.

"Oh, my God," she blurted. "That's where I know you from. That press conference last week. The Highwayman. You think this is one of *his*?"

Raquel sighed. The damned name was all over the news, since the arrest of Michael Allan Johnston and the belated admission that The Highwayman had not been some imaginary monster-under-the-bed, as they had claimed for years. Instead, a number of unsolved disappearances and murders from the seventies and eighties were indeed beginning to look connected.

Bad enough that half the jurisdictions in the Bay Area had totally overlooked a serial killer. Worse that it came on the heels of a similar revelation about ex-cop Joseph DeAngelo, whose spree of rapes and murders, hidden behind ten nicknames and multiple jurisdictions, was only found when DNA caught up with him, thirty years later.

Half the counties in the Bay Area were now scrambling to get up to speed with the Highwayman investigation. Al Hawkin had meant well, bringing Raquel to the press conference, but if he'd let her stay away as she'd asked, she would not be explaining herself to a potential witness on the Gardener Estate.

What was she supposed to tell this woman, anyway? *Yes, I'm most likely wasting your time. This body probably has nothing to do with Michael Johnston. Even if it did, San Mateo Homicide will have to go over it all again, once they're available. I'm just a cop who knows more about The Highwayman than most anyone, even if I am on medical leave (sort of) and here without my bosses knowing (some of them) and I'll wash my hands of your problem the minute I eliminate it from the Highwayman case.*

"Do you?" Jen demanded. "Think this is his?"

"I have to ask you not to talk about this, to anyone."

"But you do. Oh Christ. Poor thing. And—oh crap. We'll *have* to shut down now."

"Jen—Ms. Bachus, listen. I will be honest with you. We don't know. We have no reason to suspect any link. But he was active in the late seventies. I only want to make sure he wasn't here."

"But when word gets out . . ."

"If it does, it won't be from us."

"If I recognized you, anyone could."

"Okay, but I am with San Francisco, and I've been working with their Cold Case Unit. There are any number of investigations I could be pursuing here."

"Still."

"Ms. Bachus, we have to eliminate—"

"I know. I know, I know."

Raquel watched as the manager sat, elbows on table, dark brown hair spilling over her hands. *How did those rings not continually catch on her hair?*

"First the bones, then the Gaddo, now The Highwayman. What a shit-storm." Jen exhaled, and sat up, straightening her shoulders. "But I guess you have a job to do. And whoever that is—was—they deserve justice."

"Thank you."

"You said you hadn't identified the body, but do you have any, er, candidates?"

"That's one of the reasons why I'm here. There are a lot of tests to finish, and the bones were pretty thoroughly . . . disturbed." Crushed to bits, half-washed-away, then scattered across seventy feet of field by the crane.

"I watched it happen. And afterward, I watched those crime-scene people go over, picking up all the little bits. One of them even had the crane lift the *Eves* up again so she could slide under and check the bottom! I don't know about her, but that'll give *me* nightmares, her feet sticking out from under that slab of concrete like the wicked witch—" She shuddered. "Anyway, whoever it was, my chief responsibility is the Estate and the people who work here. We're all upset and frightened and hating that we've been walking around, oblivious of that poor soul. And whatever you find, it's going to create more trouble for us. So of course we'll help you—all of us—but don't expect us to be happy about it."

"I do understand. I'll try my best to be unobtrusive until San Mateo can take it back. But I'd like your help compiling a list of people who were here at the time."

Jen looked up as an appalling thought came to her. "You don't think it's possible that—What's his name? The Highwayman?—that he actually might have *lived* here?"

"Michael Johnston. And no, there's no evidence that he ever lived here." *Yet.*

"Well, that's something, anyway. As for a list, I can give you some names, though there will be more in the Archives. Mrs. Dalhousie will help."

Raquel closed the lid on the empty salad container and moved on to the sandwich. "What is in the Archives?"

Jen was toying with a carrot. "What isn't? The Gardeners were one of the most influential families in California. Their estate is a landmark, physically and historically. Fortunately for us, when The Commons arrived in 1975, they just—"

"Pardon," Raquel interrupted, "The Commons is, what, exactly?"

"That's what the commune called itself."

"So this place was actually a commune? Peace-and-love, changing the world, all that?"

"Absolutely—free love, brown bread, organic vegetables, and the rest. Not, as I said, a cult. In no way was it a cult. Ever."

"Okay."

"Anyway, they'd been up in Oregon, but after Rob inherited and they came here, they just shoved everything they couldn't find a use for into the attics. Which has been an untold blessing for us. There are ledgers from the Gardener gold mines, incorporation papers for the Gardener electrical and water companies, four decades of garden journals, notes and drawings from the architect. Maude Gardener—wife of the first Thaddeus Gardener, who built the house—had a real knack for bringing together unlikely people to forge political and artistic alliances. We have thank-you letters written by every president from Teddy Roosevelt to FDR. There's a short film of Albert Einstein being silly at the piano, and another of William Randolph Hearst being pushed into the reflecting pool. Maude collected Hollywood types, who would pay back her hospitality by filming a scene in the house—it appears in dozens of films. The garden alone influenced West Coast horticulture. The ballroom murals are by Thomas Hart Benton, and the foyer—well, I'm sure you saw the foyer as you came through. We get people here researching architecture, landscape design, twentieth-century art, all kinds of things. Although not many people are as fascinated by its commune era as they are the thirties and forties."

"Would you say it's common for a house like this to have a research center as well as garden tours?"

"Inspector Laing, I'm trying to tell you, there *aren't* any other houses like this. In England, maybe, but not in the United States—certainly not in California. And even here, most of what's in the Archives only survived because the Gardener family enjoyed its feuds, and no one could decide what to do with everything. I thank God for Mrs. Dalhousie, who spends far more hours than we pay her for, putting them in order."

"What kind of feuds?"

"Mrs. D could give you the details, but what it boils down to is, Rob Gardener's grandfather—Thaddeus Eugene Gardener the Second—was a true-blue, woman-hating, abusive son of a bitch, pardon my French. People called him the Old Bastard, and he lived up to it. He neglected his wife and daughter, drove his only son to suicide, and more or less kidnapped two of his grandsons—Rob and his older brother, Fort—to bring them here so he could control their upbringing. Fort—that's a nickname, for Thaddeus Gardener the Fourth—took off for India as soon as he hit his twenties and got written out of the will, but when Rob up and joined the Army, there weren't any other sons to leave it to, just the boys' cousins, David and Cynthia. And though David loves the place—and must have even as a child—he wasn't strictly speaking a Gardener.

"So because the old man didn't trust his son's sons, didn't count his daughter's children, and couldn't quite bring himself to leave the place to charity, he drew up what our lawyer describes as a stupidly convoluted will with a lot of stipulations. I don't know all the details, but in the end, Rob accepted them. And then he got back at the Old Bas—at the old man—by bringing the whole commune here with him, which I'm sure was not what Thaddeus the Second had in mind. The commune only lasted a few years, but Rob stayed on, first in the house itself and then in an off-the-grid cabin he built up on the edges of the property. That's where he lives now."

"The older brother, Fort, never claimed a share?"

"Not that I know of. Someone told me that Rob and Fort had considered giving it all away—house, land, money, the lot. Peace-and-love, the evils of capitalism and possessions, you know? But I think Jerry talked them out of it—that's Jerry Rathford, the Estate's long-time lawyer. So I guess the Old Bastard got his way in the end."

"You sound bitter."

Jen's eyes lifted to hers. "Silly, I know. Nearly half a century ago. And honestly, it would've been a shame to break up the Estate. This place is amazing."

"But there aren't any other Gardeners?"

"As far as I know, Rob—and possibly Fort, though he hasn't been heard from in years—is the last surviving Gardener." Jen's gaze wandered over to the *Eves*, and she gave a small sigh. "You want to know the people who were here in the seventies. Frankly, I'm not sure Rob has ever left them."

5

Then

Rob Gardener came home from Vietnam, like any other soldier in that spring of 1972, to a far different country from the one he'd left. He was braced for how sterile it would feel, how pale and tall its people would look after the streets of South East Asia—but when he smiled at a long-haired, miniskirted chick walking his way in the airport, he wasn't prepared for her to stop dead, glare at his uniform, and ask in a blistering voice how many babies he'd murdered. She then pursued him down the terminal, forcing him to duck into the men's room until his pulse settled.

He took care not to smile at any other women.

Outside the terminal, a bearded taxi driver drove past him like he was invisible. Rob was already jumpy, out in the open without his M16. *Idiot,* he told himself. *You should've let Marla know your flight.* The house car would've been waiting if he had, big and shiny and obvious.

Three taxi drivers in a row shook their head and said no, sorry, he was going too far outside the City for them. When the fourth one started to do the same, Rob nearly pulled the guy out of his window by the throat, but he kept the quick rage under control and offered him double. *Because yeah, think about it, Rob—what were the guy's chances of picking up a return fare from down the Peninsula?*

The guy studied his face and uniform, then jabbed his thumb at the back. Rob threw in his duffel and dove in after it.

"Thanks, man," he said, grudgingly. "I was starting to think I'd have to hitch."

The driver said sure, no problem, sorry the air-conditioning is broken but go ahead and open the window. Rob didn't tell him he felt comfortable for the first time since leaving the tropics, thirty-some hours before. The guy got onto the freeway, slid over to the fast lane, and starting talking over his shoulder, rattling on about Godfathers and George Wallace and mariners on Mars and goddamn hippies, one topic as incomprehensible as the next. The only pieces of news Rob had paid attention to in months were the drawdown of troops and Nixon going to China.

So he settled back with his eyes closed (or nearly so) and pretended to sleep. After a while, the driver noticed and shut up, and only spoke again when they were well south along the freeway.

"Uh, fella? Is this the road you wanted?"

"That's it. Three miles and then I'll tell you where to turn."

"Never been out this far before—I can see why you wouldn't want to thumb a ride. It's pretty out here, but there sure aren't a lot of houses, just that palace up there."

"There's a few, back from the road." The man was a little nervous, Rob could see. Middle-aged guy with a gut straining his shirt, driving into the middle of nowhere with an active soldier half his age and six inches taller. "Good of you to bring me out," he offered, and made a deal out of looking at the amount on the meter, then digging out his wallet. He even rubbed the bills together, to reassure the guy.

It worked. The chat resumed—deer on the hillside, the problem of wildfires, how far it was to the nearest Alpha Beta.

And then they were driving through the broad stone gates of the Gardener Estate, and the man fell silent again, through half a mile of spring-green hillside studded with native live oaks and mature imported exotics, all the way up to the "palace" at the end of the road. He slowed, and tentatively stopped before the broad entryway terrace, its manicured flower beds wrapped inside the arms of the U-shaped neoclassical brick-and-stone mansion.

Rob held the bills out over the seat. The man tore his gaze from the marble portico and took the money. "Thanks, man," he said in surprise, counting it again to check the tip.

Rob had just slung the duffel over his shoulder when the house door opened and a short, wide, gray-haired woman in an apron burst out, trotting down the stones with her arms outstretched. The young soldier dropped his load and swung the woman around in a circle, gently setting her down again as she reached both hands up to his face, tears coming down hers.

The driver was smiling as he dropped the car into gear.

"Robbie, Robbie, ah, look at you—so thin! We need to fatten you up."

"Marla-Ma, I've been saving myself for you."

Her face quivered at this childhood nickname, but she patted his face again and stepped back so he could scoop up his duffel. "You were lucky to find a taxi who would bring you—gas has gone over thirty-five cents a gallon, so they complain. You should have let us know when you were getting in."

"Planes are always late, and I didn't want Rodrigo to have to wait around for me."

"Rodrigo retired last year. Your grandfather uses a company now, it's silly to have a chauffeur here all the time. But for you, I'd have asked David."

"The kid has a license already?"

"Robbie, your cousin's all grown up and going to college, I told you. He'd have been happy to take the day off and meet you."

"I bet."

"Now, Robbie, David is a nice young man who adores you and your brother. Be generous to the boy."

"I always am, Marla. And it's good to know that one of my generation's going to college. What's he majoring in?"

"He's not the only one—Cynthia's at a university, too, back east. Davey's degree will be in business."

"Business? What kind?"

"One that will let him work for his grandfather."

"Ah, I should have known."

"What does that mean?"

"Nothing. Just that Davey's always loved this place more than Fort and me. I'm glad Grandfather will have someone he can trust around here."

She eyed him closely, for indications of sarcasm. When she could see none, she gave a sniff and changed the subject. "Was the flight home bad? How long did it take?"

"No time at all. I left tomorrow afternoon. Or maybe it was yesterday morning? I think my watch has stopped. What month is it?"

She slapped his arm. "Don't you tease me, boy, not if you expect to find anything in the cookie jar when you go looking."

"Ooh," he groaned. "Marla, I dream about your cookies. My whole squad dreamed about your cookies, after you sent that box at Christmas."

"It's the pecans," she said, as she did every time he praised them.

He was grinning as he walked into the cool perfection of the foyer, all black-and-white tiles and sea-green walls touched with gilt. Ridiculously grand, more suited to a concert hall than a home. But then, the Gardener mansion had always been more about performances than comfort.

And with that thought, the master of ceremonies himself was there.

Rob's spine went stiff, his face neutral. Marla hesitated, then turned to her boss. "Look who I found, Mr. Gardener. Doesn't he look thin? Good thing I bought that roast for dinner."

The old man looked across the chessboard floor at his grandson. "Robert."

"Sir."

"Welcome home. You might have let us know when you were arriving."

"I couldn't be sure what connections I'd make."

"There were no phones at the airport?"

"Didn't have any US change." A lie. But if you didn't push back against the Old Bastard from the get-go, you were lost.

Rob's grandfather gave a brief nod, acknowledging the declaration of battle lines more than a question of pocket change. "Join me in the Green Room."

"I need some lunch and a shower," Rob told him. "Give me a couple hours."

The faded eyes drilled into him across the space, probing his grandson's resistance for any weak spot. In the end, he simply gave another nod and turned away.

Rob knew better than to take it for a victory. Still, he felt lighthearted enough to smile at Marla as he followed her down the hallway and back to her realm, the kitchen.

A sandwich, a beer—in a glass—and his favorite kind of corn chips, which he'd never seen in any Army mess or even commissary. And yes, her Toll House cookies—soft and cake-like, the way he preferred them. With pecans.

She chattered, as always, about the goings-on of the Estate. The garden, a bad storm during the winter, some mischief a group of local kids had got up to. A mountain lion seen in the upper meadows, the number of wild turkeys this year. Any news of her own—the daughter who had married, a grandbaby on the way—always required prompting, as if he might rather hear about mildew in the rose garden and a leak in the ballroom roof instead of people he was closer to than most of his actual family.

The housekeeper's monologues, once started, made for an ongoing rhythm that did not call for any response. He'd once wondered if it was a sign of loneliness, since Marla's husband had died long ago, her kids were grown, and over the years the Gardener family employed fewer and fewer servants—only a handful now, compared with the fifteen or more full-time staff he'd grown up with. He'd decided her free-flowing conversation was more like a continuation of the radio she listened to when alone, a murmur of sound that filled the room and made it feel like home.

But every so often, she would insert a question. As she did now, setting his coffee in front of him, along with the lopsided red cookie jar he'd produced in a junior-high pottery class.

"Robbie, have you heard from your brother?"

"Yeah—one of his dumb postcards caught up with me just before I got on the plane. It's here somewhere." He dropped to his heels beside the duffel and felt around inside, coming out with the scrap of battered card stock that had made him laugh aloud. "Mailed from his ashram," he said, and handed it to Marla.

The picture postcard, cheaply printed, showed a glum-looking woman in a lot of clothes and necklaces, with the caption, Happy Dancing Girls of Bombay. The reverse had seven stamps, Rob's unit address, and the message:

HOT.

GETTING HOTTER.

HAPPY BIRTHDAY.

She frowned over the words. "Your birthday is in October."

"It's a joke. He hasn't written to you, or to the Old Bas—the old man?"

"Your grandfather has not had word from your brother since he left for India."

"And has *he* written to *Fort*?"

It was a question Marla could not answer without implied criticism, so she took a sidestep. "I wish you could get your brother to come home, even for a little time. It's been so long. And your grandfather hasn't been well."

"You told me that." Marla's letters were like her kitchen monologues, occasional bits of information dropped into meandering gossip, garden reports, and reviews of books and TV programs. Still, the boys had been hearing the housekeeper's ominous declarations of the old man's ill health ever since they'd entered their rebellious adolescence. Even if they took her seriously, her call for sympathy was doomed to failure.

"Robbie, please."

"I'll drop him a note," he relented. "Maybe the monsoon will make him want to get away for a while."

"You're a good boy, Robbie."

"No," he said. "I'm really not."

Her face changed. "Robbie, you're growing up, he's getting old. You two can start over. You're the only family he has."

"And whose fault is that? Anyway, it's not even true—Fort and David are family, too. And Cynthia, though she's a girl and we know how he feels about girls."

"Robbie—"

"Okay, Marla, yes. You're right. I'll be a good little grandson. Scrub my face and watch my language. Speaking of which, scrubbing my face sounds really good right now."

He drained his cup, thrust his hand into the jar to claim a large portion of the cookies, and bent to give her a kiss, deliberately scraping his two-day stubble against her cheek. He left the kitchen with his duffel over his shoulder and her affectionate scolding in his ears.

An hour later, clean, shaved, and in civilian clothes that were oddly tight in some places and loose in others, the cookies were a greasy weight in his stomach. He stood in front of the mirror, wondering who he was looking at. Good boy? Or Fort Gardener's pugnacious younger brother?

Rob hadn't been home since Basic. Grandfather had made it clear how he felt when Rob enlisted, and it wasn't worth having that argument again. So he'd spent all his R&Rs, including three weeks fighting a punji stick infection, on the other side of the Pacific.

Thirty-one months away, and the moment his bedroom door gave its familiar click, the Gardener Estate washed over him as if he'd never been gone. Fort's voice seemed to come from the window, punctuated by the low tones of whichever gardener he'd cornered and the higher-pitched comments from tagalong Davey. From inside came a memory of women's voices: Rosie and Gloria making up the rooms, Cook calling orders from the kitchen. And the smells—fresh-cut lawn, breakfast bacon, that lemony polish the maids had used since he was a kid. Mother's perfume drifting past, as faint and fragile as his memories of the woman herself.

How could all that survive, under two and a half years of male voices, chopper blades, and artillery, breathing in rancid sweat and fresh blood and the reek of the jungle?

He'd been tempted to put off homecoming. Why not bum his way around the country—the world, even? He was twenty-one years old, and 1972 had to have new things in it. Scenery that wasn't jungle or rice paddy, air that didn't throb with the beat of Hueys, people who weren't trying to kill him in all kinds of horrible ways.

But in the end, he'd written down San Francisco as his destination, and figured he'd decide what he wanted to do later.

That chick in the airport had been a shock. And he had to admit, he wasn't ready for what his old room would do to him—the only thing Marla had done was clean and tidy, so there he was, surrounded by meaningless sports trophies and posters for bands he could barely re-member. He should phone up his old buddies, go out for a beer. But who? There wasn't one he'd stayed in touch with. Which, for the first time, struck him as strange. Everyone else in the platoon used to hear from old girlfriends, even scribble the occasional card to the guys back home, but not Rob Gardener. Marla and Fort, that was it. And Davey, of course.

So how good were the buddies he'd had back in high school, any-way? There'd been one friend, Simeon. He and Sim were inseparable in junior year. Getting into trouble, sneaking a six-pack into the woods. Then one night, both half-drunk beneath the stars, Rob tried to ex-plain how in other families, calling a grandfather the Old Bastard might sound like an affectionate joke. How to other people, a grandfa-ther who crossed the country to rescue two young grandsons and their sickly mother from an unstable father might sound humane. How to a pair of orphaned boys, scathing criticism and unrelenting scorn could do more damage than a belt or a fist.

Sim, drunk enough not to notice that it mattered to Rob, had laughed in his face and called him a poor little rich boy. And that pretty much cooled the friendship.

Last time Rob stood in this spot, a boy had looked back at him—big and muscular, yes, but one whose rebellions were small, confined to collar-length hair and a string of tiny beads kept hidden under his shirt. July 1969. A month after he'd graduated high school. A week after Fort left for India. And one hour after Grandfather's lawyer had driven off, taking with him the new will that disowned Thaddeus Gardener the Fourth, his client's firstborn grandson and heir.

Rob's fists had been clenched the last time he stood here, too. Although then it had been a sign of upcoming decision, the boy talking himself into the recruiting office.

Now the person in the mirror was clearly a man. Not a good man, whatever Marla might think. But no longer a boy, willing to eat any plate of shit that was set before him.

He worked his hands to relax their tension—then noticed the motion, and realized that he'd done the same every time the platoon was setting out on patrol. He smiled with the face that didn't feel quite familiar, and straightened his shoulders as he turned to go downstairs. Time to let the old man know that his grandson's shit-eating days were over.

6

———

"I'm sure you learned to drink, over there," was the Old Bastard's greeting. "Pour yourself what you want. Unless they taught you drug habits, in which case I don't want you in my house."

Rob didn't think his grandfather looked sick. Just old and bitter, crouched as always in the dark green leather of his custom-made chair, in his windowless room at the center of the house.

"That's okay, Granddad, I got all the dope I need."

Thaddeus the Second had never been *Granddad,* always *Grandfather* or *Sir.* And Rob wasn't all that fond of hard liquor, but single malt was the language the old man spoke—and not that in the decanters, either. The old man kept an incredibly expensive one, in its bottle, to bring out for the few men who knew what it was. The bottle was currently tucked almost out of sight, on the small table near the old man's tweed-covered elbow.

Rob got himself a glass—reaching back for one of the treasured antiques. Only five of them now, thanks to Fort's last night here. Rob ran his thumb along the facets, remembering his brother's fury and the musical sound of heavy crystal shattering against firebrick. The brief surge of blue flame—and a few minutes later, while he and the Old Bastard were still arguing, the slam of the front door as Fort left for good.

Next, he traded the chair—an apparent twin of his grandfather's, but in fact maddeningly uncomfortable—for one of the older, more comfortable ones in the corner. Finally, he circled the table to pluck the half-hidden bottle from behind the old man's elbow, pouring more into the glass than he actually wanted. He set the bottle down on the table, took a casual swallow of the liquid gold—and only then did he sit down.

His grandfather watched it all from hooded eyes.

You can do this, Rob told himself. *If you can walk a jungle trail with Charlie sniping your ass, you can have a conversation with one old man.* "How have you been, Sir? Marla said you weren't very well."

"How would she know?"

"Marla knows everything that goes on around here. Always has."

"Nosey old thing. Time to fire her."

"You do that, old man, I'll fucking strangle you."

Rob was far more startled by his outburst than the old man seemed to be. One casual threat to a woman Rob loved—the woman who'd mothered him—and the words leapt out.

But then he registered the expression on the old man's face. Satisfaction? *Jesus,* Rob thought, *I fell for it again.* There'd been nothing casual about the threat. When it came to his grandsons, the Old Bastard always, *always* knew where to put the tip of the blade.

"Well, boy, I see the Army hasn't improved your manners any. As for your language, it was pretty foul before."

Rob took a slow breath and forced himself to meet the old man's eyes. "Sir, I apologize. I shouldn't have said that. I haven't slept in a couple of days, and my nerves may be a little raw."

That, oddly, brought a flicker of surprise. After a minute, the gray head gave a brief nod and turned to watch the fire.

Apologies, too, were a new thing here. Not that the Old Bastard was going to get more than one.

"You planning on staying here, boy?"

"If that's okay with you."

"I'll make a call in the morning, there's time to get you into Stanford come the fall."

"No. Thank you," he added, seeing the glare begin.

"What, you'd rather go to Santa Clara? I know your grades were crap, but you don't need to settle for Berkeley, like your cousin David."

"My grades were just fine, but I'm done with school."

"So you intend to sit around the house and take up navel-gazing like your idiot brother?"

"I thought I'd get a job."

"Doing what?"

The familiar scorn had Rob's hand tightening on the glass. *Don't react*, he ordered. *Keep it cool.* "Something real. Something physical, like construction work. Not for good, just for a while."

"Waste of time."

"It's my time to waste."

"You think so?"

"Look, you don't want me here, I'll move on. From what Marla says, Davey's more than happy to help you out. God forbid you should have to watch me waste my time earning an honest living."

The old man made a kind of a snort, but said no more.

They both drank, reconsidering.

"Also," Rob picked up as if nothing had been said, "I told Marla I'd see if Fort might like to come home for a little. If you don't want him here," he said, raising his voice over the old man's automatic protests, "I'll get a hotel room, Marla and I can visit him there."

To Rob's surprise, his grandfather didn't explode in a rage. Instead, he was studying Rob as if he were a stranger. "Got pretty sure of yourself over there, didn't you, boy?"

"I don't feel much like a 'boy' anymore, if that's what you mean."

"And now that Uncle Sam's made a man of you, you thought you'd come back and throw your goddamn weight around? Threaten me? You live in my house, boy, you mind your manners and follow my rules."

The old familiar anger washed through Rob, but instead of over-turning the table and storming out—instead of giving his grandfather the satisfaction—he held on to the fury for a moment, and became aware of something else, something near to gratitude. He had come home to decide what he wanted to do. It only took three hours to get the answer.

Rob downed the last half inch of his drink. "I guess this was a mistake. If you need me for anything, Marla will know where I am. See you around, Granddad."

"I should have known you'd be as much of a punk as your brother. I wrote him out of my will, I can do the same with you. Better to burn this place down than hand it over to a couple of pansies. Useless as your mother and father, the both of you."

And at last, there it was: a wave of clean, simple, purifying rage.

A quick snatch of the near-full bottle and a smash of glass, instantly followed by a *whomp* of distant artillery. This gout of flame was vastly more impressive, a billow that licked over the low table and set alight the lace of the mantelpiece scarf. In moments, his grandfather's shouts were drowned by the yammer of smoke alarms.

Seven minutes later, fire trucks with sirens and lights pulsing flew past a clean-cut young man with an Army duffel bag over his shoulder, walking calmly down the drive toward the gates of the Gardener Estate.

7

Now

Raquel watched, bemused, as Jen Bachus rummaged through her memory for names of people who might remember the Estate's commune era. Rob Gardener didn't seem to be the only person who had not left the seventies. Even this woman—the manager of a complex enterprise—seemed somewhat . . . free-spirited in the way she sorted information.

Jen had pulled out a small, chewed-looking notebook, talking to herself as she wrote. "Rob, of course. David. Jerry. And Wes—he and Rob are the only two who still live here. You might ask Rafi, our head groundsman. He wouldn't have been here himself, but his grandmother was the old man's longtime housekeeper. Let's see. There's Eddie. Artemis. And that guy in Berkeley with the pottery kiln—Sylvio? Sylvan, maybe. Oh, the weaving women, can't remember their names but I have their card in my office."

The process was entertaining, if nothing else, an apparently aimless meander through hidden byways that resulted in a growing list, even if some of the names were scratched out and others incomplete. The manager's unruly hair tumbled across her face as she bent to write, then fell back whenever she stared into the distance in thought. Twice, strands remained across her eyes, unnoticed, making Raquel's fingers twitch with the urge to tidy them back.

At last, the process ran dry, and Jen ripped out the page to hand to Raquel. "Those are people I've met over the years, though I'm sure there are loads more. Mrs. Dalhousie might help fill in some of the last names."

As Raquel frowned at the untidy edge, Jen took another dutiful mouthful of lunch, then swallowed hastily as she saw something over Raquel's shoulder.

"And speaking of Mrs. D," she said.

Raquel turned, and saw a work party coming down the path alongside the giant hedge.

"If you're finished, we should go down there. It's worth seeing." Jen stuffed the lunch remains into its bag with an air of relief, and trotted off to join the party.

At its head was a short, sturdy man in his fifties. Two younger men carried a long ladder, followed by a young woman with what looked like an armload of pillows. At the end came a tall, thin, gray-haired figure who could only be the New York art expert.

Raquel stifled her irritation and packed away her meal.

The young woman's load was indeed a pair of thick pillows, which the team duct-taped to the end of the ladder. With the conservator hovering and the men steadying the ladder, the young woman—the smallest person there—scurried up it with a pair of scissors, to snip the tape away from the offending black plastic.

The party held its collective breath as the lithe figure stretched out to ease some snag, and then the plastic was spiraling down to the grass. With the *Eves* now in view, Raquel had to agree: being glowered over by that face, and those teeth, would not make for a restful picnic.

Jen and the two older team members went quickly to the far side, followed by the others once the woman was safely on the ground. All stood, heads back, faces gone open with wonder. When Raquel had picked her way across the uneven hillside to join them, she could see why.

Despite years of dirt and some strands of long-dead ivy, the two hidden faces of *Midsummer Eves* were far from the Kali that had looked out. One wore the expression of a mother watching her child's first steps: warm, concerned, amused. The other was a bit more damaged, a little harder to interpret. It seemed to be a woman on the brink of orgasm—or perhaps, considering the distinct bulge of its torso, set for a final push in the birth process.

Seven people stared, held by fascination, until the silence was broken by someone's alarm. "Oh Lord," Jen said. "I promised I'd be in the office in ten minutes—David said he'd call to tell me what the Germans had to say. Mrs. Dalhousie, this is Inspector Laing, who's looking into our . . . into the bones. Could you give her some background, show her the Archives, help her with a list of names? Inspector, give me a shout if I can do anything—Mrs. D will give you my number so you can text me."

"Ms. Bachus, I need to set up interviews with—"

"Yes, I know. Jerry and Wes will be around tomorrow morning, David should be back on the weekend. Rob . . . I'm not sure. Let me know who else you need to see. Sorry, I have to run."

And she did.

Mrs. Dalhousie fixed her gray eyes on her new charge and nodded a greeting, but first things first: "Debs, you have the cover? If you don't mind stretching up a bit, I think the safest thing would be to roll up the edges and let it unfurl rather than risk dragging it across the surface." Safest for the statue, if less so for the young employee.

Raquel leaned on her cane while the team replaced the temporary covering with a soft, lightweight drape, made to fit neatly down to the shoulders, with a firm and professional-looking tie. The whole crew gave a small collective sigh as *Midsummer Eves* went back under its shroud. Mrs. Dalhousie thanked the others, who gathered their things and rattled off toward the house. Something about the now-faceless statue held Raquel's attention.

"Almost allegorical, isn't it?"

Raquel looked up at the older woman. "Sorry?"

"One has to wonder what Gaddo herself would have made of all this. Her work of art that explores the intersection of creation, preservation, and destruction, used to conceal a death, then rendered anonymous by a bit of canvas. She'd have had much to say on the matter. Come, I'll introduce you to the Archives."

They turned to follow the work crew, across the grass to the path that circled the formal gardens.

"The artist isn't still alive, is she?"

"She died twelve years ago."

"Why do you think she turned her statue's Destroyer face out to the world?"

"I'd love to know. Being Gaddo, there will have been a reason."

"You don't think the hedge simply grew too tall to see them?"

"The photos from that time show it nearly the same height. No, it was deliberate. But whether it was artistic choice or a political statement, I couldn't say."

"Was she a member of the Gardener commune?"

"She doesn't seem to have been. I believe she was friends with a woman named Meadow, who was Rob Gardener's partner—romantic partner, that is. Gaddo was one of a steady stream of artists and musicians who stopped in, during that time."

"It sounds like you're an expert on Gaddo."

"I wasn't, when I happened to come here and spotted them. Frankly, I was starting to find retirement just a tad boring, and the Estate and its Gaddoes gave me a project to keep busy with. The *Eves* in particular are a challenge, since there's almost nothing in the artist's own records about them. Though funnily enough, there's quite a bit about these two."

They had followed the path along the laurel and past a high brick wall to the house's grand entry, half an acre of stone terrace set with neat garden beds inside the arms of the house itself. Mrs. Dalhousie pointed at the figures on either side of the portico.

On the left, a man with a shiny red apple in one hand and the other on the shoulder of a small child; on the right, a full-skirted woman, topless but for the coils of a large snake. Her right hand held what looked like a stick with string wrapped around it, while her left cupped the brown head of a child clinging to her skirts. Recognizably by the same artist as *Midsummer Eves*—some of the tiles used were distinctive—Raquel had seen this one somewhere.

"Adam and Eve," the archivist said. With—presumably—Cain and

Abel. The *Eve* was used for the cover of a bestselling novel a few years ago." Her tone of voice said it had not been her kind of novel.

"Jen mentioned these. From the artist's early, pre-macabre phase, when she still appreciated beauty."

"Jen Bachus is a clever woman, and relentless when it comes to the Gardener Estate, but her interest in art is filtered through that lens. She likes these because the general public finds them . . . accessible."

"You don't think they're as good as the *Eves*?"

"Good? What makes art 'good'? I do know that great art is not comfortable." And with that declaration, she walked past the dismissed guardian figures to open the door.

They did not pause in the foyer—perhaps the conservator judged the mural, vibrant and enticing, as too naïve to be anything but comfortable. Halfway across the checkerboard floor, she remembered Raquel's cane and adjusted her path away from the stairs, circling down a corridor and through a fire door marked KEEP CLOSED and EMPLOYEES ONLY, inside which stood a pair of incongruous metal doors. She pressed the UP button. Rumbling began.

"You're in the kitchen wing now, which used to house some of the servants. Men downstairs, women up. The elevator is in what used to be the butler's pantry."

The ponderous doors drew back, revealing the padded-room effect of an elevator designed for moving large but delicate treasures. The doors drifted shut, and after more rumbling but almost no perceptible motion, they were on the upper floor.

The archivist led Raquel through another fire door and down a corridor that was slightly less formal than its double below, suggesting a private family realm. The right was open to the stairs and foyer, while doors on the left gave glimpses into bedrooms with four-poster beds, thick carpets, and gleaming furniture. Two of the rooms had hand-painted frescoes rather than wallpaper. They turned right again into a shorter corridor that stopped at a door posted:

ARCHIVES.

BY APPOINTMENT ONLY.

Inside had once been a bedroom—a suite, by the looks of it, though smaller than those they'd passed. Darker, too, with its only windows in the wall to the left. To the right were two doors, one showing old-fashioned bathroom tiles. The room's back wall was unbroken—at least what Raquel could see of it behind the metal storage frames fitted with acid-free flat boxes. These were labeled, arranged chronologically from GENEALOGICAL RECORDS 1816–1979 to SOCIAL MEDIA 2010–. Each box had the same prominent notice fastened to its end:

PLEASE DO NOT RE-FILE.
LEAVE BOXES AND FILES IN CENTER OF TABLE
OR ON ARCHIVIST'S DESK. THANK YOU.

The Archives room resembled an exclusive women's club taken over by college students. Delicate wallpaper, cut-glass light sconces, velveteen drapes, heavy carpets—and two long work surfaces made of Ikea dining tables set end to end, lit by an odd mix of graceful Art Deco lamps and flimsy gooseneck desk lights. Even the artwork ran the gamut, from a trio of delicate watercolors to a map dated 1781 to a psychedelic poster advertising a rock concert.

And dozens of framed black-and-white photographs: Katharine Hepburn, laughing beside an enormous Christmas tree. Cary Grant leaning out of an upstairs balcony over a sea of roses. Howard Hughes, glowering out from under the wisteria gazebo. Albert Einstein, seated at a grand piano in a ballroom. William Randolph Hearst, Franklin Delano Roosevelt, Ronald Reagan, on and on.

When she reached the far end of the room, Raquel looked down on a scattering of cars. *What had the view been before the parking lot went in?* she wondered. Those other bedrooms looked out over the formal garden, and had balconies. This room was lesser in all ways.

Mrs. Dalhousie spoke, some dry undertone in her voice suggesting that she had been listening to Raquel's thoughts. "These were the rooms given to Rob and Fort's mother, Joanna. After she and the boys were brought to live here."

"They didn't consider her important enough for one of the good rooms, I take it."

"So it would seem. Now, what can I do for you, Inspector Laing?"

Raquel began to make her way back up the room. "Like Jen said, I need some background. Who was here and what was happening in the seventies."

"This is in regards to the body under the Gaddo?"

The body under the Gaddo. Two days after it had come to light, Jen Bachus was still actively distressed, while this woman had tucked the same experience into a neat title. It occurred to Raquel that Mrs. Dalhousie's "retirement project"—no doubt a book—had just taken a big step from the academic to the popular. Not that the woman would admit to such a crass concern as book sales. Mrs. Dalhousie was the very personification of the word *steely:* tall, thin, and rigid of spine, her iron-gray hair showing no wisp out of place, her light gray eyes glinting from behind metal-rimmed glasses. She was designed, head to toe, to intimidate a short, damaged, slightly unkempt detective.

Raquel liked her already.

"Sounds like the title of a mystery novel. But yes, I'm here about the bones."

"Do you know who it is yet?"

"No. It's not directly my case, but San Mateo is, as you can guess, pretty swamped."

"Terrible thing," Mrs. Dalhousie agreed.

Three bodies, the shooter gone: *terrible* was the word.

"Their coroner and labs are working flat out, so I'm helping with the groundwork. Such as when the sculpture was installed, and who might have been here."

"June 23, 1979."

"That's very precise."

Was that faint twitch on Mrs. Dalhousie's stern face an actual smile?

"I generally have a cup of tea at this time," the archivist announced. "Would you join me? Or there's coffee, if you can abide instant."

"Tea would be fine," Raquel exaggerated, and trailed behind the very straight spine, down the hallway to a windowless space furnished as a break room.

Tea was not a bag in a mug, but leaves in a pre-warmed pot. When it was brewing, the older woman showed her first sign of uncertainty, studying Raquel with a beady eye. "Food and drink are not permitted in the Archives, although under some circumstances, I allow them at the corner table just outside my office. If you do not consider this a precedent, we can take our tea there."

"I absolutely promise not to dribble, or to consider it permission for the future."

A brisk nod, and they took their refreshment back into the dragon's realm.

8

It was a nice cup of tea, as tea went, presented with as much cere-mony as one might expect in Japan. Settled at last with a cup that had been steeped four minutes, poured through silver, garnished with milk, stirred precisely five times, and handed over along with a dry-looking cookie, Raquel admired, sipped, and set the cup and saucer down with care.

We're not in The Mission anymore, Toto.

"Where would you like to begin?" Mrs. Dalhousie asked. "With your list of names, or the family's background, or the reason for know-ing that date?"

"I'd say the date is due to that poster you see every day."

The archivist turned her head to look at the neon-hued broadside with its wild lettering advising a rock concert on the Gardener Estate. BACK TO THE GARDEN, it exclaimed, JUNE 22, 1979. Scattered around the page were names of some bands even she recognized, interspersed with topics that seemed fairly random: *Biodynamic gardening! Raku pottery! Community!* The poster's upper left corner had a spray of musical instruments; a cornucopia of summer vegetables filled its lower right.

"The date gave the title to Gaddo's piece," Mrs. Dalhousie said. "*Midsummer Eves.* The festival was the day before Midsummer, and installing the statue was supposed to be its high point. In fact, the installation itself was delayed, although the base went up on the twenty-third. We have a roll of film with the first half taken during the festival, and the rest the next morning. The last pictures show people hurrying to break down the stage while a cement truck stands waiting—for some reason, they'd built the festival stage directly over the frame. The last image shows concrete spilling down the truck's chute."

She reached for the teapot. "All those young people, so filled with excitement and purpose. One sees no indication that the commune was on the point of falling apart."

Was it because someone died here? Raquel wondered. *Did that shatter the bond? And if so, was it one of their own, or a stranger come to the festival? Did The Highwayman come riding, riding up to the old inn-door . . .*

Irritably, she shook off the compulsive rhythm of the old poem. "I understand that the commune was only here for four years."

"Not long, I agree, but life was changing at the end of the seventies. Romance died. People had children, and children need stability."

"Ms. Bachus told me that Rob Gardener installed his friends here as a way of getting back at a controlling grandfather."

The archivist frowned. "I suppose it's true that you can't really understand his decision without knowing something of the family's history." She laid down her cup with a musical *ting* and went over to the storage frames, bringing back two boxes: 1915 and 1959.

"The first Gardener in California was William Ronald, who came out from Philadelphia during the Gold Rush. He made money in the goldfields, then more money selling goods to other miners, then a small fortune buying up land in the Sierras to supply San Francisco with power and water. His only son, Thaddeus Eugene, made the fortune huge. A telephone monopoly, housing developments up and down the Peninsula, arms sales and profiteering during the First World War. Thaddeus and his wife, Maude, built this estate, intended to be a sort of Californian Versailles, but he died in 1920, before it was finished. Maude and their only child, Thaddeus the Second, put the Estate on the social and political map."

She had been leafing through the box, and now handed Raquel a formally posed photograph showing a beefy man in a high collar, a thin woman wearing an enormous flowery hat and a disapproving look, and a boy of maybe sixteen sneering down his nose at the world. Someone had printed on the white border, *Mr. and Mrs. Thaddeus Gardener I; Thaddeus Gardener II. June 1915.*

"Thaddeus the Second"—the archivist pointed at the sulky teenager—"was twenty-one when he inherited. He married a woman named Flora, but even in their wedding photographs, Flora is eclipsed by his mother. She only lived long enough to produce a son and daughter, then quietly slipped away. Maude ran the house for her son—ruled it, you might say. And once it and the garden were finished, she turned her considerable energies to the Gardener future. It was she who came up with the idea of a special train leaving Southern California every Friday, returning the guests to Los Angeles in time for the start of filming on Monday. And while the film stars were here, she could use them to charm politicians and industrialists.

"To go by Maude's letters, guest lists, and journals, she and her son intended for Thaddeus the Third to become California's governor, perhaps US senator. They may even have hoped to aim him at the White House.

"Unfortunately, the boy wanted no part of their plans. He hated the Estate, fell in love with a woman his father and grandmother both disapproved of, and married her anyway, taking her back to the family's original home, Philadelphia. His wife, Joanna, was a sickly thing, but she managed to have two sons—Thaddeus the Fourth and Robert John, later known as Fort and Rob."

She set down a black-and-white snapshot with wavy edges showing two old people and two young ones, standing in front of a gazebo that was already thick with vines. Thaddeus the Second, the sneering adolescent from 1915, was now a haughty sixty-year-old, while Maude, in her eighties, was every bit as rigid and disapproving as she had been half a lifetime before. They flanked the two boys, who stood with their shoulders touching, keeping open space between them and the adults on either side.

Raquel did not need the boys' facial expressions to read what their bodies were saying: *us against the world.* "Which boy is which?"

"The dark-headed one is Rob, who would be six or seven there. Fort is two years older."

"Were the parents still alive when this was taken?"

"Joanna was, though there's almost no pictures of her. The boys' father had died the year before. It was a sad story—Thaddeus the Second refused to support them in Philadelphia, and Thaddeus the Third refused to come home. The two boys suffered, Joanna seems to have had at least one miscarriage, and in the end, the old man went out to Philadelphia to claim his grandsons, leaving his own son there. I understand the poor fellow committed suicide—although that may have been beforehand, and the reason why the old man went to fetch the boys, it's not too clear. In any event, the boys were so young, he had to bring Joanna with them, although he and Maude between them made her life a living hell. She died in 1959, Maude the year after, leaving the boys to be raised mostly by the servants, with some help from their aunt Viola."

She took the photograph from Raquel, studying it before she returned it to the box.

"As one might expect, none of this made for an affectionate household. When the boys grew up, it was the sixties. Fort discovered meditation and drifted off to India. Rob joined the Army, leaving the old man on his own. With servants, of course."

"And his daughter, Viola."

"They don't seem to have been particularly close."

"She had children?"

"David and Cynthia. But the Gardeners were strict believers in patrilineal descent. Sons inherit, not daughters, and not a daughter's children. If their surname wasn't Gardener, the old man wasn't interested."

"Old-fashioned."

"Positively medieval. Now, you said you had a list of names I might help with?"

Mrs. Dalhousie reached for a lined pad, set with a silver pencil at her side.

A form of brisk efficiency that came as something of a relief, after the ragged, crossed-out page from the notebook of Jen Bachus.

9

_____

Raquel had got no further than taking out Jen's mangled page when her ringtone told her Al Hawkin was calling.

"I have to take this," she told Mrs. Dalhousie. "It's my partner."

"You'll get better reception on the other side of the house. Pick a room overlooking the gardens."

"Hold on, Al," Raquel said as she stumped down the corridor, "I need to find a place where the call won't drop. This should be—yes, this will work." It was one of the showy bedrooms they'd walked past, with heavy furniture, dark colors, two formal portraits on the wall. She settled into the chair without a cord across it.

"Wanted to let you know, you're off the hook for tonight," he said. "Johnston's doctor isn't happy with his blood pressure, has him back on oxygen and gave him a sedative. Says he's not to be disturbed."

"Damn it."

"I know. You find anything yet?"

"They have archives, I'm seeing what might be there. But it looks like the concrete went down on June 23, 1979."

"Well within Johnston's period."

"The archives are extensive, and there are photographs. If I find anyone who looks like Johnston, I'll make a copy. Oh, and that picture his daughter gave you—could we get it touched up with two or three kinds of facial hair? It would be useful to show it around here."

"Already sent it to my guy, he'll have it tonight."

"Any word from San Mateo?" Al was friends with the Homicide investigator officially in charge of the Gardener body, so communication went through him.

"They are officially good with our going ahead, so long as we keep them fully apprised of our findings. Privately, they're flat-out grateful that they don't even have to write any reports."

"Okay, then I'll set up interviews for tomorrow with two men who knew the place then. The archivist is helping me with other names."

"Anything you need me to do?"

"Make sure Michael Johnston keeps breathing."

Al made a noise that might have been an agreement, or a warning, and the phone went dead.

Raquel sat for a time, phone on knee and eyes on the disapproving features of the middle-aged man in the portrait. He was seated on a dark green chair, hands gripping the arms like a king on a throne. Next to it was an equally critical gray-haired woman, done by the same painter. Her hairstyle suggested the 1940s. The Old Bastard and the grande dame Maude, scheming to establish a Gardener dynasty.

It wouldn't have been easy, Raquel thought, to be a boy growing up in this house. Even with a brother, it would have taken some character to stand up to those two.

She got back to find the archival boxes from 1975 to 1979 lined up on one of the long tables.

"These are the years the commune was active," Mrs. Dalhousie said, then added, "I'm only up to 1964, so these boxes are not well collated. I also have movie film taken the day of the festival, which I can get out of storage if you want."

"I'd appreciate that."

"I am assuming you have a . . . candidate in mind. For who the bones were. Can you tell me who you think it might be?"

In fact, the face Raquel was hoping for was not victim, but perpetrator—but she did not want to go into The Highwayman. She merely shook her head.

"Sorry, I can't talk about it."

"I understand. Though of course the, er, victim could have been a stranger, who came for the festival. Am I correct in thinking that they had blond hair?"

"Blond or very light brown."

"But you don't know if it's a man, woman, or child?"

"Not a child—the teeth are adult."

"A small mercy," the archivist said. "Well, I'll let you get on with it. There's a copy machine and scanner in the next room if you want, and the wifi password is near the light switch. Please leave everything on the table when you're finished. I have to go at five, but Jen can lock up after you—oh, she asked me to give you her number. And here's mine as well." She wrote the numbers down on a neat rectangle of scratch paper. "If you have any questions, don't hesitate to ask."

Raquel looked into the indomitable gray eyes. *Personal effort should be met with personal recognition.* But in fact, it was not hard to give the archivist an honest smile. "Mrs. Dalhousie," she said, "once you finish putting the Gardener Estate in order, we could use you on the Cold Case files."

She'd judged matters nicely: the older woman turned ever so faintly pink.

Five boxes. Raquel was tempted to start with 1979, since that was when it happened. Instead, she pulled the top off 1975, and was immediately struck by the contrast with the other two boxes Mrs. Dalhousie had opened. In 1915 and 1959, photographs were in archival plastic, newspaper clippings neatly mounted on acid-free paper. Here, everything was loose: random photographs, yellowing newsprint, letters, postcards, booklets and appliance warranty sheets, lists of plant names, children's drawings, empty seed packets. The only attempt at order was an old manila envelope that bulged with bills and check registers.

Two photographs were of interest, although neither had anyone resembling Michael Johnston. One showed a collection of vehicles lined up in what looked like a dust bowl farmyard of the thirties, but was probably Oregon, with the commune about to set out for California. The second, faded and crinkled by a long-ago fold, showed five children of various ages racing after a beach ball down the long slope of what Jen had called the Great Field.

She returned them to their year, and reached for 1976. This, too, was in a relatively disordered state, but for three sets of photographs in plastic Fotomat pouches. Conveniently, the developer had put the dates on them: 3/8, 6/30, 11/1. She opened the one for March, and stepped into another world.

10

Then

Planting Day, 1976.

Annabelle *loved* the little camera her mama had sent her for Christmas. She'd shot one whole roll right away, but decided to save the next for the Planting Day celebrations.

The Commons had been debating the date for Planting Day since the morning back in September when they'd started pulling out the ugly green hedges—just ten days after the caravan of cars, pickups, and converted school buses had arrived at the Gardener Estate. Only a few of The Commons knew anything about gardening in this part of California, a place people said had no hard frost at all. But conversations with locals—including the last of the Estate's gardening crew, who really didn't know what to make of them, and the people who ran the health food store in town, who were more useful—followed by a search through the nearby library for old newspapers had Meadow thinking about planting in early March.

So in January, the biggest upstairs bedroom—one of those with paintings on the walls instead of wallpaper, which was the warmest room in the house and had good windows—was cleared of its huge bed and old-man furniture and given over to a sea of tiny pots—clay and plastic, milk cartons and cutaway plastic bottles, all filled with Meadow's mixture of sand and soil and the first batch of compost.

The kids loved the anticipation, checking for signs of life ten times a day. They came pounding down the stairs with squeals of excitement the morning the first bean leaf curled its way into the light. And with a degree of ceremony, Meadow marched them into the kitchen to turn over the commune's central calendar and write *Planting Day* on the square for March the first.

They'd long ago stripped the sunniest portions of the once-formal gardens down to bare earth, piling huge loads of those boring plants on the burn pile, planting the neglected soil with fava beans and red clover and mustard—what Meadow called green manure. A trip to the beach added seaweed. One of The Commons who worked in a café brought home endless buckets of eggshells and coffee grounds. Now all those nitrogen-rich plants and treasured amendments were dug deeply in.

The camera was a secret present from Annabelle's mother—secret from her husband, that is, who wanted nothing to do with their wayward daughter and illegitimate grandson. Her mama's small rebellion had surprised Annabelle: a simple camera, a dozen rolls of Kodachrome, and a Fotomat gift certificate to cover the developing—with a duplicate set of prints for Mama, mailed care of Auntie Rae. The first roll had been mostly of Sparrow, so his grandmother could see him grow. But honestly, *this* was Sparrow's family now, not his blood relations. So Annabelle planned to record his family here with the rest of the film, beginning with turning those sterile flower beds into an Eden to nourish their communal family.

March 1 was sunny and warm. For the first picture of the roll, she gathered the kids in the upstairs room with their dozens of sprouting young plants. The next showed Meadow, Pig, and Daisy in one of the freshly-turned beds, making holes for the little tomato plants waiting on the gravel path. Then Sparrow solemnly smashing eggshells with the other kids, his towhead gleaming white against the background of dark earth. Next, six children pushing thumbnail-sized squash seeds into the ground. By the afternoon, shirtless men were sweating as they turned over new ground and hammered in stakes for the tomatoes. The women's hair gleamed under the sun as they bent to tamp the soil, water in the plants, or admire the buds on a new bare-root fruit tree.

And when the photos were developed, Annabelle would write a description on the back of both copies, in her clear, round, schoolgirl handwriting: *Sparrow helping! Wes striping branches to make bean teepees. Pig (Peggy) turning the compost. Paolo showing Meadow how to graff apples.*

Midsummer's Day, 1976.

So hard to believe this enclosed garden paradise had been, just a few months ago, that block of brutally controlled greens and regimented colors! The beds were still geometric, of course, but the squash and nasturtium were already taking over the pathways. Where flat squares or triangles of color had stood, a hundred shades of greens rose to head height or more. Annabelle's camera again marked the day, catching glimpses of adults nearly hidden by plants, or children disappearing completely inside eight-foot-tall bean teepees.

And the harvest! Things ripened so much earlier than they had in Oregon. The big tomatoes were still green (she took a shot of one that nearly covered Wes's palm) but the cherry-sized ones filled a basket in Meadow's hands. She also lined up a row of kids, from one-year-old Dylan to thirteen-year-old Emma, and had them each hold up a green bean that matched their size, tiny to tall. In another shot, two of the men tucked some enthusiastic vines of winter squash away from the path, the fruit already the size of a tennis ball.

The last shot in that roll was of their celebration meal, with its centerpiece dish of beans and marble-sized red and yellow tomatoes. Again, she wrote captions on the backs, for her mother and for her own memory. *Sparrow likes beans,* it said on the back of one photo. *Rob inside a greenbean teepee. Meadow with 5 kinds of tomatoe! Rain with his guitar—he's really good. Mike and Wes moving the squash out of the path.*

Harvest Day, 1976.

In Central California, harvest went on nearly year-round. But like Meadow said, ritual was important when you lived off the land, and so a day in October was chosen to bring in the crops with the longest growing season, the winter squash.

Some were a little larger than a softball, others needed a grown man to lift them into the wheelbarrow. All of them had to be protected from the coming rains, so they set up benches and tables in a cool, dry corner of the never-used stables (to keep them away from the mice) and with the kids carrying the small ones and the adults the large, their harvest was preserved.

That night, they stuffed themselves on pumpkin pie (not really pumpkin, but the more flavorful Hubbard and red kuri squash). After the kids had gone to bed, the adults brought out another kind of harvest, processed in an illicit still in the woods, and made merry for a successful first year on the aptly named Gardener Estate. *Sleepy Sparrow,* said a picture of two bright blond heads nestled together on a sofa. *Ten punkin pies!!! Rob, Rain, and Meadow (isn't she pretty?).*

11

Now

The Fotomat pictures, Raquel saw, had been for a customer named Annabelle Paulson. Each set seemed to be from a single day, and centered around the garden—vegetables then, not flowers. Notes on the back in girlish handwriting often had to do with a toddler named Sparrow. Though from the size of him, *Bear* might have been more accurate.

Most of the males looked a bit bearlike, too, all hair and muscle. The March 8 photos showed a day warm enough to work shirtless—mostly the men, although two naked backs rose from wide hips, and one woman had only the bib of her overalls to keep the Fotomat attendant from censorship.

Everyone worked. Children planted seeds. Men hammered in stakes and wheeled loads around. A sturdy young woman with a long blond braid grinned as she prepared to plunge her pitchfork into a heap of leaves: *Pig,* said the note, *turning compost.* And here was Rob Gardener's partner, Meadow, wearing farmer's overalls with embroidery up the leg, frowning in concentration as a beautiful young man demonstrated how to "graff" apples (the photographer's spelling being as childish as her writing).

The June envelope showed that same garden transformed by three months of loving attention. A bearded face grinned out of a thick con-

struction of vine leaves like a modern-day Green Man: Rob—
Gardener, no doubt—in a "teepee" of bean plants. And here was
Meadow again, proudly displaying a basket of what looked like multi-
colored marbles, but which the note said were five kinds of tomatoes.
In the next shot, Meadow was pushing a bright red globe into the
middle of Rob's beard: short blond woman, tall dark man, both laughing. There were pictures of women hunkered down in the plants,
naked children racing about, a brown chicken scratching between
seedlings. One devilishly handsome man—Rain, said the note—
perched on a stump with his acoustic guitar and sang to the workers,
his hands and jeans suspiciously clean. Two men were doing something at the edge of a path. Raquel flipped it over, and her day narrowed in on a name:

Mike and Wes moving the squash out of the path.

Mike.

She laid the photograph on the table and took out her phone to retrieve the image of Michael Johnston in 1980. He was clean-shaven,
while the man in the photo . . . Raquel cursed at the unhelpful angle:
both men were hunkered on their heels. One had his back to the camera, a long, brown ponytail descending from the straw hat he wore.
The other one, his face half-hidden, had the shortest hair of any adult
in the commune, but seemed to have a beard.

She went through the other pictures in the envelope, and identified
the ponytail as Wes—with luck, the same Wes who was still on the
Estate. No other image of "Mike," unless he was one of the background figures.

She set the picture aside, along with several other blond heads, including Meadow (*isn't she pretty?*), Pig, an older woman named
Heather, and a girl who looked no older than sixteen, sitting with a lap
full of child. The caption on the back only mentioned Sparrow and his
fondness for beans. Which suggested that Annabelle was not only the
photographer, note-maker, and Fotomat customer, but the child's
mother as well.

Raquel turned to November's Fotomat envelope, but found no
other mentions of Mike, and no pictures that might be of a young Michael Johnston.

In the end, she had nine potential victims: five women, three men, and a teenager of uncertain gender who might be old enough for the teeth they'd found. Only Annabelle had a full name. The others were at best first names, some only nicknames. She knew more about the crops they had grown than the details of their lives or relationships, she could only guess at their ages. Most of her notes had question marks.

Annabelle Paulson? (16/17? mother of Sparrow?)
Meadow (30s, lover of Rob)
Heather (25—might be too tall)
Pig (Peggy, female, 25, 2 kids? Husband Paolo?)
Sarah (early 20s, v. long hair)
Kiz (teenager. Male or female?)
Stone (male, 40? Father of Kiz?)
Paul (early 20s, glasses)
Travis (early 20s, broken nose, bad teeth)

She looked at the photo on the top, showing freckle-faced Annabelle and her towheaded son, and was tempted to sweep the whole lot back into their boxes. This was beginning to feel like a dead end. The sensible thing would be to leave the job to San Mateo—or at least wait until their coroner's preliminary report. What good did it do to know that the victim had blond hair some ten or twelve inches long, without knowing if it was curly or straight, male or female, from the scalp or mixed in with beard hair? The jawbone had adult molars—but were they newly risen or a decade or more old? The nearly intact tibia they'd uncovered suggested a height within three inches of 5′8″—but there was a world of difference between 5′5″ and 5′11″. DNA had been extracted, but all labs were perennially backed up. And the bones weren't even in San Francisco, where Inspector Raquel Laing could at least harass the person in charge.

And all the while, Michael Johnston lay in his hospital bed, gloating and festering his way toward the darkness, carrying with him all those unshed secrets.

Somehow, he had turned their investigation into a game, a twisted monster's final amusement.

Johnston was terminal. He would not live to stand trial. They could prod and tempt him and hope that his own sense of glory—that same pride that reveled in the romantic title of The Highwayman—would drive him to spill out the full details before the end, but personally, Raquel did not believe he would. The previous afternoon, she'd watched him taunt an experienced Homicide detective perilously close to violence, after the cop had asked Johnston about a cold case that wasn't actually one of his.

Johnston made the rules, which amounted to: You prove a link, I'll give you the missing details. You got no proof, I'll laugh in your face.

They'd known from the start this one didn't entirely fit the High-wayman methods, but there were enough areas of similarity, and time was pressing enough, to come down and look.

But so far, there was nothing more substantial than the name "Mike" on a snapshot to suggest that The Highwayman had ever been on the Gardener Estate, much less on the day this particular blond victim was put under concrete.

She turned over her phone, to hide the man's face, and pulled over the next box.

Through 1977 and 1978, Annabelle continued her photographic ef-forts. Sparrow grew from a sturdy toddler to a suntanned boy with a grin of pure mischief, but the commune seemed to be growing as well. There were photos of new individuals and families, names on the back and occasionally the month they joined. *Katie came in* ~~March~~ *April, shes from Chicago but doesn't she look like Auntie Rae?* And on an-other, of her boy splashing furiously through a puddle, Annabelle had written, *Sparrow loves his boots he sends you a kiss.*

Fotomat had marked them all for double prints. There was no tell-ing where the other set had gone, but Raquel was grateful that the girlish handwriting kept on making its notes, giving her three more possibilities. White-blond, blue-eyed Alice, who joined in September 1977. A stoned-looking kid named Robin, two months later. And thin, nervous Janice, sagging under the weight of her boyfriend's possessive arm, whose platinum hair had dark roots: May 1978.

(Was the skeleton's hair naturally blond? Waiting for lab results was making Raquel crazy.)

The last Fotomat envelope was developed in March 1979. This one had no order for double prints. It was also considerably slimmer than the others, with only seventeen photographs instead of Annabelle's usual thirty-six or thirty-seven—a check of the negatives confirmed it. They had also been taken long before March, since the trees were bare for the winter.

Tucked in the back of the pouch was a letter, from "Aunt Rae," with the news that Annabelle's mother had died very suddenly, just after the new year.

None of these photos had notes on the back, even for the new faces.

One of the newcomers was a small, clean-shaven man in baggy Indian pants, long tunic, and vest, his hair under a knit cap. He was standing next to Rob Gardener in front of a fireplace. The two men looked nothing alike, but . . .

She laid it down and fetched the 1959 box: the black-and-white photo of two brothers, leaning away from their father and grandmother. Fort Gardener had been eight years old then, and the man in the Indian homespun had to be thirty. But for the moment, she would accept that they were the same person.

She added his photo to those on the table, and sat back to think.

Thirteen blond heads.

No sign of Michael Johnston, other than Mike on the path.

12

Raquel was not sure how long she'd been sitting there, walking the quarter up and down her knuckles as she stared into a family's dark history, when the door to the hallway came open.

"Oh—you're still . . . Hey, do you do magic tricks?" Jen was looking at the coin that had come to a rest between Raquel's thumb and first finger.

"Not really."

"Okay. Well, I was just checking that the lights were off. Are you staying much longer?"

"No, I'm finished for now." She tucked the quarter in her pocket and started gathering her things.

"I'll walk you out. Hope you found the Archives helpful?"

I found your archives a frustrating distraction, she did not say. "They're very interesting."

"I talked to Jerry, he'll be here in the morning and is happy to see you. Wes is up in Sacramento today and won't be back until late, so don't expect to get much sense out of him before noon."

"You said he lives here?"

"He has a place in the Yard—once the chauffeur's quarters. Though I'd suggest you meet up elsewhere. He's a bit . . . feral, in his habits."

Raquel paused at the word. "'Feral'?"

"Wes maybe did a little too much acid, back in the day? A bit slow, and easily distracted. We had to set down rules. If he's coming into the house or doing something around visitors, he has to shower and wear clean clothes."

"Ah."

"He's a sweet guy, with a stronger work ethic than you'd expect—he's our live-in night watchman, which is one reason why you don't see him too early in the day. As far as I know, he's absolutely clean and sober—every so often, our drive-by alarm service stops to check on him, and he's always been fine. But he does treat his rooms as a sort of pack-rat's nest."

"Noon tomorrow is fine." *Unless there's an actual development in the case.*

"I'll make sure he remembers. Jerry'll meet you in the café, down in the garden—he likes to flirt with the waitstaff. No, 'flirt' makes him sound creepy. Hang out with them, maybe? Jerry likes to feel he's still a part of the Estate family, not just our retired lawyer."

"And how do I reach Rob Gardener?"

"Ah. Well. Rob's a little more difficult. Can it wait till Monday? He'll be down to talk about Tuesday's Board meeting. He might even spend the night here—the road up to his place is pretty much impassible."

It was tempting to say no, she couldn't wait—if for no other reason than Jen's obvious wish to put her off. But she had no doubt that if she pushed, Jen would resist and go all businesslike, summoning the protection of warrants and probable cause and non-retired lawyers who would want to know why Raquel was actually here, and what the SFPD had to do with San Mateo's case.

A Pandora's box she would do well to keep well away from, at least until the need for Rob Gardener grew more immediate. "I suppose I can wait. We might even have a firm ID by Monday. And you said his cousin would be back on the weekend?" She had finished packing away her laptop and notes, and caught up her cane to make for the door.

"David's plane gets in late Saturday, but I doubt he'll talk to you before Monday. He always has trouble with jet lag."

"What is Mr. Kirkup's position on the Estate?"

"He's the Developmental Officer."

"That sounds important."

"It does, doesn't it?"

Raquel looked down at Jen, bending to lock the Archives door. "Is it not important?"

"Oh, it is, but it also makes it a little easier to isolate him from the decision-making process."

Raquel's question was silent, but Jen heard it.

"That sounds catty. I freely admit, without David's single-minded devotion, the Estate would have been sold off years ago. When the commune fell apart, Rob just hid out here and avoided making any decisions at all. The place became a kind of . . . what did they call it—crash pad? A place where friends of friends bummed off his generosity. They'd have probably burned the place down or something, but David finally stepped in. He threw out the druggies and hangers-on and brought back some of the old grounds crew. For a few years they used the house as an AIDS hospice, then an artists' community. After Rob moved up into the hills, David kept trying ways to make it pay for itself—at least as a tax write-off. But by the early 2000s, it was obvious something more permanent had to be done, and Jerry came up with the idea of the Trust. Rob said yes, and here we are. There's a Board with eleven members, including Rob, David, Jerry, and me."

"Who is the CEO?"

"We don't really have one. I suppose David is our most public face, since as family, he's often our spokesman. But in fact, he has no more authority than the other ten Board members. My vote actually counts for more than his."

"Does that create friction?"

They'd reached the kitchen wing. Jen pressed the elevator's DOWN button. "I suppose. When the Trust took over, David probably expected to be the manager, but Rob and the rest of the Board decided it was better to bring in a new face. That was me."

"Giving Mr. Kirkup the title of Developmental Officer."

"He likes it. And he mostly uses his own money for things like this Germany trip, since we can't afford much beyond his salary—even that's only half-time. We make up for it by giving him a big office with a nice carpet and some of the better artwork on the walls. There's even room for his secretary, and we pay twenty percent of her salary. He likes being able to use the Estate for his own business—he's in real estate. Big clients are impressed." The elevator door pulled open on the lower floor. "I hope Mrs. Dalhousie was helpful?"

"Very."

"That woman has been such a blessing. Not that I'd ever tell her that—she'd be mortified to know I saw through that frosty mask of hers. Did she tell you she's working on a book? She talks about it as if it's going to be a dry history published by some obscure university press, but in fact there's been some really appealing offers. It'll have loads of photos, and there's been a whole stream of big names from the seventies offering to write short pieces about the Estate in those years."

"I'll buy a copy."

"I'll give you one," Jen said.

And then she blushed.

13

Raquel thought about that blush, after Jen had ducked her head and hurried off through the formal gardens toward the parking area.

Not that there wasn't a lot to think about already. And here was a bench, weathered and substantial and thoughtfully placed for a contemplation of scenery. So she sat, and took out her well-worn quarter, and thought . . .

About a building that encapsulated the past hundred years, from the era of the robber baron to that of the social media influencer.

About the family behind those noble walls, torn apart by rivalries and expectations.

About its history of noble visions and failed attempts.

About a piece of art unlike any other, with a body laid at its feet.

And about the details of this case that were characteristic of The Highwayman, and those that were not.

Absently, she traded the coin for her phone and thumbed a preset number.

"Good evening, Corazon, this is Inspector Laing."

"Hi, Inspector, how you doing?"

"It's been a long day. I wanted to check on the patient. Al said he'd taken a turn for the worse?"

"He seems okay now. He's sleeping, but he was awake earlier and had something to eat. You want me to tell him you called?"

"No. Thanks. I just wanted to make sure . . ." To make sure what? That the slimy creature wasn't about to slip away before she could shake him down? "Never mind, you have a quiet night, Corazon."

"You too," said the nurse.

Quiet, sure. Quietly knowing that somewhere out there, a family was waiting—waiting for DNA, and for scattered bones to be pieced together, and for Raquel Laing to find something that either confirmed or denied The Highwayman's involvement here. Quietly knowing that every day's delay brought this one victim closer to being just another sad unsolved mystery.

A personal offense, to someone like Raquel Laing. Untidy, unfinished, a sign of failure.

Raquel didn't want to walk away, even for a few hours. She wanted to hunt down Jerry the lawyer and Wes the missing night watchman and squeeze what information she could out of them, but she also recognized the signs of obsession.

It was time to head for the freeway and home.

As if the obsession isn't waiting there.

This garden, though. Absolutely quiet. Empty but for the flowering beds, in the shade of that looming hedge, and the wisteria-covered building of which Jen Bachus had been so proud.

The gazebo's underlying structure was almost Japanese in its proportions. Vines thicker than Raquel's arm twined around each upright to meet on the copper roof, creating a lavender froth whose tendrils dripped like icicles around the entire circumference. Here and there, a petal drifted loose, harbinger of the approaching end to spring.

Was that why people like Jen Bachus enjoyed a garden? Not for the endless chores and dirt and backache, but for the philosophy of it? Raquel would have thought that an exact reproduction in artificial blossom and leaf would be every bit as satisfying, but perhaps she was wrong. Perhaps blisters and sweat and the transitory nature of beauty were the point, rather than unfortunate flaws.

Was that why the artist Gaddo chose to turn Eve's Destroyer face out, as a reminder that creation and preservation were ephemeral, hidden, and precious?

She should ask Jen about the garden. Come to think of it, she probably should have asked already. Her distraction must have come across as a blatant lack of interest—ah, yes: that must be what had made the Estate manager bristle. Like a mother facing someone oblivious to her baby's charm.

Raquel found that she was smiling—an unfamiliar sensation in recent weeks, and one she'd not have imagined would find her this particular day.

Perhaps there was a point to gardens after all.

The smile lingered, as she walked to her car and made her way to the freeway.

Raquel dropped her keys on the table inside the door, laid the folders beside them, added her Glock in its holster—and then sagged. After a moment, she bent down to rub at her bad knee, just as one of her housemates leapt up onto the table and sat, eye to eye with her.

"Hello, Cat," Raquel said. "Anything exciting happen today?"

The cat yawned.

A voice called from the back of the house. "Is that you, Rock?"

"No, it's the neighborhood ax murderer."

"Oh good—are you still taking requests?"

"Sure. Coffee?"

"Thanks."

Kettle on, beans through the grinder and into the French press, mugs out. Add milk, pour the cups three-quarters full so her limp doesn't send the liquid sloshing, and down the hall.

"I thought you'd be later," Dee said. "Ah, thanks for this."

"Johnston's doctor said no visitors. Are the neighbors acting up again?"

"No. Why?"

"Your suggestions for the ax murderer's list."

"Oh—more in the line of crooked politicians than noisy neighbors."

"Pretty sure there's laws against assassination. Have you eaten yet?"

"Rory came by at four with cookies. We fought off the kids and left you some in the cupboard."

"Not right now, I had a big lunch at the Gardener Estate."

"What's the place like?"

Raquel sat on the sofa, hiking up her pant leg to undo the knee brace. "Impressive. Idiosyncratic. I wish you could see it. Dee, should I know what a wisteria is?"

"The flower? Yeah, it was that purple thing that covered the back fence at Grandma's house. Why?"

"Right, and I was maybe two when Grandma died. The Estate manager said something about a wisteria today, and gave me a strange look when I didn't recognize the word. But then, the garden is a major part of her world, so . . ."

"The Estate has an interesting history. I sent you some stuff I found online."

"Slow day?"

"Slow morning, not so much this afternoon."

"Do I want to know?"

"Probably not."

Those were the rules—and if Raquel was in a difficult position at work right now, it was because she'd chosen to ignore them.

Raquel was a cop (at least, so far as she knew, she still was) and cops lived by the rigid delineations of probable cause and the need to justify search warrants. Basically, gut certainty didn't matter: if a cop couldn't hand over clean evidence to prosecutors, it might as well not exist.

For a private citizen like Dee, however, even the most aggressive snooping was legal—at least so far as being admissible in court went. But the minute a private citizen started acting on behalf of some government official—such as a sister who was a cop—the information she uncovered became poisonous, killing off any court case that depended on it.

Much of what Raquel's sister did online was, strictly speaking, against the law. The communities where Dee spent her days ranged from forums with the details of missing persons to chat groups speculating on crimes ancient and modern to groups of amateur sleuths searching for clues. Some of the communities were harmless hobby-ists, others did a lot of good and had proved themselves useful to the police.

Others were vigilantes. And some, frankly, were criminal.

Information gained from these places could be treacherous. When-ever Dee came across something she thought Raquel should know, she was scrupulous about electronic trails—no texts, no emails. She'd been known to destroy a thumb drive when Raquel was finished with it.

A few times, these anonymized tips had given Raquel the solution to a problematic case, if she could squeeze past those difficult privacy laws so the case didn't get thrown out.

And once or twice, Raquel had been faced with a situation that US law could not touch, but that Dee and her shady community, with its eyes and fingers all over the world, might help resolve. She'd dropped cautious hints, and a prudent time later, scandals had erupted, civil cases had been filed—and twice, men committed suicide.

But never open violence, and never encouraging harassment by the unbalanced. So long as the vigilante justice stayed in the realm of rep-utations and lawsuits, Raquel would turn a blind eye.

And it all worked fine until a few months ago, when she'd danced perilously close to the edge of permissible. Even then, she'd have got-ten away with it—all cops took shortcuts, from time to time—but for a leak that led the unbalanced to Inspector Raquel Laing.

While she was in the hospital, high-ranking discussions had taken place. In the end, Al's suggestion, that she quietly be seconded to Cold Case for modified duty while her leg healed, was approved.

She knew full well it was a kind of probation. She'd stepped over the line, and was now in a place where her mentor could make good use of her skills—while keeping an eye on her.

So yes, all in all, there were things going on under her roof that Raquel took care not to know.

Raquel stretched out her legs. The cat settled onto her lap. One hand dutifully patted fur, the other held her coffee, and the sisters talked about their day—the parts of their day that they could talk about. Rory, once Dee's paid assistant and now a close friend, was going through a good spot, which was encouraging. Two of Dee's online buddies, Whoops and Thatfool, were up to their usual outrageous acts of political theater, antics that always left Raquel both grinning and dreading the day the SFPD would be forced to go after the self-proclaimed Buddhist Anarchists. They were Bay Area locals, and scattered so many clues in their wake that they would not be hard to find.

Talk circled back to Raquel's day, although nothing to do with the case. She described what she could remember of the garden, then more detailed descriptions of the house, the Archives room, and the people who worked there. The walls of the foyer, the wide-open field, the Gaddo sculpture, her tasty lunch with Jen Bachus. All things Dee would never venture out for.

"Speaking of which." Raquel glanced at her watch. "I need to check my email, then I'll put dinner together. Pardon me, Cat."

"Take her some cookies."

Raquel looked at her sister in surprise. "Who, the cat?"

"The Estate manager. She likes you."

"Dee, you need to rein in your imagination. I'm a pain in the poor woman's neck, one more cop after a week of them. Plus, she's terrified of what I'm going to find there. She recognized me from the press conference."

"She knows you're after The Highwayman?"

"Unfortunately."

"All the more reason to take her some cookies."

Raquel laughed as she transferred the indignant cat to the empty cushions, and went to do battle with email.

But over dinner prep, while Raquel minced the ginger for a sort of Moroccan turkey stir-fry recipe she was trying to perfect, Dee returned to the topic of the Gardener Estate's manager.

"You like her," Dee said flatly.

"She's a likeable person."

"That's not what I mean. You're interested in her."

"Dee, I don't know anything about her. She may be happily married with eight kids."

"You could find out."

"No, I couldn't. And you won't, either."

"Okay, so just ask her out. All she can do is say no thanks."

"Dee, Jen Bachus is a potential witness."

"Witness to what? The bones are from the seventies—how old is this woman, anyway?"

"Not that old. But she's not just an employee. She seems close to the man who owns the Estate, and he was definitely there in the seventies."

"Close how?"

She looked at her sister. "That is a good question." *When I was nine, and Mom and my brother were both working, I'd wander all over,* the manager had said. *Trespassing, of course. Rob just hid out here.* Living five miles away, riding her brother's hand-me-down blue bike around the deserted Estate. All on her own, it being *a different time, then, you know?* A time when a curious and independent young girl might go exploring, and befriend a hermit in the big house, before he turned the place over to his cousin and retreated into the hills.

How close had they been, the lonely old veteran-hippie and the kid, before the grown-up Jen Bachus was hired to manage his estate? How much did she know about him, and about things that had happened when she was still being hiked around on her parents' backs?

How much of her reticence to talk about Rob Gardener was friendship, and how much was a wish to protect his secrets?

Close, how, indeed.

14

It was late by the time the dishes were clean and the morning things set out. A person with what Dee called "a good work–life balance" would go to bed with a book. But then, Dee was one to talk about obsessions.

For Raquel, it was all a matter of control. She'd found that allowing herself a fixed amount of immersion in her current preoccupation made it easier to shut it away afterward, made her less likely to lie in the dark and feel it clawing at her.

So when she sat down at the desk in her windowless office, looking at the faces of four blond women taped to the wall, she set the timer: twenty minutes, then she would leave them.

It all started, for Raquel, with a girl named Polly Lacewood, seventeen years old when she vanished in 1972, two decades before Raquel was born. Polly was a small girl with long blond hair, crooked teeth, an uneven home life, and an infectious grin. She set out one night from her mother's house in the Sunset District, planning to hitch a ride to a friend's party in Burlingame. Polly never showed. For twenty-one years, Polly was a black hole in people's lives, leaving her friends to wonder, her mother to die without knowing.

In 1993, a bulldozer was tearing up a motel on the southern edge of

San Francisco, damaged in the big 1989 earthquake. With one pass of the blade, bones came up along with the concrete floor. Polly Lacewood moved from a missing person to a cold case.

Officer Raquel Laing did not hear about Polly until 2015. She'd been on the SFPD for three years, and had submitted her application for promotion into Investigations. Competition was stiff, even for someone with double Bachelor degrees, high Academy marks, and ongoing courses in criminology. Raquel knew that no officer would be promoted that soon. But when she thought of spending her career dealing with the incomprehensible stupidities of the average criminal, amidst the impenetrable camaraderie of her fellow officers, she found it hard to pull back from despair.

Then she met Al Hawkin.

Al had been a legend in the Homicide Detail, and was on his way to becoming equally legendary in his "retirement" to Cold Case—the ideal unit for investigators who hit mandatory retirement age but are too experienced to waste, or for detectives needing a desk job while injuries heal.

Al Hawkin was well suited to Cold Case: patient, with an eye for detail and an affable manner that could gentle information out of the most repressed witness—or trick it from the most hardened suspect.

So when Officer Raquel Laing was handed a note at the station, asking her to meet him one night after her shift, she definitely knew who he was.

What she didn't know was what he could possibly want from her.

So she asked. Before the man was even in his chair.

"What do you want with me?"

His eyes, friendly as he'd greeted the waitress by name, turned to hers. Looking amused, he told Roxanne he'd have a decaf, thanks, and swung the frayed black nylon knapsack from his shoulder to the floor. Then he sat down.

"Good evening, Officer Laing. Tell me, do you find that blunt approach makes matters easier for you in the Department?"

The question was analytical, interested, with no trace of hostility that she could perceive. She blinked, and replied the only way she knew: honestly.

"No. Are matters supposed to be easy?"

"Officer Laing, you have an interesting mind. Your degrees and extracurricular courses tell me you're fully committed to a position in, I imagine, Homicide? Your partners—rather a lot of them, for someone your age—say you're dependable, but aloof and sometimes difficult to work with. Your superiors agree that you are intellectually impressive and socially stilted. Your matter-of-fact approach to both victims and suspects can be oddly effective, but is occasionally provocative, to the point of requiring your partner to intervene. Would you agree with this assessment?"

The coffee had arrived; he took a swallow as he waited for her reply.

"Why have you been talking to people about me?"

"Would you agree with the assessment?"

"I suppose."

"We've been talking about you because you're the kind of mind that doesn't come our way often. But you're also going to be forced out if you don't learn to modify your skills. Across the board, your interviews and exams give you top marks in academic competence, observational skills, problem solving, and field work. You've worked hard to compensate for your size, so that even your large male colleagues give you credit for carrying your weight in a confrontation. Your psych profile . . . well, it's no odder than anyone else's.

"It's your interpersonal skills that create a red flag. Officer Laing, since you prefer the blunt approach, let me put it this way. If you don't figure out how to listen to people, see what their body language is telling you, hear what they're really saying, then all you're ever going to get from them—whether it's a suspect, a witness, or a colleague—is the words."

The higher-ups have taken notice of me? This was not an entirely comfortable idea. But what he said made sense. And if there was one thing everyone knew about Al Hawkin, it was his people skills. The man would comfort and distract a terrified victim until they were relaxed enough to recall some key and forgotten fact, then turn around and cajole and sympathize a wary and antagonistic suspect into confessing. Any lesson from him was sure to be useful.

"What do you have in mind?"

But he only shook his head. "That's up to you. Turn that intellect of yours to it, I'm sure doors will just fall open."

He drank some more coffee.

"Was that all?" she asked. "You wanted to meet so you could suggest I learn how to get along with people and manipulate witnesses?"

"Mostly. But there's also this."

He reached down for the backpack, and drew out a thick, oversized mailing envelope, laying it on the table between them. Raquel turned down the flap, then retracted her hands and sat back.

"That's a murder book."

"A cold case, from 1972."

"I can't take that."

"You have the chief's permission."

The chief?

She considered this. Al Hawkin looked like an amiable grandfather, settling easily into his later years coaching softball and going on cruises. Except he was one of the most brilliant investigators the SFPD had known, with a clearance rate like none other.

"Okay," she said.

"First thing I want you to do is, figure out why I'm giving it to you."

"Don't you know?"

"*I* do. I'm interested in what you see."

That did not make a lot of sense to Raquel, but what did she know about murder books?

"Read it," he said. "In your spare time. Give me a call if you have any ideas."

"I don't have much spare time." It was the truth. Between the promotion exam and the class in DNA she was taking, her days were full.

"I bet you'll find time," he said. "In fact . . ." He reached into his shirt pocket and pulled out a coin, laying it on top of the mailer. "I'll bet you a quarter—a 1972 quarter—that you'll not only find the time, you'll have some ideas."

And with that, the great Al Hawkin tucked a five-dollar bill under his mug and left.

⁂

Raquel was to find, some years later, that it was common procedure to hand newly-minted detectives one or two old unsolved cases, both to familiarize them with the system and to give the victims another chance at justice. Most of the time, as the new inspector's caseload filled with urgent new murders, the files went back to Cold Case, updated, unsolved, and eventually deactivated entirely.

Not that Raquel was anywhere near to Investigations.

On the other hand, neither did she have any cases important enough to push Polly Lacewood to the back.

Raquel took the murder book home that night and started reading. She set up a small office in the house she shared with her recluse sister, taping up the photo of Polly Lacewood where she would be forced to look at it.

She spent hours going over what the reports said. Then what they didn't say. A few weeks later, Raquel looked up from the Polly Lacewood file and reached for the phone.

"Hello?" Al Hawkin's voice sounded hoarse.

"You wanted me to tell you why you gave me Polly Lacewood."

He grunted.

"It's the concrete. Nobody stumbles across that as a method of concealing a body. It's too . . . practiced. She wasn't his first."

He said nothing, although she could hear movement in the background—a rustling sound, then the pad of feet. A door closed, and then he spoke.

"You get to keep that quarter, Laing."

"So are we looking at a serial killer? From the seventies?"

"One who fell through the cracks? Some of us think so. Someone who got overlooked because he worked in different styles and multiple jurisdictions."

"'Us'? There's a task force? Why haven't I heard of it?"

"Nothing formal, there's not enough yet. Just, some of us talk. Share things we've heard. Keep an eye out for other cases."

"You're sure it's not one of the known ones? Like, Kemper, or the Night Stalker? As I remember, there were a lot of them, back in the seventies."

"We don't think so. Personally, I think this guy actually did have a presence back then, but for some reason he stopped. One or two of us think this may be the one some of the papers called The Highwayman."

"Never heard of him."

"Nobody official took it seriously, so he became a kind of bogeyman. And after a number of real-life horrors came into the light, well, this one faded."

"The Highwayman."

"There's a poem, they used to teach it in school."

"Okay. So, what comes next?"

"If you want, I'll add you into the group."

"'Group'?"

"You want to call it a network? Like I said, not a task force. Some of us working cold cases get together, have a drink, talk things over."

"What rank are the others?"

"Doesn't matter." Rank did matter, in any police department. And though she didn't know him well enough to argue, he heard the objection in her silence. "If I bring you along, Laing, nobody's going to object. Up to you."

"Okay, then, count me in."

"Just—next time you call, maybe wait till daylight."

"Why, what time is—oops."

"See you tomorrow, Inspector Laing."

"Goodnight, sir."

Raquel Laing picked up the twenty-five-cent piece that had been sitting prominently on the top of her desk, ever since the night Al Hawkin made his challenge.

There was nothing unusual about the coin: a sandwich of nickel and copper, scratched and worn, George Washington's face on one side and the eagle on the other.

Nothing unusual—except that it had been minted the year seventeen-year-old Polly Lacewood was taken.

From Inspector Al Hawkin, this was no mere coincidence.

She wrapped her hand around the quarter, and smiled.

15

Giving her the Polly Lacewood file, Raquel decided, marked the start of Al's off-the-books mentorship program.

Yes, he coached her directly, passing on a lifetime of experience and investigative techniques, but more than that, he prodded her on her "learn to listen" project. Which started in the realm of pseudoscientific corporate lie detection, but soon brought her to books from Freud to Eckman and Navarro, seminars by FBI profilers and professional card sharps, and interviews with anthropologists, anatomists, forensic psychiatrists, and experts on the brain. When she found the interrogation room cameras were no good, she bought a ridiculously expensive high-res spy camera to surreptitiously record her interviews, poring over them at slow speed for hidden revelations—though the actual work was teaching her brain to spot them in real time.

In the end, Raquel had what amounted to a do-it-yourself PhD, taking what she needed from one approach, patching in what worked for its rival, rejecting much, and inventing a few techniques along the way: body language and involuntary microexpressions, behavioral analysis and methods of interrogation, universal expressions versus individual baselines.

Not that any of it was evidence in a court of law. But it did give her a reputation for mind reading.

Al never commented on her unusually rapid progress from foot patrol into investigations, but just six years after leaving the Academy, she had a desk in Homicide. By that time, she had learned enough about reading people to see the animosity and suspicion around her when she was promoted before other, longer-serving officers.

"Sure, there's resentment," Al agreed. "You just have to prove you deserved it."

They called her Sherlock and left magnifying glasses and syringes on her desk. After one interrogation, when she'd pointed out where the suspect was lying, they took to calling her their resident polygraph. And when she tried to explain that she wasn't reading lies, she was watching for tells and giveaways—those fleeting betrayals of the unconscious that dilate the pupils, change a person's blink rate, or give an involuntary twitch to a facial muscle—the jokes shifted to Las Vegas and poker tells.

It took a couple of years, and some cases pried open by hard slog and her uncanny ability to put together unrelated facts, before the Department's agreement that Raquel Laing was either sleeping with someone or had got in as one of the SFPD's damned diversity hires began to give way. It was far from wholehearted approval, but she was finding that grudging acceptance was both more comfortable and more effective than open resentment. They'd started to consult her on interview techniques. She almost had friends now.

Polly Lacewood's murder book remained on her desk. And she and Al, along with the other members of his Cold Case not-a-task-force, opened a group folder online and put in anything they found that might be related to Polly's death.

Such as Sandra Wilson. A Cold Case investigator from down the Peninsula in Sunnyvale had discovered another young woman, found under a concrete floor in 2006. Sandra Wilson—5′8″, nineteen, cute blond pigtails, a community college student—kissed her mother goodbye one morning in 1976, set off for campus, and vanished. She, too, became a series of faded posters on Bay Area phone poles.

Until a crew renovating a popular bar pried up a slab of floor and found her.

Two victims: young, blond, both killed in the 1970s, both hidden under concrete. Al and Raquel agreed that the two victims were probably linked, others in the group did not—with no hard evidence, it could as easily be coincidence. DNA had been retrieved from semen on Sandra's clothing, but Polly's was too degraded for a good analysis.

Then a few years ago, Alameda County received a grant allowing a methodical DNA review of clothing from the evidence lockers. One of these kicked up a match for that on Sandra Wilson.

This was Demi Scott: 5′7″; light brown, shoulder-length hair; gold-rimmed glasses; lived in Mountain View with her boyfriend; left home after a fight about the baby she'd just learned she was carrying. The boyfriend, questioned at length by the police, had sworn she left with a backpack of her things to hitch a ride down to a Felton commune where some friends of hers lived. He'd peevishly turned up his music and got out his stash. Fortunately for him, the neighbor called in a noise complaint twenty minutes after hearing the door slam, so the local police gave him an alibi.

Demi didn't make it to the commune. She had been found three months after the fight, in late 1979, in a shallow grave in the opposite direction, at the edges of Alameda County.

Matching DNA took two of the deaths out of the realm of coincidence and into that of a multiple offender. However, Raquel started charting all three victims for points of commonality: hitchhiking; blond hair; concrete slab; DNA.

All were blond women known to hitch rides.

Polly and Sandra shared the concrete; Sandra and Demi were linked by DNA.

They compared the dates of their disappearances to the careers of known California serial killers, but where one or two would match, the third would not, and the methods used were not those of the Trailside Killer, Edmund Kemper, Herbert Mullin, or the others.

The cold case group went round and round over proposing these as the work of The Highwayman. The name had been a tabloid rumor for so long, it stank of romanticized danger. There'd never been any serious official recognition of such a person, and with the sharp decrease of hitchhikers in the 1980s, The Highwayman had become one of the era's urban legends.

And there it remained, until two weeks ago when Raquel caught a missing key that put a fourth face up on her office wall—and the clock began to tick.

Nineteen-year-old Windy Jackson—born Wanda Jo—had left her home in rural Texas to hitch her way out with a series of boyfriends, ending up in San Francisco just in time for the Summer of Love. Eight years later, in 1977, the flower children had dispersed, and Windy had edged into the harder corners of the drug culture.

She didn't hitch a lot anymore, too many weirdos out there, but sometimes she was stuck and there was only one way to get around. She'd been with friends in Oakland, partied, helped herself to some pricey clothes and cash, using some of that to have the roots of her hair bleached.

She'd told her friends she was getting tired of the life. Thinking of going home. Maybe staying with friends who lived near Palo Alto for a while, had a big place with a bunch of cool musicians. Time to get her shit together, you know?

Instead, Windy disappeared, like a number of other blond young women, from a freeway on-ramp. Her remains were found three years later, up in the coastal hills. Her clothing went into evidence storage in San Mateo County. And there it remained until SFPD Inspector Raquel Laing, filling her days of Cold Case secondment (not suspension, quite) by burrowing through the neighboring departments' Cold Case files, noticed something odd.

A lot of young, blond women disappeared or died in the seventies. No doubt most of them thumbed rides, from time to time. That two of them were found under concrete and two under dirt told them nothing.

But Raquel's eye caught on a small detail in the crime report—or rather, a missing detail. The list of possessions put into the evidence locker was similar to that of the others: most of their clothing, some of their things—Sandra had her books, but Demi's backpack was missing. The young women's wallets, like Demi's glasses, had been laid beside them, containing their IDs but no cash. Windy's list specifically mentioned the scraped-up state of her left shoe.

Did that mean her right shoe was undamaged? Or that the right shoe was missing altogether?

Curious, Raquel picked up the phone. Did San Mateo still have the evidence from this long-ago murder? Good—did anyone mind if she came down and had a look?

There was indeed a single tennis shoe, for the left foot.

And after she had burrowed back into the descriptions of the others, they had another point of commonality for their Venn constructions.

None of the four women on Raquel's wall had a right shoe when they were found.

16

In the meantime, during the years that young women died and the world changed, Michael Allan Johnston had gone about his life.

Johnston had grown up in the Bay Area, with an apparently normal childhood—divorced parents, but otherwise stable. Not many friends, in school or out, but some. His grades kept above C level until high school, when he couldn't be bothered, dropping out the summer before his senior year. He got a job in construction, working general labor for a series of contractors and large companies. His employment record was spotty—occasionally fired, often because he'd stirred up some trouble with his fellow workers, but more usually just failed to show up. His jobs were often short-lived and off the books.

In the late sixties, this young man with his ordinary face and not-too-long hair discovered the counterculture. In his free time, he would pick up hitchhikers, share their dope, hang out with them a while, then move on. Just like millions of freedom-loving young people were doing, all over the world. Occasionally, a freedom-loving young person would vanish. Some reappeared in Canada, others in a morgue, a few at their parents' door with a couple of scruffy children trailing behind them. Others didn't reappear.

Many years later, around the time the Gardener Estate's grounds-man was noticing that the *Midsummer Eves* statue was beginning to tilt, a woman in San Jose was clearing out her father's apartment over the family garage. He'd been deteriorating for some time, physically and mentally, and she and her husband had finally—gratefully— moved the old man into a facility that could care for him.

As she sorted through his papers, the daughter came across recent bills for a storage locker she hadn't known he rented. Her husband went the next morning to empty it, taking the old man's ring of keys in hopes that one would fit the padlock. One did. But to his surprise, when he rolled up the door, the locker was empty except for a carton of old shoes. On the top were a shiny yellow platform shoe, a beaded moccasin missing most of its beads, and a clunky high-heel with scuffed toes and a gold buckle. Pulling these aside he found one small, very worn hiking boot, one broken-strapped sandal with a plastic flower, one silver shoe suitable for disco dancing, a flat sandal with what looked like yards of narrow strapping, a brown-and-white saddle shoe, a black canvas tennie half-separated from its rubber sole, an ancient leather sandal with a loop for the big toe—and then he noticed that there wasn't a pair in the lot.

He hesitated. He'd heard of men with shoe fetishes, and one of the high heels he could see stirring a pervert's interest, but . . . those brown sandals were about as sexy as a paper bag, and that dumpy white shoe looked like something a nurse would wear.

No: more likely related to some of the boxes of odd crap they'd found in his room, from some garage sale or other.

He sighed at his father-in-law's mental state, picked up the box, and rolled down the locker door. While the desk man was closing out the bill, he laughed about the weird things he'd found in abandoned storage lockers, and the two men agreed that one box of shoes was way better than a locker stuffed to the ceiling with magazines and old junk. The desk guy took the money and handed over a receipt, and pointed to the dumpster outside the door.

Before getting rid of them, the son-in-law emptied the shoes out onto the ground just to check—but no, there was no hidden treasure in the old box. So he shoveled the footwear back in, tossed the box into the dumpster, and went home.

But first, he snapped some pictures of the collection to show his wife, as further evidence of her father's deteriorating sanity.

Two weeks later, after an uneasy conversation with a friend about whether or not dementia could be inherited, the daughter sought reassurance in the world of DNA ancestry testing. She happened to choose one of the companies that did not automatically ban reporting its results to interested law enforcement agencies.

And with that choice, the Highwayman clock was about to run out.

Her test results arrived on a Wednesday, less than a week after Raquel Laing had noticed Windy Jackson's missing shoe.

On Thursday afternoon, the San Jose police knocked at the daughter's door. Her husband was home. As they waited for his wife to get back from the hospital, he made them coffee and told them about his father-in-law's illness, how it looked like he wouldn't be around long, and he happened to mention that strange box in the old man's storage locker. They asked to see the pictures, agreed it was odd, recorded the old man's location (noting that a man hooked up to that many machines was in no way a flight risk), and included the photo with the rest of their report, which reached the Highwayman group the following day.

Nineteen shoes.

All for the right foot.

And with that, they had run out of time.

Within hours, alarm bells were beginning to go off all over the Bay Area as other informal police networks came into play. Chiefs talked to Homicide captains, mayors consulted with their chiefs, several of them spoke with the FBI, and a virtual meet-up was scheduled for Saturday morning, before the media got wind of it.

Al was there to represent the group, and the first thing he said was, "We may have as many as nineteen victims here."

Every face on the screen went stiff—even that of the FBI special agent. Eventually, the SFPD chief found his voice. "Jesus, Al, are you sure?"

"We're pretty sure about four of them, though we won't be certain until we can compare the souvenirs he took with the four evidence lockers."

"What souvenirs?"

"Shoes."

"Maybe you should explain who you mean by 'we.'"

Al gave them a quick rundown of the Highwayman group, the discovery of the shoes, and the ticking clock of Michael Johnston's rapidly progressing cancer. "So far, we're under the radar, though that won't last long. And we're assuming that one of the primary concerns is keeping that number out of the news."

All the boxes on the screen went still as the participants thought about the headlines: law enforcement had overlooked one of the most prolific serial killers in California's history.

"It'll leak," one of them said.

"Eventually. And there's no denying that there will be consequences, not the least of which will be the wannabees." Every time a spectacular crime came into the news, the phone lines filled with people whose ex-husbands or long-dead fathers had done it. "We can keep a lid on the shoes, but when it comes to the numbers, you'll have to decide if it's better to start with four known victims, or four with the possibility of fifteen others."

Their choice was obvious.

So was the next step: creating a multiagency task force. The public liked interagency task forces, based on a systematic coordination of team efforts. They'd need a list of jurisdictions for the identified victims, and perhaps some of the larger—

Al interrupted. "You're forgetting something. This man is dying. There's a good chance he'll be dead and buried before a task force can even interview him."

So . . . ?

"Use us. Our cold case group is fully up to speed, we know what to look for and what to ask. If Johnston won't talk, then he won't talk, but if we don't get around to asking him because we're still deciding who asks the questions, it makes us look like idiots."

Impossible, they said. There had to be a task force. How else to demonstrate how seriously they all took the matter? The five chiefs began to plan how best to form it, the mayors wondered who would take lead on it, Homicide had suggestions for staffing, the FBI man cleared his throat—and then Al leaned right into his laptop's camera and bluntly asked if they'd all be satisfied with losing the information Michael Johnston could give them, and letting that number of unsolved cases get leaked.

"Because if so," he said into the abruptly silent screen, "that's how we can run it. Multiple agencies, specialized teams, each with a task, regular coordination, everyone taking the time to dot their *i*'s and cross their *t*'s. And this guy'll be long dead, and every family who lost someone during those years will be asking why we thought we could take our sweet time." He let the various officials think about all those uncomfortable questions, the sort of thing that haunted careers. "Or you can let us push ahead like we have been, until the task force gets up to speed. We're small enough to keep a lid on the shoes, but there's enough of us to get as much as we can from the bastard."

"It has to be by the book," one chief of police warned.

"As if we expect a miracle cure," Al agreed. "Nobody's going free because we took shortcuts."

There was discussion, of course—no official, whether elected or appointed, would want it said they were not involved in a decision. But Al came out with their approval.

Namely, that an official Highwayman Task Force would be announced at a joint press conference on Thursday afternoon.

The press conference would avoid any mention of the specific number of victims.

And no one would say anything—anything at all—about shoes.

In the meantime, the unofficial network—which had begun to refer to itself as the Highwayman group—would move ahead. And when the official response came into being, they could turn their conclusions and evidence over to them.

The approach had got them this far; they would let it continue for the present.

Besides: whatever failures they were left with, this unorthodox group of retired cops would be a convenient place to lay the blame.

Raquel was not sure how Al had talked the chief into letting her stay an active part of the Highwayman group, considering her uncertain status. She suspected the others assumed her to be Al's secretary and occasional driver, since his dislike of driving was well known. In any event, she stayed involved, and in no time at all, the Highwayman group was scrambling to get ahead of the inevitable media explosion.

Al was sent to talk with the daughter, and as the others had known, soon had her eating out of his hand, telling him all about the father, who had separated from his wife in the seventies and dropped out of their lives entirely in the summer of 1982, when she was fourteen—only to reappear just as suddenly twenty-three years later.

Michael Johnston, they would discover from his bank records, had left the Bay Area for Mexico. It would take months to piece together those years, if they ever did, but his absence came to an end in 2005 when the man walked into a San Jose hospital with a still-unexplained, days-old gunshot wound. Police questioned him, as they would anyone with a bullet wound, but he claimed it had been done by a passing stranger, and they had no reason to keep him. He was discharged two weeks later into the care of his surprised daughter.

After all those years, it was not a fond reunion. And the daughter did remember her parents' relationship, increasingly filled with bickering, particularly over the friends he'd bring home. Still, Johnston was her only family, and he could be charming when he wanted. Besides, he let it be known that his life was long reformed from those wild days. So she and her husband relented enough to give him the apartment over their garage. There he lived, keeping to himself until his failing health led to her recent decision to put the old man into a care facility.

He was now in the hospital. It didn't look as if he'd be coming out again—which made an arrest difficult. Being discharged to the county jail, his doctor said, would kill him.

So, Al suggested, what about having him shifted into that hospital wing used for treating prisoners?

That would be fine, but there would be no harassment of this 84-year-old cancer patient, no matter what he was being accused of. Short periods of questioning, limited interaction—and no media.

The "no media" rule lasted barely twenty-four hours, but that was long enough for Al and two detectives from nearby jurisdictions to make the arrest, have the man transferred to the secure wing, and hold a first, quiet, one-on-one interview with Michael Johnston.

Johnston was surprised at the arrest. Angry, too, at his daughter and her husband, and contemptuous over the length of time he had been unnoticed, and impatient with the fussing of nurses and doctors. He mostly listened as Al told him what they had on him: the missing shoes, the jobs with concrete companies, his daughter's DNA test. A warrant on its way, for a sample from Johnston himself. All in all, plenty of evidence for a trial.

Not that any of the group, once they had seen him, thought the man would live that long.

But by the second interview, two days later, somebody had talked. The hospital was besieged by cameras, The Highwayman hit the news cycles, and Johnston decided he had nothing to lose.

He started by dismissing his lawyer. Then he said, sure, I'll take your DNA test. And sure, I'll tell you about your four girls. Why not? I got nothing else to do in here, now you've got me chained to the bed.

And sure, bring your cop friends along. The more the merrier. In fact, I'm happy to talk with all those reporters I hear you've got lining up outside.

After all, I'm going to be famous, aren't I?

And he laughed.

17

The Highwayman group's next interview with Michael Johnston took place at two in the afternoon on a perfect Monday in April—by coincidence, hours after a jawbone was brought to light on the Gardener Estate, twenty miles north of the prisoner's hospital bed.

Al wanted Raquel along for this one. So far, with the exception of that press conference, she'd stayed at the back of things. Not only was she the youngest member of the cold case group, she was one of only three women, and they were all aware that there was a potential cloud of official disapproval lingering over her head.

But Al wanted her, so she was there.

The actual Highwayman task force was still getting under way, although its creation meant that resources were suddenly available.

Half of Northern California's police departments began a close review of their cold cases, particularly any unidentified young, blond women. A phone line was set up to field calls, both from people asking for information and from those who had some to offer. Money was found to conduct searches through the old records of local concrete companies. Did you employ a man named Michael Johnston during the 1970s? If so, what jobs did you have then? Those dates and places would be set beside missing persons reports for young, blond women, and cadaver dogs or ground-penetrating radar would be sent out.

All of that information, from tips to evidence lockers, would funnel in both to the Highwayman group and to the actual task force.

But in the meantime, that Monday afternoon, the group would be interested in what lay inside Johnston's skull.

Their four known victims brought four different Bay Area jurisdictions into play, all of which should have been present. But again, this was the unofficial Highwayman group, and when Al said that Raquel would stand in for San Mateo, who were not only working that triple homicide but still getting up to speed on the Windy Jackson case, who was there to argue?

Raquel picked Al up at his house near Stanford, to review their interview plan.

"I'll tell you what I told the guys, that we need to stay on point. Johnston wants to make it a power trip, making us beg him for tidbits, and we don't have time for that."

"What about Mexico?"

"Not our job."

"For God's sake, Al, he was there for twenty-three years."

"And he may have quit when he left the Bay Area."

"How likely is that?"

"DeAngelo did. Just quit, completely."

"As far as we know."

"We'll assume Johnston did. I don't want you to distract him into Mexico." And when she did not reply, he prompted, "Raquel?"

"All right, I won't go there. But as soon as we get a chance, we open that up, too."

"Not today."

She parked in an area the hospital kept off-limits to the press, and they took the elevator to the prisoners' floor, where they found the two other members of the group waiting. Raquel knew them from emails, but had not met them in person. The white one smelled of cigarettes, and was kneading a manila envelope as if wishing he could smoke it. The Black one, whose fingernails gave him away as a recently reformed smoker, sat three chairs away.

The two stood, and Al made the introductions. "Charlie, JJ, I think you know Raquel. Rock, Charlie's from San Jose, JJ's Alameda."

Charlie's department in Santa Clara County was responsible for Sandra Wilson, JJ's for Demi Scott.

Charlie smirked and said, "Hey, if it isn't the Sherlock of San Francisco." She did not respond.

JJ gave her a nod of greeting before asking Al, "Who's taking lead here?"

"He'll be expecting me, since we've talked before."

"So maybe mix it up?"

"It's not like we've bonded, so sure. Charlie, you want to start?"

By reply, Charlie stalked down the corridor with his folder, barely acknowledging the uniformed guard as he swept past him and through the open door.

Then had to stand by while the nurse finished taking her patient's blood pressure, fetched him a jug of water, and adjusted the flow of oxygen into his nasal cannula. When she had finished raising the man's bed and gathering her things to leave, the balance of power had shifted, leaving Michael Johnston free to grant his favors to supplicants.

Charlie dropped his folder onto the sheets. *Trying to mark possession of Johnston's space,* Raquel thought. JJ stood at his left, Al at his right. Raquel took up a spot just at the edge of Johnston's peripheral vision: not far enough back to feel like a threat, but well away from his direct line of sight. She took out her notebook, as if she were a secretary, and disappeared into the background.

It also let her lean slightly against the wall, to take the weight off her leg.

"Sandra Wilson," Charlie said.

"Friend of yours?" Johnston asked. She noted his twitch of contempt, the head tilt of pride, and knew that Charlie from San Jose was not going to pry anything out of the man.

A slight sag in Al's stance showed that he knew it as well.

But taking things away from Charlie this fast would generate all kinds of hierarchical tensions and accusations of authority undermined, so she and Al stood and let him pepper the man with demands and questions.

And Michael Johnston was willing to talk about Sandra Wilson, as he had been about Polly Lacewood, Demi Scott, and Windy Jackson on Al's earlier visits. Not only willing—he positively gloated over how he'd picked her up, shared a joint, stayed the night at her crash pad, and the next night put her under where his company was scheduled to pour a concrete subfloor.

He cackled around his oxygen feed, reliving the memories, taunting them with how nervous he'd been and how satisfying it was when nothing at all happened. Wiping little Sandra from the map, like she'd never even existed. How he used to drive past the bar when it was open and think about her down there, listening to all that going on over her head. How a couple of times he'd seen cop cars there, parked right out in the open, and how tempted he'd been to go in and buy the cops a drink, on Sandra. Get it? *On* Sandra.

Then Charlie snatched up the folder and pulled out an 8x10 photograph, slapping it down on the man's legs. Raquel caught a glimpse—a forensic reconstruction showing a blond woman with slightly protruding teeth and the usual blank expression—before Johnston picked it up.

"Bit of a dog," he commented.

"Is she one of yours?"

His eyes came up—a twitch of surprise, followed by happiness and contempt—and he dropped the photo over the side of the bed to the floor. "Maybe you should tell me."

"We found her next to a swimming pool. Under concrete poured by one of your companies. Who is she?"

No need for microexpressions here—open pleasure dawned on the ravaged face and Johnston began to laugh until he choked, gesturing through tears at the glass of water on his nightstand. Al moved around to fetch it for him, while Charlie glowered and JJ looked apprehensive.

"You don't know who she is?" Johnston said, when his breath had returned. "Why the fuck should I do your job for you? You let all these girls pile up over the years, then when I come along you think you can just shove them all onto me? Shit, man, no wonder there's all these guys you never caught—the Zodiac, the Craigslist Killer, the Santa Rosa Slayer. If I'd known how crap you were at investigating, I could've stayed here all along instead of scramming off to Jalisco."

"You little shithouse," Charlie shouted, and started moving around the bed. JJ got in his way, Al grabbed his arm, and the two men hustled the San Jose cop out of the door, kicking it shut as they left.

From outside came raised voices, followed by a loud thud (which later proved to be Charlie's fist hitting the wall). Raquel studied the man in the bed.

The old man's face was a puzzle. Anyone else, and she'd have said he looked happy. But she'd seen his twitch of fear—and not when Charlie lunged at him, either.

He hadn't been afraid until the three men turned to leave the room.

As the voices died down outside, he noticed her, motionless in the background as she'd been all along.

"Hey, bitch, your masters are leaving. You don't want to be alone with the monster, do you?"

"What are you afraid of?" she wondered aloud.

"Not you, honey."

"Are you afraid of being alone? No, not that. Or not just that."

"You come a little closer, bitchy, we'll see if The Highwayman can make you afraid. Just a little closer, you and I can go riding, riding—"

"You do like the imagery, don't you? The idea of haunting people's dreams. And if the police walk out on you, that will . . . what?"

"They'll be back."

But there it was again, that tiny giveaway quirk of his eyes: *fear.*

So she followed the thought. "What if we don't come back? What happens if we leave you here by yourself until the day your heart monitor flatlines?"

This time the twitch was so pronounced, it almost qualified as a facial expression. Why? She wished she'd had time to shape a full baseline reading of the man—what was he telling her, between the words? *Monster, Highwayman, bitch, alone.* His use of the titles of three other killers.

Take a stab at it.

"You're running out of time, too, aren't you?" she said. "All these years keeping your secret. Too smart to give yourself away. You're thinking it's just chance that we found you. And now all you have left . . ." He was muttering curses and making sexual taunts, but she was watching the backs of his eyes.

And then she had it.

"Notoriety. You want us to know—you want everyone to know. You want The Highwayman to be as big a thing as the Zodiac or the Night Stalker. But you want us to work for it."

His sudden silence told her she was right.

Talk it through. "The Highwayman has been in the shadows for half a century. You must have gloated when it was dismissed as an urban myth. But it must have been frustrating, too. Down there in Mexico, knowing that your nickname was fading away up in California. And now that you've been returned to the spotlight, turns out your time is running down. Nineteen shoes, and you're going to die before we know who they all are."

Again, sneer as he might, the man's fear gave itself away in both eye and jaw.

She moved forward until her knees were resting against the foot of his bed.

"Mr. Johnston, maybe it's time to change the rules." She was close enough to see the quick dilation of his pupils.

"What rules are those, bitch?" The expression said contempt, but behind it lay interest.

"The ones for your game. The ones you worked out with my partner—that if we give you one of yours, you'll fill in all the missing details. Which makes things nice for the families, and for cops like Al who care—but honestly? Who but them gives a fuck?"

He blinked.

"We're kind of busy people, you know? And we're cops, not social workers or professional hand-holders. The only thing we really want is those missing shoes and their girls. You tell us where to find them, we might be willing to play your game."

"Fuck you."

She shrugged. "Okay. But if you don't see us again, that's why."

She tucked away her notebook, limped around the bed to recover the facial reconstruction photo the men had forgotten, and made her way to the door. Her arm was coming out for the handle before he spoke up. "What would I get out of it?"

She stopped, and turned. "Fame, I suppose. Its own kind of immortality. What else could you possibly want, in here?"

He chewed on that for a minute, studying her face nearly as intently as she'd looked at his. "Better food. A better view. Someone to talk to."

The man was on a nearly liquid diet now, and he never bothered to look out of the window he had—so no, his only interest was in conversation. "What kind of someone?" Not his daughter, surely?

"What about that reporter who tried to break in and see me? Or— how about a family member of one of my girls, that would be fun."

Fame. And cruelty. The man's twin lusts.

"Both might be possible."

"So what would I gotta do for it?"

"Give me the names."

"Nah, that's what that idiot wanted, something for nothing. You gotta find them first."

"Trade, then. I give you a name, you give me one we don't have yet."

He studied her, his watery eyes traveling over her body. She let the crawling sensation pass through her, and stood waiting.

"You're not like one of mine, but I bet you'd be fun."

"A trade?"

"Yeah, maybe."

"Good. So you owe me four, in exchange for Polly, Sandra, Demi, and Windy."

"Fuck no—you already had those."

She shrugged, and turned back to the door. This time it was half-open when he spoke.

"Let's maybe compromise. Your man's pool girl? Her name was Ta-mara. Stupid name. I met her at a bar in Half Moon Bay. First or second Friday in October 1981. She was the last one before I went to Mexico."

Raquel left the door slightly ajar and dragged a chair away from the wall to sit. Johnston pushed the controls to raise the head of his bed, watching her tuck her cane away and take out her notebook.

"What'd you do to your leg?"

"I didn't do anything to it. Which bar?"

"Just a dive, it's not there anymore. She needed a ride over the hill. So why are you limping, then?"

"Because it's how that leg works. Where did you take her?"

"She took me. She was staying in a kind of commune place, half a dozen hippies too stoned to notice the chickens shitting on their furniture. At first I thought, *Shit, I'll have to let this one go.* But the next morning started out with them smoking a joint the size of a corncob, and I thought, *Are these idiots even going to remember I was here?* And as soon as I started wondering it, it made it a little more fun, you know? Like some extra spice in the day? And so I stayed on, and then Sunday morning before they were up, I finished with Tamara and put her in the trunk and left. Had to drive around all day with her in there. Ever done that?"

"Drive around with a dead body in my car? No."

"You should try it. Makes the world seem . . . small."

Makes me feel large, she translated.

"Then after it got dark, I took her to where we had a Monday job and left her. Taking her shoe first, of course. White sandal."

"Why the shoes?"

"Why not? I'm not some pervert, if that's what you're thinking." *Shame* flashed across his face: a lie. "They're just shoes. But it seemed like I should keep some kind of souvenir. Necklaces would've been better, but what do you do when you find a girl without one? Do you have to let her go, or take a ring or a lock of hair instead? But shoes— even hippies wore shoes when they were hitching a ride."

"So, all your victims wore shoes?"

The old face seemed to come to a focus. "Why? You got a girl missing her *left* shoe?"

"Some of the older cases, evidence gets cleared away."

He seemed to accept her explanation. After a minute, he showed her his yellow teeth in a grin. "Leaves you shit out of luck on that one, I guess."

"I'll need more details on where Tamara and her friends lived."

"Just somewhere out a long road with trees. Damned if I know. So why does your leg limp? Did you break it?"

"Me? No."

"Somebody break it for you?"

"Why are you so interested in my leg?"

"Because you don't want to talk about it. And because one of my girls had a bad leg, too. She was a good one. So good, because she had spirit, tried to fight me—funny how many of them didn't, not really. But she was feisty. I liked her. I was sorry she had to be one of the quick ones, but we had a pour the next day and then the rains were coming so things were going to be slow."

"What was her name?"

"Who, the gimp? Maybe I don't remember it. But hey, did you guys find the one with the glasses under the library? I don't suppose anyone appreciated the joke with her, right? Glasses, library."

"All right, tell me *her* name instead."

"I don't know. I'm getting pretty tired. You're going to have to come back tomorrow." He did in fact look exhausted. But elated, too.

"Mr. Johnston, you owe me three more names."

"Maybe I do. And maybe I'll give you one next time. I'm taking a nap now, Inspector Bitch. See you tomorrow."

"One of us will come by."

"No. I'm not talking to them. I like you, girl. You're feisty, just like—oops. Nearly gave you the gimp's name, didn't I?"

This time, the teeth opened in a horrible grin.

He stank of death and corruption, and the thought of returning here for another name, and another, and another . . .

With great deliberation, Inspector Raquel Laing tucked her pen into her notebook and the notebook into her bag. She stood, returned the chair to its place at the wall, and went out, pulling the door shut on a joyous cackle.

And realized that she wouldn't have been able to hear the old man's laugh over the usual hospital bustle. Puzzled, she turned—and looked into a row of stunned faces.

Charlie seemed to have forgotten the pain in the hand he was cradling to his chest. JJ was gaping at the closed door. Their silence had given the nurses pause. And Al . . .

Al wore one of those difficult mixed expressions: wonder and pride, puzzlement and a review of facts, with maybe a thread of . . . not fear. Discomfort, perhaps. Concern?

"What?" she asked him.

"He gave you a name."

"And promised three more."

"Jesus, Rock. That was . . ."

"How the fuck did you do that?" Charlie demanded.

How had she done it? "I tried to think of what he'd trade for."

"Trade? Oh yeah—the reporter. Not sure that's a great idea. The bastard is already in love with the idea of being famous."

"Someone's going to tell his story eventually. We could offer an exclusive if they agree to an embargo on the shoes."

"Let's string him along, see how far we get before we have to give it. Even make it contingent on waiting for permission."

It was Al who brought up the darker promise, lowering his voice so it would not penetrate the door. "But no families. I'm not going to let that creature pull the wings off some family member, just to give us a new ID."

She looked at him in surprise, that he would imagine a promise to a man like Johnston carried any weight. "Of course not. But it's a useful piece of bait, as long as it lasts."

"It's also interesting to have another commune show up, like with Demi Scott."

"Not necessarily significant, considering he was hunting hitchhikers."

"True. But twice among the five women—possibly three times, if you count Windy's 'bunch of cool musicians' as communal—it's worth noting."

At home that night, Raquel stood at the first in the too-long line of empty pages she had taped up on her wall and printed the name, Tamara.

Fourteen blank sheets waited.

On Tuesday, in the company of Al and JJ (Charlie was home, chewing painkillers), Michael Johnston had accepted Sandra and given them Pam: met at a party in Fremont, offered a ride home, killed a short time later and left along a small road off Skyline Boulevard. May 1974.

Within hours, they matched Pam to a Jane Doe discovered in 1978.

The bones had been scattered and gnawed, stripped of most of their clothing, with no sign of any ID. They, like Windy Jackson, belonged to San Mateo County, who had created a facial reconstruction on the tenth anniversary of her discovery, to see if anyone might remember her. The county now updated the image, added the name Pam, put it onto their Twitter feed—and by Wednesday morning had a last name: Pam Waters, twenty-one, nursing student, mother. She'd been recognized by her brother. She would be claimed by her son, who had been three when his mother vanished.

Six names now on Raquel's wall, thirteen blank pages.

On Wednesday, the Highwayman group would meet up at lunch, to brainstorm ideas before their daily session with Johnston. Where could they push, how could they trigger new victims from him when they only had two names left? It frustrated the others that Johnston would only talk to Raquel—a person in administrative limbo, who wasn't even supposed to be working active cases—until Al pointed out that she was paying for this privilege by letting the creep treat her like a plaything.

She did have to admit he was right. The days she talked to Michael Johnston were the days she went home to a drink and a long, hot shower.

But Wednesday morning, Al rang to tell Raquel that bones with blond hair had been found under a statue on the Gardener Estate, down on the Peninsula. Probably from the seventies. A time when the Estate flirted with communal living. And since she was standing in for San Mateo in the group, wouldn't she like to do so for this as well?

Al would take the brainstorming lunch, while Raquel went down to start the search for any trace of Michael Johnston on the Gardener Estate.

Which had led to Jen Bachus, and Mrs. Dalhousie, and the photographic efforts of a hippie single mother named Annabelle.

Was the body under the *Eves* one of The Highwayman's?

Well, the hair was blond. It happened during Johnston's active period, and in his usual hunting ground. The company that poured the concrete was one he'd occasionally worked for.

But San Mateo's crime scene had found no shoes at all.

It didn't *feel* like his, but there could be so many reasons for that, given the small number of confirmations they'd collected, that she should put that impression aside.

The alarm Raquel had set to drag her from her obsessions was beeping, and had been for a while. Reluctantly, she lay down the 1972 quarter that she used to help her think, and walked across the room to shut it off.

She'd hoped to have victim number seven tonight, but the same row of white rectangles stared back at her. Should she claim one of them for the Gardener bones?

Raquel looked at Polly's shining high school grin, and wondered at the incredible naiveté of the times. Not that these young women would have agreed. No doubt for them, the sixties had been the time of dreamy innocence. By the mid-1970s, they'd have declared that Vietnam and Watergate stripped away any starry-eyed impulse, leaving the younger generation with a clear awareness that life was urgent and dark, and the only way to make a better world was to fight for it.

But even then, while headlines screamed about the Trailside Killer and Edmund Kemper, there were still long-haired kids standing by the freeway with their thumbs out, climbing into cars with strangers.

Had this set of bones under the *Eves* been one of them, or was Raquel wasting her time here? Until the bones were together or the DNA tests came back, they couldn't even be sure what sex the person was—anyone might have had blond hair past the shoulder, a necklace of small beads, and cotton clothing now rotted down to its white plastic buttons.

And bare feet.

In the end, Raquel took out a new sheet of paper and wrote on it the name *Eve*.

She pinned it in a separate line, close to The Highwayman's nineteen spaces, but in a row of its own.

Then turned out the light and went to bed.

18

At half-past eight Thursday morning, Raquel turned off the secondary road and in to the Gardener drive. As she went through the formal gates, a flurry of quail swept across in front of her, but other than that the grounds were quiet, since the house and garden did not open until ten. Up at the parking area, the few cars were at the far edges of the staff lot, but she pulled in near the house, where Jen Bachus had told her to park, propped the Estate permit on the dash, and sent a text to Jen's number:

I'm here.

The manager must have had her phone in her hands, because her reply came in seconds:

I'll be there in 5.

Raquel slid her phone into her pocket, grabbed her cane and the shoulder bag with her laptop in it, and got out.

She stood, listening to the morning. Far off, rush hour on the freeway, a plane on approach to San Francisco. Close in, ticking from her engine, the purring sound of a dove. A rackety motor, blessedly distant: leaf blower? No, a chain saw. Everything was still: no whisper of leaves, no babble of visitors.

Then came the quick beat of shoes on crushed gravel that she'd heard the day before, and Raquel turned with a smile.

Jen wore orange today, which suited her. Of the five rings, three were different from yesterday's. And she must have some important meeting, Raquel thought, since she was wearing makeup that emphasized her eyes.

"Good morning, Inspector. Jerry says he'll be here in half an hour, but traffic's bad so I'd count on forty minutes. And Wes is back, I told him you wanted to talk at eleven—if he doesn't show up, let me know. In the meantime, I have a phone call in about twenty minutes, but since you might be here for a while, I'm going to give you an office— there's an empty one next to the Archives, you can come and go, lock up your stuff, whatever's useful."

"That's very good of you," Raquel said.

Jen moderated her stride to the police officer's cane-assisted one, leading the way through a discreet locked gate into the garden. Once there, half her attention slid over to the flower beds. Here she bent to snap off a dead blossom; there she stepped off the path to pull up what Raquel assumed was a weed. She bent down once to run her fingers along a branch, then sniffed the scent it had left on her skin. Further on, she peered up into a tree, reading something from the tight buds on the branches. And all the time, she carried on a conversation, like a mother multitasking with her kids around her feet.

"So, I told you how I got here," she said. "What about you—how did you come to join the police? Was it a family thing?"

"Not exactly," Raquel said, amused.

Jen glanced up from tucking a sagging branch. "Why is that funny?"

"You might say that my family taught me a lot about law enforcement. Just from the other side of the equation."

The manager stopped dead. "No! Your family were criminals?"

"Only some of them." *Why am I telling her this?*

"This sounds like such a good story."

"Not very. And certainly too long a story for people with phone calls and interviews."

They had crossed the terrace to the back door of the house, which Jen pulled open for her, then followed yesterday's route with the freight elevator, Jen chatting all the while about the house, the weather, and a couple of paintings they walked past. As they rounded the last corner and the ARCHIVES sign came into view, she pointed to the room where Mrs. Dalhousie had assembled tea the previous afternoon.

"That's the break room, help yourself to anything you find in the fridge that doesn't have anyone's name on it—just don't take it into Archives, Mrs. Dalhousie will have a stroke. And here's the spare office—sorry it doesn't have a window." She pulled out a ring with two keys, choosing one and inserting it into the lock, talking all the while. "I'll also give you the key for Archives, just make sure you lock up if you leave. There's a printer, let me check and make sure the wifi password is . . . hmm." She had moved on to the Archives door and inserted the second key, but nothing happened, until she turned it the other way and they heard it lock. "That's odd, could I have left it—oh! Mrs. Dalhousie, sorry, I didn't expect you here this early."

"I came in to finish up a few things." The archivist retreated into her room, and they followed, finding her pulling sheets from the working printer. "The inspector needed a list of known residents during the Commune phase. I thought I might save her some time."

The printer wheezed to a halt. Mrs. Dalhousie added its fresh pages to the half-inch stack on the table, cracked the entire sheaf into order, and slid them into a folder.

"The image quality isn't the greatest, since they're scans, but we also have most of the negatives, if you want those. I've also given you a digital copy of the video you wanted." She added a thumb drive to the folder, and held them out to Raquel.

Each sheet had a person's face, often cropped from a group shot. The archivist had also typed in whatever pieces of information she had found on that person: first name, possible surname, the dates they had joined or left the commune, any family members, and so on.

Raquel looked up, reading the signs of fatigue in the woman's face. *Also pride.* "How long have you been here?"

"I couldn't sleep. Though I wasn't sure if you were only looking at women, or only people with blond hair, and so—well, I simply did all the commune members I could find. Will that be useful?"

Personal effort, personal recognition—and the greater the effort, the more personal the reward.

"Mrs. Dalhousie," she said, "I could kiss you."

Again, she'd hit the right response, and the older woman came very near to a dimple. "That will not be necessary, Inspector. Although if neither of you need me, I may go home now, for a while." She gathered up her laptop and keys, but at the door she paused. "The thought that someone used a piece of art to hide a murder . . . it is deeply troubling. If there is anything else I can do for you, Inspector, you need only ask."

"Thank you."

Jen gaped at the empty doorway, then at the folder. She shook her head. "Okay, then. Well. Jerry will meet you in the terrace coffee shop—it's not open yet but staff use it any time. If you're still here and free at noon, we can have lunch. Text me if you need anything."

But Raquel was already into the pages, and barely noticed Jen leave.

19

At 9:35, Raquel crossed the terrace stones to the café, carrying the folder with Mrs. Dalhousie's 102 pages, to which she'd added 5, hastily created using the same format, along with a dozen or so snapshots from the Archives. The café smelled of fresh coffee and baked goods. A group of workers were laughing over a cellphone at a corner table, but the man at the register looked more like a retired lawyer, someone who paid a lot of money to keep his thinning, once-red hair looking good, whose tanned freckles suggested regular hours on the golf links.

"Mr. Rathford?"

The vigorous way he whirled, then hurried across the room to hold out his hand, made Raquel revise her judgment: tennis, rather than golf. "Inspector Laing, good to meet you—what can we get you to drink?"

"Nothing now, thanks."

"You sure? Emmalia here makes a mean latté."

"I'm good."

They went outside, away from ears, to a table under an enormous magnolia tree. He didn't quite pull out a chair for her, but Raquel had the impression that if she'd been just a few years older, his gallantry might have got the better of him. As it was, he waited until she was seated before taking his own chair.

"Jen brought me up to speed," he said. "And although I'm sure you realize there may be things I can't divulge about my clients without their permission, I'll do everything I can to help you out."

"I appreciate that. Before we start, can I show you a photograph, see if it rings any bells?"

She handed him a page she'd printed with the image Al had forwarded the night before: Michael Johnston's 1980 photo, touched up with a short beard. He studied it, seeing the ordinary features, the eyes that could be anyone's. Even Raquel had to admit that nothing demonic peered out of that photograph. "Is this your suspect?"

"You know I can't answer that."

"Yeah. No, he doesn't look familiar, sorry."

"That's fine. So, I was hoping to get some background from you about the period when the Estate was a commune. The late seventies, I think."

"Seventy-five to seventy-nine." He listened to the words, and shook his head. "Funny to think it only lasted four years. It seemed, I don't know . . . forever."

"Your firm has been the family lawyers for a long time, I think?"

"My grandfather was the first. Just after the War. Forty-seven or -eight."

"When did you take over?"

"After my father had his first heart attack, in 1977. Though I'd been helping him out for some years, and I'd known the family forever—when I was a kid, my father used to bring me along sometimes when he had business here. The housekeeper was happy to keep me entertained."

"Did you know Rob and his brother? You seem about the same age."

"I'm a little older. I met them, sure, but only in passing. They were mostly off at boarding school."

"So you only got to know Rob after he moved back here, with his commune friends?"

"That's right—though I'd met him again in Oregon. My father was senior partner by then, and the Gardeners' lawyer. I was the one who got saddled with flying up and hiring a car to drive into the wilds and tell Rob that his grandfather had died."

"I understand the relationship was not amicable."

"You could say that."

"Politics?"

"Not really—I don't think the old man had any politics. He was just . . . he was so much older than Rob and his brother, even though he raised them. Well, he and their great-grandmother, Maude. And he always pushed them away by trying to force their obedience. Did it with Fort then tried it with Rob."

"Rob must have been pleased to learn he'd become an enormously wealthy man."

"You'd think so, wouldn't you? Especially since he figured the old man had disinherited him, too, like he did with Fort. But no. At first, he wanted nothing to do with it—especially once he saw all the stipulations that were attached. Both carrots and sticks."

"What changed his mind?"

"That was his girlfriend Meadow's doing. And, I'm afraid, mine."

Rathford fiddled with his coffee cup, then sighed. "The place in Oregon was a dump."

20

Then

Jerry had to fight to keep the rental Pontiac from sliding off the road that led to The Commons. Or at least, the road he'd been *told* led to The Commons. Though he fully expected the mucky track to end any minute at a washed-out creek, and there he'd be, working his way backward, downhill, through slick mud, in the pouring rain.

But to his surprise, the trees reluctantly parted on an open space—probably a farmyard, though it looked like some *Life* article on poverty in Appalachia.

He turned off the engine and waited, peering through the mud-smeared windshield at the house, but no one came out. The place seemed deserted.

Crap. Nothing for it, he'd have to make a dash through the rain and at least leave his card in the door. But first, he wound up the windows that he'd been forced to leave down so the windshield didn't totally steam up, and got out the umbrella his father's secretary had handed him as he left.

He looked down at what he was wearing. He'd chosen the suit as a compromise between friendly and dignified, but that was California. The people here would probably take him for a Mormon missionary.

He pushed open the car door, maneuvered the umbrella into the open, and stepped out—directly into what felt like a fresh cow pat. He cursed, pulled back, and realized that there wasn't much choice in surface.

Why the hell hadn't he thought more carefully about the idea of a commune in Oregon, and worn his old jeans and rubber boots? *Jerry, you're an idiot*, he thought, scowling at the moth-eaten wooden barn, the geodesic dome made of scraps, the junkyard of old cars and hippie-decorated school buses.

And a person, at last.

A rather ominous-looking person, he couldn't help noticing. Solitary, silent, leaning on a shovel that reminded Jerry of a movie he'd seen. Samantha Eggar, trapped and collected by Terence Stamp, picking up a shovel to bash her captor on the head.

Not that this guy looked anything like Samantha Eggar—or even Terence Stamp: big, hairy, draped in an old poncho, wearing rubber boots patched with duct tape.

Jerry came very close to getting back in the car and driving away. But— *Do you want to make partner?* He'd agreed to the job. He couldn't imagine explaining to his father and uncle that he'd been too creeped out by the whole scene to even do the notification.

So he tightened his grip on the umbrella and started off through the mud—nearly going down face-first into it. He grabbed the car door, and decided to stay where he was.

"Afternoon," he called loudly, as if the guy was deaf, or just slow. "My name's Jerry Rathford. I'm looking for Rob Gardener?"

Jerry waited, listening to the *plip-plop* of rain in mud. The guy with the shovel did look a little like Rob Gardener. Although with that beard and those clothes, it could be anyone. Any of your neighborhood mass murderers. And it wasn't like Rob Gardener didn't have a record himself . . .

The lawyer cleared his throat. "Your . . . cousin? David Kirkup? Gave me this address, and—"

The man spoke at last. "Has the Old Bastard finally died?"

"I . . . Are you . . . ?"

"I'm Rob, yeah. Is he dead?"

"I'm sorry to have to inform you, Mr. Gardener—"

"Oh Jesus. Come on, you're going to drown out here."

Jerry hesitated, just a moment. Then he tightened his grip on the attaché case and slithered his way across the yard to the farmhouse steps. They were so old they looked chewed, but they felt okay underfoot. As he walked up them, he noticed the sign nailed to the porch post: THE COMMONS. The board looked about to fall off.

The porch was big, ten feet deep and the full width of the front. Plastic chairs and handmade benches with mildewy foam cushions were pushed together at one end, with a lot of very beat-up kids' toys covering the rest of the space. Water sheeted off the porch roof. Jerry shook out his umbrella over the steps and stood back to let the man in the poncho go by.

Gardener didn't offer to shake hands, which was just as well.

A long metal tray with an assortment of shoes in it stood beside the door. Gardener stripped off his poncho and dropped it over a hook, then stepped out of his boots. His jeans were patched, and wet where the poncho had not met his boot tops. His sweater, stained but once red enough for a Christmas garment, had leather elbow patches that looked like actual mends rather than decorations, and enough holes to show the flannel shirt beneath it. As he bent to move the muddy boots into the tray, Jerry spotted the remains of a decorative embroidered butterfly on the back pocket of his jeans, and beside it, a well-worn buckskin sheath with a bone-handled knife at least ten inches long. The ancient screen door slapped shut when Gardener went inside. Reluctantly, Jerry unlaced his own shoes and left them beside the boots.

To his surprise, the linoleum floor inside looked clean, though faded and patched. He walked cautiously for a few steps until he was reassured that it would not snag his cashmere socks.

Gardener had dropped to his heels in front of a thing that Jerry had never seen outside of a Clint Eastwood movie: a genuine potbellied stove. The big man opened its door, jabbed at the embers with a bent length of steel, and fed in a handful of sticks and two logs from a pile against the wall. He shut the door and stood.

"We're out of coffee," he said. "I can offer you tea or homemade beer. The beer'll make you fart."

"Tea is fine."

"Good choice." He picked up an enormous black kettle from the patch of tile under the stove, sloshed it around to judge its contents, then set it down on the stove's top. "Lunch?"

"I ate, thanks."

"Have a seat." Gardener waved at the chairs, everything from a plaid sofa to a bentwood rocker, and walked out.

Instead of taking a chair, Jerry stood as close to the stove as he could get without setting his pant legs aflame. The house felt empty, which was strange, considering the foul weather and the amount of kids' play equipment he'd seen. There were signs that other adults lived here, too: magazines and paperbacks piled on the board-and-block shelving, a crude willow basket full of knitting projects, an entire shelf stacked with well-used sketchbooks and the pencils and pastels to go with them. Half a dozen musical instruments hung from nails driven into the peeling wallpaper—two six-string guitars and one twelve-string, a banjo, a silver flute, and a violin. On the shelves below them were baskets holding recorders, harmonicas, maracas, a tambourine, and something that resembled a miniature organ.

And on the smoke-black wall behind the stove, mounted high up beyond the reach of children, a shotgun.

The chill was leaving the room, waking up the odors of woodsmoke, marijuana, and patchouli oil, along with the overall smell of mildew. Jerry retreated a bit from the stove, moving over to the art tacked on the wall. Children's crayon stick figures were interspersed with inspirational sayings illustrated by enthusiastic amateurs—*Peace + Love = Harmony! Family is change!*—using eye-watering neon colors. There was also a beautiful watercolor landscape that, with an effort of imagination, Jerry decided might show the commune on a summer day. Next to it was a bright and intricate commercial print of a many-armed Indian goddess doing a joyous dance. And below her was a surprisingly modern record player with dozens of LP albums.

He was reaching out for a new-looking James Taylor album when he heard soft footsteps, and turned to see Rob padding in with a bowl and hunk of brown bread in one hand and a spoon in the other. The big man was scooping the bowl's contents into his mouth with the grim dedication of a starving teenager, and sat down in the rocker without a pause. In no time at all, his spoon was scraping the sides. When he had mopped the bowl with the last stub of bread, he set it on the floor with a sigh and stretched out a hand to test the kettle. Not yet hot, apparently, because he settled back in the rocker and looked at the lawyer.

Who suddenly remembered himself and fumbled in his breast pocket for his card case, stepping forward with an elegant bit of card stock. "I'm sorry—like I said, my name's Jerry Rathford, with Bishop, Avery, Johnson, Rathford, and Rathford. Your grandfather's lawyers? And yes, I'm sorry to tell you that your grandfather passed away on Monday."

"Today is . . . ?"

"Friday," Jerry said, then added, "the eighteenth of April." He glanced at the shotgun, hoping it was just an ironic decoration, then sat gingerly on a chair whose plywood seat had no obvious splinters.

Gardener studied the card as if reading a story, then dropped it into his used bowl. "How's Marla doing?"

"Marla . . . the housekeeper? She's fine, as far as I know."

"She's lived with the Old Bastard for thirty years, she won't be fine. Tell her I'll call her next time I go into town. Our phone line went down a while ago."

"Um. About that. We were hoping you would come down to the Bay Area."

"April's a busy time. Soon as the rain stops, we'll be planting, and we have a house to finish."

"You're building a house. This place is, er, rented, right?"

"Not really. We're family. Including the one whose name is on the deed."

Jerry hesitated, but decided not to mention that he'd done his homework before flying up to see this little-known client. A quick records search and some phone calls told him that the property's owner, one Aloisius Clark, had started the commune six years ago on land he'd inherited from an uncle. But Clark's wife had died last year, and according to the bank manager, their two teenagers were sick of living in the hills. The commune now sent Clark money every month so he could rent a place in Medford.

"Where are the rest of them?"

"In town. They took both cars, in case one broke down or ended up in a ditch. The girls went to pick up their food stamps and shop, one of the kids had to see a dentist, and the guys have a line on some second-hand building material. They should be back any time."

"You say kids. Any of them yours?"

"God no. More Gardeners in the world?"

Rob scooped up his empty bowl and took it away, coming back with a pair of mugs and a handmade teapot. The water in the kettle was singing now, and he used a thick, colorful square that might have been woven by a chimpanzee to pick up the uninsulated handle. In one mug, a tea bag bobbed at the surface. In the other, a straw basket did an inadequate job of containing an odd-looking bunch of leaves.

"I figured you'd take black tea," Rob said, handing his guest the one with the bag. "There's no milk."

"Sugar?"

"The girls don't believe in it. We might have some honey."

"This is fine," the lawyer lied. At least it was hot.

"Rathford," Rob said. "I went to high school with a Rathford. Tom? No—Don."

"My cousin. I met you at their house a couple of times."

"His mother was sick."

"She passed, last year."

"I'm sorry to hear that. She was cool."

The word caught at the lawyer's attention, and made the day circle around for a quick instant before it settled down again in a slightly but essentially different form. The man with the foot-long hair and the beard down his chest might look like some timeless figure from the deep woods—but in fact, Rob Gardener was twenty-four. Not all that far from the hungry teenager he'd reminded Jerry of.

He should have been driving a muscle car over to the beach on the weekends, grooving on the Stones, getting ready to sit the California Bar, maybe. Instead, the heir to one of the biggest fortunes on the West Coast slumped tiredly into a chair, ate congealed beans for lunch, and spent his day slopping mud out of ditches.

"You better get started, whatever it is you need," Rob said. "You don't look like the kind of guy who likes talking business over scream-ing kids."

"Right." Jerry set his cup on the floor and opened his attaché case on his lap, taking out a legal pad with writing on the top page, a folder with a string tie, and a sleek professional pen. After a bit of juggling, he closed the case and used it as a desk.

"First of all, the funeral home needs to arrange a date. They suggest a Saturday, so your grandfather's friends—"

"My grandfather didn't have any friends."

"His acquaintances, then. And the family."

"Why ask me? Have Davey say some words—he's always been bet-ter family to the Old Bastard than Fort and me."

Rathford stared at him. "But you're his grandson. His heir."

"I was his grandson, not his heir. He wrote me out of the will a long time ago."

"No, he didn't."

Rob tipped his hairy head, studying the lawyer. "He said he was going to."

"He may have told you that, but when my—when the firm's senior partner last saw him, two weeks ago, it was only in regards to a codicil. With the exception of minor bequests, and with certain provisions, everything was left to you."

"What about Fort?"

"The will does specify that your brother is to get nothing."

"Marla?"

"Mrs. Ramirez is to receive a pension equal to her present salary, with health insurance and annual cost of living increases. The head groundsman and Estate manager have the same arrangement. And your cousin David, who's been working for the manager, gets half sal-ary for three years."

"Huh. Way more generous than I'd have expected."

Jerry picked up the folder and shuffled through the pages. Now for the uncomfortable part. "Well, yes, um. There's a codicil. Added in late 1972. That has some effect on the provisions." He took out a stapled document. "By the way, this is a photocopy—the original is in the firm's offices and will take some considerable time to go through with you. But because of your . . . situation here, and the distances involved, I was sent to explain matters. Before—well, I think you'll understand when you've read this. The most recent codicil is at the top. The 1972 one is on the second page."

He warily held out a sheaf of paper stapled in one corner. Rob took it, every bit as reluctant. The first page made him shake his head, but as he read down the second page, his face went dark.

"Jesus Christ," he said at last. "The fucker was relentless, wasn't he?"

"Do you understand the codicil, Mr. Gardener?"

"It's pretty obvious. If I don't crawl back home with my tail between my legs, everybody else gets screwed."

"You only need to live on the Estate for a period of five years," Jerry pointed out. "My senior partner wanted me to tell you that while it is possible some of the will's provisions could be challenged in court, it would take a very long time and might mean that all the bequests are put on hold while that's going on."

"Who's the senior partner?"

"My dad. Your grandfather's lawyer."

"Yeah, it sounded like he knew me. Shit. Well, Davey will have to manage without his handout, but I'll see what I can do about sending money to Marla every month. Tell her I'm afraid it won't be as much as she's getting now." He let the pages fall shut and held the document out. "My answer is no."

"You can't be serious."

"I wouldn't eat the old man's shit when he was alive, I sure as hell won't now that he's dead. This is my home now."

"But it's only five years! He wanted ten, but my father convinced him that if you were on the Estate for five years, you'd stay forever. Surely you can force yourself to live in the mansion that long. I mean . . ." He caught himself before he could say, *look at this dump,* but his glance around the room said it all.

Gardener shook his head. "Five years, five days, doesn't matter. I'm sorry for Marla, sorry for the schools and programs that won't get their slice—sorriest of all that the money will go to that list of dirtbags he's come up with—but I can't do it. Tell your father I'll try and get down there sometime in the summer, to sign his papers. And I . . ." He paused, cocking his head at a sound. "Car coming. Good, that means you won't meet them in the road on your way out."

"But we're not—"

Rob Gardener's eyes stabbed the lawyer to silence. "We are finished. You will say nothing about this. You will get in your car and drive away, and you will tell your father that I'll let him know when I'm coming down. Are we clear?"

There was nothing peace-and-love about the bearded man in the woodsman's clothes. This was the big-knife, heavily muscled, shotgun-on-the-wall Vietnam vet looking across a too-narrow space at a city lawyer, and all Jerry could do was nod.

Rob's face relaxed and he stood up, extending his hand. "Thank you for coming, Mr. Rathford. Drive carefully as you go down the hill. The only thing that could pull you out of the creek is our tractor, and it's currently spread across half the barn floor."

21

J erry locked the papers back in the case and followed his host to the door, where Rob aimed his mismatched socks into the boots just as two cars pulled up by the porch. Eight doors came open to let out ten, eleven human beings—twelve, if one counted the babe in arms, whose mother scurried past them to the door.

Rob asked, "How's the baby?"

"Antibiotics," the woman answered darkly, and let the door slam shut.

Rob shook his head and shrugged into the damp poncho. Two small and two larger kids in handmade sweaters and too-large jackets had come to a halt halfway up the stairs, gaping at Jerry, an alien creature in a business suit. One of them wore cloth shoes with the toes out. One had a shaved head. A third had the crusts of impetigo around his mouth. All were thin.

As Rob went down the steps, he told them, "Get inside, kids. This is Jerry. He won't bite."

The quartet sidled up the steps, kicked off their footwear, and slipped inside, not taking their eyes off Jerry for an instant. A stream of full-sized hippies came next, all carrying armloads of groceries. They nodded to the intruder; he murmured greetings in return. Rob had continued on to the second car, and was standing with his hand on the nape of a woman's neck, nestled between her fair, pinned-up braids and the heathery blue Aran-knit sweater she wore. Jerry couldn't hear what she said, but she pointed toward the trunk, and Rob moved obediently around to lift out a big plastic crate, staggering off with it in the direction of the woodshed.

Jerry rescued his shoes from the growing avalanche of muddy footwear, and was settling on a bench when a voice interrupted.

"Carry this inside?"

He turned. A gangly boy of maybe nineteen was cradling a twenty-pound sack with the stencil BROWN RICE on it. Jerry looked toward the woodshed, but Rob Gardener was nowhere to be seen, so he set his shoes down beside the attaché case and took the sack.

"Hi, name's Wes," the kid said, and went back to the car.

"Um, I was just . . ." But the others were inside, and Jerry already had his shoes off—so despite Gardener's clear eviction notice, he went back into the house and followed the voices to the kitchen, where he stood waiting for someone to notice him.

The person who noticed was the woman with bound-up braids the color of wheat and a lumpy blue sweater—and, he could see now, emerald-green eyes. Other than the eyes, there was nothing out of the ordinary about her—average height, stocky build, features that on any other earth-mother type would be judged plain. But somehow she managed to be the most dynamic thing in a room that was already swirling with jostling figures, loud voices, wild hair, tie-dyed clothing, and the smells of stale sweat, fresh marijuana, and onions. Her eyes caught his, and she didn't try to make herself heard, just smiled and pointed him toward an open door.

Jerry tore his attention away from her—he hoped she hadn't seen him looking at her clearly braless chest—and carried the sack to the doorway.

It was a pantry, although most of the shelves were bare, and none looked strong enough for the rice. So he put it on the floor and stepped back into the kitchen—but the green-eyed woman was speaking with a child and didn't notice him. Reluctantly, he left.

But just outside the front door, another interruption waited.

The man on the porch boards looked even more out of place in

these rural surroundings than Jerry did, although for diametrically different reasons. Sinewy and intense, with jet-black hair and eyes, he
wore expensive rubber boots, snug black pants, and a raincoat that
actually kept out the wet. His beard was trimmed in precise, Mephis-
tophelian lines, and was the only sign of a razor Jerry had seen since
leaving civilization. More Mick Jagger than hippie farmer.

Jerry knew the man from somewhere. Or at least, he knew the face.

"Take these," Mephistopheles said in a throaty growl. "I gotta move
the car."

The brown paper bags he carried were on the verge of disintegrat-
ing, so Jerry abandoned his shoes again and allowed the unlikely figure
to press the bags into his arms. He got through the screen door without
dropping anything, and worked his way through the crowded kitchen.
"Pardon me, sorry," he said, with increasing volume, lunging for a flat
place just as the damp fiber gave way. A restaurant-sized tin of tomatoes
rolled out, heading for the floor—but the green-eyed woman caught it,
nonchalantly pulling the bag apart and scooping up three matching
tins, which she handed to one of the other women to load onto the
shelves. Up close, she was older than he'd thought, certainly over thirty.

"You guys really like tomatoes," he commented.

"Government surplus. Better than the powdered milk. The peanut
butter's not bad," she added, reaching into the other bag for a large tin
that lacked any identifying label. "Wes, honey, would you find a felt
pen and write 'chili beans' on this one? Look in that drawer.
Annabelle"—this to the woman with the small baby, who without her
enveloping rain gear turned out to be a thin, white-blond young woman
even younger than Wes—"take Sparrow up to bed and warm your-
selves up, we'll bring you a cup of tea. Who are you?"

She spoke over her shoulder as she was running water into a kettle,
so it took Jerry a moment to register that she was addressing him.
"Sorry—Jerry. Rathford. I'm the lawyer—one of the lawyers, for Mr.
Gardener's grandfather."

She switched on the gas under the kettle and turned. "The Old Bastard? Has he had a change of heart? 'Cause we're all pretty sick of this
government surplus crap. I'm Meadow, by the way. Ah, Rain, is that
the last of it? I hope you managed to keep the flour dry?"

Rain turned out to be the devilish man who'd handed Jerry the bags. "I put my coat over it—want me to leave it by the fire to make sure?"

"Good idea."

She turned the green eyes back at Jerry, waiting, although he couldn't quite remember for what. Oh, right—old Mr. Gardener's change of heart.

"Er, well, I can't . . ."

"Oh, of course. Lawyers," she said, with the same intonation people used for *pigs*.

The criticism stung. "Law is the way we smooth human interaction."

"Don't bullshit me, my friend—I used to be one. Law is the way rich people smooth their own private road."

Jerry wasn't sure he could argue with that. "What law firm did you work for?"

"Small company in Illinois, you wouldn't know it. One of the partners cornered me in the break room the same week he'd fired the two most expensive women, so I kneed him in the balls, took my severance pay from his wallet, and went off to find a new life." She looked around, and saw that the unloading of food had begun to shift into dinner preparation. "Wes, when the kettle's boiled, would you make Annabelle a cup of the raspberry leaf tea? I told her we'd take it up—put honey in it. C'mon, lawyer."

Bemused, Jerry followed her solid backside to the main room, where Rob was just coming in with a pair of cheap-looking sleeping bags. He shot Jerry a disapproving glance, but kicked the door shut behind him with a stockinged foot.

"Babe," Meadow said, "this guy can't tell me anything because he's a lawyer. Why is he here?"

The reply was interrupted by two kids scrambling up from the floor to greet Rob, then staggering back laughing as he tossed the sleeping bags into their arms. They exclaimed over the colors, shouted their thanks, then pounded off with their treasures. Rob's face had softened as he watched them go, then closed again as he remembered her question.

"He came to tell me that the old man's dead."

"Ah." She moved forward to put her arms around him—not just a comfort hug, Jerry thought, but the embrace of lovers. "Oh, sweet man. I'm sorry you didn't have a chance to set things right with him. Not good karma, to leave things unfinished. But I can't really be sorry. He didn't sound like a good person."

Which was more eulogy than the client's actual grandson had given.

She stepped back, absently patting Rob's lingering hand, then looked around to check who was in earshot. When she spoke, she kept her voice low. "Rob, I have to say, if he left you any money at all, it could make a difference. Rain and I went to see Aloisius, and like we were afraid of, he's going to sell the place. He even has a buyer, and the guy won't promise not to kick us off. Just when we're finishing the house, too. Annabelle's really freaked—if her dad finds out the baby had pneumonia, he'll blame the trailer and send someone to take them home."

Rob did not say anything, but the look on his face said that the young mother was not the only one who was feeling freaked out.

Jerry didn't intend to speak up. The future of The Commons wasn't his business. This was 1975, not 1968. All over the country, people who had gone joyously back to the land to invent a new world out of free love and shared possessions were waking up to cold reality, their dreams mowed down by a brutal Establishment. So what if this group of flower children followed the trend?

And it certainly wasn't his job. A senior partner would never have said anything. Even Jerry knew better—knew it before Rob had ordered him to silence. But then came the empty shelves and the government handouts and the appalling mud and mildew and pneumonia and the kids in rags thrilled by the gift of a cheap sleeping bag . . .

"Well, if you're going to be needing a new place anyway—" That was as far as he got before the violence in Rob Gardener's glare froze the words in his mouth. *One more word,* the big man's expression promised, *and you'll be on the floor with a broken face.*

Meadow looked from one man to the other. Rain, who'd been steaming his wet jeans beside the stove, felt the vibes and moved to stand at her side, one hand going to her shoulder. The gesture was somewhere between friendship and possession. *Free love?* Jerry wondered. The voices of children laughing upstairs seemed to come from another world.

"Rob," she said, "what's he talking about?"

Gardener did not take his angry gaze from the lawyer. "Meadow, it's nothing. Just the Old Bastard trying to blackmail me from the grave."

"By getting you to do what?" When her man didn't reply, she turned to the visitor. "What do you want Rob to do?"

Ethically, he couldn't tell her. Despite the empty pantry and the holes in the kids' shoes. Despite the green of her eyes. "Think about it," he said instead to the heir of the Gardener fortune. "You have my card. You'd only have to give it five years, and then you're free to do what you want with it."

He nodded at Meadow and Rain, then padded across the linoleum to the door. As he retrieved his abused shoes from beneath a glossy, knee-high rubber boot suitable for a day at Balmoral, a random thought fell into place and he knew who the commune's resident Mephistopheles was: ten years ago, Rain had been Reynard, a hard-driving rocker in close competition with Jagger for baddest boy in rock.

How on earth had the guy ended up here? Jerry wondered. But he wasn't about to go back inside to ask. Voices were building, an argument over the little bombshell he'd set off. He found a spot on the bench that wasn't too filthy, sat down, got one shoe tied and then the other, retrieved his umbrella—and then heard the stunned silence fall inside, followed by a gabble of cross talk with one loud and horrified cry rising above it all.

"The *Gardener* mansion? That huge place on the hill near Palo Alto? Rob, for God's sake—that family is *you*?"

Jerry did not bother to put up the umbrella. Instead, he ran, slipping across the mud and gunning the engine, spewing muck from his tires in his haste to get away before Rob Gardener came out the farmhouse door with the shotgun.

22

Now

"I never told my father exactly what I'd done," Jerry said, giving Raquel a shamefaced look. "To convince Rob to come down here, I mean. But honestly, it's one thing when a bunch of grown-ups go into the hills and live off food stamps and government handouts, but when you have a baby with pneumonia from sleeping in a trailer and kids with holes in their shoes—well, I couldn't just walk away. And I could see that Meadow was not only the most reasonable person there, but that Rob adored her. And Rain seemed to have some say in matters—I suppose I thought that the two of them might make Rob see sense. So I let them sort of overhear me telling Rob that there was not only money to be had, but a nice place to live."

"And you expected him to come after you with a shotgun."

"No—well, not really. Not an actual shotgun, of course not."

"Even though Rob Gardener did have violence in his background."

"Yeah, but that was a long time before. He was just a kid."

"Was he?"

"Sure—I mean, high school. Who doesn't get into some trouble?"

"Ah. So there was something in high school, too. I was referring to the police report his grandfather made after Rob tried to burn the house down."

"Oh, that's an exaggeration. I'm sure it was more of an accident. And the old man probably provoked him pretty hard. But violence? No. If anything, Rob's always the one to walk away from any confrontation."

"So no shotgun?"

"Not then. I mean . . . Oh jeez. No, Rob Gardener did not threaten me: not at the time, not after. He didn't even lodge a complaint with the Bar, which he'd have been justified doing, to be honest."

"And he forgave you, for putting the bait in front of his girlfriend?"

"Eventually. He must have, or he'd have changed his law firm. And it did turn out to be the right decision for everyone. Or anyway, I thought it was. For quite a long time."

23

Then

The next time Jerry Rathford drove up a road to see Rob Gardener, it was three years later and four hundred miles to the south.

When Jerry had fled the Oregon hillside that rain-drenched afternoon, he was not at all sure what the results of his bombshell would be. Both green-eyed Meadow and rock-star Rain had sounded pretty pissed off at Rob. For months, Jerry was nervous whenever he went for a jog or set off across a parking lot, sure that a furious bearded hippie would come at him with a shovel, for having revealed the Gardener family's shameful capitalist identity. Like outing Abbie Hoffman as a member of the New York Stock Exchange.

Even after Jerry's father congratulated him one afternoon, two months after the apparently unsuccessful Oregon trip, to say that Rob Gardener and his crew would be coming down to take over the Estate, he'd expected repercussions. Outright violence? A complaint lodged? A truckload of horseshit dumped in front of his apartment house?

Three years later, he was still waiting.

On the other hand, today's drive to meet the firm's client could not have been more reassuringly different.

For one thing, he was in his own car, a shiny new convertible, not some boatlike airport rental. For another, the day was hot and dry, the blue sky cloudless, and even after three years of neglect, the long driveway had not so much as a pothole in the surface. The entrance was not a tunnel of dripping fir branches, but a broad granite gate—though he was startled to see the dignified archway splashed with bright letters reading: WELCOME TO THE COMMONS. And at the end of the drive, the buildings that waited were from a different universe than the shabby farmhouse, leaky barn, and half-assed domes he'd seen that day.

Still, as the Gardener mansion came into view, evidence mounted that the Oregon commune had merely transplanted itself here, and Jerry's uneasiness began to stir.

A painted bus tucked into the oak trees was definitely the one he'd seen in Oregon. And up there near the orchard, a sprinkling of yurts, tents, domes, and cabins brought a reminder of that day. There were women in farmer john overalls or long skirts, a couple of shirtless men, children wearing nothing at all, a drift of marijuana smoke—and then at the house's front terrace, a small version of that makeshift geodesic dome, this one spilling out kids' play equipment across the close-fitted gray stones.

And yes, here was the man himself, still leaning on a heavy shovel, still waiting for him. This time in a straw hat instead of a hooded poncho, but every bit as looming as before.

Reluctantly, Jerry turned off the engine. When the man did not come storming down the terrace with the shovel raised, he opened the door, got out, closed the door. Gardener did not move. Jerry told himself he was being ridiculous and traded his baseball cap for the attaché case, then started toward the house.

Despite his nerves, it was hard to keep his eyes on the still figure, the house itself was such a shock. Like seeing your grandmother in pink satin hot pants.

The entranceway's geometrically shaved boxwood hedges and regimented flower beds were gone, replaced by beans and tomatoes staked on rough branches and zucchini vines beginning to sprawl over the stones. The monochrome of curtains in every window, which in a previous era had been arranged into a perfect sweep each morning by a maid, had either disappeared or been replaced by sheets dyed every color under the sun. The window frames themselves, formerly the same pale green as the walls of the entrance foyer, were nothing short of psychedelic, with some unfortunate dribbles of Day-Glo paint down the staid brick walls.

As for those walls themselves: twenty-foot-tall Van Gogh sunflowers now arched over the portico. A mural of purple and orange dinosaurs ambled along the ballroom wing toward the geodesic playroom. Across the terrace, the outer walls of the kitchen wing now bore a three-story-tall rainbow over a jungle scene of palm trees and giraffes.

Then there were the figures on either side of the portico: a pair of farmers? A man and a woman, eight feet tall and gazing down the terrace at arriving guests. The bearded man on the left had a bright red apple. His partner on the right, her hair a flying tangle of bright new copper strips, wore a long skirt made of glittering bits of broken tile, but was bare-breasted other than what Jerry thought at first was a demure banner. As he came closer, he realized it was an enormous snake.

He guessed, from the apple, that this was supposed to be Adam and Eve, with their two young sons. As he got closer, he noticed that Eve had green eyes. Did that make Rob the Adam?

At the reminder, Jerry pulled his attention from the figures to give his firm's client an uncertain smile.

"Good morning, Mr. Gardener. I, er, like what you've done with the place."

Rob climbed out from the bed where he'd been working and glanced at the surrounding walls. "Do you?"

"It sure is different." Which was a polite way of saying, *It sure would give your grandfather a stroke.*

"This can be an intimidating place if you're not allowed to make it your home," the owner remarked.

"But the paintings are great," Jerry said, trying not to sound too surprised. "And these sculptures, they're . . . they look really professional."

"They ought to, they're by Miriam Gaddo." The name meant nothing to Jerry until he got back to the office and asked his secretary to look it up. She didn't need to. Instead, she went wide-eyed and asked if next time she could go out with him and see them.

"It's supposed to be Adam and Eve, right? What's that she's holding?"

"A spindle. To spin yarn." Gardener pointed up at a wide metal plate mounted to the bricks above the entrance, which must have weighed half a ton. Words had been welded through it; they said:

When Adam delved and Eve span, who then was the gentleman?
From the beginning, all were created alike.
Our bondage came with the oppression of the wicked.

—JOHN BALL

"Huh," Jerry said.

"John Ball was a priest who started a peasant's revolt, in thirteen-something. We put it there as a reminder that we're here to overturn the old oppressive order." Rob leaned the shovel's handle against the portico and dropped his hat over it. "Speaking of old orders, how's your father?"

"Much better, thanks. The doctors are making him play golf instead of going to the office, and he's discovered he likes it. Though he keeps double-checking everything I do with his clients, in case I get it wrong. You're sure you're okay working with me? One of the other partners would be happy to take over."

"Why?"

"Well, it's not like you and I parted best of friends, three years ago."

"Just don't pull any shit like that again, we'll be fine."

No point in pretending he didn't know what Gardener meant. His *slip of the tongue* in front of Rob's old lady—assuming that's who Meadow was—had changed everything, and it was not entirely acci-dental. To be honest, it wasn't even a little bit accidental. But before he could try to apologize, Rob Gardener's face shifted, as he reflected on his anger.

"Look, Jerry, I was wrong. This family lives in common, like our name says. Food, work, love, money, kids, decisions—we all have an equal right to anything. I had no business deciding something that important without them. But that doesn't mean I have to like it. And it sure as hell doesn't mean I have to like the way you forced it on me."

"I understand," Jerry said, although he didn't, really. Particularly considering the reason he was here today. "So, how is everything going? Dad said you had a problem with the neighbor recently. Is that sorted out now?" Just because the senior partner had been in charge of the Gardener family needs didn't mean Jerry wasn't kept up on matters, even before the heart attack had forced the older man to turn over some of the reins.

"I think the sheriff had a word with him. Tell your dad thanks for that."

"No problem." Of course, it was a problem, and would continue to be. No one in the county was happy that the Gardener Estate had been turned into a damned hippie commune, bringing drugs, sex, long-haired weirdos, and God knows what else to the area. Who's to say that the Manson family hadn't moved in—to murder them all in their beds? Last month's full-moon drumming ceremony had flooded the sheriff's office with phone calls. A couple of the more conservative locals had taken to patrolling their property lines with shotguns.

Also, binoculars. Over drinks at the tennis club they both belonged to, the sheriff had told Jerry about a caller complaining about a couple having sex *right out in the open*—except it turned out the complainer was using a pair of binoculars so powerful, he had to brace them on a stand. Jerry suspected that a fair number of the neighbors carried similar lenses, since everyone knew that the girls worked topless in the gardens and sometimes skinny-dipped in the creek.

Drugs were a different matter. No one worried too much about the grass—hell, even Jimmy Carter was in favor of decriminalizing the stuff—but Jerry's father had to come out last winter for a conversation with Rob and the others about what could happen if there was a bust for hard drugs on the Estate. And though Rob seemed unconcerned and a few of the others laughed in the senior partner's face, Rob's woman had taken it seriously.

"How's Meadow?"

"Fine."

"The orchard looked good, as I was driving in."

"Grass needs cutting. There's talk about getting some goats."

"The mountain lions will love them."

"I told Meadow that. Not sure she believes me. You go on in, I'll find her and meet you inside. You remember where the Green Room is?"

Jerry assured him he could find it, and the two men separated—Rob, to circle the house and go through the service yard, while Jerry headed to the front door.

There he paused to look down at something else the commune had brought with it from Oregon: a long tray of dusty shoes abandoned at the door.

He considered his own spotless footwear. He could understand requiring the residents to strip to their socks when the mud was inches deep all around the house, but here? And anyway, how could hippies disapprove of anything as natural as dirt? He couldn't picture his father removing his custom-made, Italian leather shoes and walking into his client's house in his Italian wool stockings. Still, better safe than sorry, Jerry thought, picturing both Rob's threat and Meadow's scorn—and left his shoes among the moth-eaten Birkenstocks and tire-soled huaraches.

He stepped inside, and nearly staggered back out again, under the force of change.

The outside decorations were nothing compared to what had been done to the foyer. Only the black-and-white tiles on the floor suggested this was the same room that had so impressed him the first time he'd come here with his father. He'd been, what? Twelve? He'd learned what the word *elegant* meant that day, and always associated it with gilt plaster swags, pastel sea-green walls, and the gleam of polished wood.

The gilt swags were still there, but they had faded into insignificance behind the swirling clouds and the crowd of figures so busy and colorful, they made the place look like Woodstock without the mud. The mural started just to the left of the door, where a nearly life-sized motor home filled the space from door to corner. It was surrounded by a crowd of people in patchwork and tie-dye, fringe and feathers and brocade. More people leaned out of the motor home's windows. Its hairy driver, wearing a broad-brimmed hat and a prankster grin, had his elbow propped on the open window, dripping long leather fringe down the side. Half the people played guitars or violins or tambourines, and the rest were dancing, hands raised and bodies swirling, laughter on every face.

Quite a party, Jerry thought.

The next wall was a less raucous scene, and where the sky over the motor home was a brilliant blue, this took place in a dusky redwood grove strung with fairy lights, the bright white points swooping against the dark green and brown. There was dancing here, too, but only on one side, and more stylized than the gyrations of the first bunch. There was also some kind of a reading going on around a campfire, with a wild-haired man bent over a book before a fascinated audience of small children. Deeper among the trees, meanwhile, glimpses of multiple legs and strewn garments made it clear that more adult entertainments were taking place as well. And while the first wall had been mostly the work of one artist, this one had varied styles and levels of skill.

It was the third wall, surrounding the entrance to the rest of the house, that triggered Jerry's realization of what he was seeing.

White hair, startled eyes—that could only be Andy Warhol. And two figures away from him was Roy Lichtenstein, whom Jerry had met at a party in San Francisco, a month or two before.

Jerry turned for a second look at the motor home. That hairy prankster was none other than Bob Dylan. Which made the motor home his Rolling Thunder Revue. Joni Mitchell and Joan Baez were leaning out of the windows. The woman with the teeth had to be Carly Simon, which made the dark-haired guy beside her James Taylor. Up at the back, that distinctive beard had to be the rock singer Reynard-turned-commune-member Rain. He wasn't sure about the man in the cowboy hat and the big cigar, though he carried a guitar—but surely all these musicians hadn't been on the road with Dylan? That was George Harrison, wasn't it? And over there—no; he absolutely refused to believe that Brian Wilson had brought his Beach Boys sound to the Revue.

But now that Jerry knew what he was looking for, he saw them all over. Some looked like themselves, others were half-camouflaged in twenties-style evening gowns or Victorian top hats. Mostly musicians, some artists, a few writers tossed in—the man reading to the children around the campfire was Allen Ginsberg, unlikely as that seemed.

It was hard to tell how many different painters had a hand in the foyer's mural. At least three, he thought: the techniques seemed to vary deliberately, although all seemed to aim for a kind of naïve art, including those that were far too polished for that.

Even the less successful figures showed skill, humor, and a magnificent sense of color. He worked his way along the walls, studying the faces and the details of clothing, feeling as if he was being introduced to each living person as he went. Although he did want a list of characters, for those he couldn't quite put a name to.

Back at Andy Warhol, Jerry was torn between finishing the walls and seeing what else they'd done to the mansion—and then he saw his very own father, looking out from under a flowering tree. The senior partner of Bishop, Avery, Johnson, Rathford, and Rathford was wearing orange bell-bottom trousers, a red turtleneck, a fedora with a peacock feather, and the kind of embroidered Afghan vest you saw in Haight-Ashbury, with the bedraggled fur on the inside.

Jerry wondered if his father had ever noticed himself on the wall.

Puzzled, and slightly apprehensive, he walked through to the reception hall, home to cocktail parties, chamber music, and decades of behind-the-scenes political maneuvering. Here, the hippification of the Gardener house continued. A tufted velvet chaise with one high end had been turned into a sea creature. The big marble fireplace had been converted to the mouth of hell, although its red, black, and orange demon mouth seemed more friendly than threatening. In front of the French windows to the garden stood a life-sized, wide-skirted, bare-breasted figure like a modern-day Minoan goddess, her upraised hands holding lightning bolts instead of snakes. Nowhere near as proficient as the *Adam* and *Eve* outside, it nonetheless had an enthusiasm that made it appealing.

The room had been designed for circulating with a drink in hand, but now held far too much furniture for that, a wildly diverse mix of dignified leather sofas, Goodwill-reject armchairs, enormous beanbags, and cheap bentwood rockers. The room that had hosted champagne-and-caviar parties for visiting politicians, Nobel Prize winners, and movie stars seemed to have become the commune's living room.

The door on the right-hand side led to the old man's library. At first glance, it seemed remarkably little changed since the days when Thaddeus Eugene Gardener the Second had glowered from his corner desk—until Jerry noticed that the legs of the long wooden table used to display treasured texts had been sawed off, then surrounded by a lot of small plastic chairs. Behind the table, many of the lower shelves were packed with cheap children's books and basic school texts, while the ones above them were loaded with the commune's reference library: multiple editions of the *Whole Earth Catalog*, vegetarian cookbooks, *The Joy of Sex*, folk medicine herbals, Volkswagen repair, *Our Bodies, Ourselves*, and several linear feet of well-thumbed *Popular Mechanics* magazines.

Jerry went back into the reception hall–living room, pausing to glance into the formal dining room that wrapped around the corner of the house, with two fireplaces on its interior wall and windows to the garden along the outside. Its antique French chairs had been painted a cheerful mix of turquoise, magenta, and orange. The thirty-foot-long rosewood table was swathed in the kind of checked oilcloth a farmer's wife might have bought. He doubted this room had ever seen a high chair before: now there were three.

He walked down to the last door. This was the Green Room, the inner sanctum of Thaddeus Gardener the Second, tucked between corridor, reception hall, and dining room as if to better control everything that took place there. The Green Room was where the old man had gathered his chosen, dispensing cigars and whisky, settling before the fire to decide the affairs of the world, or at least of the world's business and finance.

This was the first door he'd found that was shut—including the front entrance.

Gingerly, he turned the knob, wondering what shocks this room would contain. An explosion of tropical vines and parrots? Ivy dripping from the chandeliers? Live chickens?

No. Instead, it was remarkably ordinary—well, ordinary compared with what he'd seen up to now. Its distinctive previous furniture had been cleared out, replaced by a simple desk in one corner and half a dozen mismatched armchairs—three in shades of orange, two purples, and a brown—circling a low wooden table. There were actual framed paintings on the walls, or at least print reproductions of paintings, and no eight-foot-high tile figures or leering teeth around the fireplace (and you could barely see the scorches on the mantelpiece, he saw, from the day Rob came back from Vietnam). The walls that had been papered in dark, masculine shades of green were now painted a light gray-blue. The carpet on the floor, which Jerry remembered as thick and old and hand-knotted by Third World children, had been replaced by a cheap but attractive braided oval in multiple shades of blue. The standing lamps near the chairs were now . . .

And then a thought came to him. Blue walls, blue carpet, orange and purple upholstery, framed geometric paintings . . . and Jerry laughed aloud.

There was not a touch of green in the entire room.

He turned, grinning, as he heard someone moving behind him. It was Meadow—glowing, healthy, vibrant, and barefoot, smelling of fresh sweat and sunshine. She had heard his laugh, and her eyebrows were up in a wordless question.

Even better—her stained-glass eyes supplied the missing color.

"The 'Green' Room," he explained.

Her smile went straight to his heart. "Not many people get the joke. Full points to you—with a bonus for leaving your shoes outside so we don't have to hand you a broom."

"I wasn't sure," Jerry said, "but I saw the others there. Is that what you do? Make guests sweep up after themselves?"

"Yeah, the women noticed that we were expected to clean the house while the men chopped wood and drove tractors and decided important things. So we changed the rules."

"You guys are into women's lib?"

"Bet your ass," she said.

And with that, the Gardener Estate lawyer saw that the organizing principal here—the mind, the passion, and the dedication that kept this community not only running, but flourishing—was not the owner of the Estate but his partner, who went by the deceptively soft name of Meadow.

Perhaps he'd unconsciously seen it three years ago, when he'd stood in front of her and let slip the possibility of a rent-and-food-stamp-free home.

"Who did the paintings in the foyer?" he asked.

"They're great, aren't they? We started them a couple years ago when some friends came by after a concert tour, but there's been half a dozen people working on them so far."

"Were those friends with Dylan's Rolling Thunder thing?"

"You know it? Yeah, a bunch of us went up to their last show in Vegas, and they were all so buzzed, nobody wanted to go home. So we invited them down here and hung out for a few days. Chilling out and eating and remembering how to sleep."

"You mean, Dylan and the rest were actually here? That mural's not just . . ."

"A fantasy? No. Though they weren't all here at the same time. But yeah, they're all friends. Or sometimes friends of friends. When I quit my job in Chicago, I hooked up with a band and worked as a roadie for a while, ended up managing a couple of them until I decided that the world was being taken over by this huge dark shadow of war and pollution and corruption, and the best thing I could do was live an honest and deliberate life. I had a friend—Rain, you met him in Oregon, I think—who'd just come to some hard truths of his own and was headed to a commune he knew about. I joined him. And here we are."

Rob had come in as they spoke, hands and face scrubbed clean, and waited a bit impatiently near the fireplace. "Jerry, you said you had papers to sign. Can we get on with it? I told Pig and Paolo I'd help raise the frame of their shed after lunch."

Jerry, caught up in the transition from Dylan to picturing this woman in a law office, required a moment to change gears. "Right. Yes— papers. Uh, let's use the desk."

Meadow sat down. Rob pulled a chair up to the far end of the desk from her and sat. Jerry took the chair at the back and opened up the slim attaché case, which had seen some wear since he'd carried it through the Oregon rain.

"As you know," Jerry began, "your grandfather's will covers a period of five years after his death. You have two years left. And if you die before April 1980, the alternate bequests come into effect. I can't do anything about them."

Rob gave him a grim nod. "I'll try to stick around." The punitive endowments the Old Bastard had set up would go to organizations he knew Rob would hate. No doubt why he'd picked them.

"But you asked me to put together something that would demonstrate your good intentions to your, er, housemates. This is what we've come up with."

The document was unnecessarily long and verbose, and he watched them read it. Rob went through quickly, sliding each sheet down toward Meadow. She, however, pored over the words with a frown of concentration worthy of any law student. She was only halfway through when Rob turned the last page over and looked at Jerry.

"Yeah, I know," Rob said. "You think it stinks."

"It does stink," Meadow said, to Jerry's surprise.

Rob sighed. "Babe, we've been through it a hundred times. I don't care what the will says. Without talking to Fort about it, I don't feel like I have a choice."

"So get him here."

"Easier said than done. You know what his letters are like." He looked at Jerry. "I did write him about it, this long letter like you said I should. He sent back a postcard of the Taj Mahal with two lines from the Bhagavad Gita about poverty."

Meadow turned over a page with more emphasis than necessary.

"Rob, I'm your lawyer," Jerry said. "I'll do what you tell me, but it's part of my job to make sure you understand the consequences. And you're right, I do think it would be a pity to divide up an amazing piece of California history like this estate. Like I told you, we could get the same effect by creating a trust. The more people who have a slice of ownership, the greater the chance of in-fighting. Like what happened in Oregon, on a bigger scale."

"Rob's great-grandfather built this house on stolen land, with money ripped out of the environment," Meadow said.

Rob nodded. "She's right. I'm trying to return it to the people."

It wasn't that simple, as the irritation between Rob and his woman showed. His numerous phone conversations with the Gardener heir had given Jerry a clear picture of Rob's situation: the people he lived with, whom he regarded as his family, were putting their hearts, minds, and daily sweat into transforming—as they saw it—a rich man's plaything into a creative and whole community. Every day, they looked into their future, only to see a lack of commitment from one key member.

If Rob was trustworthy, he would not cut them off. But if he really was trustworthy, why not show it by giving the other members legal rights? They'd all been betrayed in Oregon. They'd lost money and time and a home. They dreaded it happening again.

Countless hours of negotiation with the Estate lawyers had backed Rob away from his original all-or-nothing stance—which, Jerry saw, seemed to remain Meadow's now. In a small compromise, Rob had agreed that at the five-year mark, the community would take over ownership of the house, outbuildings, the once-formal gardens, and a swath of agricultural land outside the laurel hedge, while he himself would retain ownership of a small, heavily wooded corner of the Estate that he had loved and retreated to when he was a boy.

But there was one caveat that Rob, his lawyers, and against her will, Meadow would quietly fail to explain to the others—because they would see it as a reminder that he had lied to The Commons about his family wealth from the start. That caveat involved Fort. Rob was adamant: his brother, though long written out of their grandfather's will, still held moral rights to the Estate. And so, hedged about by near-impenetrable legalese, Jerry and the senior partners had created a document that seemed to say one thing, while quietly burying its key provision: that the final division of the Estate required Fort's agreement, once their grandfather's codicil expired in April 1980.

The three whose names would go on the papers today—Rob, Meadow, and Jerry—knew full well that The Commons would be outraged when they learned that Rob's absent older brother had more rights than they did. Even worse would be the realization that Rob and Meadow had deliberately kept it from them. However, Jerry and the firm had put a lot of care into the words—none of the partners wanted to spend the next two years in litigation with their client's weirdo housemates. They'd taken care that no one but a lawyer would understand the fine print. This left them two years to settle matters with Fort himself. And with luck, the day the others learned of the deception would be the day the deception was swept away for good.

Jerry put a pen down between the other two. He and Rob waited for Meadow to finish reading the pages.

She reached for the pen, used it to correct a typo, then tapped straight the edges of the document—a gesture that looked odd from a woman dressed in scissored-off overalls and a tie-dyed tank top. She laid the pages down with the pen on top, and slid them to Jerry.

He pushed them across the plywood surface to Rob, who signed his name and gave them to Meadow. She signed as witness, reluctantly using her birth name. Jerry notarized the document and put it back in his case.

"I'll make a photocopy and put it in the mail tomorrow."

"Two copies?" Meadow suggested.

"No problem."

"Want some lunch?"

He hadn't planned on it, but— "Sure. If there's plenty?"

She laughed. "We have fifty-three adults and nine kids here, and we've all been working hard since breakfast. You think *you're* going to make a dent in the food? But why don't you go stick that fancy case back in your car? Makes you look like a lawyer."

He did not state the obvious, but obediently went to the car—shoes on at the door, then off again—and came back, with the case locked in the trunk, along with his jacket and necktie.

He even rolled up his shirtsleeves as he walked through the house.

24

Not that there was a chance in hell he would blend in here, tie or no tie, Jerry thought as he stood at the kitchen door. He'd need six weeks to grow a beard, and trade his summer-weight Italian suit for denim overalls.

The kitchen had been designed for parties catered by servants, not mealtimes at a commune, but it did mean the room was fitted with multiple work surfaces, fifteen-foot ceilings, three pantries, and wide doors into the service and delivery yard. All its walls and counters were tiled in white rectangles, and the hooks and shelves were laden with a mix of heavy copper-clad pans, dented aluminum tureens, and ethnic cookware like bamboo steamers, industrial-sized woks, and a tortilla press.

The kitchen wing also held what had been the living quarters of the male house staff. Where once the butler and valet had trod, kids now raced up and down shouting. Where Jerry remembered a short-tempered Frenchman locking horns with the Gardeners' formidable housekeeper, now a couple of long-legged women in shorts gave orders, while men with clean hands and dirt-caked clothing carried out trays of sandwiches and drinks.

The chaos would have given any of the Mrs. Gardeners an attack of the vapors.

Jerry found a place to stand where he'd be out of the way. This was at the window next to the kitchen door, looking out into the service yard.

The Yard, unlike the rest of the house, hadn't changed much. It was a walled square half as big as the house: garage and stables at the far end (though as far as Jerry knew, no Gardener had ever kept a horse) and rooms that had housed the groundsman and chauffeur, with a vehicle entrance near the kitchen. At the other side, a narrow gate led through the redbrick wall to the formal garden.

A familiar face interrupted the view, holding out a tray of sandwiches. "You're Jerry the lawyer, aren't you? Remember me? I'm Wes. Wanna take these out?"

Jerry accepted the tray and followed the kid's waist-length ponytail down the servants' wing and through the French doors to the terrace, where tables were laid in the shade of two magnolia trees nearly as old as the house.

He looked at the stones, and at the $20 socks on his feet. Oh well. He could always add a pair to the Gardeners' bill.

As with most everything he had seen here, the terrace furniture was a cross between elegant garden party and thrown-together—almost literally thrown together, since three of the tables were doors laid across sawhorses. Some of the chairs were the Deco wrought iron he remembered, others folding aluminum or wobbly bistro, while some were not chairs at all, merely lengths of tree trunks or upended wooden crates.

Everyone sat down, adults and children. Wes indicated a chair for Jerry, three places down the table from Rob. As soon as all the backsides were in their seats, people reached out to load their plates.

Jerry took something from each bowl and tray as it went past, but he was more interested in the people. Quite a few dimly-remembered faces. Rain was at the adjoining table, his devilish beard as crisply delineated as it had been in Oregon. Wes, beside him, made for an interesting contrast. Between Wes and Meadow sat a young woman with near-white hair and eyebrows, her sun-browned skin and easy grin a far cry from the fearful expression and hunched shoulders he'd seen in Oregon—Annabelle, someone called her. And her baby, Sparrow, who'd then been prescribed antibiotics for his cold-induced pneumonia, was now a sturdy, nut-brown child who gobbled everything on his plate. Jerry was pleased. He'd often thought about that infant, over the years.

When he turned to his own plate, he was surprised. The food looked . . . normal. No tofu in sight, and although the bread was whole wheat rather than supermarket white, it was far from the thick, dry slabs of health-food loaves. He didn't see any meat, only eggs, cheese, beans, and some kind of paste in the sandwiches. There were loads more vegetables than he was used to, but the sandwiches were great and the salads not at all bad. He even took a second helping of the complicated-looking mix with the Chinese-flavor dressing. The people around him were mostly silent at first, digging in hungrily, and most were on their second helpings before talk rose up. General to start with—the first beets coming soon, the state of the beehives in the orchard, turkey vultures circling the upper field—but after a time the smaller kids started to drift away, and with them, to Jerry's surprise, went Rain, looking like Mephistopheles being led off by hell's cutest demons. The kids seemed to be debating whether they were on chapter seven or eight.

With the kids gone, Meadow got to her feet, asking if anyone could suggest how to get the pond filter to work, since the algae bloom was starting to kill off the fish. It took a while for Jerry to catch on, that they'd turned the reflecting pool into a farm for tilapia—a fish that to his mind was about as tasty as the mud it swam in. Talk went back and forth for a while, people mostly standing when they wanted to speak. It seemed an oddly formal but practical method, since you could hear who was saying what. Meadow ended up asking one of the men who had a friend with a successful pond to see if she'd come and look at theirs.

"If she says yes, can I use one of the cars?" he asked. "I don't want her to hitch by herself. Too many creeps out there."

This was a relatively new fear, here in the Bay Area. People were becoming aware that predators treated freeway on-ramps like watering holes where the innocent gathered. Jerry hadn't seen a solitary girl hitching for a long time, and even couples tended to look cautiously inside a car before getting in.

"The Volvo's still waiting for a part and Jackie's using the van, but the truck should be here in the afternoon. And hey, since you're headed across the Bay, could you swing past that wrecking yard in Fremont and pick up some stuff for me? They have some broken tile and a couple abandoned boxes from India that the airport gave them."

"Is this for the goddess Gaddo was talking about? Cool."

"She's thinking it's going to be big," Meadow said. "It'll need to be outside."

Jerry didn't ask if the goddess would have bare breasts.

One of the women—Debra? Donna?—then jumped up to ask if the artist intended to put these giant goddesses of hers in the garden, since it was getting awfully crowded, and if so, could they do something about the gazebo, which was pretty, sure, but pointless, especially after that purple vine was finished flowering. Someone else said they liked the purple vine, a third person offered the name wisteria, but the first woman—Daniela, that was it—ignored both of them to say that really, they ought to tear out those pointless flowers and put in grapevines, so it could be a useful space. "Every time we try to grow grapes outside the hedge, the deer eat them."

"Deer were here first," came a voice.

"And nobody minds sharing, but they don't just eat the grapes, they kill the plant. Deer aren't very good at planning ahead."

"The capitalists of the natural world," someone commented, to general laughter.

Daniela stuck to her question. "There's like a hundred feet of trellis, if you measure around the outside of the gazebo. The north side's in the shade, but the rest of it would be perfect. Even easy to pick, from the inside."

"But beauty feeds the soul." That was Meadow. She hadn't risen to say that, hadn't even put down her fork, but her posture as well as her words suggested that she and Daniela had a history of confrontation.

"Sure, but if more goddesses are moving into the garden, we'll need to extend the hedge with some kind of fence. We can't have wildlife getting into the crops."

"The goddesses can go outside the hedge, looking out over Wide Field." There were several fields on the Estate, but this one was the most impressive, the California equivalent of an English country house's manicured parkland.

"But we still need grapes. That wisteria—"

Rob shifted in his chair, then half rose apologetically. "Uh, guys? Sorry to butt in here, but the gazebo was my mother's favorite place. Could we maybe leave it, for a while longer?"

Jerry was taken aback, first by the mention of a woman he'd all but forgotten had lived here, and second by the oddly uncomfortable silence that fell across the tables. He studied the faces, trying to figure out the vibes. Some people looked embarrassed, others mildly resentful. Meadow was studying her plate, face closed. But he got the impression that the silence had less to do with the kind of vines on the gazebo than it did with the old problem—that in fact Rob Gardener didn't have to ask them for favors at all. He might be one of them, a member of a family dedicated to a communal way of life, but he was also in a very real way their landlord, representative and benefactor of a corrupt capitalist system.

Fortunately, they liked Rob well enough, that was clear. They even seemed to regard him, along with Meadow and Rain, as one of their leaders. Rob, for his part, obviously took care not to throw his weight around. And apart from any difficulties with the politics of the situation, the gazebo actually was a beautiful spot. Jerry remembered that from a childhood visit, when he'd retreated in among the protective vines and sat there breathing the heady aroma.

He also suspected that Daniela's proposal to cut down the old vines was the latest in a series of aggressively virtuous plans. She might be right, the faces said, but it didn't make her pushiness any easier to live with.

Meadow was on her feet again. "How about we use the walls of the service yard for grapes? We've talked about it, maybe we can do it this winter. All that brick, protected from the wind—it would be great to plant vines against. We could keep the main gate shut so the deer don't get in."

"But the yard's paved," Daniela objected.

"We could borrow that jackhammer again and take out the paving along the wall. And sure, the soil will be dead at first, but we have more compost than we know what to do with. Bare-root vines in the winter against the south-facing wall? We might have fruit the first year. We could even rig some plastic or glass against it, like a greenhouse, and try for early tomatoes."

Heads nodded, as the others looked grateful for the solution. Which made Jerry wonder how often the commune had been bogged down in squabbles over some plan or another. It was near to summer now, when the days were filled with work until sundown and after, but what about a rainy stretch of winter, when the nights grew long, the kids were underfoot, and nerves became just a bit stretched?

He supposed he should be grateful that the document locked in his trunk hadn't gone any further toward appeasement.

Decision made, talk moved on to whether it was too early to thin the apples, had anyone found a source for more canning jars, and did someone have enough of a background in math to help the kids with geometry, now that Robin and her old man had moved off to Tennessee?

This last roused some groans, both from the two older kids whose schooling was under discussion and the grown-ups for whom math was a foreign country filled with unfriendly natives. But a tall, thin man with a sunburned nose admitted to skills as far as trigonometry; a woman said she thought a friend was leaving for the East Coast soon and would maybe want to clear her canning supplies; and it was thought that the apples should wait a week to let some more volunteers fall (whatever that meant).

Lunch broke up soon after, dishes heading toward the house and workers in the other direction. Jerry piled a tray with used plates and carried it in, only to find himself pressed into dishwashing service. Though he was given an apron, to protect his shirt.

Teasing began, that the lawyer was going to shed his corporate self and grow his hair, drop some acid, and take on clients who were draft dodgers or Black Panthers.

By the time Jerry folded up his apron and dried his hands, he had become . . . not one of the family, but perhaps a distant cousin whose way of life wasn't entirely offensive. A few even said goodbye as he left. Rob was already gone to the shed raising, but Meadow walked Jerry to the front door, where his shoes waited.

"Thanks for lunch," he told her.

"Any time," she said, giving the impression that she meant it. "Another month and we'll give you twenty kinds of fresh produce."

"Though maybe I should wear denim and some work gloves?"

"Never a bad idea," she agreed.

He finished tying his laces and stood, looking over the transformed courtyard of the noble house, sunflowers on one side, dinosaurs on the other. "You guys are doing good things here. Let me know how I can help."

She looked surprised—but then, he'd surprised himself with the offer.

He was even more astonished when she went up on her toes and kissed him—on the mouth, paying considerable attention to the process. When she withdrew, he couldn't help glancing over her shoulders, just to make sure Rob hadn't seen. She gave him a smile, as if to say she understood, and turned back inside.

Jerry walked slowly through the courtyard, thinking about the kiss, and how even one like that didn't really mean anything here. Everything had been turned upside down in some manner. Maude's rule replaced by Meadow's. A formal entry decorated with dinosaurs. A coolly elegant foyer brought to riotous life, a library turned into a schoolroom, a Green Room that totally lacked that color. A reception hall designed to host formal events, now the messy, beating heart of a communal family.

And that wasn't even touching on the people. A multimillionaire valued for his muscles; a hippie earth mother with the political skills of a Chicago mayor; a Mephistopheles rock star who went off to read stories to other people's children.

A lawyer half in love with the whole setup.

As he drove off, Jerry was smiling.

Still, he was glad some traces of the old would remain. Replacing the Gardener wisteria with grapevines would have made him sad.

25

Now

"This Meadow," Raquel said to Jerry. "It sounds as if she was more or less running things."

"She really was. Not that anyone would have admitted it, because The Commons ran things in common. But in practice, things always seemed to circle back to her, for approval or suggestions or just to get them done."

"Not to Rob."

"Rob was always in the loop, sure. But with everything going on, different people tended to focus on different things. Like, anything to do with the gardens was Meadow. Rain was great when it came to the outside world, especially music. Pig and Paolo mostly were in charge of the kids, and Eddie was the machinery expert, from pumps to car repair. A couple of the women—Donna? Daniela, that's right—and a friend of hers who was a weaver, forget her name . . . anyway, some of the women were pretty organized politically, they brought The Commons into play for demonstrations and things."

"So, where did that leave Rob?"

"Rob was happy to do whatever people needed."

"That sounds awfully passive, for the man who actually owned everything."

"Well, think about it. If he threw his weight around, what would that say to the others? There were already points against him, for having been in Vietnam."

"The others didn't trust him?"

"I think . . . This was all a long time ago," he said. "And I was only here as a visitor. But I'd say, looking back, Rob may have deliberately chosen to stay in the background."

"Passive."

"Nonconfrontational, certainly."

"Unlike Meadow."

"She was the most amazing woman. Beautiful and alive and smart and fearless. You should've seen her standing in front of the city council, convincing them that having a huge rock festival in their backyard was just what they wanted. Do you think that's her they found? The bones? Yeah, yeah—ongoing investigation, I know you can't tell me. But do you?"

"As you say, Mr. Rathford, I can't talk about it. Meadow can't have been her real name."

"No, it was Christine . . . something. I had to notarize her signature one time and needed to make sure she wasn't using a nickname. Rob would remember."

Raquel flipped through the folder of printouts—naturally, Mrs. Dalhousie had put them in alphabetical order—and found the page for Meadow. She added the name Christine, and closed the folder before the lawyer's eyes got any sharper.

"Couldn't you retrieve the name?"

"I'm sure my old notary books are in storage, though it might take a while to lay hands on them. You might ask Mrs. Dalhousie if she's seen the document itself in the Archives—it was an agreement that once Rob inherited the Estate, five years after his grandfather died, The Commons would take over ownership. Or at any rate, it seemed to say that, although in fact it was a little less clear-cut—deliberately so, since Rob wanted to leave a loophole open in case Fort had an opinion. Anyway, it might be here, since I gave copies to both Rob and Meadow."

"I'll ask. I did notice another agreement, covering how the commune would vote on any visitors who wanted to stay. Do you know if a vote was ever used to get rid of a guest?"

She'd noticed the document because it was so uncharacteristically formal, worded like a contract, and she'd wondered if one of the would-be guests up for approval had been named Michael Johnston.

He frowned. "I know they used it sometimes to *approve* people—they even voted on Fort, when he came back, though you wonder what would've happened if they'd decided against him. Yes, they drew that document up after they realized that the old open system wasn't the greatest. Basically, anyone could bring anyone in, who could then bring friends—which meant people helping themselves to things other people might need, and always expecting to eat, even if they weren't really into work."

"Was the agreement Meadow's idea?"

He laughed. "She wrote the thing! Do you know, she actually asked me once about setting up as a nonprofit? Can you imagine any of the others even thinking of that?"

"When did you last see her?"

"That rock festival—the Midsummer Fair. Which was really something, especially considering the size of it and how fast they'd put it together. Again, thanks to Meadow. In a few weeks, she got the permits, organized bands, food, equipment—that woman could've been running California, if she wanted to. But then, when it was over, she just took off. And without her, nobody seemed to know what to do. So people started leaving. By the end of summer, most of them were gone, even those who'd been with The Commons from the start. Rain, Annabelle. Pig and Paolo. Even Fort took off."

"All at once?"

"Mostly a few at a time."

"But Meadow was one of the first to leave."

"Her and Fort, yeah."

"Together?"

Jerry shook his head. "He went back to India. He used to write, sometimes."

"And she couldn't have joined him?"

After a minute, he had to shrug. "Meadow never seemed the ashram type, but what do I know? I'm just a lawyer."

"Tell me about these problems they had. That led to the approval agreement."

26

Then

In the months after that first lunch, Jerry Rathford drove out to the Gardener Estate at least half a dozen times.

In July, Rob asked him to come and explain to a new family what the consequences were of not registering their infant's birth. Jerry sat down with the bearded boy and the glowing new mother, describing for them how no, it would not be a crime, but it would create such a series of hassles for the newborn that, hippie child or not, the child (Boy? Or girl? The mother refused to participate in the misogyny of the patriarchy by telling him) would end up hating Mommy and Daddy. Yes, a child without a birth certificate or Social Security number could not be drafted, tracked down, or billed for taxes. But that child also could not go to college, could be jailed for driving without a license, and would only find jobs that paid under the table—which would leave him (her?) open to exploitation by The Man.

He—or she—could never travel outside the United States.

The new parents insisted that they were fine with all that—until Jerry added that without a birth certificate on record, a father had no rights to his own child. If something happened to the mother, the law would consider the child an orphan.

So, how did they feel about handing their baby to its mother's parents to raise?

The two young people looked at each other, and filled out the papers to register the birth.

(It was a boy.)

In early September, Jerry picked up his office phone and heard shouting. "Who is—Rob?" He raised his own voice. "Rob, is that you? What the hell is going—"

"We got cops at the door, Jerry, how soon can you get here?"

"Cops? What happened?"

"A friend of Ronnie's picked up a hitchhiker yesterday and he's—"

Rob's voice gave way to a series of authoritative bellows that could only be the police, commanding him to put the phone down, to stand up, to keep still, and other contradictory orders.

Now Jerry shouted, as loud as he could into the receiver. "Don't hang up, don't tell them anything except that your lawyer will be right over!"

But the line was dead.

He nearly collided with his secretary in the doorway. "Mr. Rathford, what—?"

"Something's going on at the Gardener place, the police are there."

"A drug raid?"

"I don't know. Cancel my morning appointments, I'll phone you from the Estate. Tell my father where I am. And, who are we using for criminal cases now?" The Rathford law firm dealt with Estate matters, not crimes that caused the police to break down a man's door.

"Tim Benedict."

"Let him know we might need him later."

For once, Jerry didn't strip off his tie as he approached the Gardener house. Instead, he made sure it was absolutely straight and his jacket without a speck, and marched toward the front door as if he were blind to the uniformed cop standing outside it.

"Sir, I—"

"I am Mr. Gardener's lawyer. Your boss has no right to question him without me present."

"Okay, but Rob's not here."

Jerry stopped aiming himself at the door and turned his attention to the young officer. "Where is he?"

"They went downtown. He's helping—oops."

The door behind him had opened without his noticing, and a small child pushed past his legs, turning a gap-toothed grin at Jerry before toddling off into the courtyard.

Both men watched the small person, who seemed intent on the parked cars in the drive.

"Uh, do you think—oh, sorry."

This time, the person pushing past them was one of the men, who trotted after the wanderer and scooped him up, walking back to the house with the toddler tucked under his arm like a giggling football.

"Hi, Jerry," he said.

The lawyer looked under the bush of hair and saw a pair of blue eyes that looked familiar. "Hi, er, Eddie? Do you know what's going on?"

"It's freakin' weird, man. One of our guys, Ronnie, picked up a hitcher a while ago and brought him back, and that was cool, but then *he* brought one of *his* friends and there was some heavy dope involved and, well, this morning all shit breaks loose and the pigs come crashing through the door—guns, man: not cool around the kids." This last was directed at the uniform, who did look abashed at the accusation. "They think Ronnie's hitchhiker ra—" He looked down at the interested child, then opened the door, deposited him inside, and closed it again. "They said the guy raped a chick in Berkeley last week, beat her up bad. Anyway, somebody spotted him from a poster, when he stopped in town to pick up his buddy, and the cops tracked down our truck's license plate and raided the place."

"Was he still here?"

"Up in Ronnie's trailer. Got to say, the idea of a slime like that hanging out here . . . freaked everybody out. Anyway, Rob went down to give the story. The head cop was pretty cool about it, actually."

Jerry looked at the uniformed officer. "They'd have gone downtown?"

"Yeah. But I heard Sheriff Dales say they'd bring the two men back after they gave their statements."

Eddie nodded his hair and went inside. After a moment, Jerry followed.

The escaped child was nowhere in sight, but he could hear distant voices, tracing them back to the kitchen.

Every woman in the commune seemed to be here, seated at the long wooden table. For once, their hands were occupied with half-empty cups rather than tasks. Meadow sat at the head of the table, and looked up at the movement in the doorway.

"Jerry—hi. I phoned your office to let them know we didn't need you, but you'd already left."

"I saw Eddie at the door, he told me what happened. You okay? Anything I can do?"

"We're fine," she said, as if he'd been asking about the other women as well. "Creeped out, but he wasn't here long. And nothing happened." None of them seemed too reassured. But then she sat upright. "Come to think of it, there is something you might be able to do. It's not like the cops never get things wrong. So could you ask them about the guy? Just so we're sure, before we decide if there's anything we should be doing different."

"You want to know if he really did rape that girl?"

"Yeah."

"I might be able to find out how sure the police are about it, and maybe if he's got a record."

"Thank you, Jerry, that would be helpful."

He became aware that the roomful of women were fixing him with their *You can leave now* expressions, so he started to retreat, then thought of something. "Okay to use your phone?"

"In the Green Room, help yourself."

He reported in to his secretary and told her that she could have Tim Benedict stand down. "But Donna, I also need to know how sure they are about the guy they arrested. The people here are kind of freaked out, and it would be good if they could be certain, one way or another. Do you still have that friend who works in the sheriff's office?"

"I'll give her a ring, see if she knows anything."

"Thanks. I should be back for my afternoon appointments, I'll let you know if not."

But by the time he got to the sheriff's office, it was all over. Arrest made, statements taken, Rob was calm and Ronnie was free to go. So

Jerry drove them, hearing the details not only of what the man had done and said while with the commune, but things Rob had overheard from the cops.

Yes, the cops had the right man.

And yes, it maybe should change how the commune did things in the future, when it came to welcoming in strangers.

27

Now

Raquel interrupted Jerry's story. "There was a convicted rapist living here?"

"He hadn't been convicted when he was here, but yes, afterward."

"What was his name?"

"Oh, man. Something Irish sounding. O'Donnell, maybe? And he wasn't living here. He'd been hitching a ride and one of the guys brought him back. I think he was only here for a couple days."

"When was that?"

"Toward the end of 1978, I'd guess. And like I say, that was why they drew up the residency agreement. The women especially were really not happy."

"I can imagine."

28

Then

Over the following months, Jerry's work with The Commons was nothing if not varied. A visiting musician had overstayed his US visa: could Jerry help? What about their negotiations with the county to replace half a dozen porta-potties with septic systems? And could he look over the new agreement The Commons was considering, requiring community approval for anyone wanting to stay more than two months? It felt like a cop-out, setting up rules like that, but . . .

Three births, two weddings, a car registration gone awry, a tricky negotiation with the fire marshal over the commune's full-moon campfires, a mental competency hearing brought by a pregnant girl's parents—even a will, when one of the residents had some strange health problems. None of these were exactly Jerry's responsibility, but as 1978 wore on, he gradually became the commune's go-to guy for any legal matters. He learned early on not to wear a suit, after the kids started greeting him with a hug around the legs. He let Meadow post his home number on the Green Room phone, in case anyone needed help too urgently for business hours. They'd tease him about his hair, offer him a toke from their burning joints, send him concert tickets, or invite him by whenever some counterculture celebrity was visiting. Someone stuck a QUESTION AUTHORITY bumper sticker on his car, which stayed on until one of the partners noticed it. He drove out with a carful of presents for the kids on Christmas morning. He froze his ass off the night of the Midwinter Fest, and happily nursed the resulting headache. He even took a couple of the women out on dates.

Then one night, three weeks into the new year of 1979, Jerry got a call from the Estate.

Fort Gardener had come home from India.

29

As homecomings went, that of Thaddeus Eugene Gardener the Fourth didn't get off to a promising start.

At two o'clock on a rainy January afternoon, an old three-quarter-ton pickup bearing a hand-built wood cabin turned in to the Gardener drive, then braked to a stop. Faces peered through the bug-spattered windshield at the closed gate. On this side, parked every which way, were a dozen cars and vans, some plastered with the logos of television stations. On the other side of the gate, foursquare in the drive, sat a sheriff's car.

A lot of well-dressed men and a few women were huddling under foldout shelters and giant umbrellas. As one, they turned to look at the truck. Cameras with foot-long lenses were raised, more from boredom than interest. No one cared enough to venture out into the wet.

After a minute, the truck slowly reversed back onto the main road, continuing the way it had been going, up into the hills. Twenty minutes later, it drove past again, heading toward the freeway.

Nearly an hour later, a sodden figure came through the gate in the laurel hedge and stopped dead, staring at the mulched-over beds of the winter vegetable garden. He made a survey, from the bare vines on the gazebo to what remained of the rose walk near the house, then shifted the backpack on his shoulders and continued down the path to the gate through the brick wall, and across the service yard to the kitchen door.

It was locked.

This seemed to startle him more than the garden beds had. He took a step back, glanced toward the yard's wide vehicle entrance as if considering going around to the front door, then seemed to hear something from inside. He stepped forward and knocked. When nothing happened, he made a fist and pounded.

The door cracked open, but whoever had answered was not about to welcome this dripping stranger inside. A certain amount of discussion followed, with the newcomer's hand gestures indicating his growing temper—then suddenly the door flew open and a big man stepped out. He seized the shoulders of the rain-soaked coat, then flung his arms around the smaller figure.

Both Gardener brothers were home.

"God, it's good to see you, Fort." The brothers sat on either side of the Green Room fireplace, feet stretched out to the heat, glasses in hands. They were alone, the doors closed against the rest of the household.

The two could not have made a greater contrast. One brother was small, slim, light-haired, and clean-shaven, dressed in a long tunic and snug-legged trousers made of homespun cotton, with a thick Nehru-collar vest against the chill and soft leather slippers on his feet. The other brother was big, muscular, dark-haired, and fully bearded, wearing striped bell-bottoms, a bright green Mexican pullover sweater, and lumpy hand-knit socks.

"You too, Rob. You look good. Happy."

"I am, mostly. Busy, for sure."

"I bet."

"Sometimes too busy. I had to turn over a lot of the crap stuff to Davey and the lawyer—remember old man Rathford, used to come out and smoke cigars with the Old Bastard? His son, Jerry, took over, and he's actually kind of cool. Anyway, the two of them are good with all the Establishment hassle, I just have to sign the papers. Which is great, because we seem to have got on the art world's must-see list now. Meadow's musician friends are fun, since they're usually on tour so they only stay for a night or two, but lately it seems like every painter and writer who passes through the Bay Area now stops in for a night and stays for ten."

"Is that why there's reporters at the gate? Some famous painter?"

"Crap, are they still there?"

"I had to have my ride drop me up at the bridge and walk."

"No wonder you were soaked! Sorry, I'd have driven down if I'd known. No, in this case it was music—they got wind that George Harrison was here."

"Is he?"

"He was, left a couple days ago. Nice guy. Said he knew you."

"We were at the same ashram for a while. I liked him a lot."

"He and Meadow spent most of their time talking about gardening."

"Meadow is so gorgeous. None of those kids I saw are yours, right?"

"No kids."

"Not yet."

"Not ever. Not in this world."

"Really? Huh. So you and I are the end of the Gardener line. Grandfather would roll over in his grave."

"Here's to the Old Bastard's grave," Rob said, raising his glass.

The two brothers watched the fire for a time, listening to the patter of rain on the windows and the noises of children trapped inside by the weather. After a time, Rob stirred. "You think you'll stay for a while?"

"My guru has instructed me to take a few months away from the ashram. So I can meditate on the next step in my journey. Would that be possible?"

"Possible? Fort, that would be so great!"

"But I don't need Mom's room—though there are some good vibes in there. It almost smells like her."

"There's only been two places I asked to have left as they are—that and her gazebo."

"Her favorite reading place. I was glad to see the wisteria is still there."

"It's amazing, in the spring."

"When you say you *asked* to have things left. Do the others give you a hard time?"

"I try not to push things. The Commons decides. Fortunately, people like the gazebo as it is—well, nearly everyone does. As for Mom's room, we do sometimes get a visitor who needs a proper room. Believe it or not, some people get freaked out if there's no bed or you have to go outside to the toilet, or if mice run over their face at night."

"I'm surprised you didn't keep Maude's rooms for guests. That and Grandfather's are the fancy ones."

"Not anymore. We put up the kids in Maude's room the first year, they had lots of fun adding crayon to the frescoes."

"Good for you. Anyway, I'm happy to sleep in a trailer or the stables or something."

"No rush."

"How many people do you have here, anyway?"

"Let's see. Full-time, sixty, maybe sixty-five adults and nine or ten kids—oldest is seventeen, youngest just turned one. There's some people away at the moment, one on a yoga retreat and two of the adults took their twins off for Christmas in Wisconsin. There's a couple of hitchhiking musicians one of the women thought needed feeding, and a guy who's working on the electricity in exchange for room and board. Meadow's friend Miriam Gaddo—do you know her? Famous artist, known by her last name, she did a couple of figures I'll show you in the morning. The two of them have a big project planned for the summer, so Gaddo is in and out a lot, we ended up just giving her Rodrigo's old space, in the Yard. And there's a glassblower thinking about doing an installation in the garden, but he's only here for a couple days. Oh, and our pet writer—I always forget her because she lives up in the attic and only comes down at night."

"Sounds like you're running a hotel. Or a summer camp."

"Yeah, except Meadow makes it very clear to anyone staying here that they change their own sheets and clean their own toilets. And if they eat, they work—garden, buildings, the kitchen. You've never lived till you've seen Kurt Vonnegut in a flowered apron scrubbing pans."

"Women's lib at work."

"You got it."

"Must be a pain, having to lock the doors. I nearly broke my nose when it didn't open."

"We don't do that often. A while back, we found some bastard with a camera right in the house, so we have Jerry let us know whenever we're in the news, and there might be people poking around. Those reporters will take off as soon as somebody spots George getting onto a plane."

"Sounds like Maude and her parties. All those Hollywood people."

"I don't remember parties."

"You were too young. And I didn't have a clue who everyone was, I just knew that Marla and the others were excited. How is Marla?"

"Getting old, but fighting it. She has two grandkids now, she brings them up sometimes to play."

"What does she make of . . . everything?"

"She's cool. Wanted to know if we were using drugs and when I told her we weren't, not the hard stuff, anyway, she just sort of shook her head and got on with it. She's taken a couple of the younger members under her wing—we have a single mom here who's nineteen now, but came to us three years ago when she was pregnant. I heard her little boy call Marla 'Grandma' the other day. And she and Meadow get along great, had a lot of fun doing a Solstice dinner—Christmas for Marla, of course—in the ballroom, with a tree that nearly touched the roof. We must've had a hundred people here."

Fort studied his brother. "I'm happy for you, Rob."

"Fort, look. You were always the one who loved this place. I don't mean as a possession, but as a place, where you felt at home."

"Yeah, and you were always tromping around the hills."

"We don't need to get into this now, but as far as I'm concerned, the house is yours. Always has been. I mean, fuck the Old Bastard—when the five years are up, his will gets flushed down the tubes. But I should tell you that it's a little complicated, and you might not want to bring it up in front of the others. You see, when we first came here and every-one started pouring their energy into making the place usable, it didn't seem right to them that everything they saw was mine. And I mean, sure, they knew I wasn't going to kick them off the land, but it had already happened to them in Oregon, and a place like this, it carries with it some pretty heavy capitalist karma, you know? So I had Jerry write up a statement saying they'll have rights when I'm free to give them. But . . . he didn't like it, and the firm's partners liked it even less, and plus that, I wasn't about to just write you out when you weren't here, so in the end, what it says is that you need to give your approval when things get renegotiated at the five-year mark. Which is next April."

"The Rig Veda says, 'Hoarded wealth leads to ruin.' In this case, what it might ruin is your friendship with these people."

"God, don't I know it! Anyway, Meadow and I have been careful not to point out that the agreement doesn't really say anything. Jerry wrote it in this legal bullshit that *looks* like it says, 'In April 1980, this place belongs to the collective,' while what it really says is, 'In April 1980, we can talk about who it belongs to.' Anyway, now you're here, you and I have till then to settle what we want to do."

"I won't talk about it to the others, no."

"Like I say, we don't need to get into it tonight, but out of curiosity, can you see yourself stepping into the Gardener shoes and living here, like the Old Bastard wanted us to?"

"Rob, it's not my karma to be a householder. I've gone from student to forest dweller without pausing to fulfill the life of the *Grihastha*. The next step for me is *Sannyasa*," he said. "Renunciation."

"C'mon, Fort, you're only thirty. You can't tell me you're giving up the world yet."

"I already have. Rob, I'm an Indian citizen now, passport and everything. I even have a new name—Farhat Mali, which is pretty much my old one translated into Hindi. But as part of being *Sannyasa*, it is my dharma to give to charity. And my guru is a good man."

Rob stared at his brother. "Your guru? Jesus, Fort, you want to move your guru here? Set up your ashram in California? Come on now—"

"Rob, no, don't worry. He's not some Rajneesh, eager to suck at the teat of the West. He belongs in Rishikesh—it's a holy place. But that doesn't mean I don't want to lay something at my master's feet. Even a holy man has to pay for food and a roof over his disciples' heads."

Rob took a deliberate swallow from his glass, placed it slowly on the table. The fire crackled for a few minutes before he spoke again. "So, we need to figure some arrangement that keeps The Commons se-cure, but also frees up some cash for your ashram. That's what you're saying?"

"If we can."

"Is that why you came home, Fort? To get your hands on a slice of the Estate?"

"I came home to see my brother. And to spend time meditating on whether I am making the right choices."

"Okay. Well, we'll have to talk to Jerry, see what he thinks. It's going to mean selling off some land. I hope we don't end up having to stare at a mile of suburban ticky-tackies, that'd be the shits."

"People need to live somewhere," Fort said.

"Maybe Jerry can figure something out. Just remember, it's better you and I come up with a couple clear alternatives to put in front of the others, rather than come out and ask everyone what they think."

"You, me, and Meadow, then. Right?"

"I . . ." The fire sounds returned, for a time. "Maybe we should leave Meadow out of it, for the moment."

If Rob noticed his brother's surprise, or felt Fort's gaze on him, he did not show it.

"You guys okay?"

"Yeah. Just . . . it's complicated."

Fort might have spent the last decade holed up in an ashram, but his expression made it clear that he hadn't forgotten the language.

It's complicated was what men said when they meant *It's falling apart.*

30

Fort settled in, moving out of their mother's suite to a storage room next to the stables. People got used to coming across him sitting in full lotus, eyes half-shut, murmuring the low buzz of his mantra. The kids ignored him. It wasn't the weirdest thing adults did around the place.

As the weather warmed, Fort was often to be found in the gazebo or just outside the garden, with the laurel hedge at his back and the sweep of Wide Field and wood-covered hills before him.

Someone spotted him doing a headstand one morning at dawn, and asked to be shown how. He soon had a little tribe of students, learning yoga positions and listening to his thoughts on nature, and poverty, and being human.

Not that he spent his every hour in meditation and yoga. His willingness to work surprised those who'd expected him to act like a privileged guest. He was happy to do the tedious or dirty jobs others grumbled at, like hanging out laundry or helping empty the portable toilets used by those living in the woods. He was often found immersed in the endless chore of weeding. Rain swore he'd overheard the newcomer asking each tiny weed's forgiveness, but frankly, nobody cared much about Fort's karma if it meant the vegetables thrived.

The men were less certain about him at first. It's all well and good to stand on your head for an hour or demonstrate the holy qualities of fetching wood and carrying water, but what about the hard work?

Then the nights warmed enough to start serious planting, and double-digging the beds required muscles—at which point the men discovered that yoga built those, too. Give the guy a digging fork and tell him what to do, and man, it really gets done. Murmuring chants all the while and apologizing to the exposed earthworms, sure, but without pause.

When the time came to approve his continued residence in The Commons, there was not one vote against him.

By the end of April, Fort Gardener was as much a part of the commune as his brother was. With one exception: he wasn't sharing his bed. Not that some of the women hadn't offered—and one of the men who was happy to swing both ways—but he merely thanked them all and went on with whatever he was doing. And when the commune went a little nuts with the Beltane–May Day celebrations, he volunteered to keep the kids out of the way while the adults celebrated the fertility of spring. Sex was a natural part of life, they all agreed, but nobody wanted some busybody neighbor with binoculars reporting them to Child Services.

The following week, The Commons residents finally reached an agreement on the long-discussed plans for Midsummer.

Gaddo's three-faced statue was nearly ready for installation. She'd been a regular during the spring months, working with Meadow, spending hours talking to Fort about Hindu belief, making changes to the sculpture as a result. They'd chosen a site, were working on the final stages, and had found a crane company to lift it into place.

Why not, Meadow proposed, make the installation the centerpiece of the Midsummer celebrations?

Gaddo even had the perfect name for what she'd originally envisioned as a trio of semi-Minoan goddesses but might, like the *Eve* at the house entrance, be as easily thought of as firmly Judeo-Christian: a three-faced Eve, just outside the garden, venturing into a new world at the height of summer.

She could call it *Midsummer Eves*.

Nearly every member of The Commons had contributed in some small way, from bending rebar for the base to breaking up the tiles for the figure's skirts. This would be a sculpture the entire community could be proud of—and the larger community as well, since an accident of the landscape meant that patch of hillside was visible for miles in all directions.

In fact, the discussion went, why *not* let the wider community claim it? *Midsummer Eves* could be a coming-out party for The Commons. Invite the neighbors in, along with friends from near and far, make it a day on the green (or rather, considering summer in California, on the brown). A band or two, a feast from their own garden, festivities of all sorts: a declaration of who we are, of how we have nothing to hide, open our arms to all.

And more—it could be used to convert people! Show them what a properly lived life could do—the lushness of the garden, the art they produced, their plans for responsible living when it came to the resources of the world. Why, they could even try to finish the schoolroom conversion for the kids. Display before-and-after pictures, to show how sterility could be made to bloom.

Some of the friends they invited could bring their bands, and make it a festival.

It would take a huge amount of work, and more money than The Commons had spent on any other project.

The first problem was solved when Meadow declared herself in favor. The Commons might be a collective, but some votes were more equal than others, and Meadow's carried more weight than anyone else's, including Rob's—mostly because everyone knew that anything Meadow threw herself into would get done, period.

True, many of those who were the most vocally enthusiastic, brushing aside the labor, money, and sheer endless hassle of putting on what was in effect a small Renaissance Faire (and just when the demands of the gardens were at a peak, too), were also the ones who tended to be missing when the big, dull jobs came along. But dragging people out of bed and getting them to work was nothing new.

Because if you were serious about showing the emptiness of Establishment values by converting an estate that was the very essence of capitalist history into a place of egalitarian community resources—and that, after all, was why they were here in the first place—then what better way of proclaiming that message than a spectacular piece of street theater like a music, art, and garden festival? The public splash would send a message far beyond their normal reach. Even better, using celebrities and the media to attract attention would let them point out the flawed foundation those celebrities and media stood on.

This brought the discussion around to money. Some residents embraced the lilies-of-the-field attitude, certain that beauty would rise up from the earth regardless of checkbooks, parking control, and porta-potties. But again, more experienced minds knew that, despite the impression of those grooving in the mud, a lot of planning had gone into Woodstock, and the pots of soup and emergency medical care hadn't just appeared from the goodwill of the crowds.

In any case, something the size of what they were envisioning would never be allowed to go on in the Bay Area if The Commons hadn't rented the tents, bought the food, and paid for the damned permits.

At this point, late one smoke-filled night on the terrace, someone stood up and said that they should actually give *all* the money away. Empty the Estate bank accounts, cash in the Gardener stocks, hand it all out, show how absurd and useless those scraps of paper were compared to real things like good food and beautiful art and music.

The meeting broke up shortly after that, with those in favor of the Great Potlach Giveaway dancing off to their beds, elevated by nobility and community and some high-quality weed.

The next morning, as calmer heads had known it would, reality set in. They actually couldn't cash in the Gardener riches yet, even if they had the lawyer's approval. And there was a growing awareness that Rob, who might have been able to talk Jerry into freeing up *some* of the money, was nowhere near as enthusiastic about the idea as some of his fellow Commoners.

Rob did have a personal bank account—that is, there was a checkbook with his name on it that every adult member of The Commons could use, with the approval of their fellow members. But draining that account to give the money away to strangers would mean nothing left for a festival.

One or the other: give out cash, or celebrate, inform, and inspire?

Had it been possible to strip the Gardener coffers entirely, they might have been tempted. But as a half-assed gesture, to make a far lesser point? And afterward, how would they pay for car repairs and electricity and property taxes? Would they have to put off buying books and shoes for the kids?

With grumbles and a sense of being forced to pander, the Midsummer's Eve Fest was back on and the topic of cash handouts tabled until next April, when the lawyers' grubby hands would be off the Estate for good. And they'd donate any money the festival made to a group trying to build organic gardens on empty lots in central Oakland.

The festival even acquired a name, playing on that of the Estate and the centerpiece of Gaddo's sculpture: Back to the Garden.

But like a poisonous snake in an untended corner of Eden, resentments stirred.

Six weeks to pull off a small miracle.

Anyone unattached to the Gardener name would not have stood a chance—an irony not lost on Meadow, during the long hours she spent with Jerry Rathford in any number of public offices, wheedling permits out of the bureaucracy.

Spring was not a good time to neglect the garden. So Fort stepped in, cutting down his long hours of meditation and pausing the yoga classes entirely to oversee weeding and planting. In the evenings, he and Meadow, usually with Rain, occasionally with Rob or one of the longer-term residents, would meet up to review what had been done and what needed doing.

Jobs fell to those best suited to them. Meadow was their sweet, organized, implacable representative to the outer world. David, young as he was, proved surprisingly useful, his degree having taught him how to write proposals in the language spoken by bureaucrats. Rain made sure that the permits and agreements the two of them came back with had responsible members of The Commons in charge of implementation. Fort quietly summoned and encouraged the vital work in the garden. Rob headed up the work crews.

Music? Meadow and Rain put out the word to friends, and soon had half a dozen bands. Food? The kitchen could manage, but they'd need tables and tents and plates for people to eat off. And yes—unless they wanted people pissing on the zucchini plants, more portable toilets. All those details in addition to finishing the conversion of the stables into a self-contained schoolhouse—four classrooms in the upper level that had once been the hayloft, and a single open area below that could be shaped into whatever the students decided.

It would do their neighbors good to see how proud The Commons were of their kids.

Two weeks into this whole process, the sheriff drove up. Rob went out to meet him, and the two men walked off into the field where the festival would take place and *Midsummer Eves* would rise.

The sheriff was not a regular Commons visitor, but he'd known Rob a little back in high school, and in recent years, he'd been out here enough to see that the residents, peculiar as they were, weren't likely to make a lot of trouble for him. The drugs they used were not the kinds that were followed by guns and violence, and though he did not approve of marijuana—far less the LSD they probably used—the hippie commune took care of their kids and gave his office less trouble than half the city bars.

Still.

"That nice lady of yours came in to talk about a permit for this festival thing you're looking to hold."

"She said she was going to."

"Lotta people might drop in."

"That was the idea."

The sheriff looked over at him. "You don't sound too keen."

"I'm not all that great with crowds. But the community wants it, so I'm doing my part."

"Yeah, well, it's the crowds we need to talk about. I need to have some deputies here."

"Can't do it. No guns, no uniforms."

The sheriff chewed his lip for a minute, looking out over the hills. "What if they wear regular clothes?"

"No guns."

"I put a car at the gate, to remind people we're here. And my plainclothes have radios, in case."

"My people won't like it."

"You gotta have some kind of security, or I can't sign off on it."

"What about private?"

"What, like Hells Angels?"

"Yeah, because that worked so well at Altamont. No, just men who know how to handle themselves without having to push people around."

"Vets?"

"Maybe."

"I get their names beforehand, so I can check their records. Make sure you don't have someone with a habit of beating people up."

"Agreed."

"So, three or four of my guys inside, two armed and uniformed at the gate, and at least half a dozen of yours. Can you put yours in matching T-shirts or something, so people know who to ask for help?"

"I'll let Meadow know."

"But Rob? I hear of anyone tripping or selling, I come in and shut you down."

"I'll let her know that, too."

His wording suggested that an occasional whiff of dope would be overlooked unless things got problematic. Rob figured The Commons could handle that degree of oppression, just for a day.

The weeks went past. Key permits came in, large checks went out, posters were designed and sent to the printer, equipment started to arrive.

Then the first major hitch.

Half The Commons heard Meadow's voice.

"You gotta be fucking kidding me! What do you mean, we can't put it up the next morning? No, I thought— But you said— Wait one goddamned minute, we had an *agreement*. Yeah, I— But that was the whole point! So what—" There followed a lengthy silence, although those close to the Green Room could hear her occasional grunt and "yeah."

Then true silence. After a time, Meadow was seen walking through the garden deep in conversation with Rain, and out through the laurel hedge.

31

Now

Raquel flipped back some pages in her notebook. "According to
Mrs. Dalhousie, they'd planned to install the statue the morning
after the festival." Although as Jen had pointed out, the commune was
more likely to have researched strains of cannabis than how to engi-
neer a large statue.

"That's right," Jerry said. "The idea was that the Fest would end at
dawn, then the trucks would arrive. But a few days before, they discovered that wouldn't be possible. It needed to be done in two stages, and
there wasn't enough time between them."

"A lack of planning sounds uncharacteristic of Meadow."

"I suppose she couldn't manage everything. That spring was just
overwhelmingly busy for everyone—too much work, not enough sleep,
nothing getting done but the festival. By June, people were snapping
at each other—I even saw little Annabelle give her kid a swat on the
rear, though she was the one who burst into tears."

"What about Fort? Did he snap at people?"

"He may have been the only one who didn't. Though I imagine even
he had to take a deep breath every so often."

She thought about the dynamics Jerry was sketching out: Rob,
Meadow, Fort, and Rain. Four people deeply committed to the belief
that love was to be free, that possessions were evil, that all living beings

were to be given a voice. The central characters in a story about creating Paradise.

"When you met them in Oregon, your impression was that Meadow and Rob were lovers."

"Oh, they were, definitely."

"And after three years in California?"

"They were still, sure."

"But?"

"But more like an old married couple. They loved each other, you could see that, but maybe not so much *in* love, if you know what I mean."

Paradise lost, or just grown too familiar?

In Raquel's experience, every Eden had a serpent. And love did not innoculate against its venom.

32

Then

Rain and Meadow let themselves out through the hidden gate and went down to the line of half-buried tree trunks the commune used for watching deer graze at the field's edges or stars turn in the night sky. The kids called it Nature's drive-in.

The air was pungent with the smell of fresh-sawed wood, from the timber stacked and ready for stage construction. After a minute, Rain dug out his stash and built a small joint, lighting it up. They passed it back and forth for a while, watching a pair of red-tailed hawks.

The joint was half gone when Meadow waved it away. Rain, taking care not to let any embers fall, crushed it out and put it back into the pouch.

Meadow lowered her gaze from the hawks to the site where the *Eves* waited. They were all but finished, and currently hedged in by an elaborate support network of two-by-fours, on the ground just behind what looked like a jungle gym for pixies made of bent rebar inside a stout wooden fence.

She sighed. "You'd think somebody might have mentioned it, don't you? Like, maybe to Gaddo herself? I mean, how could we be expected to know it would take two whole weeks for the damned concrete to set?"

"What if we just put it up anyway?"

"We'd never get it up there without a crane, and we'd never get a crane without the contractor's approval."

"More fucking permits," Rain grumbled. "Couldn't we just, I don't know, raise them ourselves? The Incas and Aztecs built whole temples without cranes. Egypt and its pyramids."

"The *Eves* are designed to drop down over the fittings. We can't tip them up like a barn raising. And if we just stick them up there, they're sure to fall over on someone. Do you really want to be famous for killing Joni Mitchell, halfway through her set?"

"Guess not," Rain said dutifully.

"But God, that rebar is ugly. Do we have a tarp big enough to cover it?"

"What if we put the stage in front of it?"

"The ground's sloping so much right there, the stage would have to be made a lot taller. And we'd then have to put railings all the way around—remember what's-his-face going off that stage in Albany? Scared the hell out of me, and he'd probably have broken his neck if he hadn't been so stoned. But . . . wait. What if we built the stage on top of the frame?"

The two tried to picture it: the golden surface of Wide Field stretching out below, the high laurel hedge behind, an oak tree on one side and the three-faced *Eves* on the other—Creator Eve smiling toward Wide Field, a place rich with life and potential; Preserver Eve keeping a watchful eye on the gardens and house; Destroyer Eve, her baleful glare directed at the world beyond the gates.

"It would still have to be high, to clear those uprights," Meadow went on. "But if Gaddo let us take some of the scaffolding down, to show the faces, we could drape the rest of the scaffold with bedsheets or something. Instead of installing *Eve herself,* we could say that the Fest is preparing the way. Blessing the ground, as it were. Then we could at least pour the cement as soon as the stage comes down. Take all the time it needs to cure before the *Eves* are lifted into place."

"Works for me," Rain said.

"It would mean that the hillside isn't all chewed up from the heavy equipment," Meadow added, sounding happier about things. She leaned forward to kiss Rain, a long, leisurely embrace that—on a less crowded day or a more private spot—might have progressed. She broke away first, and ran an affectionate finger over the sharp line between shaved skin and beard hair.

"I can't believe you still do this every morning."

"It's kind of a meditation, you know?"

"You started it in . . . was it Chicago?"

"Philly."

"Was that the concert where the light tower fell over?"

"Just after that. Some chick handed me a picture to sign and I couldn't tell which one was me."

"So you became the bad boy."

"Hey, if it fits."

"It does suit you, babe."

"So how is Rob, anyway?" he asked. "I never see him unless I'm on one of his work gangs."

"Rob's going through some heavy shit. I think his brother coming back is making him wonder about his own path. I think he has unresolved matters that have nothing to do with you or me or anyone here. I think his family, and whatever he did in Vietnam, those are things he needs to face. I think he's angry and scared and trying hard to keep it together. When the Fest is over with, I'll take him to bed and screw him silly, but then I think . . . I don't know, Rain. I get the feeling that after Midsummer, we're all going to be stepping back to see where we are. Things are beginning to feel like they did before you and I took off to Oregon. Remember? New and old, light and heavy—change, you know? I could be wrong, this could be just a chapter ending and there's another one waiting on the next page. But I do know that as soon as this is over, we're all going to have to circle around and see if we can help Rob get rid of the ghosts. We owe him that."

Silence held for a while.

"Ghosts, man," Rain pronounced. "They're a bummer."

Meadow was stoned enough to find this funny, and fell off her tree trunk with laughter.

Rain hauled her to her feet, and the two stood side by side, arms draped across each other's shoulders.

The red-tails had moved on. With another sigh, Meadow turned, and the two went back through the hedge and into another day of bureaucratic hassles and organizing a lot of organization-averse people.

33

Now

"How did Meadow and Rob meet?" Raquel asked.

Jerry drained the last of his coffee. "After he got back from Vietnam, Rob just took to the road, thumbing rides, staying places for a while, and moving on. I'm not sure when he turned up at the Oregon place, but Meadow was already there. She and Rain knew the guy who started it, and when the two of them gave up the music scene, that's where they went."

"They were musicians?"

"Not Meadow, she didn't have much of a voice—one of the few things she couldn't do—but she ran the business side of things for others. Everybody loved her. I remember a rumor that the song 'Green-Eyed Lady' was about her, but that may have been just a story.

"But Rain was. Ever hear of Reynard? He had a couple of top-ten songs and was looking to become another Jagger or Sting until a girl died at one of his concerts, and he just couldn't get over it. I don't think he even knew the girl, she was just a fan, but after the inquiry was over, he canceled the next tour and said he had to go find himself. Which I guess he did, because he never went back."

"When was that?"

"Not sure, but it was after Altamont. Maybe 1970? Early '71? Anyway, he and Meadow had been in Oregon for a couple of years before Rob got there."

"As lovers?"

"Probably. Though by the time I met them, they were mostly friends."

"Mostly."

"Meadow was not what you'd call exclusive. She and Rain had been a thing, so they might have continued, I don't know."

"Was that a problem, between her and Rob?"

"Didn't seem to be. And I never got the sense that Rob had any trouble with Rain."

"What about his brother, Fort? Were he and Meadow sleeping together?"

"Fort? Huh. My instinct is to say no, but I'm not sure why. I guess he just never seemed a very sexual sort of guy. Overtly, anyway. But he and Meadow did have a lot in common, and they spent loads of time together, so . . . maybe? From Meadow's side, it wouldn't have surprised me. If you weren't there, it's hard to understand how different sex was, back in the seventies. The Pill was new, AIDS hadn't started up yet, marriage was a bourgeois construct, so why not sleep around? And Meadow was big on equality. If women could chop firewood and weld things, they could also sleep with whoever they wanted.

"The two of them were definitely close, I can say that. Fort was really interested in the garden, and that was Meadow's baby. When it came to other things, Rain was Meadow's right-hand guy, and Rob would take over whatever she pointed him at, but neither of them were much into the garden. Fort was. Maybe not as mystical about growing as Meadow could be, but I'm sure she was happy to have someone to take over some of the work that spring. Even with everything going on, she had time to breathe. Time to help Gaddo with her sculpture—that's when they were finishing the *Eves*."

"It sounds like everything was going well."

"I thought it was. And the festival was incredible. The idea was to use a day of big-name music and bring people in, then turn them on to what The Commons was doing with the Estate—philosophically, po-

litically, and ecologically. And they all seemed really happy and excited, and then, well . . ." He made a gesture like a seedpod dispersing
on the wind.

"The commune fell apart."

"Not instantly. But yes, pretty soon. Like I said, Meadow and Fort
went, and Rain—or did he wait till the *Eves* were up? I think so. Things
were a little chaotic, and Rob was hiding out in the house—yeah, Rain
stuck around. I remember him and Gaddo having some kind of argument about the statue while this whacking great crane was sitting there
charging by the hour. She wanted it one way, the guy said he didn't
think it would work, she made it work. Anyway, that would've been a
couple weeks after the Fest."

"Was Rob there?"

"No. For some reason, Gaddo was well and truly pissed off with
Rob, so he made himself scarce. Not just that day, either, but the rest
of the summer. Like he knew the rest of them were blaming him for
Meadow leaving, too."

"Do you think he was to blame?"

"I figured he was, somehow. But on the other hand . . . how to put
this? Meadow liked to be needed. She didn't have kids, but she was a
sort of mother figure to the rest of the commune. It was the sort of
place where wounded people ended up, and she was a big reason for
that. But you know how mother dogs go through this stage with pup-
pies, of getting up and walking away? And if they're too persistent,
she'll take a snap at them? Sometimes Meadow would get this look.
Like she was getting fed up with her children and wondering if they
wouldn't be better off if she just walked off and forced them to grow
up."

"Was there anyone she didn't look at that way?"

"Fort. Rain. Pig, one or two of the other women."

"Not Rob?"

"Rob got that look a lot. He'd done something to get on her shit
list."

"Perhaps he'd shown his jealousy?"

Jerry shrugged.

"Did he know? About Meadow's promiscuity?"

"Now, there's a word that didn't get used much in the seventies. Rob would've known if she was sleeping around, sure. People didn't tend to keep that kind of thing a secret. But I'd have thought that, if he objected, it would have led to all kinds of discussion—like what they used to call encounter groups, with everybody chiming in. Frankly, I think Rob would've hated being the target of that kind of attention and concern. I'd say if he knew, and if he wasn't happy about it, he'd still have kept it to himself."

"What about you? Did you sleep with Meadow?"

"I . . . wouldn't call it sleeping. We had sex, yes. Once. I'd brought some papers by for Rob to sign and he wasn't there. She just said she was horny and reached for my belt. Didn't even close the door."

Yes, Raquel thought, *the seventies were a different world. Hitch a ride, share your body, give away your money.*

But the seventies didn't last. And even during the decade, unacknowledged hostility and resentment had to have been bubbling away under the surface, waiting to erupt.

"What if he found out that she was sleeping with Fort? His older brother, who'd come back from India and charmed the whole commune with his winning ways?"

"Funny, I'd never thought of it that way. I guess Fort did impress everyone with his . . ."

"Holiness?"

"Actually, I was going to say his dependability, but sure, the spiritual thing was a big part of his appeal for them. 'Chop wood, carry water,' you know? And there's no denying he was good-looking, in the kind of delicate way that would've got him beaten up in redneck country. Wiry, half a foot shorter than Rob, with long Jesus hair and blue eyes. He was the only guy on the commune who shaved, other than Rain."

"Did a lot of the women sleep with him?"

"I'm pretty sure they were willing, but as far I know, nobody did."

"What about Rain?"

"Sleeping with Fort? God, no. If either of them had been gay, every third person on the place would have come up and told me, just so they could show how completely cool they were with it."

"Not a lot of gay people here, then?"

"About as many as there were Black people or Hispanics. Not that The Commons wouldn't have welcomed them with open arms, but like any commune, pretty much everyone here was white-bread, middle-class, heterosexual. People who could give everything up because they had parents in the background, to bail them out of trouble."

"Cynical."

He shrugged.

"But actually, I wasn't asking if Rain and Fort were having sex. I was wondering how Rain felt about matters. He and Meadow were close until Fort, the Indian guru, showed up, weren't they?"

"Yeah, but again, I'm not sure any of them would have thought like that. Jealousy was a thing that belonged on a shelf with capitalism, patriarchy, Watergate, and the people who stole land from the Native Americans. There was no room for jealousy at The Commons."

"In my experience, Mr. Rathford, jealousy has a way of making room for itself anywhere. And what about Rob Gardener? As you admit, he had a history of violence, from high school troubles to nearly burning the house down when he came home from Vietnam. He even turned a shotgun on some trespassers, just a few months ago. Why should I not think that he lost his temper in 1979 and put the resulting body where he knew it would disappear?"

"Are you talking about Meadow? But he loved her."

Raquel did not bother to reply to that, merely raised an eyebrow at him.

Jerry sighed. "Yeah, I know. And I'll admit, the man did make me nervous once or twice, but that was mostly because he was strong, and could be kind of intense. In actual fact, he almost never so much as raised his voice."

"What about since the commune days? What has he been up to?"

"Nothing."

"You can't tell me that in forty years, he's never ventured outside his house."

"I suppose he must have at some point, but for the most part, he's here. Not here in the main house, of course, not since the Trust took over. But after that summer, I can't remember ever seeing him outside the Estate."

"Funerals, marriages, parties?"

Jerry shook his head. "It's possible, but he doesn't have a car, and it's a long walk to town. I do know that he's never showed up at anything I invited him to. He wasn't at his niece's wedding last year."

Raquel looked up sharply. "His niece? Did Fort have children?"

"Sorry, no—I tend to think of David as a third brother. His daughter . . . would she be Rob's first cousin once removed? Something like that. Anyway, I'm sure they invited Rob."

"What about Fort? Is he still alive?" Jen had seemed doubtful about it.

"We don't really know. It was sad, the way he left. He and Rob used to be close, orphaned early and living with their grandfather, but whatever happened during the festival, it was a final break. He wrote a few times over the years, but to Marla, the housekeeper, not Rob. He liked to send these cheap postcards with enigmatic messages on them. Anyway, he'd be in his seventies now, and there's a lot of things to die from, in India."

"I'd have thought the death of a US citizen would come to someone's attention."

"Oh, Fort took Indian citizenship before he came back that last time. Changed his name, even."

"To what?"

"God knows."

"God doesn't tend to help me much, Mr. Rathford."

"Well, I'm not sure who can. I don't think I've ever come across it in the Estate's papers. You might ask Rob."

"What about Rob's will? Does it include his brother in its bequests? Assuming he's still alive."

"It—look, that's something I can't tell you. Not without Rob's agreement."

She nodded, having expected that line to be drawn, and took out the folder of snapshots and printouts—Mrs. Dalhousie's pages, three that she'd made with random faces and names, and two showing Michael Johnston, one with a small mustache, the other with a beard.

Jerry treated it as a walk down Memory Lane, exclaiming over the clothes and hair, laughing over his sideburns—and more to the point, supplying details for several names missing from the archived folders. Three of the people he had seen in recent years. Three others he knew to have died.

He studied the face of Michael Johnston, but shook his head and went on.

When he had finished with the printout pages, he went back to the glossy photos, picking up the one showing what seemed to be most of The Commons sprawled out on a hillside. Acres of hair, colorful clothes, strong bodies, facing the future absolutely convinced of the joy it would hold.

"That might have been the morning of the festival. They all got together to watch the sun come up. Though I'm not sure they'd been to bed the night before." His finger touched some of the faces, as he recited the names: Meadow, Wes, David, Annabelle, Fort, Rain, Pig, Paolo.

"Every time I'd come out here during those years," he reflected, "I wouldn't want to leave. I'd sit and eat their fresh tomatoes and whole wheat bread, smell the sweat and watch the kids race around, and I'd think to myself, *This life has got to be better than a paper-filled office with fluorescent lights.*"

He slid the pictures back across the table, and said sadly, "I think if Meadow had asked me to stay, or even Rob, I'd have dumped it all and let my hair grow. I'd probably still be here, living next to Wes in the Yard, frying my last brain cells on homegrown."

34

"Hi, Al, something interesting came up in one of the interviews that we might want to look into."

Raquel had thanked Jerry and sent him on his way, and was now headed back to her borrowed office to meet Wes Albright.

"Interesting bad, or interesting hopeful?"

"I don't know. In the fall of 1978, somebody here picked up a hitch-hiker and brought him home. A few days later, the guy—the stranger, that is—was arrested for an attack on a woman in Berkeley. His name was something like O'Donnell, but the lawyer wasn't too sure about it. I thought maybe you'd like to ask your friends in San Mateo to look through their arrest records, see if we can find the guy."

"You think it might be Johnston?"

"No, it doesn't sound like him, and Jerry—the lawyer—didn't recognize the photo."

"So not a rush, then."

"Not unless we have two multiple offenders who are both terminally ill."

"I think we're safe there. Okay, I'll send it to San Mateo, but I won't flag it as having to do with Johnston."

"Call you later," she said. "Mr. Albright?"

This last was to a man with a long gray ponytail, standing at the end of the hallway looking a bit lost.

"Um, you're the inspector lady? Jen asked me to come?"

"I am—Inspector Laing. Come on in."

Raquel was relieved she hadn't had to track him down in his den. And even more relieved to find him freshly showered and in a relatively clean T-shirt.

She laid her things on the desk and turned to study her next interviewee.

Jerry Rathford had aged well. Wes had not. The boy from the photographs, cheerful and not terribly bright, looked older than the lawyer did, although she knew he had to be at least ten years younger. Skin mottled from the sun, eyes that would need cataract surgery before long, and bald on top, his tonsure gathered at the back of his skull into a bright pink elastic.

Nervous at Authority: put him at ease. She smiled and said, "Thanks so much for coming, I'm sorry to interrupt your day—let's go down to the break room, we can have a coffee or something. Have you eaten yet?"

"Not really."

"Good, there seem to be a huge number of sandwiches in the fridge, left over from something, I imagine. You want to help yourself? I'll put on some coffee—or would you rather have tea?"

Prattle and food took some of the terror from his face, although he'd probably never feel comfortable talking to a cop. She even took care to spill some milk, and mop it up with an exclamation.

Casual talk, then slip in the questions. "This is such a great place— I live in San Francisco and it's so *noisy* there compared to this. Have you been here long?" When dither and drink had done their job and his body had lost its tension, she shifted into recent events on the Estate, and the discovery of the bones.

The man's face concealed little. He was troubled by the bones, but not ashamed or guilty.

"Wes, you understand that I'm here to try and find who did it? And to figure out which of your friends the body might be?"

"That's what Jen said."

"I know it's a long time ago, but I'm hoping one of you who was here will remember something that helps me."

"I don't forget a lot," he said. "But sometimes it takes a while to dig things out." The smile he gave her was an echo of his expression in one of the photos—sweet, sad, and very aware of how she saw him. She revised her earlier judgment: less stupid than deliberate.

As with Jerry, she started with the photograph of Michael Johnston—and again, he hesitated, but didn't recognize him. She put it away, and sat back with her coffee.

"Mr. Albright, I'd like to know about the last days of the commune. Around the time of the Midsummer Fair."

"Midsummer's Eve Fest," he corrected.

"Of course, thanks. I understand a lot of things changed after that day. How did it begin?"

She'd meant, how did things start to change after that day, but he took the question literally—how did that day begin?

35

Then

Before dawn, on Midsummer's eve, most of The Commons adults gathered on the far side of Wide Field to watch the sun come up. All were riding high on exhaustion and exhilaration, ready for the day and already dreading it being over. Meadow passed around still-warm bread rolls and the first of the orchard's white peaches. Fort handed out mugs and thermoses of coffee or herb tea. Rain brought out a joint fully six inches long and, once he'd managed to get it going, they passed it around as a ceremonial bond, one puff each.

When it had gone the rounds, Meadow intercepted its second circuit and put it away, saying firmly that they'd have the rest tonight, once the day was over.

The morning was too beautiful to spend arguing. They sat or lay back, watching the sky go lavender, while Rain dug into the rucksack he'd brought and pulled out a boxy little device.

"I borrowed this from a friend," he told them. "This day needs to be recorded, forever." He fiddled with the camera, then stood, holding it to his eye to run it slowly across the raised faces at his feet, then going on to pan along the tree line to the hills beyond. He then moved the focus back, showing Wide Field topped by the waiting stage, its dramatic height (they'd been forced to raise it above the rebar protrusions, ready for the base of the *Eves*) emphasized by the colorful skirt stapled to its edge, flanked by tall lights and six-foot-high speakers. (The generator was behind the hedge, the wires buried to please the county inspector.) Then up to the face of Creator Eve, looking out over her scaffold-concealing drapes, with the dark laurel wall behind.

As a joke—he could always edit this out—he flipped the camera around to grin into the lens.

Then with a sigh of satisfaction, he lowered the camera. When the others turned back to the sunrise, they discovered that while they'd been watching the budding cinematographer, the sun had come up, unnoticed. Annoyed, Meadow tossed out the dregs of her cup and got to her feet. "Well, this was nice, anyway. So has everybody checked the batteries in their walkie-talkies? We all clear on what we're doing? Remember: I'm food and drink, Rain is anything to do with the music, Fort helps people find each other, and Davey is bringing his motorbike to help fetch and carry. At least *he*'s guaranteed to be sober." The others laughed. David grinned shyly. "And speaking of which, if you find anyone drunk or tripping or making problems of any kind, call Rob."

"Where's Rob now?"

"He better be down there, getting his goon squad ready." She raised her head. "Is that a truck?"

It was a truck, growling its way up the drive. The day had begun.

The afternoon's first music was acoustic, individual and group, more folk than rock. One band—the third, starting at 4:00—was local and not very good, so Rain went up and took the mic early, thanking them so profusely they didn't realize they'd been kicked off. The next group was rock enough to kick the big speakers to life. Sound began to bounce off the hills, overcoming the annoying buzz of David's little scooter running food down to the gate and bits of lost equipment up to those who needed it. As soon as the serious music started, people abandoned the demonstrations of organic gardening, raku pottery, and homeschooling to gather before the speakers and groove to the beat.

By 6:00, the family groups were starting to leave. At the same time, the line of cars on the road coming in was getting longer, and the guys in charge of parking were directing the drivers into the overflow field.

At 7:00, the only children on the Estate were those who lived there.

At 8:00, a fistfight at the back of the Great Field had men running in from all sides, smothering the alcohol-fueled anger under the sheer weight of responders. The combatants were hauled apart, marched down to the car park, and turned over, along with their keys, to their more sober friends.

Just before 9:00, Rob's voice came crackling over the walkie-talkie on Meadow's belt.

"Which of you fuckers left the goddamn front door open?"

She snatched up the device and turned down the volume, nearly tripping as her foot caught on an ill-buried wire as she walked away from the speakers. "Shit—damn it, they were supposed to bury those. Rob, this is Meadow, what's the matter? Over."

But Rob was paying no attention to the mechanics of one-way communication, and had just kept talking.

"—heard the voices and there they were right in my mother's fucking room, poking around like they owned the place! Jesus, I told everybody they had to—"

"Rob! Rob, Rob, *Rob*." Her voice finally got through to him.

"*What?*"

"You didn't hit anyone, did you? Over."

Silence.

"Robbie, are you okay, did you hit anyone? Over."

"Yeah—I mean no. No, I didn't hit them. But they were moving fast when they left." Silence. "Over."

"Okay, so what do you want me to do? Bring you a stick? Send one of the sheriff's guys to arrest them? What were they doing there anyway, stealing her old dresses? It's just a bedroom, Rob. Over."

Silence. It went on.

"Rob, I got things to do, if you don't need me to hold your hand. Just lock the front door and everything will be fine. Okay? Over."

No reply.

"Out," she snapped in irritation, and went back to the food tent.

Pausing first to catch up the shovel leaning against the back of the stage and bury the cables correctly.

❧

It wasn't until after 10:00 that things began to go sideways. The permit said the music was supposed to stop at 10:00, but all the bands had gone overtime, and the hard-rocking guys who were meant to start at 9:00 had only been on for about five minutes. Rain was fine with that, Meadow was not, and Fort found the two of them arguing behind the stage, with David and Wes in the background looking uncomfortable.

"Sorry," Fort broke in, "I don't want to add to your problems, but there's some weird shit building out there, and I can't find Rob. You know where he is?"

"I saw him going into the Yard a while ago," David offered.

Rain pulled out his walkie-talkie and spoke Rob's name. Meadow asked what kind of weird shit.

"Let's just say I wouldn't want to see a single girl or a Black dude heading in that direction. They're high on something, though it could just be booze."

Meadow pulled out her walkie-talkie and keyed it on. "Rob? Rob, are you there? Rob, damn it, where are you? Do your fucking job, man." She turned to Rain. "What's the name of his guy, the one who brought the others? Lennie, right." She keyed the speaker again to say, "Lennie, this is Meadow, I can't find Rob and there's a problem brewing in the crowd, are you up here? Over."

They waited. The music pounded. She was lifting the thing to her face again when it crackled. "Hey, this's Lennie. What's the problem? Over."

She handed it to Fort, who identified himself and described where to find the group giving out the aggressive vibes, adding, "A couple of us will head up there and just move other people down a ways, put some space between them. You want the sheriff's guys? Over."

"They're with me, no problem, see you up there, Fort, over out."

Fort handed Meadow back her walkie-talkie. "Lennie's cool, don't worry, he knows how to pour cold water on hotheads. And most people have already come down closer to the lights, anyway. Rain and I will round up anyone else and tell them it's time to pack up."

"You're sure? I was at Altamont, Fort, it was . . . I have nightmares."

He took her hand. "That's not going to happen here, Meadow. Things will stay cool. Promise."

She flung her arms around him, her blond hair pressing into his, and held him close for a minute, then kissed his cheek and let him go. He and Rain trotted off, Wes following along more reluctantly. After a minute, David started his scooter and buzzed away. Meadow scowled at the silent walkie-talkie, then hooked it on her belt and turned to go—only to jerk back with an exclamation of surprise.

36

Now

"Before we go on," Raquel interrupted, "can I ask you about Rob and violence? Was this a common concern, that he would beat up someone?"

"Rob? No! Never."

"Not even a trespasser?"

"Not that I ever heard about."

"So why did Meadow think he would?"

He puffed out his cheeks and blew out a long, slow breath. "I honestly don't know. That festival—don't get me wrong, it was really cool, but it also just . . . changed everything. When we started it, everything was all sharing and beautiful, but then it got buried under this endless pile of permits and inspectors and crap. These outsider bureaucrats having to approve of every little thing. Made us all crazy, you know? There were so many weird vibes by the end of it, and everybody seemed to be falling apart. Like I say, I never did understand exactly why, but something must have gone totally wrong, somewhere. And before you knew it, everybody was gone."

37

Then

Meadow jerked back. "Rob! Jeez, sneak up on a person, why don't you? Isn't your radio working? We called and you didn't hear."

"It's working, but you wouldn't have heard me over the noise, so I came instead. Meadow, are you screwing my brother?"

"Am I—what's *wrong* with you, Rob? What does it matter, anyway? My body doesn't belong to you."

"We had an agreement. We'd tell the other before we slept with anyone."

"Rob, look, there's a problem up at—"

"I mean, you're sleeping with Rain and Jerry and probably Gaddo and—"

"For fuck's sake, Rob, do we have to do this right now? Can we just fix this problem before the county sends in their riot squad? The guys are up there now, doing *your* fucking job—could you *please* just help out for once? And if you dare hit me, you bastard," she said, meeting his hunched muscles with fury of her own, "I will *bury* you." The two glared at each other, the short blond woman and the tall dark man, and an onlooker would have found it hard to decide which was about to erupt into violence first.

But Rob clawed back control. "I've never hit you, Meadow, and I'm not going to now. Where are they?"

"Up near the viewing rock. I called your guy Lennie, he and the others are up there."

"I'll go."

"Wait," she said.

"*What?*"

"I . . . Robbie, love, this really isn't working. You and me. Is it?"

Guitars throbbed, drums crashed, the smell of pot drifted by. "No. I guess it isn't."

She stepped forward, going on her toes to kiss him full on the mouth, light but lingering. Her hands rested on his shirtfront for a moment, then she drew away, meeting his surprise with a sad smile.

"Go," she said.

His fists were not quite so tightly clenched as he stalked off toward the distant conflict.

It took those fists to clear out the knot of drunks, Rob's along with Lennie's and two of the other vets'. When the band finally finished and the blast of music was replaced by the sound of Rain's voice thanking people for coming and inviting them to move on home, Fort raised the walkie-talkie and phoned down to the sheriff's deputies at the gate.

Ten minutes later, the two uniforms got out of their wagon and stood, hands on hips, surveying the aftermath of this battlefield. The only sign of who had won was that the five losers were sitting. One of them was snoring.

"If they weren't so drunk," Fort told the uniforms, "we'd have let them drive home. But they'll need to sober up, either here or down at your place."

His offer was a compromise between The Commons residents, who'd wanted to lock the drunks in a shed until morning, and Lennie's guys, eager to drag them down to the main road and make them walk home. Fort pointed out that locking them up could be counted as kidnapping, and that turning drunks loose on the road just invited a different set of problems, so why not use the people paid to clean up society's garbage? The two deputies looked at each other, and started loading the five losers into the back of their wagon.

When the door was shut, the older of the two looked at Rob and Lennie. "You guys might want to see if that nurse is still in the medical tent. She could put in a few stitches for you."

Rob had his with no anesthetic, and the two men went to supervise the departure of the last visitors. It was well after one in the morning before the last car had left the parking area.

"My ears are ringing," Lennie said into the silence.

"It was a good day," Rob said. "Thanks for having our back. And thank your guys. Can we send you a check, to divvy up?"

"We'd have done it for nothing, but the bread's nice, too."

They shook hands, and Lennie went off to retrieve his Harley from behind some bushes, while Rob walked up the familiar nighttime road to the house. As he got closer, an echo of the day's beat grew. Inside the front door, he followed the sound to the ballroom, and found a party going on—most of the bands were there, half their roadies, and nearly all the residents. The air was thick with smoke, the Stones were wailing through the speakers, and David was happily deejaying a heap of records on the stereo. Meadow was laughing uproariously with Gaddo and a couple of rockers, passing around a joint the size of one of Grandfather's Havana cigars. Rain had his camera going, recording the night for posterity, but when the lens turned his way, Rob backed out of the room.

The thump of the bass, Mick's wails, and the wall of talk and laughter followed him down the hallway and through the reception room. It dropped further when the door to the Green Room nearly shut, though he could still feel the vibration.

He switched on the light and crossed over to where the drinks were kept, filling one of the two surviving antique glasses to the brim. He swallowed the top couple of inches at a go, then nearly choked as a voice spoke.

"Hey."

Rob whirled around, staring at the figure hidden by the back of the tall chair. "Fort, what are you doing here?"

"I was going to bed, but there were a couple people there already. I said they could have it for an hour or so."

"Shoulda joined them."

"Not really my thing, Rob."

"Yeah, sure." He took another mighty swig and dropped into the chair behind the desk, across the room from his brother.

"What does that mean, 'Yeah, sure'?"

"The holy man act, Fort. Gets a little tiresome."

The two brothers sat in the throbbing room for some minutes before the older one spoke again. "Rob, why do I get the feeling that today marks the end of things, rather than a beginning?"

"We were fine until you came."

"I don't think you were fine. I think you just didn't notice."

"Ah, right, and if I treated her better, she wouldn't need anyone else, is that what you're saying?"

"Are we talking about Meadow, here?"

"Who else is there you've been fucking around with? Coming here, all yoga and helpful, and all the time you've got your goddamn ashram lined up to move in next April—or force us to sell up so you can have yours. I don't mind, Fort—like I say, it's your house, too. Just that the sneakiness of it pisses me off."

Jagger finished telling the world that he was shattered, and after a pause and a guitar riff, Stephen Stills began to describe how he'd come across a child of God, hitching to an upstate farm.

"Yeah," Fort said, and got to his feet. "It's time I was going."

"Ah, screw it, man, I need some sleep." Rob finished his drink and, feeling as if he were standing at the edge of a cliff, walked with care across the room and opened the door. "See you tomorrow."

Fort said something in reply, but with the rush of sound, Rob didn't hear it. Halfway across the foyer, somebody ripped the needle off the CSNY album. He stopped, swaying a little as the voices rose in what sounded like anger. But no: the gentle harmonies David had set to play were replaced by Jimmy Page's guitar. A roar of approval, and laughter rose again as Rob Gardener climbed the stairs to his bed.

He slept late the next day. When he finally woke to make his bleary-headed way downstairs, the house was silent, and everyone who mattered was gone.

38

Now

Raquel looked across the break-room table at Wes. "When you said everyone left, you don't mean that nearly eighty adults and children just cleared out overnight?" That hadn't been Jerry Rathford's version of events.

"Oh, no—people were here, just not the ones that mattered. To Rob, I mean. Fort went back to India. Not that anyone even noticed at first, because Meadow took off, too, her and that weird artist lady. Gaddo. Man, the whole day was just nuts. We'd all crashed, because we'd been up for like two days, and then one of the parents—Pig, maybe? Yeah, I think it was her, her kids woke her up and she looked out and saw that the stage was still up. We had to take it down before the concrete guy could do his thing, so she and Paolo started waking everyone up to see if we knew where Meadow was. I mean, she was supposed to be running the whole installation thing for Gaddo, but nobody could find her and the cement truck was coming at noon. And Gaddo's pickup was gone, too, and we'd all seen her and Meadow hanging around together, and I guess we all just figured, you know— far out, the two chicks have gone off to have a good time."

"Really? I'd have thought that, even with the distractions, people might have been a bit more worried. Meadow sounds to me like a responsible sort of person, not someone who'd just take off like that."

"Sure, but some of her stuff was missing. You know, the kind of stuff you'd take if you left, purse and clothes and shit. And then somebody said Meadow'd banged on her door really early to say she was going and to tell everyone she loved them."

"Who was that?"

But he could only shake his head. "It would've been one of the girls—women, sorry. I only remember people thinking she might as well have left a note on the fridge or something. Anyway, *then* we found out that she and Rob had a fight, so it all kind of made sense. That she'd take off for a while. Though you're right, we still thought it was a kinda shitty thing to do."

"A physical fight?"

"Physical? Like, him hitting her? God no, Rob wouldn't do that."

"But he did hit people?"

"He sure pounded on some guys that were making trouble during the festival, but that was different. I never saw him hit one of us.

"Anyway, most of us wanted to go back to bed because, hell, if Gaddo and Meadow didn't care enough to be there, why should we? But you know, we were up by then and still half-stoned and we all knew what to do. And anyway, it's kinda fun to really rip something apart, you know? So we all grabbed tools and the cement guy came and he knew where to pour it so that was cool, and we figured Meadow would come back when she was ready. Except she didn't. And then a couple weeks later, when Gaddo came to show the crane how to put the *Eves* on the base, she said she hadn't seen Meadow since that night after the festival."

"How was Gaddo?"

"What do you mean, how was she? I told you she was weird."

"But that day. Was she angry?"

"Maybe? She could be pretty impatient with some of us. Mostly the guys. And yeah, she was kinda pissed off at the crane driver, something about the way she wanted the statue to go up. They had a big argument and she ended up whacking some of the things that stuck up from the concrete so they fit better. Anyway, as soon as it was up, she left."

"What about Meadow? Did anyone try to find her?"

"I guess, but what could we do? I mean, we all knew she and Rob were getting on each other's nerves, but Meadow was a free spirit, you know? And people came and went all the time. We thought she'd show up when she got tired of doing whatever.

"But you know, after the festival, nothing seemed to work right. It was partly because Meadow was gone. I mean, she had such great energy and knew how to get stuff done, but it was other shit as well. Rob was drinking and Jerry was hassling everybody about paying the bills, and somebody left a gate open so deer got into the garden and people started bitching at each other about whose turn it was to cook and why hadn't someone done the shopping.

"And so people began to go, you know? Just a couple at first, people with kids who decided to go back to wherever they came from so their kids could go to actual school, with a teacher who knew things. Somebody else got a job with one of the bands that came through, so he and his old lady left. A bunch of others heard about this amazing commune down in New Mexico, and—well, you get the picture.

"By the end, it was really sad, maybe ten people still there, living in the woods mostly."

"Can you remember who?"

"Let's see. Rob, of course, in the house. I think Davey was staying here, too, for a while—Rob's cousin, you know? But not long. Rob seemed to like being alone. Paolo and Pig were in the big school bus with the kids. Gary and Chet were in the two yurts, and Heather was in the dead motor home with somebody I didn't know. Oh, and the Airstream, there were two guys in that. Cowboy was one, the other . . . I don't remember, probably someone new. And there might've been a couple other new guys in the rooms inside the Yard."

"Not Rain?"

"Rain took off when the *Eves* were up. Him and Meadow had a thing, you know?"

"I thought Meadow was with Rob?"

"She was, mostly. And he was cool with it, but as time went on, it was . . . it's hard to explain. It was like . . . like this house took Rob over, you know? Like the walls were a whole different life that pulled him back in. Turned him from free and open and a believer in the power of love to someone who'd be pissed if you scratched the floors."

"Sounds like there were some resentments building."

"I suppose. I mean, look—the whole back-to-the-earth thing was such a beautiful time, you know? It was sharing and good vibes and healthy living, everything the world wasn't. But it's really hard to live that way, long-term. Like, it's cool to live in a tent and raise your own vegetables, but then the gophers eat the beans and your clothes are always wet because the roof leaks and somebody gets sick because the toilets got blocked up and people were shitting in the woods, and it turns out that what you thought was a permanent thing was only borrowed, and the owner wants it back."

"Are you talking about Rob and the Estate?"

"Yeah, I guess. There was some complicated arrangement that got screwed up. I don't remember exactly what it was, just that people found out that he'd been lying to everyone."

Maybe his legalese didn't keep things as invisible as Jerry thought. "Tell me what you do remember."

Wes's memory for human interactions was better than things to do with legal documents, but he tried his best.

"It was something to do with this agreement Rob made. That the Estate belonged to The Commons. Or it would—that's right: Jerry said he couldn't sign things over to us yet, but they made this agreement that he would when he could, which would've been the next year, after all this went down. That we'd all own it, with equal say in how things were done. Which would have been so cool, right? But then that summer, I remember somebody explaining that what it really said was that Rob and Fort would *think* about giving it to us. Which is pretty bullshit, you have to agree, after you've been pretending it's a done deal.

"Anyway, without Meadow and Rain and some of the others to work things out, that was sort of the nail in the coffin, and pretty much everybody left."

"But not you?"

"Oh, I took off, too, for a while. I mean, we were family, and when your family packs up and moves away, you do, too. But I kept thinking about Rob and the garden and stuff, and after a while I just sort of found myself back here. And it was kinda empty-feeling, with everyone missing, but really, Rob needed somebody around who wasn't ripping him off, so I moved in. Jerry even gave me a kind of allowance. Or maybe it was David? Anyway, me and Rob have been here ever since. And just me, after the Trust."

"You ever see any of the other members of The Commons?"

"Sure, time to time they wash up here. And every so often I see a name on Facebook or something and realize it's someone who was there, so I get in touch, but you know, it was the past. Another country, like they say." He looked at her sadly, the thin, wistful boy of the snapshots peering out from an old man's face. "I guess we all grew up, and got busy with our lives."

"Can I ask you to look at some pictures, see if you can tell me anything about the people?"

"Sure." He patted his clothing and pulled out a pair of cheap reading glasses, settling them on his nose to bend over the first picture.

"Wow, that takes me back. We all look about ten years old."

"Who are those in the photograph, Mr. Albright?"

"Call me Wes. That's Rob and Meadow at the old place, in Oregon. Jeez, even in the summer it was kind of a mess, wasn't it? Those two kids belonged to Paolo and Pig." He looked up, startled. "Listen to me— 'belonged to.' Paolo would've beat the crap out of me for saying that kids 'belong' to their parents. Anyway, they did. And that's their mom, Pig. She used to snort so funny when she laughed. She laughed a lot."

"What about the other two men?"

He shook his head. "I don't remember them. It was Oregon, I guess those guys didn't come with us."

"Were there many who stayed behind?"

"Oh yeah, mostly the survivalists. You know about them? Didn't call them that then—but the guys with guns and revolution and end-of-the-world shit—real paranoia. It's one of the reasons Meadow and Pig and some of the others were happy to get out. The Estate was really mellow, all gardens and pot and sunshine instead of guns and hard stuff and mud."

"So there wasn't a lot of drug use here?"

"Not really, Rob and Meadow didn't like it," he said. "Just grass and acid. Someone brought peyote once—Jesus, that stuff's nasty."

She stifled a smile: he'd forgotten he was talking to a cop. She handed him the next photo, from Planting Day.

"Hey, here's me in the garden—man, it sure has changed, hasn't it?"

This was Annabelle's photo of the two men shifting the squash vines off the path. The one with the person who might be Michael Johnston. "Do you remember that other man?"

He squinted, raised it to the light. "We all had beards, we all dressed like that. Could be anyone."

"The note says his name is Mike," she prompted.

He turned it over, read the childlike script aloud: "'Mike and Wes moving the squash out of the path.' Nah, I don't remember him."

She handed him the next one, then started on the printouts. Some of his identifications confirmed what she had, but he did add several first names and even two surnames to the pages.

Her three random identities and both versions of Michael Johnston, mixed in with Mrs. Dalhousie's records, merely brought a shake of his head.

When he had finished, she retrieved the one of the path. "You're sure you don't remember this man?"

"Could've been someone who was just visiting. But Annabelle—oh, definitely. She was so great."

She was also on Raquel's list of blond potential victims. "Do you know how long after the festival she stayed?"

"Nah, she—wait. She had a kid, right? Sparrow, but we all called him The Bruiser. There was an aunt who showed up, I think just before. Nice lady. I think . . . did she maybe talk Annabelle into going home with her? Something about letting the kid spend the summer with his cousins. So yeah, it might've been then."

At the end, he handed the photos back with some reluctance. "I don't suppose you could give me copies of those?"

"You could ask Mrs. Dalhousie, these came from the Archives."

"Really? Huh, right here all the time. I'll ask Jen—Mrs. D is kind of scary. Anyway, you never said. Who is it that they found, under the statue?"

"We don't know yet. But whoever it was, they died right around the Midsummer's Eve festival."

"There was a ton of people here, that's for sure. And there was that fight, that Rob and the others had to break up? Maybe those guys . . . Nah, they couldn't have done anything like that, the cops came up and took them away. And I don't remember anybody coming to look for a friend who didn't make it home, like lost and found."

"So as far as you remember, it was only Meadow and Annabelle who disappeared that first day. And Fort."

"Yeah, but at least we heard from him. He used to send these really dumb picture postcards, elephants and temples and stuff, that said things like 'Wish you were here,' or 'Happy Christmas' in the middle of summer. But Meadow never even wrote, not that I ever heard."

"It must have been hard on Rob, to have his brother and his girl-friend go at the same time."

"I guess. He was drinking a lot. We wouldn't see him for days, and then when he did come down, he'd just argue with people. Even Rain only stuck around long enough to get the statue up, and then, like I say, everyone else split, too."

Wes was holding one of the snapshots. Its faded colors showed Meadow sitting on the terrace wall, the thriving gardens rising behind her. She was dressed in a short-sleeved dress heavy with Mexican em-broidery, her hair falling in the typical fashion of women in the seven-ties, glossy and parted in the center. She looked humorous and vital and absolutely certain of herself.

And the longing on Wes Albright's weather-beaten face made it per-fectly clear that he'd been in love with her his whole life.

"So, Meadow was Rob's lover," Raquel said, "though she'd been with Rain before Oregon. Did she share herself around?"

He blushed and put the photograph down. "She was mostly with Rob. And the two of them were so good together. He loved her so much. And she helped him through some weird shit."

"What weird shit?"

He looked away, clearly unwilling to talk about it.

"How was Rob weird, Wes?"

"Well, you know I said that in Oregon, there were the guys who turned into survivalists? For a while, in some ways, Rob seemed closer to them than the others."

"And yet you say he wasn't violent?"

"He wasn't. He'd get pissed off at something, but he'd go off to the woods for a while, or go chop a whole lot of firewood. It was more like—we all lived pretty close together then, even at night. And we'd sometimes hear him—nightmares, I guess. Meadow said it was because of Vietnam, and I know that happened, because I had a friend who came back just a heap of nerves, ended up killing himself. Rob wasn't like that, but he had problems. Just sometimes, until he learned to mellow out. Meadow helped him with that—we all did."

Until the mother dog snapped at the demands of her young? "Didn't she lose patience with him, sometimes?"

"She lost patience with everyone, some time or another. I mean, she was what I guess you'd call a feminist—we called them women's libbers. So one time, back in Oregon, she and some of the other girls got together and said it wasn't fair they did all the cooking and cleaning. That if we guys wanted to eat, we'd have to help out in the kitchen. And that was cool, but after that, they used to band together when time came to vote on things, even when the men wanted to do things one way. Like the way Rob didn't really want to leave Oregon until Meadow said he had to. But he was fine with it once everyone decided."

"Did that apply to Meadow sharing her affections with other men as well?"

Again with the blush.

"We all kind of shared, right? Moved around a little? I mean, it would've been weird if everyone but the two of them did. Tell you the truth, I don't know if Rob slept with anyone else. But yeah, Meadow did. She was mostly with him, but it was like she was proving something to him by sleeping with Rain or Paolo or . . . or me. Limiting yourself was wrong. Love was the whole world. Anyway, that's what we believed, back then." He thought about his words, and shook his head.

"Man, the world sure has changed, hasn't it?"

39

When Raquel had run out of questions for Wes, he sat for a minute, as if to realign his attention, then drifted away toward a vaguely described job that needed doing. One of the gardeners spotted him, approached, talked for a bit, and then Wes went off with him, job forgotten.

She took out her phone and texted Al.

Finished here.

Al was not a man to live with his phone in his hand, and she'd learned to expect a delay in his response. She gathered her things and made her way cautiously down the stairway to take another look at the house. Two women were talking loudly about the hell-mouth fireplace. Voices from the library suggested a school group. She paused in the foyer to study its idiosyncratic murals.

Dozens of faces looked out from its walls: rock stars and pop artists, commune farmers and literary oddities. Meadow and Rain, frozen in time. Wes, a ridiculously young version of the fuzzy gray-haired man she'd talked to. And was that Jerry? Yes, it had to be, hair red then instead of mostly white—clean-shaven, one of only half a dozen wearing a tie, but still looking comfortable among the longhairs and rebels.

What about cousin David, the not-quite-a-Gardener? She knew what he looked like, since his photo was in the Archives, but she didn't see him here. He'd have been younger than his two cousins, but was surely in his mid-twenties. Perhaps that person with the mustache, half-turned to speak to a woman dressed as a Renaissance queen.

She checked the detailed key that translated the foyer walls into outlines with numbers and identities, but the young man was one of the many unidentified.

The queen he was talking to, however, whose breasts threatened to spill out of their tight, low brocade, had become a US senator known for her rigidly conservative views.

Thoughtful, Raquel continued her circuit of the foyer. At the foot of the stairway, a huge slab of rusty steel was bolted to the wall, with words welded through the metal:

When Adam delved and Eve span, who then was the gentleman?
From the beginning, all were created alike.
Our bondage came with the oppression of the wicked.

—JOHN BALL

Adam and Eve. A new Eden, flowering from the bones of the old order.

A time of innocence.

A time with few defenses.

She thought about belief, how people could come together in the absolute and joyous conviction that what they did mattered. That the minutiae of their daily lives—the bean seeds they planted, the bread they ate—could change the world. Absurd, childlike, rendered melancholy by the intervening years.

Voices ebbed and flowed around her. The schoolkids were being lectured about the Green Room; the two women had moved on to discuss the library shelves. She ventured through an open door and found the ballroom, its Thomas Hart Benton panels on the upper half of the back wall looking slightly incongruous amidst the rococo trim. Beneath the figures was a low stage, complete with footlights. The ballroom seemed to be waiting for the curtains to rise and a merry crowd to wash in—and that corner, she realized, was where Katharine Hepburn had laughed in front of the Christmas tree, although there was no sign of Einstein's grand piano.

The suite given to the boys' mother must be on the other side of the Benton mural. Raquel wondered how often the woman had lain in her bed, listening to the tumult of an event through that wall.

Another door at the side of the stage led to a hallway with two locked doors, then to the library, dark and dignified, heavy with leather-bound volumes. Reception hall, restored to its 1930s glory but with a large picture of the fireplace when it was painted to resemble the mouth of hell. A note explained that the paint used had not proved long-lived, and restoration to its seventies state had proved, sadly, impossible.

Raquel, studying the gaping maw, could imagine the Trustees taking some care to ensure that the paint could not be restored.

Next came the dining room, thirty feet of gleaming mahogany and rigidly placed chairs. Paintings in gilt frames from the eighteenth and nineteenth centuries, crystal chandeliers, a small marble fireplace at either end, velveteen drapes arranged in perfect rhythm along the outer walls of French doors, leading out to the terrace and garden.

The stars and tycoons of forties Hollywood, she thought, *would have felt right at home.*

Her phone pinged. Al:

Me too. Pick me up, we can talk before MJ?

She hesitated. Their appointment with Johnston was not until four o'clock. That left plenty of time for lunch with Jen Bachus. She liked Jen, and certainly there was much she could still learn from her about this place.

So why the hesitation? Why the . . .

Distaste, her mind provided.

Because cops didn't socialize with witnesses?

No. Because this cop did not want to look across a table at Jen Bachus while knowing what waited for her in a hospital room twenty miles to the south.

Because she didn't want to create a link of any kind between the manager of the Gardener Estate and a man who collected shoes from the feet of dead women.

Raquel thumbed in her response:

Half an hour.

And dropped her phone in her pocket.

She paused briefly at the door to the Green Room—a windowless hideaway with dark green armchairs, pale sage walls, and generous touches of emerald in the carpets. Even the doily thing along the length of the mantelpiece was tinted aqua.

And that was the Gardener mansion. She walked down the hallway and through the door marked EMPLOYEES ONLY, to the manager's office.

Jen sat with her head in her hands, her desk strewn with the contents of an international-express mailer: glossy brochures, colorful folders, and assorted tourist-shop odds and ends. The manager was either deep in thought or gathering her strength.

Before Raquel could decide whether to knock or go quietly away, voices rang out from down the hall. Jen straightened and saw Raquel in the doorway.

"Hi, sorry, I was miles away. What can I—oh, lunch. I offered you lunch. What time is it? Heavens, you should have come and got me. You must be starving."

She was already on her feet and moving around her desk, ignoring Raquel's raised hand.

"No, I just came to tell you that I have to go. Something came up."

"Oh. I'm sorry. When will—I mean, are you coming back?"

"I imagine so. I still need to speak with David and Rob."

"Of course. Monday, then. Though any time you want a personal tour. Or something."

"That's very nice of you, but I can see how busy you are."

"God, no, if I don't get away from this, I'll commit murder. Hmm, probably not the best thing to say to a Homicide detective. What I mean is, I'd be happy for a distraction."

"Is this to do with those brochures and decorative keychains?"

Jen looked at her in surprise. "How did you guess?"

"They appear to trouble you."

"Certainly they depress me." She scooped up the mailing box and began to shovel the booklets and keychains back inside. "This place costs a fortune to maintain. We manage to just break even, most years, but it's always close, and the last two years have been a real problem. David came up with the idea to turn us into a combination concert venue and corporate retreat center. Part of that involves, as he puts it, 'establishing the Gardener brand.'"

She jabbed a pen in on top of the rest, and dropped the box into a desk drawer, looking up with a crooked smile.

"I just want people to come and enjoy the garden."

That afternoon, Michael Johnston gave them Laurel: blond, hippie, hitchhiking down in Monterey. She'd taken him to the commune she lived in near Tassajara. He'd stayed a few days and moved on, tipping her body over the cliffs into the ocean. She'd washed up in Cambria a few days later: September 1980.

40

Jen Bachus sat back in her chair, eyes shut, and listened as the long day ebbed away from the Gardener Estate. Voices went past at a distance—two of the garden staff making weekend plans, their energy undimmed by eight hours of physical labor. Had she ever been that young? A vacuum cleaner somewhere, cutting off when a door closed. Slow footsteps on the gravel path outside her window: Rafi taking his customary end-of-day survey, checking his beloved beds for dropped possessions, offending litter, and signs of illicit cuttings.

And beneath the human intrusions, the weight of a solid old house settling in for the night.

Every so often, Jen would stay here overnight. It was against the rules, but neither Wes nor the drive-by guard service had ever asked why her car stayed in the parking lot. She didn't do it often, and always tidied away any signs of her intrusion, but there were times when going home was just more than she could face. Times when she wanted to lose herself in other people's lives, sleep in their beds, breathe in the faint trace of lavender that the pillows retained. Listen to the echoes of their voices, stern or loving.

Not tonight.

She sighed, and opened the office laptop. While it loaded up the afternoon's email, she walked down to the kitchen to make a cup of instant coffee and raid the fridge for leftovers that would do for dinner.

Business emails about group reservations, arguments over the cost of a tour, a plea to fit in a last-minute wedding because any later and the bride would be showing. A brisk and friendly email from a counterpart in Britain, a longer friendly chat from another colleague in Australia (winter there, hence more time on the woman's hands). Confirmation from David that he was flying back to California on Saturday and would see her Monday. A note from Mrs. Dalhousie that would have startled someone who only knew the archivist professionally, since its grasp of social media and modern slang would have done justice to a high school student.

Jen liked her job. She loved the Estate, she was proud of its history and its future, and the other longtime employees felt like family. She even enjoyed the wild variety of tasks and voices she found in her in-box every day, which sometimes made her crazy, but never made her bored.

Her quick typing shot replies around the globe, forwarded messages to other people on the Estate, transferred dates to half a dozen different calendars. At the end of the hour, she had two emails in the drafts folder and an otherwise empty in-box.

She sat back, looking through the window at the dusk. Only the white flowers stood out, mostly the long, uneven cloud of the climbing Noisette cultivar named after Maude Gardener (by what Rafi claimed was a grudging head gardener, who'd wanted to call it after his own wife). And then it, too, began to fade, until all Jen saw was the reflection of her desk light in the glass.

She gave another sigh, and turned back to the screen-saver image of that same garden on her computer. After a minute, she opened a browser and typed a name into the search bar: Raquel Laing, SFPD.

The top links were recent articles about The Highwayman, which included Inspector Laing in a list of contacts to write with information regarding Michael Johnston or one of the victims. Beneath them was a YouTube link of the recent Highwayman press conference, which the search engine seemed to have kicked up because of the SFPD reference, rather than the investigator's name.

Jen clicked on it, and watched it for a minute before speeding forward through speeches by the mayor of San Francisco, the FBI, and various police officers, announcing the arrest of a suspect and something about a task force—and then she stopped, and reversed it.

A short, amber-eyed woman with a cane was standing at the back, mostly hidden from the camera behind an older man with a nice face. She'd moved forward to hear something he was saying. They talked for a minute, his head tucked down behind one hand, her eyes staying on the podium. After a brief conversation, she nodded at something he said, then faded into the background again.

Jen let the video run to its end, then went back to the search page, hovering the cursor over the IMAGES button.

Then she closed it out and shut the laptop.

Don't be a stalker, she told herself.

41

When Raquel pulled to the curb in front of Al's house, she left the engine running.

"Why don't you come in," he said.

"If I do, it'll just spoil Jani's evening."

"Jani's off with the grandkids on spring break, and you don't look fit to drive home. Did you eat today?"

"Sure."

"Which means you don't remember. Take the keys out of the car, Inspector Laing, and come inside."

If she went home, she could have a shower and a drink. On the other hand, if she went home, she'd have to look at twelve blank pages on the wall. She took out the keys, and followed him in.

Al's wife still taught the occasional seminar at Stanford, and often invited groups of students home. It was a place of ideas and fellowship, untidy but clean, colorful but oddly soothing.

It smelled of family.

Raquel excused herself to spend a long time in Al's guest bathroom, scrubbing her hands and face, rubbing in some faintly lemony hand cream that helped take the hospital out of her pores. When she came out, he was dividing a large pan of scrambled eggs onto two plates, with toast that glittered with butter.

"What did the sheriff—" she started, but he cut her off.

"Eat first, then talk," he ordered, and handed her a fork.

Neither of them said a word until the plates were empty and Al was pouring coffee into a pair of mugs.

"No sign yet of an O'Donnell arrested for rape on San Mateo's books," he said. "They're going to look for similar names, see if we can find him, and if not I'll reach out to Berkeley."

"If this one turns out not to be Johnston, we can at least give your friend an alternative."

"Tell me about the Gardener Estate," he said.

"It's quite a setup. Hard to imagine it filled with hippies."

"It really was a commune, then? Long hair, free love?"

"Oh yes. You haven't been there?"

"Jani took me to some function, a million years ago. A wedding maybe? But I think it was mostly in the garden."

"It was a working commune, organic vegetables and all. But it was also a place where important musicians and artists stopped by, on their way through the Bay Area. In fact—would you like to look at a video? The archivist gave me a thumb drive this morning, I haven't had a chance to watch it."

"Sure," he said.

She dug out the drive and her laptop, and a minute later, the screen filled with a video version of the photo she'd seen, of hippies sitting on the ground, wearing jeans and vests and ankle-length skirts. She froze it, enlarging the display to zero in on some of the key characters—there was Meadow, and Wes. That pale head must be Annabelle. No sign of Rain's distinctive beard, although there was a nearly clean-shaven young man in the background, looking awkward. Nor did she see anyone resembling Michael Johnston. She pointed out those she recognized, then returned the picture to full screen and let it play.

Dramatic views of the hills, a sweep along the grasslands, that solid-looking hedge concealing the formal gardens, the hidden gate that she and Jen Bachus had come through—and a stage, as incongruous as a beached fishing boat, where the body had been found.

She stopped the play again, and told Al what he was seeing. "That's where they found the bones. The stage was temporary, over where the concrete base was going."

But between the stage itself and its fabric skirt, there was nothing to see of what lay underneath. She started it up again, paused it when the camera flipped around and was filled with the diabolically grinning face of Rain, and ran it again.

The next forty minutes were taken up with the festival itself, primarily the music. After a bit, she speeded it up, and let it run until the scenery changed: an interior setting. She stopped the play and recognized the ballroom, where a party was going on. A woman with big hair and smeared makeup blew a cloud of dope at the camera. In the background, someone was bent over a mirror with white lines on it. The center of the room was a sea of dancing figures, pulsing to the beat of recorded music.

She caught glimpses of those she knew, with the camera lingering on Meadow, sharing a joint with an alarmingly thin, crop-haired woman, both of them laughing. One bearded man at the edge of things turned away just as the camera came to him: was that Rob Gardener? But he was gone, and the ballroom's stage passed by, occupied by a remarkably clean-cut David Kirkup and the music system. A few minutes later, the Rolling Stones gave way to the Woodstock song—which wasn't popular with the dancers or the person filming. After some catcalls, the picture flew back and forth, then shut off entirely.

That was the end.

"Well, that sure makes me feel old," Al said.

"I'll go over it more closely, and I'll see if I can narrow down the time frame, but for sure Meadow was still alive. However, I didn't see Michael Johnston, in either section of it."

"I didn't, either."

"There was one person in a photo that might be him, but neither of the people I talked to today recognized him. The last surviving Gardener and his cousin aren't available till Monday, but I do have a list of others who lived there, to start in on." *I may need to go back to the Estate before Monday,* she thought. "I'm tempted to push matters, and insist on seeing Rob Gardener. He was the owner during the commune time—he's a hermit now, lives in a far corner of the Estate. But he can't be completely unreachable."

"Why not push?"

"Both the Estate manager and its lawyer are very protective of him. If I insist, they may start talking about warrants."

Al nodded. "Probably better to hold off."

"Tomorrow we give Johnston our last name. I don't think we can wait."

"I just had a message from Los Gatos saying that their cadaver dog may have found something."

"What, already?"

"Another bar. An outside patio, fortunately, and it went in in 1973, so they're not screaming about tearing it up."

"That's two bars now, and a motel. You think he picked them because of the poem? 'The Highwayman comes riding, riding, up to the old inn-door'?"

"If so, you'd expect him to stick to women with raven hair."

"But even if the dogs have found something, that would only take us to Saturday."

"Unless he gets sick again and his doctor won't let us in."

Or unless he dies. "I'll start on Jen's list first thing in the morning, her weaver and glassblower. If any of them recognize Johnston's face, I say we give him Eve."

"Who's Eve?"

"Sorry—shorthand. The Gardener body was found under a statue of Eve."

"Got it. Sure, and I'm happy to divide your list or go with, either one. More coffee?"

"No, that was enough. Thank you for the food."

"Fresh start tomorrow."

"Always." She watched him clear away the cups, load the dishwasher, wipe up the crumbs from the table. "Al, you were too young for Vietnam, weren't you?"

"By a few years, yeah. My older brother went."

"So, Rob Gardener. He enlisted after high school, served in the final years, came home in 1972, had a slightly violent falling-out with his grandfather and left home, ended up at a commune in Oregon, and then, when the grandfather died in 1975, moved that commune down to the Estate. Four years later, something happened that changed it all: His lover left him, his brother moved permanently off to India, and the commune disbanded. Gardener lived in the house, mostly on his own, until he gave it over to a trust and moved to his cabin up in the woods. Where, as I understand, he sometimes waves a shotgun at would-be intruders."

"Okay."

"So what should I expect, when I talk with him? Would you say there are some PTSD issues at play?"

"There's sure to be, to some extent."

"Well, I suppose that if he's gone fifty years without going on a rampage, he's probably not going to turn his shotgun on me."

"Don't bet on it."

"Al, the man's seventy-some years old."

"Yeah, and there may be a reason why he's lived by himself in the woods. Just because you don't see any fire in old men doesn't mean it's not smoldering underground, waiting for air."

"Really?"

He grinned at her. "Nah, probably not. But if you're talking to him and things start feeling wrong, thank the man nicely and walk away. You can always return with backup."

42

Friday.

There was no point in driving back down to the Gardener Estate. Raquel had the names—recalled by Jen and filled out by Wes, Jerry, and Mrs. Dalhousie—of people who might remember life during the commune years.

She reminded herself that, this early in an investigation, she should feel that she was drifting aimlessly. Drifting was an essential, if frustrating, part of the process, allowing her to map the actual contours and characteristics of the landscape instead of setting off in a pre-chosen direction. Yes, this left her torn, between a tight commitment to Michael Johnston and a broad sweep of what the Gardener Estate had to tell her, but facts would become clear and a route would take shape.

Unless it turned out that there was no link at all between the man and the place.

She retrieved Jen's torn-out page, and ran her thumb along the left side where she'd hidden the ragged edge with a sharp fold. She laid beside it the lined page with her own writing, noting the details she'd found. *Rob, of course,* Jen had started, bent over the picnic table with her hair across her face. David Kirkup, Jerry Rathford, Wes Albright.

Rafi Bautista, the groundsman, whose grandmother had worked for the Gardeners for decades. "Ned" had a line through it, when Jerry said he'd died two years ago. Travis Patterson, an organic farmer near Gilroy. Sylvan Tracy, the Berkeley potter, and two weavers who lived up near Tahoe, Sarah and Kim, whose surnames were not on the card they'd left with Jen one summer.

The ones she really wanted were Meadow, Rain, and Annabelle— but Rain-formerly-Reynard had died in 2005, while Annabelle Paulson and Meadow aka Christine (Jerry Rathford's secretary had yet to dig her surname out from the files) could be anywhere.

Still, she began with those, typing up all the information she had, attaching any photographs she'd scanned or snapped from the Archives, and adding it to the task force folder.

By which time an email had dropped into her in-box, with a sender name Arachne Weaving:

> Hi Raquel, yes definitely I'm the weaver who lived on the Gardener commune during the 70s—what a long time ago that seems! I'm up here in Truckee with my partner, Kim, who was also there for a couple of years, and we'd be happy to talk. (Though I don't think Kim will be much help, she's not doing too great, poor love, and her memory goes in and out.)
>   Like you said in your note, it's a long drive from the Bay Area, and video is fine—our wifi isn't great, but we can try, and mornings seem a little better (both for the machine and for Kim).

Forty seconds later, Sarah herself was on Raquel's laptop screen: a surprised old woman in a bright purple bathrobe, sitting at a kitchen table with a handmade mug, her wispy white hair having not seen a comb yet that day.

"Well," the weaver said. "No time like the present, I see."

Should I have confirmed first? "I can call back later, if you like."

"If you don't mind looking at me, this is as good as any. You're Raquel Laing?"

"With the San Francisco Police Department, yes. The manager of the Gardener Estate showed me the card you'd left with her, a year or two ago."

"Kim and I went down for a couple of days—MOMA had a show with one of her pieces, and we spent the weekend poking around our old haunts. Our last trip out before she had her stroke."

"I'm sorry." *Was that the right response?* It seemed to be.

"Don't be, we had a lovely time. Jen Whatsis showed us all around."

"Bachus."

"Right. How different the place looks now. So formal and cold. A bit sad, really."

"How long did you live there?"

"I came down from Oregon with the others, nineteen seventy . . . five, I think it was? I met Kim two years later, she lived there, too, for a year or so, but after that we moved to Berkeley."

"So you weren't there that last spring, in 1979?" *Disappointment.*

"On and off, sure. Just not full-time. Oops, hold on a minute, I have to help— Kimmy?" The purple robe flew across the screen and disappeared, leaving Raquel with a view of a farmhouse kitchen that was either a deliberate parody, or had not been changed since it was last remodeled in the era of avocado appliances. She could hear their voices, Sarah's calm and low, the other woman's higher-pitched. After a minute, the bathrobe was back, joined by another woman who was even thinner, older, and more unkempt.

"Sit down and talk to this nice lady for a minute, sweetheart, while I get you some tea," Sarah said. "Her name is Raquel. She's interested in the Gardener place. The Commons, remember?"

The ancient face came close to the screen, screwed up to study Raquel's features. She was missing some of her front teeth. "Hello," Raquel said, stifling the urge to move back.

"Raquel," the terrible old woman said. "Gorgeous eyes you have."

"Er, thank you."

The face abruptly grew smaller as their camera lens was pulled away. From the side came a hand holding a pair of fluorescent pink glasses. "Kimmy, don't tease the poor girl, put on your specs and talk to her nicely."

The old lady cackled, slid on the circular frames, and transformed from a dreadful harbinger of deterioration to a maker of mischief.

"But you do have nice eyes," she said, her own crinkling up with the joke.

"So I am told," Raquel said.

Sarah came back to the table, adjusted the camera to show them both, two old partners, shoulder to shoulder with their steaming cups.

"I'm looking for someone who might have been a visitor, or even a resident, during that last year of the commune, 1979."

The glasses turned to the other woman. "Were we still there?"

"No, we were with the collective by then, but that was when they were putting together the big festival, and we went over a few times for that."

"The *Eves*!" Kim exclaimed. "What fun that was! What was that madwoman's name?"

"Gaddo," her partner reminded her.

"Right—we called her Gadabout. She hated that."

"She wanted everyone to think of her as Solemn and Important."

Fortunately, Sarah dragged the discussion back to where Raquel needed it. "But Raquel isn't interested in Gaddo, I don't think. Who was it you were after, honey?"

"Let me show you his face." Raquel retrieved the two images of Michael Johnston—one with a mustache, the other with a beard—and transferred them onto the screen.

Two white heads came forward, two sets of eyes squinted at their device on the table.

Sarah sat back first, shaking her head. "It's not someone I remember."

Kim tipped back her head—bifocals?—and said, "Can you make it . . . ?" Sarah's hand came near the camera to expand the image. "The mustache, maybe."

Raquel retrieved the single image of Johnston with the mustache and replaced the composite with that. But Kim ended up shaking her head. "He looks, I don't know. Little bells, maybe, but I couldn't tell you where I'd seen him."

"Or even if?" Sarah asked.

"Or even if," her partner agreed, sadly.

The two women agreed to think about it, and if anything came to mind, they would get in touch. And they'd make a search through the old photos they had, though there weren't many from that period. "We weren't really into possessions, you know?" Neither had any idea what had become of Meadow or Annabelle, although they did come up with a number for Joni Longwood, daughter of Paolo and Pig, who might have kept in touch with the younger generation.

Raquel added Joni to her list, thanked the women, and went on to the next name.

But the possible "little bells" memory of one dotty old stroke victim was the closest she came to Michael Johnston that day. At two in the afternoon, she closed her laptop and sat, feeling the buzz of frustration.

Nearly half the pages Mrs. Dalhousie had printed out now had the laconic word *Deceased* at the top.

Of the eleven men and women she'd talked to that day, four thought the guy with the mustache looked vaguely familiar, two said the same of the bearded version, and five just shook their heads and told her it was too long ago. All promised to look through their old photos and let Raquel know what showed up.

About the other residents, two of them agreed: Annabelle Paulson had been from Texas. One had been in touch with her for a few years, but not since the nineties.

All eleven remembered Meadow. Only one produced the name Chris as an alternative, but no surname. Two had seen her after The Commons years, one of those across a crowded airport, probably Atlanta, the other at a village in the south of France. This one started out quite hopeful, as he launched into detail about the conversation they'd had, but as the topics of that conversation began to wind on—Meadow had talked about honey, and cheesemaking, or perhaps it was candles? Or was hers that stall in the market that sold local jams, rather than honey?—the lead became less firm than she had hoped.

Before leaving the house, she made another call: the bar patio in

Los Gatos where the cadaver dog had showed interest was being slowly peeled back, but nothing yet.

Friday afternoon traffic was building, as she drove south to pick up Al and continue to the hospital.

In the hallway outside Johnston's room, Al made his own call to the Los Gatos team. His face told her the answer.

"Nothing?"

"Floor's mostly up, they're working their way down now."

"They do know there's a time factor?"

"They know." He put away his phone and looked at the door. "And if the bastard gives us that bar as his bonus name, it's going to get them all fired."

But Michael Johnston did not get the team fired. Instead, the withering creature in the bed accepted the task force's last identified Highwayman victim, Windy Jackson, and gave them a girl named Mandy, picked up outside a health food store in Redwood City, left beneath a huge parking lot job in Milpitas, June 1978.

He'd cut that one short, he said, because it was his daughter's birthday, and he'd promised to take her out for dinner.

Raquel drove home, and printed the name Mandy on the next blank sheet.

Eleven pages yet to fill.

43

Saturday.

Raquel hadn't really slept last night. The stir of dread, the buzz of tension, the tick of the clock, time pressing close. Johnston's eyes, already bloodshot, had been going yellow, a sign that his organs were beginning to fail.

She drank coffee, checked the group's shared folder, looked through her junk mail in case a witness response had gone astray. Nothing.

The Los Gatos team would start again at nine o'clock.

At ten, she'd heard nothing, and started working her way through a Google search linking Annabelle, Meadow, or Christine with the name Gardener.

At eleven, she had a note from Al to say that the "O'Donnell" they were looking for was Max O'Connor, currently serving a ten-year sentence for aggravated assault, having bashed his neighbor over the head in a drunken argument over dog shit.

Noon.

She made more coffee. Dee came in as she was waiting for it to brew, and stood, saying nothing.

"No," Raquel said, not looking at her. "I don't want your help."

"I understand. But the Señora next door needs yours. You promised to walk her dog, every week."

"I don't have time."

"You do. And you need air or you're going to explode. Take your phone, you won't miss anything."

"I hate you."

"Go."

The dog was so old, even Raquel's short and hampered pace had it half dragging behind her at the end of its leash. She stopped three times to check her in-box. On the third stop, the creature just looked at her from its collapse on the ground. If it didn't smell so bad, she'd have picked it up . . . but instead she used the moment of hesitation to think.

And sat on the low wall nearby.

Michael Johnston.

Nineteen shoes.

Concrete. Hitchhiking.

(*Had he worked for a contractor during his years in Mexico?*)

The Gardener Estate.

A victim laid under *Midsummer Eves*.

The join between them did not feel seamless, although Raquel could not have said why.

The dog snored. Kids ran around the playground across the way. San Francisco on a sunny weekend.

Her phone rang. The caller's name showed as Gardener Estate.

"Raquel Laing," she answered.

"Oh hi, I wasn't sure if you'd be working or—this is Jen. Bachus."

"Yes, Jen."

"I know it's the weekend, and you're probably busy, but I just wanted to say that if you *weren't* busy, and if you felt like taking me up on my offer of a tour of the Estate, I'll be here all weekend. Backup, you know—although things seem to be going fairly smoothly today, thank goodness. Anyway, the garden is so spectacular, even with the crowds, plus that there's a kind of grotto up along the creek that never gets as many people and the native azalea up there might be in bloom, which can be just magical. There's a road most of the way," she hastened to add. "You wouldn't have to hike cross-country, just some path and it's not very—"

But the phone had begun to beep in her ear, another call coming in.

"Jen, I need to put you on hold," she interrupted. Then, "This is Raquel."

"Los Gatos found her," Al said.

"Shoes?"

"No sign of a right shoe."

Raquel had to rest her phone on her leg for a minute, under the surge of relief. When she raised it, Al was in the middle of a sentence.

"—he swore he'd talk to the press himself and tell them how we were mistreating a prisoner."

"Can you repeat that, Al? There was a bus. Going by."

"I said, his doctor wants to give him a transfusion and sedate him for the rest of the day. And says if we show up and attempt to interview him, he'll report us to the press."

"You think Johnston is playing us?"

"The doctor doesn't, so there's not much we can do unless we want to try and get him taken off the case."

"When we come to an end, which one of us gets to hold a pillow over his face?"

"Assuming you mean Johnston, you'll have to join the line."

"Tomorrow, then. What time?"

"Doctor says noon."

"Pick you up at half-past eleven?"

"See you then."

Raquel lifted her face to the sun. The girl in Los Gatos would be number nine, and reward them with a tenth name as well.

If Johnston was still alive at noon tomorrow.

She remembered Jen then, but there was no call, patiently waiting for her to return. Her thumb hovered over redial, but then she closed out the phone and shifted to text:

Things are a little crazy, magical azaleas will have to wait.

Jen's response came:

Sorry to hear, but I understand.

Well, she thought as she tugged the old dog to his feet, *at least I've heard of azaleas.*

That text was as good as Saturday got.

On Sunday, three teams of cadaver dogs would set out, to three possible sites that Michael Johnston might have worked on. She didn't need Al to point out how lucky they'd been with the Los Gatos girl. Between the years that had gone by and the arbitrary nature of their search, the odds were minuscule that they would find another that way.

She and Dee had argued on Saturday night, and Raquel intended to keep out of her sister's way. Instead, early in the morning, Dee opened the office door and walked in—a thing she never, ever did. This was Raquel's private world, 120 square feet of official SFPD values and structures. Dee's eyes flicked briefly over the precise line of pages on the wall before she picked up the cat's chair and moved it across the desk from Raquel.

"Rock, what is going on?"

"I can't tell you, Dee, you know that."

"I'm not asking you for case details. I know it's The Highwayman. But you have to tell me what has you jumping out of your skin."

Raquel straightened the cards on her desk, then consulted the ten awful blank sheets. In the end, she lowered her gaze to meet Dee's concerned eyes. "You can't tell. If it gets out, I'm finished."

"Of course not."

She jerked her chin at the line on the wall. "He's claiming nineteen."

"*Nineteen* victims? Jesus, Rock."

At least her online buddies hadn't picked up on that yet, Raquel thought. Small satisfaction. "We've caught four, maybe five. I found a way to get four or five more out of him. But we might not get the rest."

"Is there anything—"

"No. We have people on it, Dee. Hands off."

"Just saying, if."

"If I can't do this by the rules, I can't do it period."

Her sister nodded and stood, replacing the chair in the corner. But she paused to study Raquel's detailed craniofacial map, like a flayed homicide victim looking over the detective's shoulder. "You need a way to take your mind off it for a bit. You know that helps."

"I'm not taking the Señora's dog for another walk."

"Drive out and throw rocks in the ocean. Walk down to that burrito place and bring back lunch. Go to the shooting range and demolish some paper targets. Anything, to let your mind step back."

The door closed.

After a while, Raquel reached for her phone and found the number.

"Hi," Jen answered.

"Do you like cookies?"

"For breakfast? Sure."

"Breakfast?" *What time is it, anyway?* "Were you asleep?"

"No, I had to answer the phone. Or lunch, whatever's good for you."

"I have to be in San Jose at noon."

"Breakfast, then, on your way down. I'll buy the coffee."

"What time?"

"We open at ten. I'll be on the café terrace."

Raquel found her under the big magnolia, the table next to the one where she and Jerry had talked. But when she handed Jen the box of cookies she'd stopped to buy, breakfast nearly ended up on the ground. Jen caught the box, set it on the table, then raised its lid to study the contents with what seemed a great deal of attention.

Maybe packing a large-sized box to the brim was a little . . . exces-sive, Raquel thought.

"I found it hard to choose," she explained.

"I thought maybe, a couple of croissants."

"Do you prefer croissants?"

"These look great. Though I may leave some of them in the break room, afterward."

"Good idea."

"What kind of coffee you want?"

Some ninety minutes later, Raquel decided that her sister had been right.

Her brain was clear, her mood improved, and she could face the drive south without a sensation that the dread was going to suffocate her.

And all she'd done was eat sweet things and listen to Jen talk. About the Estate and her brother and a short-lived marriage some years before, about the long summer in Europe that had changed her life and all the places on her dream list. About why she loved this garden—any garden, really, but given her limited income—"I have a manor-house taste but an apartment-house salary"—this had become hers by proxy, to be groomed and encouraged and created alongside the gardening staff, with all the suffering and apprehension and celebration growing things entailed.

A waitress refreshed their cups. Jen ate three cookies—she liked oatmeal raisin and the things with peanuts on the top, Raquel noted— and told her about the book she was writing about Isabella Worn, an early California landscape gardener who had worked with Julia Morgan on Hearst Castle, and consulted here with the Terrible Maude.

And when Raquel's eyes slid over to her phone, Jen broke off. "You have to go."

"I do."

"I didn't show you the azaleas."

"Another time."

"Well, I guess we'll see you tomorrow, anyway. So you can talk to David and Rob. David made it home, by the way, jet-lagged as hell though he swears he'll be fine in the morning. And Rob will hike down in the afternoon, though please don't keep him any later than five— I hate to think of him wandering around the hills after dark. But look, as for today, do you know when you'll be finished? I know you live in San Francisco, and you probably have things you need to get back to there, but if you happen to be just turning around and heading back after your appointment, you could, you know . . . hop off the freeway again and come look at the azaleas. If you feel like it. Anyway, I'll be around till closing. If you're coming by, just shoot me a text." She smiled shyly. "Just a thought."

44

Michael Johnston accepted the bones under the Los Gatos bar as one of his. "She was one of the early ones—number two, I think it was. Spring of 1970. Stupid chick called herself Janis, but I'm sure that wasn't her name. She was hitching out of Santa Cruz with this massive guitar and a bottle of that booze. Southern Comfort. Sang songs and swigged from the bottle all the way over 17, drove me crazy. That was before I used to keep a shovel in the trunk, so I had to stop at a hardware store and get one. She was snoring when I got back to the car. Ugly sound that is, a drunk woman snoring. Anyway, there was a place on the pour schedule just down the road—talk about meant to be. So I left her as soon as it was dark, and I helped smooth the concrete over her, first thing Monday morning. I gave her guitar to the secretary at the company. Used to make me laugh, every time she thanked me."

Raquel kept any reaction from her face as she noted down the details of date and shoes and the rest. When information had descended to mere swagger, she asked for his matching name.

"Which one?"

"Well, if Janis was an early one, give us a later one."

"Why?"

"Contrast? It doesn't matter, you choose."

"No, okay, the second from last."

"The one before Tamara. Who was your last before leaving for Mexico."

"Sweet of you to remember my girls," he leered.

Oh, Mr. Johnston, she thought. *The rest of my life, I will remember every word you say, every shift in your voice, every faint twitch on your face.*

"That was a really good one. A hippie chick, even though the hippies were mostly gone by then. All the girls were big hair and giant shoulder pads. Either that or exercise clothing, Jane Fonda wannabees. Ugly as shit. Anyway, this one was like something from the sixties, all flowers and beads and even a headband—not that she was old enough. She couldn't have been more than twenty, though she acted about twelve. Come to think of it, there might have been something wrong with her. At the time, I figured she was just stoned out of her gourd. Anyway, she called herself Rainbow Joy, so good luck finding her with that."

"Was she hitching a ride?"

"By that time, there weren't a lot of girls thumbing rides all on their lonesome. Few years earlier, we all hitched, all over the place. That made it so easy, when you had a car. No, by then I had to keep my ear out for chicks looking for rides. Like, headed for LA or something, you'd tell them hey, I'm going to San Diego, want a lift? By the time anyone noticed she hadn't shown up, they'd forgotten what you looked like. Anyway, Rainbow girl had a sister in Portland, good old friendly Mike is going to Seattle, can he drop you off?"

"Where is she now?"

"You'll love this one. She's under a statue." Raquel felt Al stiffen, but— "They were pouring at a playground and had this thing like a pirate ship for kids to climb on. I thought good old Rainbow would like the mermaid."

"When was this?"

"Couple weeks before Christmas, 1979. Took six months or so for people to notice she hadn't got to Portland. That's when the Highwayman name started getting tossed around a lot. And frankly, things started getting more difficult. I hung on till the next year, then a buddy invited me to this place he had in Guadalajara. I liked it there, so I stayed for a while."

And with that, as if a switch had been turned, Johnston ran out of energy. His mottled scalp sagged into the pillow, his jaw dropped, he panted, looking ten years older.

Raquel hesitated, and met Al's eyes. He cocked his head at the door, and she had to agree.

On the elevator down, Raquel did a Google search, turning her phone to show Al. "There's two kids' parks with pirate ships. The one in Sunnyvale has a mermaid."

"Good work."

"There was something else. Something he said."

"What?"

"I don't know. It caught the corner of my mind, but it didn't stick."

"It'll come. At three A.M."

Not a lot of girls thumbing rides.

We all hitched, all over. That made it so easy.

Something . . .

Let your mind step back.

She drove Al home, aware that he was talking about Jani, aware too that it was nothing she needed to reply to beyond the occasional grunt of encouragement. The one thing she did register was that he'd heard that the San Mateo coroner hoped to work on the bones on Tuesday, or Wednesday at the latest. She shook her head, but said nothing.

Then she was alone in the car, out in front of his house. *Let your mind step back,* Dee had said.

And maybe she'd been wrong, to force a distance between Michael Johnston and the Gardener Estate. Jen Bachus moved through a world where gardens grew, where beauty waited, where men and women had tried to create a new world. Maybe building a wall acknowledged a danger, giving it power. Maybe Jen was strong enough to stand on her own. Maybe Michael Johnston and his Highwayman fantasies could not touch her.

Trust your emotions, Dee would suggest. The problem was, how to pin down what those emotions were. By way of experiment, she thumbed in a text:

I'm free to look at azaleas, if you're there in half an hour?

And studied it for a while. How was her body reacting to the idea of pressing SEND? Panic and dread, or confidence? She let her thumb hover over the button, waiting for the pulse of reaction to snatch it away. Instead, it touched the button, and off the message went.

To which Jen replied:

Pick me up in front of the house.

The carrier bag at Jen's feet was well filled and emblazoned with the Gardener Estate logo. She dropped it onto the backseat and got in beside Raquel. "Figured you might be ready for something more substantial than cookies. Though I brought those, too. Go back down the drive toward the gates, I'll show you where to turn off."

Past the brick wall enclosing the service yard, away from the laurel hedge and the faceless *Midsummer Eves,* a sprinkling of families at the picnic tables, walking the Great Field.

"Here, where it says NO ACCESS."

The surface was uneven, but passable, ending in a small graveled parking lot. "This is my second-favorite place on the Estate," Jen told her, and got out to fetch the bag.

The path was long-established, and came out in what could indeed best be described as a grotto. There would be a stream running through here in the rainy season, and everything was still damp enough to smell of water.

Here and there, tiny splashes of orange were opening up, but the sight made Jen sigh with disappointment. "Oh, sorry, it hasn't been quite warm enough. Another week and it'll be spectacular."

Raquel leaned on her cane, breathing in the air, listening to her companion's feet crunching across to the rustic table.

"Not spectacular," she agreed. "But I can see the magic."

From the intensity of pleasure on the manager's face, Raquel might have handed her a small and adorable kitten. The expression made her think back, to an earlier look of pleasure broken by a quick twitch of disappointment.

"Your second-favorite place. Is your favorite just outside the hedge, at the top of the hill?"

The small and adorable kitten might have just sprouted gossamer wings. "Yes! I love that moment, stepping through the hidden gate into the outer world. It gets me, every time."

Jen turned and happily began to unpack the bag, setting out a bottle of white wine and two glasses, a block of creamy-looking cheese and a bag of crackers. "Everyone gobbled up the strawberries, I should've grabbed a box earlier. Though I should have asked—do you drink?"

"A small glass, thanks."

Raquel sat, Jen poured, they picked up their glasses, and Jen raised hers. "To friendship."

But as Raquel drank to the sentiment, she wondered if there had been just the briefest hesitation between the two words. As if Jen Bachus wasn't too sure about the nature of this . . . friendship, either.

The cheese was good, the crackers baked in the Estate kitchen. The natural history of azaleas was discussed. The more recent history of this particular place was also given: the commune used to use this grove as a full-moon drumming circle—the Trust had to remove the fire pit in the center, for fear of encouraging modern visitors—but they'd also found signs of Native American occupancy right here, including a mortar and pestle that was now in the Bancroft Museum.

"We were happy for them to take it," Jen said. "We have a bunch of them already—the commune used to find them all over."

"Do you suppose they tried grinding their own grain with them?"

"I think the Native Americans used them for acorns, and I can't imagine even hippies would have been hungry enough to eat those. Anyway, the men would have considered it beneath them and the women were too feminist to spend their days bent over a pestle. What do you think," Jen asked, reaching for the bottle to refill her glass. "If you'd been young in the seventies, would you have joined a commune?"

"God, no."

"Why not?"

The untidiness, the constant press of people, the need to be nice to them? "I don't like dirt under my fingernails."

Jen nearly snorted out her mouthful of wine. "You could wear gloves," she said, laughing.

Raquel thought for a minute. "The only pair of gloves I remember in those Archive snapshots were on two men putting up a very rough-looking wooden fence."

"You think skin-to-skin contact with the earth would have been mandatory? You may be right. Too bad, they could have used someone like you to keep things in line."

"A commune with a cop?"

"I was thinking more of your knack for cutting through bullshit. Because that's what would have driven *me* crazy—the endless discussions. What to plant and where to put it and when's the celebration and whether it's ethical to kill the extra roosters and put them in the soup pot."

"The woman Meadow seems to have got around it by just taking charge."

"Did she? Good for her, I'll have to ask Rob about how that worked. Though I remember Jerry telling me how frustrating it was whenever the commune had to agree on something, so she didn't always just get her way."

The Commons had to agree . . . The sensation of some idea, caught in the corner of her mind, returned more strongly. "The two-month agreement," she said, thinking aloud.

"Two months? Oh, right, Jerry told me about that. How it took weeks of back-and-forth for them to decide that they needed some way of getting rid of people they didn't like. And that was *after* one of them had brought in this guy he barely knew, and they found out he was wanted for attacking some woman. Can you imagine?"

Hitchhiking.

We all hitched, all over, Johnston had said. *That made it so easy.* We.

And Jerry, earlier: *Anyone could bring anyone in. Helping themselves to things. Expecting to eat, even if they weren't really into work.*

"Who was it?"

"Who was who?" Jen asked. "Raquel?"

But Raquel had already pulled out her phone.

Jerry would—but no. It was the women of The Commons who had taken charge. And the women would remember all the scary details of what had brought them together in solidarity around the commune's big kitchen table. Of what had made it necessary to draw back from complete freedom and build a door to keep themselves safe.

"Arachne Weaving," the voice said.

"Sarah, this is Inspector Laing."

"Hello, there, Raquel. Kimmy and I have been having a grand time picking over our past, but I'm afraid we haven't found much yet."

"The police came one day, to the commune."

"They were here a lot, especially near to weed harvest time."

"This was a raid. In the fall of 1978. They were looking for a man who had raped and beaten a woman in Berkeley."

"Oh God, I remember that." Her voice faded as she lowered the phone for a moment. "It's our friend the inspector, she's asking about that time Ronnie brought home the rapist."

"Tell me everything you can remember," Raquel asked, and sat unseeing in the magical grotto as the woman's story unfolded.

45

Then

In the early days, The Commons was all about growing: planting food, raising children, making ourselves whole.

In the second year, word got around, and people started dropping by. Tents would get set up in the orchard, names would be added to the work schedules, but most of the newcomers weren't interested in growing—or, in growing anything you couldn't smoke. Most of them got bored and moved on. Sometimes, they'd help themselves to things as they went. Twice, people unaccustomed to California summers made cookfires that got loose and brought in the fire service.

But it wasn't until Ronnie brought home the rapist that we decided something had to change.

Ronnie had lived there for maybe a year or so, and he was a bit of a jerk—the kind of guy who was always missing when there was heavy work to be done, but always there when someone was needed to drive out and fetch something. And when he eventually came back from fetching, he'd often bring some useless friend—male or female—and we'd be stuck with them for a while.

The rapist was one of those. Not that we knew he was a rapist—and to be fair, I'm sure Ronnie didn't know, either. But like usual, the guy moved into the old trailer with Ronnie.

And it must have been a few days later that somebody gave the guy their car keys and he made his own trip into town. And when he came back, he brought a friend.

It was the three men all together that created the weirdness. Our days were filled with hard work and good food, we didn't have a lot of energy left for partying. But these guys up in the trailer, it was like a little hot spot of trouble. Booze, noise, music all night, and drugs a lot harder than the rest of us used. We had kids, you know?

But before we could decide what to do about it, the cops came. Must have been a dozen cars, guns drawn, shouting. The kids were terrified—hell, we were all terrified. And no clue what was going on. I mean, the sheriff knew us, by that time. He knew we weren't up to any weird shit.

But once they showed us a picture of the guy they were looking for, half of us turned around and pointed them at Ronnie's trailer.

It was the women who had to change how The Commons did things, of course. Like it or not, we women usually have to be the responsible ones. But the men agreed, things did have to change. And after that, the drop-ins got screened a little, with any creeps or troublemakers invited to go.

Ronnie and the third guy—the guy the rapist had brought in—were let go after a few days. Ronnie came back to clear out his stuff from the trailer, and that was the end of them.

And it was sad, in a way. We'd all wanted to think that surrounding ourselves with good thoughts and a clean life would change the world, but in the end, the cops had to come and save us.

It felt like the universe was saying, *Enough playing around, kids. Time to grow up.*

46

Now

Raquel sat, waiting for Al's reaction over the phone.

She felt she'd put together her thoughts in a logical sequence, and presented them clearly. When she finished, she waited for her partner to seize her conclusions and start down the path she had opened up.

She waited, first puzzled, then concerned. She finally broke the unaccustomed silence herself. "Don't you agree that if the three men were held for several days, that would mean they were arrested rather than just held? Unless they did things differently in the seventies?"

"No, it would've been a forty-eight-hour hold."

"So do you think the booking photos would be available?"

"Most likely. You're thinking the third man is Michael Johnston?"

Raquel wished she could see Al's face. His voice sounded noncommittal.

"I'm thinking it's worth asking. His daughter told you she and her mother didn't like Johnston's friends. And yesterday he mentioned thumbing for rides himself, not just picking people up. He also said that as time went on and girls got more cautious, he was forced to change his system—to get inside places his kind of girls could be found, and take them from there. You have to wonder if maybe he used a partner, sometimes, to smooth his way."

"Ronnie."

"Or the rapist himself. It's not unheard of for men to work in pairs."

"This was the year before the Gardener's statue went up?"

"Six or seven months before. But if Johnston knew his way around the Estate from having spent some time there, and if he knew that one of his concrete companies had the job on Midsummer's Day . . ."

"I'll reach out to the sheriff. That far back, things may not be digitized, but they should still be in Records."

"If we can place Johnston on the Estate, I say we take him the *Eves* one tomorrow." *That would give us eleven and twelve.* "But if I'm wrong . . ."

"Then the others stay lost. But it's going to come to that pretty soon, anyway."

She hung up.

At some point—before she started talking to Al, she hoped—she'd had the sense to walk away from Jen, ending up at the car. *My God, I'm being rude to this poor woman,* she thought.

But as she got out, intending to retrieve her drinking companion from the once-magical grotto, she saw that Jen had followed her and was now sitting on a tree stump, happily finishing off the bottle of wine.

As she watched Raquel approach, she nudged open the top of a pink box and drew out something brown and sticky-looking.

"Finished?" she asked.

"My sister tells me I have terrible manners. She's right."

"You have a sister?"

"You'd like her."

"Bring her down sometime."

That was not going to happen.

"Anyway, I apologize."

"Your job is demanding, today mine isn't, plus I got the chance to sit and look at the flowers, all by myself. Don't worry about it."

She set aside the box and wineglass, brushed off her hands, and hopped off the tree stump. "But you should come back when things are less . . . fraught? Is that the word I want? And the azaleas really are worth the trip."

47

The next morning, Raquel woke feeling rested, which was a surprise. She'd expected the added complication of . . . whatever was happening with Jen Bachus to make matters even worse. And objectively speaking, with the snarl of half-related threads and uncertain ties and the massive pressure of impending death and the silence that lay beyond, she should have been staring up at the ceiling all night.

Instead, the impenetrable snarl felt as if it was about to unknot itself in her hands. Although she couldn't see how.

An early text informed the team that one of the cadaver dogs was showing interest in a site over in Milpitas; a radar crew would join them there.

Soon after, Al wrote saying that he was heading up to see Max O'Connor in San Quentin, to show him a picture of Michael Johnston. If he knew him, and if he had any information they could use, the prisoner might trade it for a positive word at his next parole hearing.

Then, just as she was leaving the house, two old black-and-white booking photographs arrived. One was Maxwell John O'Connor, 5´8˝ with thin, shifty features and greasy-looking hair.

The other photo showed a young Michael Johnston.

David Kirkup had that jet-lagged appearance of a person who'd been swigging coffee all night in an attempt to convince his body it was morning. His desk was littered with the kind of old-fashioned pink phone memos that Raquel hadn't seen in years, and his eyes, much the same color, looked somewhat frantic.

"Jen!" he exclaimed, as he spotted her in the doorway. "Thank God, do you know where the Germany folder has got to?"

"Not being your secretary, no, I don't," Jen told him. "Ruth should be here at ten, as usual."

"I phoned her three times and she's not answering."

"She's probably on the freeway."

"She needs to get hands-free. Who's this?"

"David Kirkup, Raquel Laing, San Francisco Police Department."

"Really? What can we do for the SFPD, Ms. Laing?"

"David, it's *Inspector* Laing, and I did tell you—she's here about the body under the *Eves*."

He looked startled, his bloodshot eyes darting between the two women—and then his brain came to life and he ran a hand over his face. "God. I'm sorry, of course. The skeleton. Any idea who it is yet?"

"You were here in the seventies, weren't you, Mr. Kirkup?"

"I was around, yes. I didn't live here."

"I'd like to speak to you about some of the people who did."

"Uh, sure. Sure. But not right this minute, I have a call to Berlin and they're only available until seven their time. Ten ours. Maybe this afternoon? Or what about tomorrow?"

"I'll come back at ten," Raquel told him.

He squinted at his sleek watch, clearly thinking of telling her that wouldn't do, then reconsidered. "Yeah, good, this shouldn't take me more than half an hour."

Jen spoke up. "David, I hope you're not committing us to anything with the German people."

"Of course not. But honest, the Trust is going to love it, it's an incredible opportunity to put the Estate on the cultural map. I'm just trying to get the outlines of their proposal firmed up so I can put it in front of the Board tomorrow. Good to meet you, Rachel, see you in a bit."

"It's not—" Jen stopped at the touch of Raquel's hand.

"We probably should keep things on a formal basis, Mr. Kirkup," Raquel said. "'Inspector Laing' will do fine. And I'll see you in forty minutes."

The Estate manager was grinning when the door shut. "Well done."

"Do you have problems with Mr. Kirkup?"

"MeToo problems, you mean? No, David's fine, even with the younger staff. Just a little clueless, and he lets his enthusiasm carry him away. Which, like I told you the other day, has been good for the Estate. Rob certainly wouldn't have fought as hard to keep things together. But it also takes some reining in, and I'm anticipating a challenging session tomorrow with the Board.

"But look," she said abruptly. "I enjoyed yesterday. I'd like to go for coffee sometime. Or a drink would be even better—but with our phones off, and not here."

Raquel studied Jen's face, seeing both determination and a blush. "Are you asking me on a . . . date?" Jen's blush deepened, but she also raised her chin.

"Maybe. Or I could just be asking you for coffee."

Raquel nodded. "Let's start with the coffee, then."

"Great. But next time, I'm in charge of the cookies. And now we've settled that, I promised Mrs. Dalhousie I'd bring you by Archives. She has something you'll be interested in."

What Mrs. Dalhousie had was a leather-bound sketchbook kept by the artist Gaddo during her weeks of residence, which the archivist said was one of the most valuable things the Estate owned. It was usually housed off-site, but she'd retrieved it that morning for Raquel to see.

And although Raquel had no wish to spend her time on art, the woman had given up her sleep on Wednesday to compile the residents' pages. The least Raquel could do was give her half an hour of appreciation.

Anyway, until San Mateo's coroner came to life and David Kirkup found a minute for her, what else did she have to do?

Mrs. Dalhousie made Raquel scrub her hands, then laid the book reverently down on the table. "Touch only the edges," she ordered. "Pencil can smear."

Raquel promised.

Despite the leather cover, the pages inside were worksheets rather than finished treasures, and brought to life many of the faces Raquel was coming to know through the snapshots.

Here was Wes, for example, wearing farmer's overalls with no shirt as he squatted to examine something with two little boys, all three faces bearing the same childlike enthusiasm. And Rob Gardener, tall, hairy, watchful, patriarchal. Several pages were devoted to Rain, his devilish features clear even in the quickest sketches. One closely worked drawing showed him shirtless, starting the downswing of an ax at a chopping block, the muscles of his chest clear as an anatomy drawing. Fort Gardener, on the other hand, was seated in lotus position. He was the only man in the book with no facial hair at all—even Jerry Rathford, caught getting out of a convertible in front of the house, had a mustache, as did the young David Kirkup, standing behind him. She found David in several of the drawings, mostly in the background, looking on. One page showed a remarkably young Sarah, weaving at a complicated loom, followed by several studies and partial studies of a woman breastfeeding her infant.

But the person who appeared most in the pages was Meadow. Strong, vivid, and always busy, the woman was a distinctive personality even when rendered with a few lines on a page. Many were partial sketches—the side of her head, some brief pencil strokes denoting a smile, a study of her shoulder as she reached down for a load. Almost as if the artist was trying to piece her together, or figure her out. There were no particularly erotic overtones to the images, no loving preoccupation and careful reworking of the shapes—if anything, Raquel would have said the drawings of Rain showed the only traces of lust.

But Gaddo was clearly intrigued by Meadow. And after a time, a viewer could not help being as well.

She was startled, what felt like a short time later, to realize it was nearly ten o'clock. She closed the book and carried it to Mrs. Dalhousie's office.

"Are you finished with it, then?"

"I've looked through it, although I feel I could spend a lot more time studying them."

"The portraits are extraordinary, aren't they? Especially considering that Gaddo was never known for her representational art."

"They're more telling than photographs, in a way. It's too bad you can't display them openly."

"I agree. Unfortunately, the Estate's insurance agent does not." The archivist smiled, and locked her treasure away.

48

David Kirkup's secretary had arrived. Raquel found her in the awkwardly proportioned space in front of his office, at a desk with filing cabinets pressing in on all sides.

"Raquel Laing," she told the gray-haired woman. "Mr. Kirkup is expecting me."

"Is he? Just a moment." She leaned forward to push a switch on a large, vintage intercom box. "Mr. Kirkup, your ten o'clock is here. Mr. Kirkup?" Nothing happened, so with a shake of the head, she got up and edged past Raquel to go knock on his door and, without waiting for a reply, stick her head in. "You had a ten o'clock?"

"Right, Inspector Laing. I guess—sure, send her in." But by that time, the secretary had already retreated and Raquel was halfway through the doorway.

Coffee, eyedrops, and the German conversation had restored a degree of sparkle to Kirkup's mood. He rolled back his expensive ergonomic desk chair and stood, offering his hand, but was taken aback slightly by the cane. "Hurt your leg?"

"A while ago. Thank you for seeing me, Mr. Kirkup, I won't take up much of your time." She sat. He sat.

"That's okay, I'm happy to do what I can for the SFPD. I was talking to your chief a couple months ago about hosting an event for you guys."

That ticked off the *I Know Your Boss (So Watch Yourself)* box on Raquel's inner power-play checklist. Earlier, he had checked the one for *I'm Far Too Busy and Important for You*, and tried for a dual attempt on *You Won't Mind if I Call You by Your First Name*, supplemented by *I Got Your Name Slightly Wrong*.

She gave him her most confident smile. "How nice of you, I'm sure our two thousand patrol officers and their families will enjoy a day here." His face fell at the thought of a swarm of lowly officers and their brats, but she went on before he could respond. "However, what I need at the moment is information regarding the period when the body was put under the concrete. As I understand it, the concrete was actually poured on Saturday, June 23, 1979. That would have been the day after the Estate hosted its Midsummer's Eve Fest?"

"Wow. Um, yeah. I mean, I don't remember the dates, but that sounds about right."

"You do remember the festival?"

"Of course I remember it, I worked like a dog all day. I couldn't tell you what time I left, but it was long over by then."

"You didn't stay for the after-party?"

"Oh, sure. Well, most of it, anyway."

Discomfort. She studied him for a moment, wondering where that came from. It wasn't a lie—he had been there, she'd glimpsed him throughout Rain's video—but something about the party, or the night, made him uneasy. Still, human beings were complicated, and this was a man who would be loath to admit that he'd been left out of any important event in the family's life. Such as an after-party with famous musicians.

"How old were you, in 1979?"

"I'd have been twenty-five, or thereabouts."

"Were you working for your cousin Rob at the time?"

"Not really. Well, sort of, although mostly that came later, after the rest of them took off. Before that, it was kind of informal. I did a load of stuff for him—you wouldn't believe the bureaucratic wrangling it takes to run a place like this, and did even during the commune days. And we set it up so the Estate contributed money to my rent and gas and stuff. But I don't think either of us thought of it as me working for him. Not then, anyway. Though later, like I say, we formalized things."

"But you didn't live here."

"No. I've stayed here on and off over the years, naturally, but it's more convenient to be in town."

"Convenient." With a man like this, word repetitions and flat statements were more effective than actual questions, since he'd rather correct than inform.

"To be honest, the whole hippie vibe wasn't, as we used to say, my 'thing.' I like a shower every morning, and the smell of pot gives me a headache." He grinned at the admission of being non-cool. Which might offer insight into his discomfort in talking about a party with drugs.

"What about the free love?"

His grin widened. "We were young, so sure. Free love was a big plus."

"Did you ever sleep with Meadow?"

Another twitch of discomfort.

"You mean—you're talking about Rob's girlfriend, right?"

"She seems to have been committed to the practice of free love."

"If you say so."

"Did you sleep with her?"

"I don't know that it's your business, but maybe I did. Once or twice. She was very willing."

"Twice?"

"Once, maybe. Why are you asking?"

"Have you heard from Meadow since the festival?"

"I don't think so, but then, she wouldn't have any reason to get in touch with me. Like I say, it was just the once, and that was a while before she left. You know that summer was the end of the commune, right? Pretty much everyone was gone by fall. Some of them we did hear from. My cousin Fort—Rob's brother—used to send notes from India. Just silly cards, to say hi, basically. And every so often, someone who'd lived here would stop by. Wes, of course—he came back before too long. Even now people show up every so often on a tour. But I don't remember anything from Meadow. You could ask Rob."

"I'll do that. What about the day after the festival?"

"What about it? Everyone was pretty trashed."

"And then the concrete truck showed up. On a Saturday."

"I'll take your word for it."

"You don't remember?"

"Do I remember the day of the week, forty-odd years later? No." He laughed, but to Raquel's ears, the sound was slightly forced. There was deception here: because of the drugs that were no doubt a part of that weekend, or something else?

"If you were all feeling 'trashed,' why not send the truck away?"

"Because it was there, because it cost money. And I guess because it was easier just to deal with it. And—wait. It was something Gaddo wanted. That sculptress. Oh, of course: the name of the piece is *Midsummer Eves,* so it just *had* to go in that day."

"Except that the sculpture itself wasn't installed for a couple of weeks."

"Wasn't it?" He frowned, staring off into the past. "You're right. Something about the concrete having to get hard. Probably nobody wanted to tell her that we'd sent the truck away."

"Gaddo came back to install it, didn't she?"

"And what a pain in the ass *that* was. She didn't want to be there in the first place, then she had to mess around with it for hours to get it to fit—the guy with the crane wanted to take off for another job. Huge drama."

"Why didn't it fit?"

"Because she was a crap amateur, maybe?"

"Was she?"

"I guess—no, wait. She changed her mind! That's right—I forgot, that's why the crane guy was so ticked off. The thing was supposed to go one way, but for some reason she decided she wanted it the other way, and it took forever to whack the rebar into place."

"And Meadow wasn't there to sort it out."

"You're right about that—Meadow was surprisingly good at making things work smoothly, but she wasn't there. In fact . . . wasn't that why Gaddo was so angry in the first place?" Raquel let him stare out of his window for a time, dredging up memories from his youth—and she could see them come back when his face lit up and his gaze returned to her. "Because of Rob. Gaddo was snarky when she got there because Rob had done something to infuriate Meadow, and she and Meadow were good friends."

"So you're sure Meadow wasn't there?"

"Of course she wasn't there," he said impatiently. "If she had been, we wouldn't have had all the problems."

"Was she at the party after the festival was over?"

"I'm sure she—" He stopped. "Are you saying . . ." His hand came up to cover the lower half of his face. "You think that body is *Meadow*?"

"Could it be?"

He stared at Raquel, then rose so fast, his chair spun into the wall. He stood with his back to her, gazing out the window, tense and drawn in and silent. Raquel wished she could see his face.

"Meadow?" he said after a moment, trying it out.

"She was missing, the day after the party."

The tension took a while to leave his shoulders. Replaced by . . . decision? Acceptance? Eventually, he turned back to the room. "I thought there would be tests and things you people would do."

"There are. We're doing them. But they're slow and there are some . . . external considerations. If we can eliminate her by confirming that she was seen after the concrete was poured, we can move on."

He retrieved his chair, rubbing at the invisible mark on the paint, then sat. He placed his hands together on the desk. "I see why you were asking about her. And as far as I know, none of us saw Meadow after the night of the party. But I don't remember anyone being worried about her, at the time. We were all pretty sure she took off on her own."

"Is there anyone else who went missing around that same time?"

"Who knows? There were dozens of people here helping—a bunch of Diggers came down from San Francisco to feed the crowd, all the bands had their own roadies, Rob had some Vietnam buddies to help keep the crowd in line. All kinds of people. Most of them left pretty soon after. As for ours? Let's see. Gaddo was already gone, she needed to be in . . . Rome, was it? Florence? Anyway, when Meadow took off, we figured she'd gone with Gaddo. They were great friends, had a lot in common—politics, feminism, art, you name it. And, am I right in thinking that some of her stuff was missing? Passport and things?" He was either a first-rate actor, or he was honestly deep in the recall process. And his memory did confirm what Wes had told her. "I remember people feeling more resentful than worried, so probably so. Who else? Like I said, Fort went back to India, sent those cards. And there was a pregnant girl . . . called herself Butterfly—Bonnie, I think. Her sister had come for the Fest and talked her into going home with her."

"What color hair did Bonnie have?"

But he shook his head. "Couldn't tell you, all I remember is the vast size of her. Someone said it was twins."

"Tell me about Fort." Raquel couldn't tell if David's mentions of his older cousin were brief as a means of burying the name, or because he had little to say about the wayward Gardener.

"My cousin? His name wasn't really Fort—but I suppose you know that. Thaddeus the Fourth, meant to be heir to the Estate and head of the family, until he discovered navel-gazing and went off to join the Beatles wannabees in India. And basically never came home, other than that spring."

Familiar ground from Jerry, but the answers were worth comparing. "You ever hear from him?"

"Only the postcards. Though those stopped a long time ago. We figured he must have died." That agreed with what Jen and Jerry had told her.

"Wouldn't the family have been notified?"

"Not if they didn't know who he was. He actually became an Indian citizen—changed his name, his passport, the whole thing. And his ashram closed up in the nineties—when Rob was looking to turn things over to the Trust, we sent someone over to look for his brother, but everyone was long gone. We were lucky that their grandfather's will had already left Fort out, or Rob would've been wrapped up in endless legal problems. And speaking of which." He looked pointedly at the high-tech watch on his wrist. "I have an appointment with a donor."

"Nearly finished," she said. "I just need you to look through these and tell me what you remember of them."

He was irritated at the thickness of her folder, and demonstrated it by the speed with which he went through the pages. "Wes you already know. Don't know her. Or him. This one's name was Robin, she wasn't here long. That's Peggy, married to Paolo—or whatever passed for married in those days—with a bunch of kids. Sarah, though I think she was gone before the festival days. This kid called herself Kismet, lived with her father, Stone. Don't know him, or him. Her . . . Dani? Daniela? Something like that. Bit of a—she was a little pushy. No, don't know her, or him."

The page for "Mike"—Johnston with the beard—was one of those turned over with an unhesitating "Don't know him." Still, she retrieved it and laid it in front of him again.

"Does this face seem at all familiar?"

"No, sorry. Who is it?"

"Someone who may have visited during those years."

He shook his head and pushed the papers across the desk at her. "Sorry. Now, I really have to go."

He stood at the door until she had passed through it, then hurried past her to his donor appointment.

49

The house seemed oddly silent. By contrast, Raquel's thoughts seemed remarkably noisy. She walked through the halls, absently heading toward open air.

David Kirkup and Wes Albright agreed: Meadow's possessions—ID, checkbook—disappeared when she did.

Wes thought someone had seen her on her way out, though he didn't know who it was.

The Commons as a whole, despite the turmoil caused by their mother figure's absence, quickly accepted her departure as voluntary.

Which either meant that the woman had indeed packed her things and gone, or someone made it look as if she had. And although the place had been crawling with outsiders that night, any stranger who found his way to the woman's passport and clothes could not have gone on to plant the idea that someone had seen her go—and certainly not in the brief time before the confusion at her absence could turn to worry.

So: either Meadow left under her own power that day and the bones belonged to someone else, or one of The Commons had covered her death as only a family member could.

Raquel found that she was standing in the garden. It was as quiet as the house had been, despite the spectacle of the spring blooms. Right, a distant part of her brain noted—Monday: the Estate was closed.

Which freed her to walk unimpeded through the garden to Jen's wisteria gazebo, up its three shallow steps to the cave of blossoms.

The gazebo held a garden bench, a wooden chair, and a small table with a child's ornament: a jam jar with a sprig of blossoms. Raquel was about to sit down on the bench when she noticed a small metal rectangle set into the back of the chair. It read:

IN MEMORY OF JOANNA GARDENER
WHO LOVED THIS SPOT

Joanna, wife of a suicide, mother of Rob and Fort. No doubt this place offered an escape from her dark, enclosed rooms and the disapproval of her father-in-law and Maude. Raquel's thumb came out to rub at the plaque, and she sat on the chair instead, to look at the spot this woman had loved.

For a cop, love could be a warning sign. Men stole and manipulated and killed for love. Women returned to their abusers, children forgave their parents, beaten dogs crept back and licked their owners' shoes for love.

For people like Raquel, inclined by nature to mistrust strong emotion, love was as likely to be a tool for intimidation or a justification for violence as it was a sign of trust and respect. Someone had called it grit in a sensitive instrument, and that was true. Any personal involvement— with a case, a victim, even a witness—could affect an investigator's clarity of vision.

Suspects and witnesses had emotions. Seeing and understanding those emotions, especially the buried ones, could solve a case. But a Homicide cop who got too caught up in a case was a Homicide cop who was not seeing clearly, and not serving the victim.

Joanna Gardener had loved this small corner of her prison, yet her sons had fled, one to the other side of the world, the other to a far corner of the family lands. During the short years of The Commons, people had come together to build a new kind of family, spending their love and respect on each other—yet one of them ended up under a concrete slab.

Any emotion could be dangerous, especially in an investigation. Happiness could distract. Boredom dulled the eyes. An angry cop forgot to think. A contemptuous cop was neither hearing nor seeing. An impatient cop could get herself shot, or get a partner killed.

Raquel Laing always—*always*—took care to think, and hear, and see. Inspector Laing was known for her cold-blooded approach, her refusal to be led astray, her dedication to balance, even when it led her away from a prime suspect.

So why had that small word—*loved*—on a metal plaque set off such a reverberation in her thoughts? The idea of that long-dead woman's love as a worthy goal, as a small triumph, as a tiny consolation?

The question came with its answer: because what Raquel was feeling just now was love's opposite. The emotion that was causing her thoughts to tumble and her teeth to clench was nothing less than sheer loathing.

Admit it: she loathed Michael Johnston. She loathed his actions, his gestures, the way he played with the cops who came to his room. She wanted to erase him from the world, to smear him into nothingness—but first, she wanted to win.

She wanted to claim back the remaining faces on her wall—and not just those, but any unknown horrors that Johnston had left behind in Mexico. For the first time, she understood—she felt it in her entire body—the urge to torture, the belief that inflicting pain could produce information, that here was a case that justified crossing the line separating cop from crime.

And with that, her phone shouted out Al's ringtone—a physical shock, as if her mentor, her partner, the man she owed everything to, had been listening to her thoughts.

She let it ring three times before she could be sure her voice would remain steady.

"Hi, Al."

"There's been some . . ." He paused. "You okay?"

Maybe not as steady as she thought. "I'm fine, what's up? Any luck with the sheriff's records?"

"There's been an interesting development—two of them. The Los Gatos girl, Janis, is Janet Esposito—I'll put her picture in the group folder. And Max O'Connor. He says he might know something, and he's up for parole in six weeks."

"You're thinking of a deal."

"I'm thinking that if he gives us anything good on Johnston, we offer to speak on his behalf."

"That'll take too long."

"I know. But we're doing all we can with the dogs and the rest—and those are long shots, anyway. Even if Johnston admits to your Eve and gives us another for her, we're still left with seven."

Torture, pain.

"And Mexico," she said. A breath of wind stirred the trailing blossoms, scattering petals across the painted wood.

"Mexico?"

"He was there for twenty-three years, Al. You honestly think he stopped?"

"Rock, you cannot start thinking that way. We do what we can that lets us sleep at night. If we don't get the names from him, we'll get them some other way. In no way is Mexico our responsibility. Raquel, are you hearing me?"

"Yes, Al. I understand. It's just . . . I guess I'm a little distracted."

"Don't be," he said sharply. "Inspector Laing, do we have to take you off the case?"

"No. Of course not. Al, I want to take the *Eves* to Johnston."

"I'm going to be tied up here, most of the day."

"Let me go. I'll see if Charlie or JJ is free."

The phone was silent. That in itself was a sign of Al's consternation.

"One of them has to be there," he said in the end.

"I know that. Should I ask Johnston about O'Connor, too?"

"Be interesting to see his reaction."

"Want me to wait, till you're here?"

"No, I'd miss it anyway, my old eyes."

"I could record it, show you afterward slowed down."

"You and JJ will be fine. Just don't give Johnston any details about the plea bargain."

"I'll keep it cryptic."

"Good luck."

"You too," she said. She texted JJ, who said sure, he was available.

"Give me an hour," she told him. There were some things she needed to do first.

50

JJ was waiting when the elevator doors came open.

"I hear Al may have a line on a snitch," he said.

"Possibly. But we don't want to give Johnston too many details."

"'Course not. How sure are you with your body? The one up on that estate?"

"Not at all sure. But I need you to do me a favor. Just stand back and don't say anything. Pretend you're in on it."

"Unless you plan on beating him up, sure. Not that I think the bastard doesn't need it."

"No violence," she said. "I'm just showing him some pictures, and I need to concentrate on his reactions."

The first was Janet Esposito—not a good photo, but he recognized her. "Ah, you found Janis. Bet that wasn't her name, was I right?"

She did not reply, merely held up the next photograph, all her attention on the tiny movements underneath the old man's skin. "Sure, that's Mandy, her hair was a little lighter then."

The next. "That's Sandra, you showed me her before."

The next. "What is this, old home week? That's Pam."

The next photograph showed Meadow: good resolution, her green eyes and blond hair absolutely distinctive. Raquel absorbed every faint movement in Johnston's body when he saw her, which ended in a frown of concentration. "She's not one of mine, but I'm sure I met her, somewhere. One of the hippie places, by the looks of it."

Next photo. "Yeah, that's Rainbow. You found her?"

Next: Annabelle, blond and smiling. He studied her, but shook his head. "No. You're just tossing out lost girls at me, aren't you? I told you, I'm not going to—"

Then the 1978 booking photo of the rapist, Max O'Connor.

Fear. Just a quick spasm, instantly replaced by anger. "What's this? I don't know who—"

She slid that page aside and let him see the next one, of Johnston himself, four decades younger and thirty pounds heavier. His expression in the photo was every bit as wary as it was now.

"Get out of here," he growled.

Raquel showed the two booking photos to JJ. "You'll recognize Mr. Johnston, here. Max O'Connor is a friend of his who is currently doing time for aggravated assault, although this photo was taken the day he was arrested for rape, when he, Mr. Johnston, and another man were removed from the Gardener Estate. O'Connor is currently interested in parole. And he says he has things to tell about his friend, Michael Johnston."

"He doesn't. He doesn't know anything. He's full of shit—I mean, I didn't know him well, but that's how he acted. He'll tell you whatever you want to hear."

Raquel began to tidy the pages. "Not being in charge of the case, I can't be certain, but I also understand that Mr. O'Connor has some interesting claims of his own. He is saying that he, in fact, is The Highwayman, not you. That you are trying to ride into the books of famous murderers on his work. I don't know why anyone would do that, but then, I often don't understand why the people I arrest do things."

She put the folder into her bag, closed its top, and looked down at him. "So, any names you'd like to add before Mr. O'Connor gets a chance, Mr. Johnston? Any locations?"

Someone who spent years analyzing the body's involuntary giveaways often learned how to show nothing on her own face. Her stance reflected only the long day of a cop. Her voice held no tension whatsoever. Her expression, slightly bored, was that of someone whose only interest was in getting home to dinner.

JJ was a very different matter. Raquel could see his clenched fist at the corner of her eye.

Fortunately, the old monster did not notice JJ's fist.

Instead, his predator's eyes ate up her face, seeking out the faintest suggestion of a lie, of manipulation or resistance. She gave him nothing but a growing hint of impatience. Nothing but an absolute confidence in the strength of her case without him.

And she showed no trace of reaction as she saw him waver. The old man was tired. He could feel the end pressing in on him. Was it more important for him to continue taunting the cops, or to step forward and claim his place in the history of murder? His breath wheezed in and out past the oxygen tubes for a minute, and then:

"I might," he said.

Twenty minutes later, a nurse came in, took one look at her patient, and ordered the two cops to leave.

Three steps into the hallway, Raquel was yanked off her feet by a large man who whirled her in a circle.

"Holy shit, girl, you're a magician!" he said, when he'd set her down.

She took a wary step back. "I didn't find O'Connor, that was Al."

"But you used him to get Johnston to open up. All *nine*? Jesus, I didn't think we'd get any of them—and then I saw his face change, and *boom!*"

She peeled back the corner of her folder and slid out the top sheet. "Do you want to take care of this, then?"

His jaw dropped. "You don't . . . what?"

"The search, for the others. The sooner we find them, the better."

JJ looked at the sheet of notes concerning Johnston's remaining victims: names, dates, and where they would be found. Then he looked up at her. "You need to take that."

"Why—what else do you have going?"

"I don't have anything. That's the point, girl. I'm retired. You most definitely are not."

"But I have to . . ." She stopped.

He was right. That piece of paper represented triumph. It would make headlines, and could establish a reputation to rival the great Al Hawkin's. JJ's career, though solid, was behind him. Hers was not.

Slowly, she shook her head. "There's something I have to do. Can you at least get things started?"

He reluctantly put out his hand for the sheet of paper.

"Great. Thank you," she said, meaning it. Then she sat down to begin writing on the back of one of the pages she had showed Johnston. After a minute, she realized that the Alameda County detective hadn't moved.

"Sorry, did I forget something?"

"A person would think you weren't interested in these girls."

"Of course I'm interested. But I need to write up my notes while my impressions are fresh."

"What notes?"

"My baseline. Of Michael Johnston. His giveaways."

JJ kept standing there, but Raquel had already lost twenty minutes to the distraction, so she gave him a polite smile and bent over the page with her pencil.

After a bit, the elevator doors opened and shut, and the life of the hospital resumed around her.

51

When Raquel surfaced from her writing, she found several texts waiting. Three were from Al: thoughts about Max O'Connor; the results of a preliminary talk with the DA; then one that fairly leapt off the screen:

> We may have struck gold w/Oconnor—there's indications he
> spent the 90s in Puerto Vallarta!

JJ would say, *Get in there, girl.* And he'd be right. Anyone with the least concern for her professional future would drop everything and head north. Because, as the notes she'd just finished writing up said, Johnston's giveaways had been clear: if the bones were either Meadow or Annabelle—her two leading candidates at present—then he was not responsible. And if he hadn't done it, then the bones belonged entirely to San Mateo Homicide, with no reason for the Highwayman group to be involved.

She should let go. Or at least put the Gardener body on pause until the coroner got back to her.

And she should be happy to be freed up, not only because the Johnston case was cracking open—with his time in Mexico as a bonus—but because her involvement would get her out of this oppressive semi-probation she was in with the department. She'd be a hero, and they'd be eager to bring her back into the fold.

So why did she find her thoughts circling back to whether she could perhaps take a different approach with the Gardener bones? Thinking about how she'd used the faces of his victims to trigger Johnston's reactions, so maybe a photograph of the place he'd left this one would trigger the guilt signs equally well? If, for example, she lifted a still from the video that showed the stage ready for the festival . . .

Any happiness she felt—and she did, she realized, feel happy—was not because the Highwayman case was opening and her future with it, but because turning things over to JJ would leave her free to focus on the Gardener Estate.

Because the Gardener case was where her interest lay.

She didn't like the idea of Jen—and the others, of course—left not knowing. *We've been walking around, oblivious of that poor soul.* And now that they knew, an open case would leave them haunted.

Besides, if Raquel didn't pursue it, how many months—years, even—would it be before San Mateo managed to turn their attention to it? That nameless body would become another Polly Lacewood, a case gone colder than the bones themselves.

Of course, if she didn't know for certain that the victim wasn't connected to The Highwayman, that left the door very much open. Didn't it? And surely she'd have an answer one way or the other soon. Wouldn't she?

She started to put away her phone, then noticed another message waiting, this one from Jen Bachus:

Rob's here, so any time.

She texted back that she'd be half an hour. The reply came when the elevator reached the parking level:

We'll be in the green room. Jerry's here too.

The Gardener hermit had come out of the hills at last.

❦

Raquel went in through the terrace doors and down the corridor to the closed-in room with the green walls.

Jerry was half sitting on the edge of the big desk. Jen was in the chair behind it.

And there, standing in front of the formal marble fireplace as if warming his backside against nonexistent flames, was Rob Gardener.

She'd built up the mental picture of an ancient hippie, beard to his waist and yellowing fingernails. Instead, he looked like a retired academic who spent his weekends splitting wood: thick white hair gathered into a neat ponytail, close-trimmed gray beard, flannel shirt, jeans, and hiking boots that had seen a lot of miles. In his early seventies, but incredibly fit. And clean—the rustic cabin must include a water heater and washing machine.

"Rob, this is Raquel Laing—Inspector Laing," Jen said. "And as you can see, Raquel, this is Rob Gardener."

The hand that closed gently around hers was powerful enough to break bones, and the forearms exposed by rolled-up sleeves might have belonged to a blacksmith. He smelled of fresh air and masculinity.

"Mr. Gardener."

"Call me Rob."

"I was beginning to think I'd have to go hiking to see you—though I understand that your cousin David is the only person who can approach your house without having a shotgun turned on him."

"Not the only. Jen comes up, sometimes."

Raquel turned an accusing eye at the manager, who had definitely not offered her services last week, but Jen was shaking her head. "Rob, I told you I wasn't going to drive that road again until you let us have it graded. Not even in the Land Rover."

"Yeah, the rains really did a number on it," he said, sounding apologetic. "But I haven't had so much as a dirt bike come up for weeks."

"How did you know I wanted to talk to you?" Raquel asked. Smoke signals? Carrier pigeons?

"Jen texted."

Raquel laughed: so much for assumptions.

"I see. Well, yes, I did need to speak with you." She hung her cane and laptop bag over the back of a chair and sat down. Then waited expectantly, until he realized that he was looming. He pulled himself away from the fireplace and settled onto the chair across from her.

"Mr. Gardener, do you know what's been going on here in the past week?"

"They found a skeleton. Under the *Eves* statue."

"That's right. We're currently trying to figure out who it might be. Any ideas?"

"It's not Meadow."

Raquel felt her eyebrows rise.

"Jen said," he explained, "that you thought it might be."

"Why don't you think so?"

"Because I talked to Meadow last week."

Jerry jerked upright. "What? She's still alive? Be damned. Where is she?"

"France," Rob told him. "A village. In the south."

Had the man been this terse before he became a hermit, Raquel wondered, or had he just forgotten how to put a full sentence together?

"How the hell did she end up there?" Jerry demanded. "What is she—oh, duh. I was going to ask what she was doing, but at our age, I hope she's enjoying the sun."

"Meadow, retire? No, she's farming. Greens for Michelin chefs. Organic."

"Man, I always wanted to know what became of her. I'm glad she stayed in touch with you, at least."

"She didn't. Not till I went to Gaddo's memorial. In Florence."

Raquel stepped into this trip down memory lane. "She and the artist remained close?"

"They lived together. Worked together. From the time Meadow left until Gaddo died."

"As lovers?"

"Maybe? Friends, for sure."

"Did you know that was where she'd gone? With Gaddo?"

Rob frowned in thought. "I'm not sure I'd have *known* anything that summer, I was so out of it. But I remember everyone else sort of deciding that the two of them must have gone off together."

Raquel watched him closely. A witness's claim to memory loss often got them moved over to the suspect side of the equation. And yet, both Jerry and Wes had said that Rob spent the summer of 1979 in an alcoholic stupor. Plus that, his face did show thought, not deception.

"I didn't find out for sure until three or four years later. Everyone was gone by then. I was out in the garden one morning and it was such a mess, overgrown and neglected, that it hit me just how much I missed her. So I had David hunt down the name of the gallery in New York that Gaddo used, and I sent them a letter to pass on to her, asking if she knew where Meadow was. It came back ripped into tiny pieces. After that I paid a guy. Friend of a friend. He found out where Gaddo lived, in Italy. He went to see, took a long lens, brought back pictures. And there was Meadow. She looked happy. So I wrote her there. She didn't answer, but she didn't send it back all torn up, either. So about once a year, I'd write her. Just to say hi. Thirty years—crazy, huh? And she never wrote back until Gaddo was gone."

Jerry cut in. "Why didn't Gaddo tell us, when she came back to install the *Eves*?"

"Man, she was so pissed off at me. Way more than Meadow was. She wasn't going to come at all, but Meadow made her. Didn't you ever wonder why the statue was the wrong way around?" Remembering the artist's fury had triggered a relative flood of words from the laconic man.

"Was it?"

"Sure. It was supposed to have one of the other faces out, but like I say, she was really angry. Putting that face on the outside was her revenge on me."

"Hah!" Jen exclaimed, from her chair behind the desk. "Mrs. Dalhousie's been trying to figure that out ever since we saw the other faces."

"Sorry. Anyway, yes, Meadow is fine. Well, she's got arthritis and some blood pressure thing, but she was definitely alive last week."

"Man, Rob," Jerry said. "All these years. Why didn't she get in touch—and why didn't you tell us?"

"She said not to. I don't know how well you remember Meadow, but she was never about half measures. The way she approached things— you give yourself heart and soul, but if it ends, you cut your ties and you walk away. Never look back. Like, before I knew her, she was this lawyer, headed for the big time—until she changed her mind and flat-out quit. Then she was a roadie and a band manager, until one day she wasn't that, either. She lived with The Commons, first in Oregon and then here, but when she realized it wasn't a good fit anymore, she pulled up her roots and went. Every time: change your mind, change your heart—change your name, even."

"But to France?"

"Italy, at first. Gaddo had this women's community near Florence. Meadow decided that we men were fucking up the world, so women-only was where she wanted to be. *Who* she wanted to be. You know what name she took, when she moved there?" Jerry shook his head. "Eve. She said because 'Meadow' was passive, a place where other things grew, but Eve was the one who set everything in motion. Anyway, they stayed in Florence until Gaddo died, then she and a couple of others went off to France and bought a place there. Though she still calls herself Eve."

"I'm so glad to hear she's doing okay. When you talk to her, tell her I said hi."

The lawyer had been doing an efficient job of asking Raquel's questions while she sat quietly and composed a mental follow-up list, beginning with: get a warrant for Rob Gardener's phone records. Now, as Rob turned back to her, she resumed the questioning.

"Mr. Gardener, unlike your lawyer, I will need to actually speak with your friend Meadow."

"You can try. I'll bring you her number tomorrow. There's a Board meeting I'm coming back down for."

"You don't have it on your phone?"

"I don't carry my phone with me. Down here, it just bings at me all the time."

Jen spoke up. "Rob, I'm glad you're coming tomorrow, but it makes for a crazy amount of walking. Spend the night here. We'll call out for pizza, or Chinese."

"Thanks, Jen, but I like my own bed."

"Okay. But I'm going to drive the Rover up in the morning and meet you at the turnaround. It'll save your feet a few miles, anyway."

Enough, Raquel thought. "Jen, Jerry, could you two leave us alone for a while? I'm sure you have plenty to do, even on a Monday."

Jen rose. Jerry did not. "As Mr. Gardener's lawyer, I should remain present."

But Rob said, "It's okay, Jerry, we'll be fine. I'll see you tomorrow."

"Rob—"

"Go. Please."

The lawyer pulled himself off the desk. "Okay, but if any of her questions bother you, or if she seems to be suspecting you of a crime— *any* crime—stop talking immediately and call me in."

"And Rob, I can give you a ride up to the turnaround, too, when you're finished," Jen said over her shoulder.

And closed the door.

Instantly, Rob got up to open it again, leaving it a few inches ajar. Walking back, he gave Raquel an apologetic look. "This room always makes me claustrophobic. With all the windows in the house, all the great views, I could never figure out why the old man would spend his days locked away in here. Anyway—coffee?" he asked. "Should still be warm."

"I'm fine, thanks."

He had stopped next to a tray set with a carafe and mugs, where he filled one and brought it back to the chair, resting the cup on its arm. He glanced down at Raquel's leg, and she braced herself for questions— but the one that came was not what she'd expected.

"Is that chair comfortable?"

"It's fine, thanks."

"It was my grandfather's. He had another one that looked just like it, but was designed to make the person sitting in it really uncomfortable. Says a lot about him."

"I thought I recognized the chair, from his portrait in the bedroom upstairs."

"Is that where they put the thing? It's a copy. We let the kids use the original for an archery target."

"There's another with it, a portrait of his mother, I think?"

"Maude. What a team. I hope you don't want to talk about them."

"No. I'm interested in the period leading up to June 23, 1979."

"Ah. So, the body was . . . fresh, when we put up the statue?"

"Certainly when the concrete was poured."

"There were hundreds of people around. For the festival."

"Did you ever hear any talk of someone going missing? Even rumors?"

"No. But like I said, I wasn't paying much attention to real life just then."

"What about the fight?"

A quick flash of wariness. "Which fight was that?"

"I understand there was trouble that night. Arrests were made."

His face cleared. "Ah, *that* fight. Just some kids who had too much to drink and started harassing people. We stopped it, and held on to them until the cops could take them away."

"What fight did you think I meant?"

Shame, a glimpse, as he swiveled the cup on the arm of the chair, then raised his eyes. "I thought maybe you heard about the argument I had with Meadow. The one where I should have apologized and didn't. The one where I stood there and saw full well what I was doing and went ahead and did it anyway. The one that ended everything."

"What was it about?"

"What are fights like that ever about? Even when you're living a life wrapped up in freedom and equality and the rights of others, the ugly things persist, and you find yourself accusing someone of something you know damned well they would never do."

"Mr. Gard—"

"Jealousy. Can you believe it? Our fight was about jealousy. And I can't even call it a fight, really. It should have been. It should have been furious and loud and gone on for days, but instead, it was like— *poof*! There and gone. I mean, looking back, there'd been all kinds of minor irritations and snarky comments building up. And not as much affection, of any kind. But then, there was a lot going on, and by the time the festival started up, everyone was a little on edge. I didn't think much about it, until all of a sudden, there we were squabbling about

something and she just looked up at me and said, 'It's over, isn't it?'
And I didn't even have the sense to say no.

"Because she was right. If I was feeling jealous, after all that time
and everything I knew about her, then I'd failed. Failed her, failed me,
failed everyone."

"Who were you jealous of?"

"Who *wasn't* I jealous of?" His face was a study in sadness. "That's
the thing about the male ego. If it's feeling weak, then everything in
the world is to blame. This man, that woman, those kids. The piece of
art that's taking up her interest. The cat that settles into her lap. And
that's what killed off The Commons. Meadow leaving was bad enough,
but when I basically blamed everyone else for her going, that pulled
the trigger. Rain left, Eddie and Paolo—they'd been with The Commons before I showed up. Even Fort walked away—from *me*. Never
came back from India, never answered my letters. He'd write, but only
to Marla—the housekeeper who basically raised us."

"And yet, he'd come back that spring. Why?"

"He said his guru wanted him to be sure that the ashram was what
he wanted to do with the rest of his life, so he came here to think about
it. And I guess he decided what we were doing with the place was
worthwhile, because he left a note to say that he wouldn't be wanting
the money I'd offered him."

"How much, may I ask?"

"I don't think we'd pinned it down, but basically, he wanted to give
his guru whatever we could get by selling off a corner of land that's
across the road. He deserved more than that, but in the end he didn't
want it."

Raquel fished the image of Michael Johnston with a beard out of
her folder. "Does this man look familiar?"

The woodsman patted his shirt pocket and drew out a pair of half-
glasses, perching them on his nose. "Not really."

"A little familiar, or not at all?"

"Maybe a little, but I couldn't tell you from where."

"What about this one?" This was the picture of Max O'Connor.

It being a booking photo helped to prompt his memory. "That's the
scum who was arrested for attacking a woman. He was hiding out here

until someone saw him. One of the newer guys brought him home one day. Man, that was such a disturbing episode. But—wait. Wasn't that other—yeah, him."

She'd offered him the second booking photo, the one of Michael Johnston. Gardener held it next to the doctored one with the beard. "That's where I know him from—he was here at the same time, with Ronnie and the creep. But I don't think he had anything to do with it. At least, as I remember, the cops let him go."

Raquel merely took the pages back and moved on to the others in her folder, her candidates: seventeen blond or light-headed men, nineteen women—and a couple of near adults. She'd folded the pages so only the pictures showed, not the names.

His face softened. "That's Pig. Peggy was her name. She played the dulcimer. Last name was Long-something. And Heather—she wasn't here for long, and she may have left before that summer. This one . . . Sally? Susan? Lesbian, she and a girlfriend lived here for a while. Sharon?" He shook his head, and went to the next. "Ah, Kiz—she was great, an amazing kid. She was maybe eleven or twelve when I got to Oregon. She and her father were there, the mother was in prison, some political thing. That last summer she'd have been around eighteen, you could tell she was going to be beautiful. And so smart—that's right, they were going to leave anyway, she'd been accepted at some big college back east. Her father was Stone—but that wasn't his name. Oh, Peter. Pete Talley. God, what corner of the brain do these things hide in, all these years? And Annabelle. What a love. Single mother, so young—she couldn't have been more than fifteen when she got pregnant. Her father threw her out. Her mother sent money sometimes, presents for the kid—Sparrow. He was a hoot. She never said who the father was. This one . . . sorry, she was around, don't remember her name, but she used to squint because she needed glasses. That kid's Pat—Padraic, he called himself, but nobody else did. Really great voice, though he sometimes forgot the accent when he got stoned. This woman I don't remember at all. But that guy's Bear—not because he was big, but his name was Barry. He got a job with some guys we used for security during the festival. And that's Julia . . . Crowsomething. Cromarty? Artist—parts of the foyer are by her. She and Pig were friends before, and I'm pretty sure they all left together."

His memory, for events nearly half a century ago and clouded by substances, was surprisingly good—several pieces of new information, no glaring gaps, and the only person he did not recognize was one Raquel had created. She went more closely over the list, trying to narrow down who had been seen after the festival, and ended up with three women who could have disappeared that day: Annabelle, Heather, and the nameless squinting woman. Three blond heads who might readily have slipped between the cracks, when the commune was breaking up—no partner, no close friend, just one small child.

Unless he was lying about Meadow.

"Tell me about Annabelle," she said.

He looked up. "You think it could be her?"

"She had a son called Sparrow. You think that was the child's legal name?"

"I don't think the kid was legal. She was scared of her father. Convinced he was going to swoop down and grab the boy."

"You think he might have done so?"

"No." But he heard the dismissive tone in his voice, and thought about it. "I'm pretty sure I'd remember if any of us thought she was actually under threat. And that day? There were a lot of people around."

"She was in photographs taken that morning," Raquel told him. "But not the kids. Where were the children, during the festival?"

"I think Pig had them? So they wouldn't get underfoot. I remember seeing a bunch of them in the Yard, around the schoolhouse. The house was closed—it was supposed to be closed, anyway—but the Yard was an open area, so yeah, anyone could have come in."

"I expect there would have been a panic, if either Annabelle or her boy went missing. But what if they both disappeared, at the same time?"

"I'm sure somebody would have said something. I mean, things were crazy that day, but surely somebody would have noticed?"

The phrase "I'm sure" generally meant "I hope."

There was a tap on the door before it pushed open and Jen's head appeared. "If you're going to be much longer, Rob, I will insist on driving you up to the turnaround. I do not want you walking home in the dark."

"Yes, Mother." He looked at Raquel, who had to admit that she had nothing else to ask him for the moment. "I'll be there in a minute, Jen."

The manager nodded and withdrew, leaving the door open.

"I hope you can figure out who it is, under the statue. Let me know what I can do."

"You could send me Meadow's contact number, when you get back to your phone."

"Depends on how late it is. There's a hill I have to hike up to get a signal, and it's tricky in the dark. If I break my leg, Mother Hen there will never let me hear the end of it. But I promise I'll bring my phone with me tomorrow, and send you the number as soon as I get into range."

"What time will that be?"

"The Board meeting starts at ten, so around nine if Jen picks me up halfway, closer to eight if I'm walking."

She was struck anew by the incongruity of this ponytailed hippie sitting down to a Board meeting. And why had everyone wanted her to think that the man never came out of the deep woods? "Do you usually come in for these meetings?"

"God, no. First one. Well, first since the Trust took over."

"Why now?"

"Jen asked me. They're talking about some big decisions, she thought I should know."

Decisions to do with keychains and German brochures, Raquel thought.

"Let me give you my number," she said, and printed it on one of her cards. "Phone or text, as early as possible."

He slid it into the pocket of his flannel shirt, and politely followed her out of his grandfather's windowless inner sanctum.

52

Never theorize ahead of the facts. The most basic dictum of all. Yet even after Michael Johnston's face had failed to react to the woman with the green eyes, Raquel had persisted in trying to cover the bones with that striking personality.

Unless Rob Gardener was better at lying than Raquel was at seeing, the body was not Meadow.

Annabelle?

She slid out her phone and opened up Facebook, only to find a lengthy list of variations on the name. She knew that San Mateo would do this, eventually. Probably. Her fingertip hesitated on the first one with gray hair . . . and then she closed out Facebook and made a phone call instead.

"Yup?"

"Dee, do me a favor? If you have the time."

"For you, yes."

"Annabelle Paulson, early sixties, possibly from Texas, son named Sparrow. Start with Facebook, there's about fifty of them to go through. I only need to know if she's alive."

"Connected with your Highwayman?"

"Purposes of elimination."

"Will do. Anything else?"

"No, I . . ." Raquel's voice trailed off.

"Rock?" Dee asked. And when the silence went on: "Rock, is there something else you want me to do?"

In no way is Mexico our responsibility. Bad enough she was walking around on San Mateo's toes . . .

"Your missing persons forums. The international ones." Now it was Dee's turn to go silent. "1982 to 2005. Mexico, start with Jalisco. Guadalajara, Puerto Vallarta. Young women. Probably blond. Possibly . . ."

No. So far, they'd kept Johnston's collection of shoes away from the media. Handing her sister that information would cross Al Hawkin's line. "See what you can find."

"That's not much of a—"

"That's all I can give you," she said, and ended the call.

What was she thinking? *Here's the cliff Al told you not to go near, let's step off it and take his reputation with us, shall we?*

On the other hand, why the hell couldn't that coroner at least give her some preliminary answers?

She shook off the irritation and made her way upstairs to the borrowed office, translating the hasty notes she'd made sitting in the hospital hallway into an actual report, bristling with technical terminology and cross-references to fundamental works. The result would be incomprehensible to the rest of the Highwayman group, but she would put a copy in their common folder anyway, in case Al felt like sitting down with a chart of craniofacial muscles and trying to visualize a quarter-second contraction of Johnston's zygomaticus minor.

It would be of no use whatsoever in a court of law. Its significance would be snuffed out entirely when Michael Johnston's heart ceased to beat. And anyone without Raquel Laing's talent and training would need a slowed-down video to have any idea what she meant.

But if they made such a recording and went through it with her notes, they could not fail to see the absolutely distinctive reaction that flickered across The Highwayman's face whenever he laid eyes on one of his victims.

53

"Good heavens, you're still here?"

Raquel caught the traveling quarter between her fingers and looked up.

"What time—oh, sorry, I got involved in something."

"I can see that. I was putting the Rover away in the Yard when I noticed the light was still on. Good thing I didn't lock you in for the night."

"I'll go."

"Look, I'm going to forage through the kitchen for a bite, before I leave. Want to join me?"

"That's okay, I'll stop and grab something on my way home."

"I doubt that. Come on, there's sure to be plenty."

"Why does everyone seem to think I need feeding?"

"I wonder," Jen said dryly.

"What does that mean?"

"Inspector Laing, I've known you for five days, and I could tell on day one that you were the kind to get absolutely sucked into whatever was on your mind. Even now you're not entirely here. Though that could be low blood sugar. Come. Eat."

She should just check her emails first . . .

Raquel smiled into Jen's eyes, and shut her laptop. "Food would be great, thanks."

She managed to keep her hands off both laptop and phone the whole time Jen was foraging—vegetables and bits of leftover chicken—and stir-frying them with a dash of sesame oil from an industrial-sized jar. She heard three pings while they were eating, but forced her attention to stay on the plate and the woman across from her until the last forkful disappeared.

"Okay, now you can check your messages," Jen said, and got up to transfer the dishes to the sink.

From Dee:

Annabelle now Anna Paulson age 63, son Sparrow age 48, living in Austin Texas. Big Insta acct of nature photos. Sound like your lady?

Then ten minutes later, she'd sent:

Dozens of Jalisco mispers and Jane Does under your given specs. You want them all?

And a while after that:

Any way you can narrow down this search?

Raquel's thumb traveled up and down the edge of the phone as she thought about her reply.

In no way is Mexico our responsibility.

A cup of coffee appeared in front of her. Raquel deliberately set the phone aside and looked across the table at Jen Bachus.

"How does a person decide what's right?" she asked.

Jen, about to take a sip from her cup, paused. "What is this about?"

"Oh, one of those things that's sucking my mind in."

"To do with your job."

"Yes. Although it won't stop there."

"Well, personally, I usually find it easier to figure out what would be wrong, and do the opposite."

Raquel said nothing. After a minute, Jen set down the cup. "I'm a great believer in the wisdom of the body. Sometimes the brain gets in the way. Like, you're hiking around the hills and you get turned around, and you have no idea where you are. First, you panic. Then your mind starts coming up with options and facts and theories. But underneath, if you wait out the panic and the theories, you'll find that one direction just doesn't *feel* right. You visualize yourself going off to the left and you feel vaguely uncomfortable. So you go right."

"And they find you starving and hypothermic days later."

"I admit it may not work for everyone. But if you're faced with a choice—and I'm assuming that you're talking about a moral choice, here—and heading one way makes you feel vaguely unclean, there may be a reason for that."

Unclean.

In no way is Mexico our responsibility.

I'm not some pervert, if that's what you're thinking.

She picked up her phone, and keyed in:

Were any of them missing their right shoe?

Her thumb hesitated. Compliance versus responsibility. What felt right as opposed to what felt unclean. What she owed Al Hawkin, and what she owed twenty-three years of potential victims. The self-protection of giving this to Dee verbally, as opposed to the traceable defiance of something sent on a screen.

Her thumb came down on SEND.

She laid the device on the table, facedown, and looked at Jen.

Whose forehead was folded into worry lines. "Um, did I just get you in trouble?"

"*You* didn't, no."

"Raquel, what's going on?"

"I'll tell you about it someday. But now I should go. You have a busy day tomorrow."

"Are you coming back down?"

"Probably not. I'm hoping Mr. Gardener will send me a contact number for Meadow, as soon as he comes into range of a cell tower." *And once I've talked to her, I'll be off the case. If not off the force entirely.*

"I'm meeting him around 8:30, halfway up the road. I'll remind him."

"Thank you."

"I'm glad to know it's not Meadow. I mean, it's awful that it's anyone, but the pictures of her make her seem so . . . alive."

"I am looking forward to talking with her."

"Have you any idea who it might be, if not her?"

"Several ideas, but the coroner should have a preliminary report—" Raquel looked at the time: not quite as late as she thought. "—tomorrow."

"Well, good luck."

"And you. With your Board meeting."

Jen shook her head wryly. "I told the kitchen to add wine to the lunch menu. We're all going to need a drink by then."

They went through the dark house and into the garden, where the pathways were gently lit by solar-powered lights. Raquel's car was just outside the gate; Jen's was farther back, where the employees parked.

"I need to check my email," Raquel told her. "Don't wait for me."

"Don't get sucked in," Jen warned, and wished her a good night.

The moon was half-full, the night warm and fragrant with something from inside the garden wall. Feeling a lot older than her years, Raquel lowered herself into the seat, pulling her bad leg inside.

Across the parking lot, an engine started. Headlights went on, and after a brief pause, shadows slid and danced over the tarmac. A horn gave two quick beeps, and Jen was gone.

Two minutes later, her own car's lights automatically shut off, leaving Raquel in darkness.

Figure out what's wrong, and do the opposite. Explaining her actions to Al Hawkin was going to be hard enough, but if she had to stand in her captain's office, or that of the chief . . .

But she felt clean. For a first step on the path, that would have to be sufficient.

She slid her hand into her bag and tugged out her laptop, wondering if the Archives wifi would reach through the walls. The car interior brightened as the screen went on, and after a moment, her in-box came to life.

The most recent email was from Dee—one of Dee's many identities. It had seven attachments. The message read:

R, we found seven possible missing women so far, with lists of their clothing that caught the names in a first pass-through. Only one specifically mentions a missing right shoe, the others just say a single shoe was found.

I've only looped in two of the others on this, and told them not to say anything about the right shoe element. You can trust them.

D

Raquel began to open the attachments, which started in 1988: Veronica Baxter, twenty-seven, from Chicago, in Puerto Vallarta for a bachelorette party. Big hair, oversized clothes, long bare legs, and an oversized margarita in one hand; 1994: Maria Torres, twenty-two, worked in a bar, bright bleached hair contradicting her dark eyes and heavy eyebrows; 1985: Sueanne Dyer, seventeen, on vacation with her family from Atlanta . . .

All were his type.

No, Michael Johnston had not simply stopped, like the Golden State Killer.

She looked at the corner of the screen—nearly midnight. Whether she trusted Dee's fellow amateurs was beside the point. Tomorrow, she would have to tell Al what she had done. Her modified duty status would become a suspension, removing her from the Highwayman group and the Gardener Estate.

The Department would consider her act a disgrace. Certainly a firing offense. Raquel could not argue with that.

But before talking to Al, she wanted to reach the woman once known as Meadow.

And because Rob had not texted her the number before darkness had fallen, that meant she had time for something else tonight.

She found a twenty-four-hour print shop in a strip mall near the hospital, and ran off the seven attachments, along with three more that Dee had sent later, and three that she mocked up using anonymous faces.

She parked in front of the hospital and went in through the front door, empty and echoing at that hour.

She took the elevator up and walked as briskly as possible to Michael Johnston's room, startling the dozing guard but holding out her badge to keep him in his chair.

Johnston's machines murmured and beeped quietly to themselves. His breath rattled under his oxygen mask. She switched on the lights and said his name.

He startled awake, blinking and coughing, squinting at the figure standing at the foot of his bed. "What the fuck? What time is it?"

She merely held up one of her fakes for him to look at.

"Who's that?" he complained. "Are we doing this again, you giving me your strays? I'm calling the nurse—"

She stretched out her cane and flipped his controls off the side of the bed, then held up the picture of Veronica Baxter, twenty-seven, from Chicago.

And there it was. The Highwayman's giveaway twitch.

Johnston said nothing. But it was the same for Maria Torres. And Sueanne Dyer. Not until her second fake was held up in front of him did he protest.

She was on the last page when the door burst open and the nurse and guard came through it, scolding and protesting. Raquel wordlessly gathered her pages and walked out.

Neither of the staff knew quite what to do with her. Nobody stopped her from leaving.

In the elevator down, she took her phone from her pocket and stopped the recording.

In her car, she sat and wrote up the results.

But she didn't put it into the group's folder yet.

Instead, she drove home, feeling at peace for the first time in many days. There she slept, deeply, for nearly four hours, and awoke to a new day.

"You going to tell me what we did last night?" Dee asked her as the coffee brewed.

"We made a decision."

"Yeah, I sort of gathered that. How much shit will you be in if they find out?"

"We'll know when I tell Al. And I'm going to do that as soon as I've made a phone call." Assuming the hermit remembered to send her the number. And if he didn't—or if the woman in France refused to talk to her? Well, it wasn't necessary, she supposed. But she would admit, she was deeply curious about Meadow-turned-Eve, and hoped to have a conversation with her before she had to remove herself from the case.

She'd left her laptop bag at the front door when she got in, and fetched it now, propping open the lid on the kitchen table so it would download her email. "Want some toast?"

"There's some nice bread that Rory brought. I think she's going to marry that baker of hers. Look, there's no reason for Al to know. We've been careful."

"I'm not going to lie to him, Dee. I owe him too much."

"Will you be fired?"

"I won't wait for that."

"Ah. He's going to be disappointed."

"I know. But I don't think he'll be very surprised."

"So, those women we found. Were they killed by that Johnston creature?"

"Seven of the ten you sent me were. Any others you come up with, I'll hand over with my report, and they can find another behavioral investigator to follow up. If they hurry."

Raquel's phone started to ring: Al's tone. She made no move to get it. Instead, she took the slices from the toaster and spread them with butter and jam. When she carried hers back to the table, she saw that the call had gone to voicemail.

She sat, took a bite, washed it down with coffee, and brushed the crumbs from her hands before scrolling up her in-box.

Then the landline rang. She and Dee looked at it in surprise, but since the calls there were nearly always junk, they waited: anyone who mattered would leave a message, when she could interrupt to take the call if she wanted.

Raquel's attention went back to the email, where a sender's name caught her eye. She clicked it open.

I know you're waiting for this and it'll take me a while to write everything up, but if you want a verbal report, give me a call before hours.

It was from the San Mateo coroner's private email address, cc'ing Al, and had a phone number attached.

Raquel was dimly aware that the rings had ended and Al's voice was recording a message on the landline, but he could wait.

"This is Raquel Laing, you said I could— Yes, thanks, I would. Yeah. *What?*" She listened as, with a few brief phrases, her case turned upside down and her mind began to jump rapidly forward. "I agree. Yes, I understand. Let me guess: India. Okay, thanks."

She hung up. Her sister said something, but Raquel did not hear her. Her fingertips located the old quarter and set it into motion. Back and forth.

The much-shattered pelvis had belonged to a male.

The skull, though missing some small pieces, showed a massive fracture, two or three blows from a hard, flat object like a board or a shovel.

One section of jawbone was missing, but the rest had been reconstructed enough to make a dental identification, if they could locate old X-rays.

And although the ME planned to call in a forensic dentist to be sure, she'd thought that one of the fillings had been done in an area with technology that was outdated even at the time.

Such as, yes, India.

54

Not Meadow. Not Annabelle or Heather or Peggy.

And not linked in any way to Michael Johnston.

Fort Gardener.

If postcards came from India, they hadn't been from him.

And if the body under *Midsummer Eves* was Thaddeus Gardener the Fourth, that opened up a whole new realm of questions and motivations.

Multiple blows meant murder, not an accident hidden from the authorities by a group of antiauthoritarians, or incorporated under a piece of art by a woman known for macabre imagery.

What would bring murder to a communal family?

Jealousy? The Bible blamed it for the first murder, in the first family. Cain and Abel—who stood with their parents at the very door of the Gardener house—had brought gifts to God, and when God preferred what Abel had given, Cain murdered his brother in a jealous rage.

Am I my brother's keeper?

Rob had even confessed to jealousy—although his twitches of guilt had been linked to Meadow and The Commons, not to his brother. Unless she wanted to consider a drug-induced rage followed by the haze of alcohol, she did not think the man would forget killing his brother.

Although, what if Fort had been secondary, almost incidental compared to the true target, Meadow? Say that Meadow, the community's mother figure, had preferred what Fort had to offer. If she had turned from Rain to Rob, how would he have taken it if she then chose Fort? Sex plus approval was a powerful message.

But that would be true for others as well. Rain, for example: what if he'd found a second Gardener taking Rob's place . . . ? Or some other member of The Commons who resented Meadow's shared affections?

If not jealousy, then what? Money? An infuriated member of the commune who'd discovered what the agreement really said—that they were secretly being left out? But why attack Fort, instead of Rob, who'd set up the deception? Unless they thought that Fort was still in line for a piece of the Estate. If that was the case, then what about the other members of the family? Why not go after David or his sister . . . ?

The coin paused as the name snagged at Raquel's mind, then resumed. Cousin David. A Kirkup, not a Gardener—never a Gardener, in name or in acceptance. Always there, always overlooked.

Always overlooked.

I tend to think of David as a third brother.

Cain, Abel . . . and another brother too invisible to name?

As a boy, Davey tagging along behind the two Gardener brothers. When they were away at boarding school, Davey trying to make himself useful to the family tyrant. As a young man—*he's spent his whole life working here*—shaping his professional life around the Estate, dedicating his energies to making it run smoothly, first for Thaddeus the Second, then for Rob the hippie—both of whom kept him at a distance, treating him with a trace of disdain. Others would make the decisions, and David—as he saw it—would make them possible. Even decisions he disagreed with.

Without David's single-minded devotion, the Estate would have been sold off years ago . . .

Selling off a corner of land across the road.

Cousin David might have been resigned to being considered a lesser Gardener, and would have known his whole life that he had little chance of inheriting any portion of his beloved Estate. It must have rankled, to see the influx of The Commons—but at least they'd respected the land and made no effort to sell it.

But how would he have felt on learning that one of the brothers intended to tear off a piece of the Estate to provide some Indian guru with a handout?

If David had learned, back in 1979, that the Estate he loved was under threat, would he have accepted that decision, too? Or would it have seemed to him that removing Fort would remove the threat? Fort Gardener: a man who had turned his back on the house and land he'd grown up in. Cousin Fort, whom David, in his interview, had tucked in behind Meadow's missing passport and the details of the statue going in and the Diggers and the roadies and a pregnant girl named Butterfly or Bonnie . . .

The only thing he'd contributed about his cousin Fort was that he'd continued to send postcards, well after he'd left the Estate. He'd taken care to mention the cards twice—no, three times.

It didn't have to be a planned murder. Cain deliberately drew Abel out into the fields, but she could easily envision a fervent plea from 25-year-old David Kirkup to his older cousin getting out of hand. Moving from *"You can't be thinking of doing this"* to *"You really mustn't do this"* and finally *"I won't let you do this."*

A young man who had devoted his life to a family that consistently patronized and overlooked him, that ignored his skills and commitment, that kept him at arm's length, refused to hear his voice, outvoted his every proposal—

Raquel went still, completely unaware of the old quarter falling off her fingers and rolling away to the floor.

Outvoted his every proposal.

A Board meeting. The Trustees considering a plan to transform the Gardener Estate into a place of enormous influence on the world stage. A proposal that would ensure its survival, would shore up its boundaries for decades against the encroachment of the house-hungry Bay Area.

She could hear Jen's voice: *My vote actually counts for more than his.*

Surely not. Kirkup was in his sixties now. Youthful rage and resentments would have been long put aside. Right?

Just because you don't see any fire in old men doesn't mean it's not smoldering underground.

She snatched her phone and hit the CALL icon. Three rings . . . then Jen's voice.

One instant of huge relief jarred up against the realization that she was hearing a recording, Jen's voice inviting her to leave a message after the beep. "Jen, hon, are you—I hope—" She stopped, feeling Dee's alarmed gaze. She took a breath, started again. "Jen, this is Raquel Laing, you need to phone me, right now. Please, the instant you get this, call me, on this number. Thanks."

Hon?

She ended the call and dialed the Estate's main number, but there was Jen's voice again, more formal this time, telling her that the Gardener Estate was not yet open.

Jerry Rathford was next—and he, at least, replied.

By now, Raquel had herself under control. "Morning, Mr. Rathford, this is Inspector Laing. I'm trying to reach Jen Bachus and she's not picking up. Do you know where she is?"

"She's probably gone up to get Rob. I know she wanted to get back by—"

"Where are you?"

"I'm at home. About to eat br—"

She broke the connection and pawed through her bag for David Kirkup's card. She tapped in the number, listened to it ring. It, too, went to voicemail.

She hung up and redialed the lawyer.

"What?" he answered, sounding annoyed.

"I'm sorry, Mr. Rathford, we got cut off. I can't reach Mr. Kirkup, either."

Apologies and a blame on technology soothed his irritation. "Maybe he and Jen went up together? She might have asked him to drive her up to Rob's place—David doesn't mind that road as much as she does, not in the Rover."

"Could I have Mr. Gardener's cell number, please?"

"Rob doesn't answer his phone."

"I'll try a text. There's something important I need to check."

"Hold on a sec," he said. "Yeah, here it is—got a pencil?"

This time, she thanked him before hanging up.

Rob Gardener, as expected, did not answer, but she left a voice message that she urgently needed to speak with him. Then she did the same as a text, since those often reached obscure corners of the world when a clear phone link did not.

And finally, she looked up at her sister.

There was no reason for her to feel as if a tsunami was about to crest over her head, Raquel told herself. No logic behind the unbearable tension that was stretching all the nerves in her body.

No reason at all. But she couldn't stay here, not for another moment.

Her chair scraped back and she was talking over her shoulder.

"Dee, I need you to locate a cabin that's up at the far edges of the Gardener Estate. It's off the grid—no power, no phone, but I suspect not off the books. Probably built in the nineties. There's a place that may be it on Google Earth, but I could only see the little road up from the main house. I need you to find me a back way in."

"Why do you think it has one?"

"Because his grandfather's windowless study makes Rob Gardener claustrophobic."

The front door slammed as Raquel hurried, cursing her leg, toward the car that she'd parked halfway down the next block.

Dee retrieved her sister's talisman coin from the kitchen floor and laid it on the table, then went to work.

55

Then

Three hours after the last of the festival bands had left the outdoor stage, David stood at the back of the pounding ballroom, watching Rain take over his DJ job at the record player. What was wrong with the Woodstock song, anyway? Sure, he liked the Stones, but you didn't have to be rude about it.

Maybe he wasn't the only one to feel that way? Now that he wasn't busy with the records, David could see that most of the people in the ballroom were outsiders—band members and backup crews, some newer members of The Commons. Rain and Wes and Paolo were here, and he'd seen Rob a little while ago, but where were all the others? Did it have something to do with everyone's short temper today? You'd think they'd all be happy to have got through it, but he didn't even see Meadow, who was always in the center of everything. Maybe she went off with that high-and-mighty artist.

Or maybe they were just tired.

The air was thick with dope smoke, and some of the strangers were doing lines of coke, but to be honest, David didn't really like either one—pot made him paranoid and coke kept him from sleeping for days. He just wasn't cool enough for this crowd, he guessed—and with that, his headache was back.

Screw 'em, he was going home.

Someone was going up the stairs as he came into the foyer—Rob, it looked like. He nearly called a good night to his cousin, but decided not to. Rob had been in a bad mood earlier, David didn't need another downer added to his night. Instead, he continued through the house to the kitchen, scene of so many happy childhood hours, drank a big glass of cold water, then rummaged around for some leftovers and ate them, standing at the window. Two indistinct figures crossed the Yard, close enough that they must have been holding hands, but since they were headed out, he didn't worry about them. He drank some more water, left the glass in the sink for someone else to clean up, and let himself out the door.

Halfway across the Yard, he was startled at a sound behind him—the gate to the gardens. A pale shape appeared.

"Who's that?" he demanded.

The figure paused. "It's just me—Fort. Davey, is that you?"

Why couldn't they call him David? "Yeah, sorry, there's so many strangers here tonight, I didn't think we wanted them poking around."

"Well, there's already been people in my room," Fort said. "If anyone else wants to steal something, they're welcome to it."

The holy man speaks, David thought sourly. "Okay, but maybe not everybody is keen on having someone steal their shit."

"You're right. And it's good of you to watch out for them."

Jesus Christ, David nearly said aloud, *rub my nose in it, why don't you?* You couldn't even argue with a man so selfless, he'd stand by and watch a stranger take his belongings. Both his cousins drove him nuts sometimes. And speaking of acting so superior—"Hey, do you know what's bugging Rob so hard? He's been snapping at people all day. Everyone except those Army buddies of his."

Fort started to reply, then glanced at the dark windows along the side of the Yard. "I think there's kids trying to sleep here—let's take a walk, I'll tell you about it."

They left the Yard and turned onto the path toward the Great Field. There was no moon tonight, but between a couple of lights left burning in the kitchen tent and the pale gravel of the path, the way was clear enough for two men who had spent their childhoods running up and down the grounds.

They passed the lingering smells of grease and spices, stepping cautiously over the uneven ground to the far side of the stage, where clean night air drifted off the grassland below.

Fort drew a deep breath, slowly let it out. "The first time I came out to the Great Field at night was about two weeks after Grandfather brought Rob and me here. I was scared shitless, sure that a bear was going to eat me. But I wanted to see the stars. You never see them, in a city."

"Is that what you came here to tell me?"

"Good old Davey, always to the point. Here, sit down."

There were crates and pieces of equipment, abandoned along the edge of the bare stage. The giant speakers and lights had been taken away, though the buried electrical cables and crates of lesser equipment had yet to be cleared off. Fort settled onto a trunk with a band name painted on it, kicking off his beat-up Indian sandals and tucking his feet underneath him. David chose a nearby crate and sat more conventionally.

The field was nothing but darkness, and the hills rising up were a dim silhouette. Over their shoulders, Gaddo's *Eves* loomed, waiting for their final home. But the stars overhead were dazzling.

Fort gave a little sigh. "It's wrong to love a possession," he mused. "But I'm not sure it's wrong to love a place. It has always seemed to me that loving a place means embracing Creation itself."

"I guess" was the only response David could think of.

"On the other hand, if a person loves a place because it's *his* and he controls it, doesn't that make it just another possession? The Bhagavad Gita teaches us that hoarded wealth is the cause of ruin. That sharing wealth brings merit. You have to wonder if wealth comes in forms other than just money."

"Fort, I don't know what you're talking about."

"Yeah, I know, I'm being sentimental. Rob and I have been discussing matters, and it seems to me we should let you know. I mean, this place might not be your home, but it's always been important to you, and God knows you've put a lot of energy into it. More than Rob and me, to be honest. Anyway, when I came back in January, Rob wanted to know if I was staying, and he said, flat out, that he'd always thought of the place as mine, no matter what Grandfather's will said.

"I told him I wasn't planning on staying, that I wasn't interested in becoming a householder, but I did ask him to think about freeing up some portion of the inheritance so I could take it back to India with me. For my guru, and the ashram. We didn't go into any details, since I knew I'd be here for a while, but now the festival's over and things are settling down, he doesn't need me here. I'm thinking of going back at the end of summer, but Rob and I will need to settle the question of money before I go."

"Fort, there aren't a lot of liquid assets anymore. Not unless Rob's got some secret bank account hidden away." David laughed at the idea.

"Yeah, that's not very likely. No, I was thinking more of selling a small piece of the land. Like that section on the other side of the main road. It's already divided off—Grandfather bought it after the rest, and—"

But David hadn't heard anything past the words, "selling the land." He stared at the pale shape that was his cousin. "What? Fort, no, you can't sell off the Estate."

"Not the whole thing, Davey, of course not. But that one section, the fifty acres across the road. It's barely visible from the house, and nobody's using it other than the farmer who turns his steers out on it. You know someone would pay a small fortune for it."

"You can't be serious. You want to let some developer put up a sub-division right outside the front gate? Just so you can give some damned guru a check? Fort, you're nuts."

"Davey, man, life moves on. You can't live in a walled garden forever. And really, what right do we have to fence out the world, anyway? Isn't that just what our great-grandparents tried to do—build a castle and keep the rabble at bay? Sharing the wealth may mean sharing the things that make it. Like land."

Fort continued talking, his voice spilling down over the silent grassland, but David couldn't—wouldn't—hear the words over the pounding in his ears. *Sell?* Cut the Estate into pieces so some vulture could throw up cheap housing? He'd got to his feet, only realizing it when

Fort stopped talking and turned to look up at him. "Are you *insane*? Do you imagine you can just chop a hunk off the family's land and hand it to some . . . some charlatan cult leader off in India? You have no right to any part of this place—there was a reason Grandfather wrote you out of his will. Ask Jerry if you don't believe it—you have no rights here anymore. Your damn guru will just have to make do with what he gets out of his other gullible Americans."

"David, what Jerry thinks doesn't matter. I've talked to Rob, and he agreed."

"I don't believe you."

"He wanted to give me the entire place. I told him a part of it would do."

David was never entirely sure what happened next. He was tired and stressed and he'd been breathing in other people's dope for hours, and somehow the night had narrowed itself down to this tiny point. It was hard to breathe. He walked away a few steps—he remembered that. And he recalled turning to look at his cousin, sitting there with his back to David, looking down over the precious legacy he was planning to give away. Fort was bareheaded for once, his pale hair falling to his shoulders.

After that, all David remembered were blows that jarred his arms down to his hips, and a sound like a weight hitting the ground.

Then he was panting, leaning upright on some wooden handle. His eyes were shut tight, he swayed with the wildness of his pulse, so he let go of whatever it was (dimly conscious of it falling) to sit down hard on the crate, letting his head drop between his knees.

It took a long time for the dizziness to pass. When it did, he lifted his head to stare up at the stars, then finally, unwillingly, looked down at his cousin's body, sprawled on the dry summer ground.

After a while, he picked up the thing he'd dropped—a shovel, it was—and looked around. Under the stage, the ground would be soft enough to dig. And they'd built it high enough over the rebar frame that he could nearly stand upright. When he was finished, he shoved the rebar into place, and put the shovel back where he'd found it.

Up at the kitchen tent, he found the flashlights the county had required along with the fire extinguishers, and used one to check.

It looked pretty much like it had before.

And a few kicks of his shoes sent dust and grass over the wetness by the band's crate.

But around its side, the flashlight beam caught on a pair of sandals. Unmistakable Indian sandals that anyone on the place would know belonged to Fort.

He snatched them up, took them over to the rebar frame, and then decided, Why bother? There was a gigantic dumpster full of garbage that would go on Monday morning. All he had to do was push them down a little.

So he did.

As he approached the house, the thump of music went on. But in the Yard, no one stirred. No one saw him go into Fort's room. No one noticed him come out with Fort's backpack.

And the next day, the scramble to tear down the stage and let the cement truck do its job meant that no one noticed any disturbance of soil under the rebar before the gray slurry poured down over it. The stain in the grass disappeared entirely in minutes.

David wasn't there. Instead, he drove to the airport, bought a postcard, printed a message, and dropped it in the terminal's mailbox.

GONE HOME TO MY ASHRAM.
LOVE YOU ALL, AND I NEED NOTHING FROM YOU.
FORT

The card was delivered, read by half The Commons, and sat on the mantelpiece for a few days, until one of the kids needed the picture of an airplane for a project.

The things from the backpack went into various garbage cans. The passport and driver's license he burned.

A few months later, David found someone who made regular trips to India, and paid him to mail the occasional card. Half a dozen of them, and after that he didn't bother.

But sometimes, especially after the Trust took over and Rob wasn't around to notice, David would take one of the kitchen's excellent picnic lunches up to sit at the foot of the *Eves,* on the concrete base just to the side of where Fort lay. He wasn't sure why. He took no pride or pleasure in what he'd done—really, other than the postcards, it didn't feel like something he'd done at all.

It was almost as if the Gardener Estate itself had used him. Chosen him over the brothers, to act as its champion and save the house and its land for the future.

56

Raquel cursed the traffic. Why hadn't she thought to get magnetic revolving lights for the car roof? Honks and rude gestures followed her through the city streets, but at last she was spilling on to the freeway, where in ten seconds she could ride bumpers in the fast lane, free to sit back and visualize the problem before her.

The Gardener Estate was immense, the largest piece of undeveloped private land on the Peninsula. Its east and south sides were bordered by a busy two-lane road. West and north followed the small, rural road circling past the Estate's entrance.

If there was a back way to Rob Gardener's cabin, it could only be from that smaller road. And now that she'd met the man, she did not believe that he'd spent every day of the past twenty years holed up among the trees, no matter what the others thought.

Gardener was a man who liked his privacy, and who did not like to be shut in. He would have a back door—one that, like the invisible gate through the laurel hedge, only appeared if you knew it was there.

Twenty-eight minutes after she'd pulled on to the freeway, a mile short of the turnoff, her phone pinged. She made herself wait to check it until she was safely away from traffic, and smiled grimly when she saw the satellite image Dee had sent—one with far better resolution than the Google Earth screen Raquel had studied the previous week.

Dee had dropped a circle around a building in a small clearing with what might be a vegetable garden, up at the northeastern edge of the Estate. The dirt road that led to the main Gardener house was a narrow, twisty brown line—according to Jen, currently all but impassable, even with four-wheel drive.

Dee had also put two arrows along the rural road, one near the Estate's northwest corner, the other all the way around where the road took an abrupt turn north, to head for a small lake some miles away. The first arrow pointed to a bridge over a stream, where a small parking area led to a path following the water course to the Great Field and the Gardener house beyond. The other arrow, though directly north of the cabin, lay across a mile or so of what seemed to be unbroken forest. However, Dee had made a second, closer-up image, onto which she'd sketched a dotted line between the cabin and the road.

Raquel hit her sister's number and put it on speaker, pulling back on to the tarmac.

"Does that look like it?" Dee's voice came.

"I guess."

"Building permits were issued in 1993, final inspection two years later. No power or phone lines, but it has its own well. The roof has solar panels."

"How sure are you about that dotted line you drew?"

"Not at all. You can see three or four bits of what might be dirt road showing through the trees—but it could also be bare hillside. Hang on, I was just looking at something."

The entrance to the Gardener Estate flashed by, but Raquel kept her foot down, even when the road began to climb and curve. Finally, Dee said, "I can't be sure, but there might be some kind of shed, at the edge of that wide spot where the little road jogs north toward the reservoir. It's almost completely hidden by trees, but there's a corner of what might be a roof."

"A lot of ifs and mights. How far is it from the cabin?"

"A mile, mile and a quarter."

I can walk that, if I have to. "Dee, I'm about to lose my connection. Do me a favor and call Al? Tell him where I am and what I'm doing.

Tell him I'm afraid Jen Bachus has gone to pick up Rob, and has his cousin David with her. Tell him David may be our man."

"Do you want Al there?"

"He'll come whether I—"

The phone chirped, and the connection dropped.

Whether I want him or not.

57

The wide spot was about where Dee had said, off to the right just as the road kinked left into the hills. It was rough and unwelcoming, but behind a small mountain of blackberry vines, it widened out and led to—yes, a run-down-looking shack with a pair of doors wide enough to take a vehicle, next to a weed-grown dirt track blocked by a lichen-covered metal gate.

Like the shack, the gate looked ancient, but its posts were straight, the hinges hefty, and the padlocks on both structures were robust. Once, Raquel would have jumped over the gate and trotted across the mile of uneven ground in minutes. Not now.

Jen, what time did you leave?

She eased forward until her bumper came into contact with the gate—and kept her foot down.

The padlock and chain held; one of her headlights went; the gate and both posts began to buckle—but a link in the chain gave way first. The gate flew back on its hinges and rebounded, cracking the passenger-side window as she went by.

She barely noticed. *Three-quarters of a mile,* she thought, setting her odometer. Slow enough to conceal the engine noise, then walk the rest—she could manage that.

These mountains were filled with fire trails, bulldozed for access, cleared every twenty years or so—and kept clear: a young fallen tree had been hauled to the side, recently enough that the cut was still pale. Farther on, a minor landslide was crossed by tire tracks, long enough ago that weeds were sprouting in the indentations.

Just short of the three-quarter-mile mark, she put on the brakes and shut off the engine. The keys she left in the ignition—wouldn't want the car blocking the way of any backup.

Or ambulance.

She tucked her gun in her belt, made sure her cuffs were in her pocket, and set off as fast as her cane would take her.

She fell once, crossing a particularly rough stretch. Later, she froze at a crashing in the undergrowth, until a deer bounced across the way ahead. As she struggled up a steep hill, a blue jay began to scold, making her wonder if a woodsman would take warning. Then she came around a bend—and quickly stepped back under the trees.

It was a log cabin, sitting at the north side of a clearing, but even from the back it was obvious that *off the grid* did not mean *lacking the basics*. Solar panels, big windows, a second story over one section, and at least two fireplaces. About half the clearing was surrounded by a high wire fence around vegetable beds and a chicken run. The far corner of the house seemed to have a roofed-over porch. The windows, all of which were bare of curtains, showed a room with a wall full of books. The whole place was neat, rustic, but far from primitive. Rather like its owner.

The actual drive entered the clearing on the other side of the cabin, but she could not see its end. Could not tell if the Estate's four-wheel-drive Land Rover had got here first.

There was no way to circle the house and remain entirely hidden—at least, not for someone with a limited ability to clamber over trees and through shrubs. At least she was wearing dull clothing—and two small sheds and a woodpile offered some cover. The house was silent, though she could smell woodsmoke. She kept an eye on the windows, and set off around the edge of the clearing.

Eventually, after several snags and a bloody wound from an unnoticed twig, she had edged her way far enough around to see the front of the house.

No Land Rover, thank God.

She heard a sound from the direction she'd come in, and fought her way back through the undergrowth, arriving in time to see Rob Gardener, one big hand cradling a bunch of eggs, step out of the henhouse and head toward his back door. He was dressed in jeans and a blue plaid shirt, the sleeves rolled up on his forearms, and paused to pull a few leaves off some plant, then again to look at something on a bush. He let himself out through the wire fence, taking care to drop the gate latch as he went.

Raquel opened her mouth to call his name—and stopped. A motor, alarmingly near, far too close to risk stepping out into the open. And yes, a bare fifteen seconds later the car itself came into view, an old but polished Land Rover, dropping down the last section of drive and circling around to the front of the house.

It stopped with the passenger side facing the porch. Raquel, pressed against a tree, did not know whether to be relieved or frightened when she saw Jen get out.

She was alive. And not afraid, although neither did she seem happy as she walked up the steps. The distance between her and the car grew. Raquel slipped her handgun from its holster, waiting . . .

But when the other car door slammed, David Kirkup walked around the back of the Land Rover, his white shirt flitting briefly across her field of vision as he followed Jen up the stairs. No way to intercept him before he reached the others.

Raquel shoved her gun into its holster and struggled back to the fire road, oblivious of snags and jabs. She scurried across it as fast as she could, hearing voices—not raised, just speaking. Past the fence and the henhouse, down the path to the back door, up two steps, panting as she bent down under the window, laying her hand on the doorknob.

Blessed relief—it turned, noiselessly. She eased it open, just enough to confirm that the voices were in a more distant room, then opened it fully to step into Rob Gardener's kitchen.

It smelled of frying onions and fresh coffee from a French-press pot. Five brown eggs sat in a shallow basket next to the wood-burning stove where a black iron skillet warmed. A wooden cutting board held the spinach he'd picked as he went through the garden—half chopped before he'd been interrupted by Jen coming through the front door.

Raquel winced at the click of her cane on the tile floor, and lurched across the rest of the room without it, abandoning it behind an old-fashioned sideboard laden with plates. From here on out, she would need hands more than support for her legs.

Near the doorway now, she could hear the words.

"—didn't think you'd be coming all the way up, or this early. I was just making breakfast. You two want some?"

"We need to talk." That was David, his voice gone high with tension.

Yes, he would need to talk—and it occurred to Raquel that she'd even counted on it. This man would need to justify his grievances and work himself up to whatever it was he had in mind. That was why she hadn't panicked and stepped out into the open with her gun drawn.

The wisdom of the body . . .

But Gardener was asking the others if they wanted coffee, and though David was protesting, Rob's voice was already closer than it had been—"Hold on, I need to take the pan off the heat. Jen, you sure you don't want a cup?"—and the only thing for it was to open the closed door beside her and step into darkness.

It was a storage room, its shelves laden with glass jars and anonymous boxes, and she left the door open a crack, which darkened as Gardener walked past. A metallic scrape: the frying pan moving off its heat source. Other small noises, followed by half a dozen footsteps and the sound of liquid going into a cup. The small tap of the French-press pot being set down, two more steps . . .

Then silence.

With caution, Raquel craned around the door to see what he was doing.

Gardener was standing with a cup in his hand, looking straight at her. And though he had clearly seen the motion, he said nothing. Instead, his eyes narrowed in thought, then moved deliberately sideways to the far end of the sideboard, before returning to the crack.

He'd seen her cane. He knew she was here.

She let the door come open enough to show her face, touching one finger to her lips and giving a slow shake of the head.

His eyes flicked over to the door he'd come through, then back to her. She nodded.

As if a switch had gone on, everything about the man went instantly sharp, alert, wary. He might have been a platoon leader about to set off into the trees. He set down his steaming mug and used the hand to shape a pointing handgun. She pulled her Glock from its holster and held it to the opening. He jabbed a finger toward the living room, then made a come-here gesture with his fingers: *You want them out there, or in here?*

Not an easy choice, without having seen the other room. She would assume that Kirkup was armed, though she doubted he spent hours on a shooting range. And the bigger the space, the greater the distance between Jen and his gun. On the other hand . . .

She jerked her head to the right: *Bring him here.*

The soldier in the kitchen nodded, did an automatic survey of his surroundings, and moved on silent feet to the stove. The iron skillet went back onto the heat and he picked up the knife from the cutting board, raising his voice as if the sound of chopping was too great to be heard over. "Davey, sorry, but I've been up for hours and I gotta eat before I face the Board. If you want to come in here while I'm cooking my eggs, you can tell me what's so important it can't wait till we're driving down."

His voice managed to be casual, although his body looked like a catapult ready for launching, and his grip on the knife was in no way suitable for chopping spinach.

Raquel closed the door down to three inches: left hand on the knob, ready to fling it open; right hand holding the sidearm against her chest, ready to follow through. Safety off. Something from the pan drew Rob's attention, and he moved it aside without looking, rather than trying to stir the contents.

They waited, soon-to-be ex-cop and the longtime ex-soldier, for the enemy to show himself.

What they got was Jen.

58

Raquel felt motion, but Rob saw the person in the doorway, and immediately spoke up. "Hey, Jen, nice dress. Say, do me a favor and open the back door? I kinda burned the onions."

"Is the hood fan broken?" she asked, obediently continuing across the room. Raquel heard the door open.

"In fact," he said, ignoring her question, "could you go out and grab me another handful of spinach? This one has bugs or something."

"Can't you just pick them off?"

"Jen, please."

"Okay, but I'm going to steal some of your lettuce while I'm there."

No clue, Raquel thought. *She has no idea. Could I be wrong about him? Could this be an innocent—*

"Don't go out, Jen," came the command from the doorway.

No. Nothing innocent in that voice.

"I don't mind, David, I know just where— What the hell? Why do you have a *gun*?"

"I don't have a gun, Jen. You have a gun. You brought it with you, because you planned a murder-suicide with Rob, here. Your old lover, about to sell you out, turn the Estate over to a moneymaking proposition, undercutting your authority. You're consumed by rage, furious at his betrayal, the old story. I think you should sit down at the table."

"*What?* David, are you *insane,* or—ah, this is some elaborate joke, isn't it? That's Raquel's cane, she's put you up to it."

Kirkup had been standing just inside the door to the living room, where Raquel could see the old revolver in his hand—aimed directly at Rob, so close even an amateur could not miss. It shifted briefly when he gestured at the table, but that only took it closer to Jen. Now, however, he was distracted, moving forward to see what Jen was looking at. As he went past, a small corner of Raquel's mind gave out a small, sardonic thought—*All the clever insight in the world sometimes isn't enough*—but her body was already in motion.

Door going back, the Glock coming up, she opened her mouth to say the words *Put the gun down, Mr. Kirkup*—but before she could move into place behind him, the world exploded.

Shouts and a scream and the deafening crack of a gun came too fast to sort it out. She lunged clear of the doorway and into a stink of gunshot, a blur of motion, and more noise—a hard clang and a cry and a second deafening *BLAM* and more screaming, all whirled together.

For a breathless moment, the blur paused, resolving into: Rob Gardener with a big black skillet poised above his shoulder; David Kirkup, hunched crooning around his right hand; in the corner of her eye, an old revolver on the floor with a spatter of fried onions over it all.

Then the brief pause ended as Rob swung the skillet down in a backhand stroke, flat against his cousin's skull.

Plates vomited from the sideboard as Kirkup bounced against it and collapsed, a cacophony of breaking glass and crockery fading to the single, anticlimactic spin of a pan lid on tiles and the faint plop of onions coming off the ceiling.

The cop recovered first. Raquel jammed away her gun and grabbed the handcuffs, bending over the unconscious man as she shouted over her shoulder, straining to hear over the whine in her ears. "Are you hit? Jen, are you okay?"

Not that she could hear a reply, but when she'd straightened and her eyes found the terrified figure outlined against the shattered window, Jen was shaking her head.

The lack of blood made Raquel feel light-headed. It took a moment to pull her gaze to her other responsibility. "Are you hit?" she asked Rob.

He saw the question and shook his head, but she looked him over to be sure. No blood, and no indication of injury as he stepped over his cousin's legs to retrieve the gun, placing it atop the sideboard.

Then Raquel was free to cross the room and wrap her arms around the other woman, murmuring words of comfort that could gradually be heard over the muffled ringing of the shots. Over and over: "It's okay, I've got you, it's okay, Jen, I'm here. I'm here."

59

Two weeks later

They met in the same coffee shop they'd used a hundred times, back to when Raquel Laing was a lowly patrol officer responding to a superior officer's invitation. Now she was not even that.

"How's it feel, not to have a badge?" Al asked, when his favorite waitress had brought his decaf and her regular.

"A bit like foot patrol without a vest."

"They'll take you back. Give them a while."

"No. The chief was right, I'm not a good fit. Although after the stink has blown away, assuming it does, I might put my name down as a consultant."

"Sherlock for hire."

"Say that again if you want coffee in your lap."

"They'll hire you. Nobody could have got what you did out of Michael Johnston."

"I heard he's in a coma?"

"Yesterday. His daughter signed a DNR, so when he's gone, that's it."

"Good."

"Looks like eleven women in Mexico. They're still looking for four of them. The last was in 1997, and then he just stopped."

"I hear they do that, sometimes. What about David Kirkup? I saw he was charged, but nothing since then."

"He's out of the hospital, though he'll have headaches for a while. I forgot to ask—what was it that Gardener hit him with?"

"A frying pan."

"What, that massive cast-iron thing he was cooking breakfast on?"

"The very same." Al had reached the cabin about twenty minutes after Gardener had knocked his cousin out—during which time the veteran had decided that none of them should face a long, difficult day on an empty stomach.

"Well, that explains the state of Kirkup's skull. Anyway, his lawyer is asking about a plea bargain."

"What, second degree? God, don't tell me they're thinking manslaughter."

"No, sounds like he's willing to do the full time if the DA promises prison camp rather than high security."

"I suppose waiving a trial would make things easier on the Estate."

"How's Ms. Bachus?"

"She's good. Back at work. Mrs. Dalhousie has all kinds of ideas for the *Midsummer Eves* statue."

They talked about Jen and Mrs. Dalhousie, about Al's summer plans with his grandchildren, and about some recent happenings with mutual friends in the Department. She made him laugh recounting her conversation with Meadow-turned-Eve, who'd seen nothing odd about a life's path from law office to rock music to organic commune to European art world and back to organic greens. "It's all been about making the world a better place, hasn't it?" she'd told Raquel, and admitted that she might be returning to the Bay Area for a while, before too long.

Al then caught her up on the work of the Highwayman group and its rivalry-slash-cooperation with the actual task force. She offered suggestions for officers the Department might train to take her place when it came to mind reading in the interrogation room. They touched lightly on Raquel's own thoughts about her future—although neither of them brought up Dee and how much her shadowy world might be involved.

When their cups were empty for the last time, Raquel reached under her seat for a carrier bag, laying it on the table between them.

"And here's for you," she told him. "One last piece of unfinished business."

He lifted the edge of the bag, and saw the distinctive cover of an old murder book.

After all these years, the SFPD could put Polly Lacewood to rest.

Afterword / Thanks

Thanks to everyone who helped dig an author out of a hard time with this one, especially Karen Lynch (*Good Cop, Bad Daughter*, find her at http://www.karenrlynch.com), whose patience and eye for detail prove how good she was as a street cop and Homicide investigator in the SFPD. And Inspector Daniel Cunningham, also of the SFPD, who fit my questions in among some serious breaking investigations of his own. Dr. Judy Melinek and her partner T. J. Mitchell (*Working Stiff; First Cut; Aftershock*) were similarly generous with their time and expertise in the field of forensic pathology, and are missed here in Northern California.

It need hardly be said, none of these people are to blame for any mistakes, even willful ones, on the part of the author. If a department or jurisdiction doesn't do things the way they're described here, well, I'm sorry.

And as always, my gratitude to the energy, talent, and goodwill of the various parts of Team LRK: my agent, Alec Shane, my friends and beta readers Alice, Merrily, Karen, Sabrina, Erin, John, Mary Alice, Anna, Zoë, and all of the Beekeeper's Apprentices on Facebook. And of course, the ladies and gents of Penguin Random House, who believe in my stories: Hilary, Erin, Allison, Kim, Melissa, Emma, Caroline, Jessica, Rachel, and a thousand others, as well as my buddies at Recorded Books, especially Brian Sweany and Jenny Sterlin.

Bless, too, the booksellers and librarians, determined to put words into the hands of readers.

It truly takes a small city to raise a book onto the shelves.

ABOUT THE AUTHOR

LAURIE R. KING is the award-winning, bestselling author of seventeen Mary Russell mysteries, five contemporary novels featuring Kate Martinelli, and many acclaimed stand-alone novels such as *Folly, Touchstone, The Bones of Paris,* and *Lockdown.* She lives on California's Central Coast, where she is at work on her next Mary Russell mystery.

LaurieRKing.com
Facebook.com/LaurieRKing
Twitter: @LaurieRKing and @Mary_Russell

ABOUT THE TYPE

This book was set in Caledonia, a typeface designed in 1939 by W. A. Dwiggins (1880–1956) for the Merganthaler Linotype Company. Its name is the ancient Roman term for Scotland, because the face was intended to have a Scottish-Roman flavor. Caledonia is considered to be a well-proportioned, businesslike face with little contrast between its thick and thin lines.